KANSAS CITY COUNTDOWN

BY
JULIE MILLER

First Published in Great Britain 2016
By Mills & Boon, an imprint of HarperCollins*Publishers*
1 London Bridge Street, London, SE1 9GF

ISBN: 978-0-263-91925-7

46-1216

Our policy is to use papers that are natural, renewable and recyclable products and made from wood grown in sustainable forests. The logging and manufacturing processes conform to the legal environmental regulations of the country of origin.

Printed and bound in Spain
by CPI, Barcelona

Julie Miller is an award-winning *USA TODAY* best-selling author of breathtaking romantic suspense—with a National Readers' Choice Award and a Daphne du Maurier Award, among other prizes. She has also earned an *RT Book Reviews* Career Achievement Award. For a complete list of her books, monthly newsletter and more, go to www.juliemiller.org.

To my fellow Whovians.
You know who you are.
(And please don't ask me to pick a favorite Doctor!)

Prologue

"You're a bad boy, Detective Watson."

Keir Watson laughed at the teasing gibe from Natalie Fensom Parker, the bridesmaid he was escorting down the aisle at his sister's wedding. He adjusted the cherry-red bow tie that matched the vest he wore with his black tuxedo and doffed a salute to Al Junkert as they walked past. Al was an old family friend and KCPD senior officer who'd once partnered with Keir's father, Thomas, before a shattered leg had forced Thomas into early retirement from the department. "No, ma'am. I'm a truth teller. You are absolutely the prettiest pregnant lady here today. The guests can't keep their eyes off you."

Natalie's bouquet of red and white carnations seemed to rest on her swollen belly as she giggled. "Everyone's eyes will be on your sister and Gabe today. Nobody is watching me waddle down the aisle."

"Your husband is."

"Maybe Jim is watching *you*." She beamed a smile to her husband as they walked by. "He and your sister, Olivia, have been partners for some time now. I've got the scoop on all three of you Watson boys. Third generation cops like your father and grandfather before you. He knows your reputation around the precinct offices."

"That I'm a sharp-eyed detective who is as tough as he is resourceful? That I'll make sergeant detective and be running my own task force before I turn thirty-five?"

"No, that you're a flirt." Her fingers squeezed his arm to take the sting out of the accusation. "But Jim assures me you're harmless."

"Natalie, you wound me."

"Well, better me than my husband."

"The warning is duly noted." Keir patted Natalie's hand and grinned. Jim Parker was a lucky man to have this woman love him. His soon-to-be brother-in-law, Gabe Knight, was lucky to have Liv so head over heels for him. And though Keir modestly suspected that there was at least one single woman in the crowded church he could charm into going home with him by the end of the wedding reception, he instead felt a stab of envy that these good people had found their happily-ever-afters. Not that he'd ever admit that little taste of bitterness out loud.

Marriage vows and 2.5 children just weren't in the cards for the youngest Watson brother.

Once he'd wanted what his father and late mother had had until she'd been torn from their lives by her senseless murder by a doped-up thief. He'd seen how devastated his father had been. Keir had felt the grief just as keenly, though as an eleven-year-old he hadn't quite understood why his mother wasn't coming home or why Grandpa Seamus and a new housekeeper/cook were coming to live with them.

Once he'd wanted that goofy smile kind of happiness Natalie and Jim Parker shared. Like them, he'd imagined starting his own family one day. A few years back he'd almost taken the plunge. But patience wasn't always a virtue. He'd waited too long to put his heart on the line. He'd let the high standard of his mother's example of what he wanted in a wife and his ambitious career plans with KCPD get in the way of grasping happiness when the opportunity presented itself.

With the engagement ring he'd hoped to give her buried in his pocket, Keir had waited hours for Sophie Collins to meet him at the restaurant where he'd planned to propose, only to find out the next day that she'd eloped with a friend of his from the police academy—the same man who'd introduced them two years earlier. While he'd been busy studying for his detective's exam and taking extra training courses to be ready for any assignment opportunity, letting the relationship slide to the back burner, the other two had been spending lots of time together. Sophie considered Keir to be the friend, expected him to be happy for her. So he'd kissed her cheek, said all the right words and walked away.

He'd been walking away ever since.

That day, he'd picked his pride up off the floor and closed off his heart to that kind of loss and humiliation ever again. He wasn't averse to enjoying a woman's company, and took pride in being a gentleman and showing a lady a good time—whichever she preferred. But let anything get too serious, too close to feeling like he was giving a woman control over his heart, and Keir moved on. He had plenty of friends, and his career at KCPD was taking off. He'd made detective that first year he was eligible and he'd gotten several plum assignments, including his position now with the major case squad.

What more could a man need to have a successful life?

Right. Family. As Keir neared the front of the church, he reached out and squeezed his hand over the shoulder of his grandpa, Seamus Watson. The eighty-year-old retired KCPD desk sergeant laid his bony fingers over Keir's and smiled, and Keir knew he had all the love a man could need with this close, supportive family. He caught the smile of the plump, silver-haired woman sitting behind Seamus and winked. Grinning at the blush that colored her cheeks, Keir blew a kiss to Millie Leighter, the woman who'd raised him and his brothers and sister after their mother's death. More aunt or grandmother than housekeeper and cook, Millie was family, too.

Yeah. Keir Watson had enough for his life to be a success. The past was what it was. He was moving on.

He released Natalie as they'd rehearsed the night before and joined his older brothers—Duff, the detective, and Niall, an autopsy doctor at the KCPD Crime Lab—on the top step of the altar. A grin curved his lips as he saw Niall adjusting the dark frames of his glasses and nailing him with a piercing glare.

"Natalie is married to Liv's partner, you know," Niall whispered.

"Relax, Charm School Dropout." Keir clapped his tallest brother on the shoulder of his matching black tuxedo and moved in behind him. "Young or old, married or not—it never hurts to be friendly."

Olivia must have given Niall a directive about keeping his brothers in line, because the bespectacled medical examiner now turned his attention to Keir's oldest brother, Duff. "Seriously? Are you packing today?"

Duff's massive shoulders shifted as he turned to whisper a response. "Hey. You wear your glasses every day, Poindexter. I wear my gun."

"I wasn't aware that you knew what the term *Poindexter* meant."

"I'm smarter than I look," was Duff's terse response.

Keir couldn't let that straight line go without saying something. "He'd have to be."

Duff turned his square jaw toward Keir. "So help me, baby brother, if you give me any grief today, I will lay you out flat."

He probably could. If Niall was the brains of the family, Duff was definitely the brawn. But Keir had vowed from a tender age to never go down without a fight—or at least without a smart-aleck protest or two.

But before he could utter the barb on the tip of his tongue, Niall was shushing them. "Zip it. Both of you. You, mind your manners." Keir put up a hand, acquiescing to the terse command, while Niall got on Duff's case, too. "And you stop fidgeting like a little kid."

Then the organ music coming from the wall of pipes in the church's balcony changed and all three brothers turned their attention to the archway at the back of the church. Everyone in the congregation stood and watched Olivia Mary Watson and their father, Thomas, pause a moment before heading down the long aisle together.

Keir's breath caught in his chest as he watched his sister and father approach. They both carried themselves proudly and walked with a purpose, despite Thomas Watson's limping gait. Good grief! When had his tomboy little sister grown up to be such a beautiful woman? She was a detective like him, for Pete's sake, and usually sported jeans and leather jackets. But today, sparkles and lace clung to curves sisters weren't supposed to have. The veil of Irish lace that sat on her dark hair framed blue eyes like his own, and took Keir back several years to the pictures he remembered seeing of their mother and father's wedding day.

"Dude." Duff was about to wax poetic, giving voice to a sentiment similar to what Keir was feeling. "Gabe, you are one lucky son of a—"

"Duff." Leave it to Niall to maintain a necessary sense of decorum.

"You'd better treat her right." Duff whispered a warning to the groom.

"We've already had this conversation, Duff," Niall pointed out. "I'm convinced he loves her."

Gabe never took his eyes off Olivia as he leaned back toward his soon-to-be brothers-in-law. "He does."

This conversation was pointless to Keir's way of thinking. "Anyway, Liv's made her choice. You think any one of us could change her mind? I'd be scared to try."

The minister hushed the lot of them as father and bride approached.

"Ah, hell." Duff was tearing up. "This is not happening to me."

Keir blinked rapidly. If he wasn't careful, he might embarrass himself and do the same thing. "She looks the way I remember Mom."

Niall slipped Duff a handkerchief while Olivia shared a tight hug with their father. Keir gave her a thumbs-up when she smiled at the three of them, then turned his attention to the exchanging of vows and rings.

By the end of the ceremony, Keir was feeling that sting of envy again, a hollowness that seemed to fill the area of his chest right around his heart.

"You may now kiss the bride."

But he'd made his choices. He was genuinely happy for his sister. While Liv's new husband planted an embarrassingly thorough kiss on her lips, the guests applauded and Keir whistled a cheer between his teeth. Then the recessional started and the happy couple proceeded down the aisle to acknowledge all the family, friends and coworkers gathered here. Duff followed with the matron of honor. Niall took the arm of his bridesmaid and Keir extended his arm to walk Natalie back to her husband and get going to the party to find someone who could make him forget, for a little while, at least, that he wasn't missing a thing by not putting his heart on the line again.

He even danced the first few steps in time with the music until he caught a glimpse of movement up in the balcony. A door opened beside a limestone buttress near the organist. The man who stepped in was dressed in black from head to toe. That was no guest.

"What the...?"

By the time Niall shouted, "Gun!" and the recessional ended on an abrupt, dissonant chord, the masked man upstairs had pulled a rifle from beneath his long coat and opened fire down into the church. Keir cursed as he reached for a gun at his waist that wasn't there and pulled Natalie to the floor behind the front pew.

Gunfire exploded in the air and chips of wood

blasted over their heads and rained down as the shooter emptied his rifle into the congregation.

Keir was calling Dispatch for a SWAT unit when he heard Duff yell for everybody to get down and heard more chatter among the many police officers in the crowd—getting guests to safety, pinpointing the shooter's location, making plans to go after the man. A matter of seconds passed as the shooter emptied his clip. The momentary pause meant he was reloading, pulling another gun or running. Now was the time to move.

"Stay put," Keir warned Natalie, turning on the camera on his phone. He raised the device over the pew, snapping pictures and getting a position on the shooter before crawling into the aisle. "Damn." New gun. Keir scrambled toward his father, grandfather and Millie as the man pulled a semiautomatic pistol from his belt and sprayed the church with more bullets. A chunk of marble spit off the floor and smacked into Keir's leg.

What the hell was the guy aiming at? Was he blind? Going for chaos over accuracy? The minister at the front of the church was crouched behind the pulpit, and though there were children crying and shouts of panic, Keir couldn't see signs that anyone was hurt or administering first aid. He didn't intend to give the guy the opportunity to improve his aim. He might only have milliseconds to reach his family before the shooter turned his gun back in this direction. "Dad? Grandpa? Millie?"

Keir reached his family, ducking between the seats as a bullet shredded the lacy bow decorating the pew beside him. He pushed Millie to the floor and reached over the seat to help the others. Seamus's cane clattered to the floor.

"Grandpa!" Keir felt the spatter of warm blood hit his cheek a split second before the old man crumpled against Thomas. "Ah, hell."

Seamus Watson had been hit.

Keir shrugged out of his jacket and tossed it on the marble floor beneath his grandfather as his father lowered him to the floor. The rage of bullets fell silent and he spared a glance up at the door closing in the balcony as the shooter escaped, silently swearing to track down the bastard. He pulled a shocked, weeping Millie into his chest and turned her away from the blood pooling on the floor as his brother Niall worked on their grandfather's wound.

Keir had already made one call to Dispatch, but he dialed the number a second time and repeated the call for help, making sure an ambulance was en route. "I need a bus. Now. Officer down. I repeat officer down."

Chapter One

May

Keir dropped the shot of whiskey into his mug of beer and picked it up before the drink foamed over. "Here's to the Terminator."

His partner, Hudson Kramer, dressed in work boots and blue jeans, lowered his bottle of beer to the bar top. "Please tell me that's sarcasm."

"Loud and bitter, my friend." The Shamrock Bar tonight was loud with Irish music, conversation, laughter, the periodic clinks of glassware and the sharp smacks of pool balls caroming off each other. The frenetic, celebratory energy was typical for a Friday night where several denizens from the KCPD and surrounding downtown neighborhood liked to hang out. They'd survived another week of long hours and hard work that could be, at turns, tedious and dangerous. Some of his fellow cops here had broken cases wide-open this week or arrested criminals or even just kept a drunk driver off the streets, where he could be a threat to the citizens they'd all sworn to serve and protect.

But Keir and Hud, yin and yang in both style and background, yet as close as Keir was to his own brothers, had nothing to celebrate. Keir was feeling the need to either get drunk or get laid to ease the tension coiling inside him.

Sure, some of it had to do with his frustration over the slow-moving investigation into the shooting at the church where his grandfather had nearly died—an investigation that he and his two older brothers weren't allowed to be a part of in any official capacity. Not that departmental restrictions were going to stop Keir and his brothers from pursuing answers for themselves. A masked shooter who threatened a building full of cops on a happy occasion and then disappeared into thin air made every officer in the department an investigator until the perp who'd targeted Keir's family could be identified and caught.

No, tonight's extra-special foray into moody sarcasm all had to do with a leggy, ash-blond defense attorney who'd made mincemeat out of the attempted murder-for-hire investigation he and Hud had turned over to the DA's office on Monday. It had taken Kenna Parker only five days of motions and court appearances to punch holes in their airtight case. The hoity-toity plastic surgeon who'd talked to Keir in an undercover op about hiring him to kill his estranged wife before she could divorce him and cost him a fortune in alimony had gotten off with little more than a slap on the wrist.

Yes, the guy was now under an ethics investigation by the state medical board—a sidebar that could cost him his license or, at the very least, put a dent in his lucrative medical practice. But that wasn't the same as a judge acknowledging that Detective Keir Watson had done his job right. Kenna "the Terminator" Parker hadn't even really cleared Dr. Andrew Colbern of conspiracy to commit murder—she'd just raised enough doubts about Keir's competence and a few seconds of static on the recording he'd made of the conversation that Colbern was walking.

"Did you see how she booked it out of the courtroom right after the judge announced his ruling?" Hud punctuated his condemning tone with a long swallow of his beer. "That's just rubbing her victory in our faces."

Keir eyed the foamy amber liquid in his mug. "She probably went off to pop open a magnum of champagne at our expense."

Hud turned the brown bottle in his hand, then grinned. "Well, then let's just hope she's drinkin' it alone, my friend."

"You got that right." Keir clinked his mug against Hud's bottle, but he couldn't match his partner's good humor.

They'd failed to prove Colbern's guilt beyond a reasonable doubt, according to the Terminator. Interesting what kind of justice a lot of money and a killer law firm could buy.

Well, reputation meant everything to him, too. Keir Watson didn't botch cases. When he investigated a crime, he got answers. No matter how long it took, he got the job done.

"I swear that woman is going to make me a better cop," Keir vowed, remembering the smug smile on her copper-tinted lips as she'd packed up her briefcase and passed him on her way out of the courtroom. "Next time she shows up in court, she won't be able to raise the issue of entrapment and question technicalities or make her client look more like the victim than the woman he tried to have killed. The next time I'm testifying against one of her clients, I'll make her look like the idiot."

Hud raised his bottle again. "Then, to the downfall of the Terminator."

"Amen." Keir swallowed a healthy portion of the beer and whiskey, savoring the heat seeping down his gullet. Half a drink later, Keir still couldn't erase the tension in him and felt himself turning inward, replaying each step of the case he'd put together, and each trick Kenna Parker had used to pull it apart.

He loosened his tie and unbuttoned his collar, only half listening to Hud regale him with a story about his first encounter with an attorney as a teenager, protesting a ticket in his small-town traffic court. Something about the lawyer being the judge's second cousin's daughter's boyfriend, and the judge declaring a conflict of interest and dismissing the speeding ticket because the guy was family, and there wasn't anyone else in town who wasn't related who could represent him. Hardly a problem someone with Kenna Parker's legal eagle pedigree would ever have to face.

Sitting here tonight, fuming over the case that had gotten tossed, Keir knew he wasn't very good company. Hud, on the other hand, could blow off the tension once he was away from the job in ways that Keir wasn't able to. Maybe he'd better cut his partner loose to play a game of pool or share a drink with one of the local ladies who had a thing for cops. Keir downed the last of his beer and Bushmill's and pushed the mug away, intent on heading home where he could stew in silence—or more likely, pull out his case file against Andrew Colbern and reread the transcript of his undercover conversation to figure out exactly where he'd misspoken so he wouldn't make the same mistake again.

He clapped Hud on the shoulder of his plaid flannel shirt and stood. "Hey, buddy, I'm heading home."

Hud threw up his hands and frowned. "You're kiddin' me, right? The night is young and this place is crawlin' with opportunities." His brown eyes swept the bar, indicating the disproportionate number of female to male customers. "I need you to be my wingman."

Chuckling at his partner's humorous determination, Keir tossed a couple of bills onto the bar to pay for their drinks. "Sorry. Guess I'm lousy company tonight."

"Tell me about it. I'm givin' you my best stuff and all I've gotten out of you is a smirk."

Keir conceded the truth with a nod. "It's not your job to make things right when a case goes wrong."

"The hell it isn't." Hud polished off the last of his beer and swiped his knuckles over his mouth to erase the foamy mustache. "You'll still be in a mood when you come back to work on Monday, and I'm the guy who has to look at you all day." He pushed aside the money Keir had put on the bar and set a twenty-dollar bill in its place. "I dare you to stay and have a little fun. I know there's a lady here tonight who can put a full-blown smile on your face and make you forget all about the Terminator. In fact, I'll bet you that last round of drinks that I can score some action and be smiling before you."

"Really?" Hud knew his weakness for refusing to back down from a dare. Keir's older brothers had given him plenty of practice at holding his own growing up. Still, he was about to tell his partner that he'd take that bet on some other night when he wasn't quite so tired or distracted, when the Shamrock's owner, Robbie Nichols, set a beer and shot on the bar in front of him. Keir frowned. "I didn't order this."

The bushy-bearded Irishman nodded toward someone behind Keir's back and winked. "She did. Good luck to you, Detective."

Keir turned to see a sweet little strawberry blonde smiling at him as she wove her way through the maze of tables to reach him. Maybe he should take a lesson from his laid-back partner and blow off a little steam. Suddenly, spending Friday night at home with work wasn't as appealing as it had sounded a minute ago. "Are you responsible for this?" he asked the man staring, openmouthed, beside him.

"I wish." Hud had turned, too, and was shaking his head. "Even on your worst night, the ladies love you. Why don't I have that kind of luck?"

"Because you're half hillbilly. And—" Keir buttoned his collar and adjusted his tie as the young woman approached "—a man in a well tailored suit is like catnip to the ladies." Keir picked up the drink. "I promise you, my friend—if you're going to bet me, you're going to lose."

Robbie returned, popping the cap off a chilled bottle of beer and setting it in front of Hud. "Not to worry, Detective Kramer. The ladies got you one, too."

"Ladies? As in plural?" Quickly tucking his shirt into his jeans, Hud stood beside Keir, focusing in on the burgundy-haired woman with glasses trailing after her friend. "Game on, catnip boy."

The strawberry blonde reached them before Keir could respond to Hud's challenge. "Hi. I'm Tammy.

I hope you're not leaving. My sister and I took a vote and decided you were the cutest guy here."

Cute? Well, now, didn't that make him feel about twice this girl's age and a little less eager to win the bet? Still, from a very young age, his mama had taught him to have manners, so Keir extended his hand. "I'm flattered. Keir Watson. Thank you for the drink."

"Keir? That's an unusual name."

"It's Irish. My mother was born in Ireland."

"Awesome."

The shy redhead at her shoulder looked a few years older and a little less enthusiastic about picking up a guy in a bar. She nudged her friend and glanced at Hud. "Tammy, it's getting late. How long is this going to take?"

Poor Hud. He had his work cut out for him if he wanted to win the bet.

Instead of answering, Tammy beamed a smile at Keir's partner. "This is Gigi. My older sister." Tammy emphasized the age difference, as if the three or four years that must separate them meant big sis was over the hill and that she was the prime catch. *Awkward.* Clearly, Tammy was pawning her sister off on Hud, and had eyes only for Keir. "I'll let Gigi tell you what it's short for."

But Hud wasn't complaining. Once the introductions had been completed, he pulled out the stool Keir had vacated and invited Gigi to sit beside him.

Keir smiled down at the strawberry blonde. Whether her sister was shy about men or genuinely tired, Tammy was determined to hit on him. And Gigi seemed to be sufficiently entertained as Hud launched into his good ol' boy spiel. "All right, then. Shall we?"

He picked up his drinks and escorted Tammy to a private table while she asked if the gun and badge he wore were real. Feeling older by the minute and wishing he'd trusted his gut and headed home, Keir briefly considered if this woman might be underage. But he was certain Robbie and his staff would have carded both women before selling them alcohol. Something about running a bar frequented by cops kept a man from bending the rules.

Still, the momentary rush of proving to Hud that (a) he always had his game on with the ladies, and (b) his partner didn't need to worry about his mood, quickly faded. An hour passed and Keir was beginning to feel as though he was watching out for a friend's kid sister rather than seriously considering extending the evening into something more. True, his thoughts kept straying back to those moments in the courtroom when the judge had chastised his unit for not making sure all their ducks were in a row in their case against Dr. Colbern.

But it seemed Tammy couldn't sustain a conversation beyond flirty come-on lines, the classes she was taking at UMKC and all the adventures at bars she and her sister were having now that she'd turned twenty-one. Tammy was pretty. She was sweet. And he had a feeling she was sincere in her interest in him. But twenty-one was too young for a man in his early thirties, and Keir wisely kept the evening platonic until the cocktail waitress announced last call and he decided to call it a night.

Hud and the less animated Gigi had moved over to the pool tables, where he was teaching her some tricks of the game. A quick text exchange with Keir's partner confirmed that they'd hit it off as friends and that Hud was fine giving the young lady a ride home after they finished their last set. Keir conceded the bet and paid for all their drinks.

Tammy was obviously disappointed that Keir decided to call it a night instead of inviting her out on a date or even asking for her number. He tried to soften the blow to her ego. "It's been a long week for me and I'm tired. Plus, if you've got an exam Monday, you'd better try to get a little sleep so you can study this weekend." He stood and took her hand. "Come on. I'll walk you to your car."

He traded a salute with Hud and led Tammy through the dwindling crowd outside the front door. The days had been warming up with the advent of spring, but the hour was late and there was a chill in the air that elicited an audible shiver from the young woman beside him. Whether her reaction was legit or one last attempt to stir his interest in her, Keir shrugged out of his suit jacket and draped it around her shoulders. "Which way?"

There might be a dozen or more cops inside the bar, but the downtown streets of Kansas City—even in neighborhoods that were being reclaimed like this one—were no place for a woman to be walking alone at night. She pointed past the neon shamrock in the bar's window to the curb on the next block. Making a brief scan of the street and sidewalks, Keir dropped his hand to the small of Tammy's back and headed past the bar's parking lot, the valet stand for a nearby restaurant, past a north-south alley and the sports bar beyond it, then across the intersection to reach her car.

"I'll wait until you get in and get it started," he said, taking back his jacket and slipping into it.

"You're a nice guy, Detective Watson." Tammy latched on to the lapels of his coat and stretched up on tiptoe as he straightened the collar. "Are you sure I can't change your mind about coming home with me? It looks like Gigi and your friend will be a while."

He pried her hands loose and leaned down to kiss her forehead. "Good night, Tammy." He grinned when she slipped a piece of paper into his pocket, suspecting it was the phone number he hadn't asked for. He closed the door behind her once she'd started the engine, and stepped back onto the curb. "Be safe."

Waving as she drove away, Keir loosened his tie and collar again. Time to call it a night. He hadn't gotten drunk. He hadn't gotten laid. And he sure as hell hadn't figured out any answers to the unresolved cases weighing on his mind. Deciding that the night wasn't going to get any better, and his day couldn't get any worse, he turned and strode back toward the parking lot behind the Shamrock where he'd parked his own car.

He nodded to the trio of college-aged men bemoaning a call in the baseball game they'd been watching inside as they exited the sports bar. Then he stepped around the group of suits and dresses waiting for their ride outside the South American restaurant, shrugging at their fancy outfits in this workingman's neighborhood. Keir's attention shifted to a man standing on the sidewalk across the street. Hanging back in the shadows, wearing a dark hoodie, his shoulders hunched over with his hands buried in the pockets of his baggy jeans, the man's face was unreadable. But his focus was unmistakable. There was something about the restaurant, something about the people walking down the street as the bars and restaurants let out, something or someone on this side of the street he was watching so intently that the hood over his head never even moved.

And that's why you walk a lady to her car.

His suspicions pinging with an alert, Keir slowed his pace and stopped, discreetly pulling his phone from his pocket and snapping a picture while pretending to text. He doubted he'd get a clear shot, but he could at least record a location and vague description. But Hoodie Guy saw that he'd been noticed, and quickly spun away and shuffled on down the street.

"That's right, buddy, I'm a cop." Keir watched the man until he turned at the next intersection and disappeared around the corner of a closed-up building. "You're not causing any trouble tonight."

Detouring for a moment, Keir retraced his steps, wondering if there was anything in particular Hoodie Guy had been watching. Maybe he'd been waiting for someone to separate from the pack—someone to mug for drug money or mooch a drink from. Maybe he'd been watching an old girlfriend on a date with someone new. And maybe the guy just had a creepy sense of fashion and poor timing when it came to choosing where he wanted to loiter. There was no way for Keir to get answers unless he wanted to chase the guy down. And, technically, the guy hadn't done anything to warrant such a response.

Satisfied for the moment that the street was safe, Keir turned around and resumed the walk to his car. Keeping one eye on the cars and empty spaces and drivers and pedestrians to see if Hoodie Guy reappeared, he pulled up his messages. Maybe he'd find a victorious text from Hud or news from his family about Seamus Watson's shooting or his health as his eighty-year-old grandfather recovered from the brain injury that had left him relearning how to speak and use the left side of his body. Nothing. Not even an update from the detectives working the investigation.

Keir scrolled through the case notes he sent himself as texts on his phone as he stepped over the cable marking off a neighborhood parking area and cut through the public space to reach the Shamrock's parking lot. He stepped over the cable at the back end of the lot, ignored the retching sounds of a drunk in the alley he passed and climbed a couple of steps over a short concrete wall to reach the lot where his Dodge Charger was parked.

He was considering sending a text to Hud about their failed pickup bet when he heard the scrabble of footsteps and a slurred, feminine voice from the alley behind him.

"One. One. One is the wrong number."

Keir swung around at the garbled words, leaving the text half-finished and pulling back his jacket to rest his hand on his holstered weapon.

A tall, slender woman stumbled to the edge of the alley. "Three… Two… One isn't right."

"Ma'am?" She wasn't drunk and she wasn't a threat. She was hurt. Seriously hurt, judging by the blood on her face and clothes.

She tried to raise her head, but she groaned and braced her hand against the brick wall as she swayed. "Please. Help me."

Keir leaped over the concrete barrier, taking in several details as he ran to assist the injured woman. Dark silvery blond hair bounced against her chin and clung to the bloody hash marks on one side of her face. The skirt of her fancy tan suit was ripped along one seam and there were dirty smudges on both sleeves of her jacket. She wore one ridiculously sexy leather pump on her right foot, and nothing but a torn silky stocking over the scraped-up knee and toes on her left foot.

"Ma'am, are you all right?" Keir slipped his arm behind her waist, taking her weight and guiding her to the concrete wall. Hoodie Guy's curiosity about something Keir had missed was screaming at him now. Damn it. He should have followed up on his suspicions and stopped the guy for questioning. He helped the lady sit on the edge of the wall, wondering if Hoodie Guy was responsible for this. "What happened?"

"I woke up. I got sick. Everything…spinning."

"Are you alone? Is anyone else hurt?"

She opened her mouth to answer, turned her chin toward the alley, then looked away. "I don't remember."

"Okay." Clearly, she was a little disoriented. "Stay put. I'll be right back."

Once he was certain she wasn't going to collapse on him, Keir pulled his weapon and darted back into the alley, making a cursory sweep of the trash bins and power poles. He startled a rat from its hiding place. But there was no one else in the alley. No signs of a struggle. Not even the missing shoe. This was a dump site. Whatever had happened to her hadn't happened here.

Maybe Hoodie Guy hadn't attacked her, after all. He'd moved away on foot, and it would be impossible to transport an injured woman through this maze of back alleys without a vehicle or someone noticing the two of them together.

Holstering his Glock, Keir jogged back out of the alley to find her on her feet, limping over to meet him. So much for staying put. "Is anyone else hurt?"

Keir caught her by the elbows and turned her back toward the wall and the nearest lamp in the middle of the lot. "Just you. I thought I told you to wait for me."

"I don't know where I…" she muttered beside him. "I don't know how long I was there." She flattened her hand over her stomach and bent forward, as if she was going to be ill. "I don't feel so good."

"Ma'am?" He stopped her beneath the light and waited for her to nod that she could stand straight again before brushing the angled line of bangs off her forehead. Keir swore under his breath as he tilted her face to the yellowish light. He knew this woman. "Kenna Parker? What the hell are you doing—"

"Who are you?" She squinted against the light shining in her eyes and backed away from him, fear making her skin pale.

He raised a placating hand to stop her wobbly retreat and pulled his badge from his belt. "I'm Detective Keir Watson, KCPD. Ms. Parker, how badly are you hurt? Can you tell me what happened?"

She shook her head. But the motion made her dizzy and she grabbed the sides of her head and tumbled.

"Watch out." Keir caught her before she hit the ground and scooped her up into his arms. Her cheek fell against his shoulder and she curled into him without a protest as he stepped over the short wall and carried her to his car. "What does *one* mean?" he asked. Maybe her attacker had been wearing a jersey with a number on it, or she'd seen part of a license plate. "Why is it the wrong number?"

"What?" Her fingers curled into the lapel of his jacket. "I don't understand."

"You kept saying… Never mind." Once he got the passenger door open, he set her feet on the pavement and helped her onto the edge of the seat before pulling the first-aid kit out of the glove compartment. "You were mugged. Assaulted. I can't tell how badly yet. Can you tell me who did this to you? Do you know how you got into that alley? I don't think the attack happened there."

He dabbed at the cuts on her face, tried to assess how well her eyes were tracking the movement of his hands as he knelt in front of her. Besides their sensitivity to the light, her pupils were dilated, both signs that she had a concussion. "I should have a purse. Or a briefcase or something. Where are my things? I always carry…" Her voice trailed away and the thought escaped her.

"I didn't see anything like that in the alley. Is *one* part of a phone number? If you need to call someone, you can borrow my phone."

"Who do I need to call?"

He didn't think she was married. There was no ring, nor any sign that she'd ever worn one, on her left hand. "A boyfriend? Any friend? Your doctor? Someone you work with?"

She touched her finger to the drops of blood staining the knobby silk of her jacket and blouse, as if discovering the spots distracted her from the conversation.

Stay with me, lady. Keir slipped two fingers beneath her chin and tilted her face back to his. "Do you want me to call them for you?"

"I can't think of names right now." Her fingertips

tickled the back of his wrist as they danced against the skin there. "Aren't you my boyfriend? Isn't that why you're here?"

"No, ma'am." He carefully plucked a stray lock of hair from the wound on her cheek and tucked it behind her ear. "Detective Watson, remember? I showed you my badge."

Instead of answering, she raised her fingers to touch the seeping gash. But Keir ripped open a gauze pad and batted her hand away to stanch the wound. This was more than a mugging or purse snatch. These cuts were fine and deep, made by something with a short, sharp blade. She was damn lucky she still had her eye. Carving up half her face like this indicated a lot of rage, and something very personal. The senseless brutality of this attack wasn't something he'd wish even on the woman who'd humiliated him in court. "Here. Can you hold that there while I check the rest of your injuries?"

"It hurts." Her shaking fingers brushed against his as she reached up to apply pressure against the cut. Her eyes were pale gray, almost like starlight, in the dim illumination of the car's overhead light. But though her voice sounded far less steady and sure than it had in the courtroom that afternoon, she was determined to hold his gaze. "My thoughts aren't very clear, Detective. I can't seem to concentrate. I don't think that's like me."

"It's not."

"So you do know me."

"Yes, ma'am." Keir gently tunneled his fingers into the straight, silky curtain of her chin-length hair, probing her scalp until he found the goose egg and oozy warmth of blood at the base of her skull. She winced and he quickly pulled away to open an emergency ice pack and crush the chemicals together between his hands to activate its frosty chill. He placed the ice pack over the knot on her scalp and tried to estimate if he had enough gauze or something else to anchor it into place. He sought out her starlit eyes again. “Looks like you suffered a pretty good blow to the head. Tell me what you *can* remember.”

Although concentrating on the answer seemed to cause her pain, she bravely came up with an answer. “I was going to a meeting. Dinner. A dinner meeting.”

Dinner would have been hours ago. “Who was your meeting with?”

“I don’t know.”

“Where did you eat? Were you walking to your car? Do you remember where you parked? Did a chauffeur or taxi pick you up?”

“I don’t know.” Seeming to grow more agitated, she pulled the gauze pad from her face and saw the scarlet stain on it. “Is all this blood mine?”

“I need to get you to an ER.” She leaned over against the seat, closing her eyes as he placed a call to Dispatch and gave his name, location and badge number. “I need an ambulance…” He dropped the phone into her lap and cupped his palm over the uninjured side of her face. “No, no. Don’t close your eyes. Ms. Parker? Kenna? Kenna, open your eyes.”

Her silvery eyes popped open. “Stop saying that.”

Now, *that* tone sounded like the Terminator. “Are you kidding me? You’re going to the hospital if I have to drive you myself.”

“What’s happened to me? I don’t understand.”

“Ah, hell.” He swung her legs into the car and buckled her in. “That’s it. We’ll make sense of this later.”

He snatched up the phone and relayed the necessary information to complete the call before shrugging out of his jackct and draping it over her like a blanket. "We're going to the hospital, Kenna."

She grabbed the front of his shirt as he leaned over her, pulling her injured face close to his. "Why do you keep calling me that?"

"Fine," he snapped. "You're Ms. Parker. Don't suppose I can get away with calling you the Terminator to your face."

Her pale lips trembled. "Why would you do that?"

He was a sorry SOB for losing his temper for even one moment with this woman. She was probably five or six years older than Keir, and had been his enemy in the courtroom. He had less in common with her than that Tammy Too-Young from the bar. But he couldn't look at the tragedy that marred her beautiful face or the fear that darted in the corner of her eyes and not feel something. He covered her hands where she still held on to him and eased her back into the seat. "I'm sorry. I don't mean to be a jackass. But you're the last person I expected to be helping tonight."

"You don't like me, do you?" She gave him a graceful out for that question by asking another. "You know who I am?"

"Yes, ma'am. Kenna Parker. You're a criminal defense attorney."

Her fingertips dug into the muscle beneath the cotton of his shirt, holding on when he would have pulled away. "How do you know? You said you couldn't find my purse."

She wanted to argue with him? *Patience, Watson. The woman is scared.* "You shredded a case of mine in court this afternoon. But I'm a cop before anything else. Now something terrible has happened to you tonight. I don't know what exactly, but I'm going to help you."

Her posture sagged, although her grip on him barely eased. He couldn't tell if she was frightened or angry or some combination of both.

"Detective Watson. I don't remember what happened to me tonight, much less this afternoon. I don't know how I got into that alley. I don't know why someone wanted to hurt me like this.

"I don't even remember my name."

Chapter Two

Kenna Parker.

Shivering in an immodest gown in the sterile hospital air, she silently worked the name around her tongue and wondered if she was truly remembering her name or if she'd simply heard it said to her so many times over the past few hours that she was now accepting it as fact.

Kenna.

She was Kenna Parker. She'd been named after her late father, Kenneth. She was [illegible] only child, a surprise gift to older parents who'd [illegible] expected to have children at all. No one had to [illegible] that tonight—or make that the early hours of S[illegible]ay morning. Kenna breathed a cautious sigh of [illegible]. She was remembering. Some of her life [illegible] like the growing-up [illegible] the reception desk [illegible] questions from [illegible] the admitting nurse [illegible] criminologist who'd scr[illegible]d beneath her fingernails and taken pictures of [illegible] injuries before the attending physician went to [illegible].

She couldn't remember [illegible]ther or not she was in a relationship. She couldn't [illegible] where she'd eaten dinner or even if she had eaten. And hard as she tried, she had absolutely no memory of being brutalized and left for dead, no image of her attacker haunting her thoughts. She had no memory of who hated her or something she represented or had done so much that splitting her head open and taking a sharp blade to the left side of her face seemed justifiable. The nicks on her hands, and the scrapes on her knee and foot, indicated she'd put up a fight. Surely she'd eventually remember a face or mask or height or voice or something if she'd done that kind of battle with her assailant.

But there was a black void in place of where any memory of the assault should be. Bits and pieces of her life before whatever had happened to her tonight were coming together like an old film reel being spliced together. Yet Kenna was afraid some parts of the movie would never be recovered. Even the last few hours after the assault were fi[illegible]d with holes. According to the doctor, scrambled [illegible]ins were a side effect of the head trauma she'd recei[illegible]d. Plus, he'd said that the amnesia could be psycho[illegible]cal, as *well*—that whatever she'd been through ha[illegible]een so awful that her mind might be protecting he[illegible]m the shock of remembering.

That didn't se[illegible]ght, though. She wasn't sure why, but Kenna got th[illegible]lin[illegible] from her defensive injuries, and her inability t[illegible]lax unt[illegible] figured out at [illegible] some part of what h[illegible] happened [illegible] that Kenneth [illegible]t she had a strong will to surviv[illegible]—that [illegible] some-one in her past had ta[illegible]ght her to think a[illegible] surrender to a weakn[illegible] like hysterical amnesia. [illegible]

A glimpse of somet[illegible]ng sharp and silver glinted in the corner of her eye an[illegible] Kenna shrieked. "Stop it!" Throwing up her hands, s[illegible]e snatched the man's wrist to stop the sharp object coming at her face.

"Nurse."

"Yes, Doctor." Small hands tugged at her shoulder and Kenna twisted away. "Easy, Ms. Parker. We're trying to help you."

"Get away from me!" Kenna evaded the hands and shoved the weapon away, fighting to sit up.

"Kenna." A firmer hand clasped her shoulder, refusing to be shrugged off. "You're safe. I've got your back."

Kenna froze at the deeply articulate male voice. She tilted her gaze to the dark-haired man with the badge and gun on his belt. Blue eyes. She knew those blue eyes. He was Detective…? The name that went with the piercing gaze escaped her for the moment. Still, she appreciated the clip of authority in his tone. If he said so, she believed he would keep her safe.

"The last thing we need is for her to panic. Isn't that right, Doc?"

The other man chuckled beside her. "It's never a good thing in the ER."

Kenna turned to the gentler voice and looked into the black man's warm brown eyes.

"That's where you are now. St. Luke's Hospital emergency room. You have a concussion, several abrasions and some deep cuts. I'm in the process of treating now that I know what medications I can use."

Kenna took a deep breath to calm the pulse pounding in her ears and nodded. She dropped her gaze to the plastic ID badge the doctor in the white lab coat wore around his neck. "Dr. McBride." She realized she still had his forearm clenched between her hands and quickly opened her grip. "I'm sorry. I thought you were… That someone was… I don't know what I thought."

"Did you remember something about the attack?" Detective Blue Eyes asked. "Is the syringe significant?"

"There was no evidence of drugs in her preliminary blood work," the doctor offered.

Keir nodded. "But there are some drugs that leave the system quickly."

"That's true. And I estimate these injuries occurred eight to ten hours ago."

"I don't think that's it," Kenna interrupted. "Something was coming at my face. I could see…" A black void filled the space where the memory should be. She shook her head. A syringe? She eyed the object in the doctor's hand and frowned. She couldn't have been cut with a syringe. Her focus narrowed to the tiny hash marks and numbers marking the syringe—*3 ml. 2.5 ml. 2 ml. 1.5…* A door slammed shut in her head and she wanted to scream.

So what did that mean? She tried to recall what it was that had triggered her panicked reaction. But when she closed her eyes to concentrate, she was greeted by the frightening abyss of her amnesia. Kenna quickly opened her eyes to focus on things she could recognize and shook her head. "Sorr[illegible]ve still got nothing."

"Not to worry." The detective p[illegible] away, retreating to the doorway where he must have[illegible] out of the doctor's and nurse's way. "We'[illegible]waiting [illegible] it out."

"I hope you're right."

He winked. "I'm always right."

His confidence surprised her for a moment before

she felt a smile softening her bruised, swollen face. His roguish charm distracted her from her fears and gave her back some of her own confidence. "Then we'd better get to it. I'll do my best not to freak out on anyone again."

While the nurse tucked a warm blanket around her, Dr. McBride rolled his stool back to the examination table and pointed to the items on the stainless steel tray beside him as he explained the procedure. She watched him pick up the syringe again, and her chest grew tight. Kenna breathed in deeply to dispel the uneasiness quaking inside her. Maybe she just had a thing about needles. With the nurse's help, she turned onto her side, looking away from the doctor as he went to work. "Go ahead, Doctor."

"I need you to relax. This is the same localized numbing agent I used on your scalp when I stitched that up. You'll feel three little pinches before I'm done."

Kenna nodded her understanding. If she wasn't going to have any useful kind of flashback, why bother trying to understand? Forcing her jumbled thoughts to organize themselves was only aggravating the headache throbbing against her skull. Maybe if she stopped fighting so hard to remember and didn't focus on anything except her present surroundings, the answers would finally come to her.

Dr. McBr[illegible] blessed patient with her and co[illegible] his treatment of her wounds. The nurs[illegible] around the ER room, setting equipment and medicines on the tray beside the doctor and taking away discarded items. Detective Blue Eyes—no, wait…Keir Watson. His name fell into place and she smiled inside. Finally. A memory that seemed to stick.

Detective Watson was either standing guard at the door or waiting to get the full report on her injuries from the doctor. Kenna wasn't sure why the younger man with the take-charge voice would still be here if it wasn't for some official reason. He'd explained more than once that they didn't have a personal connection. Instead, he'd described them as adversaries from work.

It was a shame to have forgotten a compelling face like Keir's. Chiseled bone structure that was perhaps a bit too sharp to be traditionally handsome was softened by a dusting of tobacco-brown beard stubble and a sexy half-grin. Those impossibly blue eyes narrowed with a question when he caught her studying him and she held his gaze until he folded his arms over his chest. The movement drew her attention lower. He'd put his jacket back on and she acknowledged another memory. Seeing how the dark gray wool hugged his shoulders and biceps, Kenna recalled Keir's body heat, and how quickly she'd warmed up with his jacket draped over her in his car. She remembered the faint scents of something oakish and bitter that had clung to the material, too, making her think he'd enjoyed some kind of drink before they'd met.

Or met again.

Or something like that.

Oh, how she hated being at s[illegible] a disad[illegible] Why was Keir her enemy? She'd do[illegible]omething to him. *Shredded a case* of his in court? Jus[illegible]at kind of attorney was she? Not one who worked for th[illegible]od guys, apparently.

Now, didn't that conjure up all kinds of possibilities as to who might want to hurt her? A client unsatisfied with her representation? The family member of a criminal who'd been sent to prison despite her best efforts? A victim upset because she'd kept someone *out* of prison? Was she trying a controversial case? Had she learned a dangerous secret from one of her clients that someone else was anxious to keep silent?

She didn't think this kind of violence could be random. Maybe the attack had nothing to do with her job. Did she have a jealous ex? A rival at work? It was impossible to evaluate her choices when she couldn't yet recall all the details of her life.

Kenna winced as the needle pricked the skin near her temple and closed her eyes when she felt a second pinch in her hairline. She gritted her teeth when she felt the third shot sting her jaw, and her breathing grew a little more rapid. How much more would she have to endure tonight?

She'd kept herself as calm and focused as she could, under the extreme circumstances. But the emergency room at St. Luke's Hospital in downtown Kansas City was a noisy, overwhelming place, especially for a woman who couldn't answer many of the questions the admitting clerk, attending nurse, emergency room physician or KCPD criminologist who'd left earlier had asked her over the last several hours.

Keir Watson's badge had gotten her through the red tape of checking in, but without an insurance card or a driver's license, the staff couldn't check her medical records. Dr. McBride had refused to give her anything for the pain or even antibiotics until he'd received a fax to back up her shaky assertion that she didn't *think* she was allergic to any medications. She was worn out. There wasn't any part of her that didn't hurt. And the wound to her memory wasn't something that Dr. McBride and his nurse could treat.

Were those tears chafing her eyelids? She wasn't a crier, was she? She'd hate that if she was. Exhaustion and frustration were finally winning the battle against the sheer will to keep it all together.

"Need something to hold on to?"

Kenna's eyes popped open when she felt a warm hand sliding over hers.

Keir Watson's grasp was as sure as the hug of his arms around her body had been when he carried her to his car. It was just as warm and reassuring, too, reminding her she wasn't alone and that someone strong and capable truly did have her back—even if it was only for tonight.

Kenna nodded her thanks and squeezed her fingers around the detective's solid grip. "Thank you. Again."

"Don't worry, Counselor. I'm keeping tabs on what you owe me."

Kenna hoped that his teasing tone was genuine, because she felt like smiling. Only, the shots had deadened the left side of her face and she couldn't tell if she'd smiled or not. The stiffness from the swelling and the raw ache of the open wounds finally disappeared with a numbing relief.

She squeezed her eyes shut and held on while the doctor worked on the long, deep cuts. He'd already pulled her hair off her forehead and cheek and anchored it off her face with one of those caps she'd seen doctors wear into surgery. Although she couldn't actually see what the doctor was doing, she felt the warmth of the sterile solution he squirted over her cuts and tasted miniscule grit and the coppery tang of her own blood at the corner of her lips before someone wiped it away. She felt the tugs on her skin and heard a couple of concerned sighs and quick orders to the nurse while he glued and sutured and applied tiny butterfly bandages to the wounds.

"I think we're finally done." The doctor rolled his stool away from the table and stood.

The left side of Kenna's face was still numb, her eyelid droopy from the anesthetic, when she finally let go of Keir's hand. He and the nurse helped her sit up and swing her legs over the edge of the table while Dr. McBride rattled off wound-care instructions and washed his hands. He shone a light into her eyes one more time, checking her pupil reaction, before smiling and giving her permission to leave on the proviso that she contact her personal physician Monday morning.

The nurse rolled aside the stainless steel tray piled with bloodied gauze and various tubes of antibiotics and skin glue. After depositing the sharps on the tray in the disposal bin, the nurse handed her several sheets of printed instructions and a package of sterile gauze pads and tape. Meanwhile the doctor reminded her of the symptoms to watch out for that might indicate the injury to her brain was getting worse.

"Thank you, Dr. McBride." Kenna spoke slowly to articulate around the numbness beside her mouth. "I appreciate everything you've done for me."

"You're lucky you can't remember what happened to you, Ms. Parker." He reached out and shook her hand, holding on for a few compassionate seconds. "If the amnesia turns out to be permanent, perhaps that's a good thing. I can't imagine how frightening an attack like that would be. You take care."

After Dr. McBride and the nurse had gone, Kenna tilted her gaze to the detective still standing beside the examination table. “So why don’t I feel lucky?”

“Because you don’t know who did this to you. And you’re afraid he or she might come back to finish the job.”

Exactly. “I think I liked you better when you held my hand and didn’t say anything.”

Keir slid his hands into the pockets of his charcoal slacks and grinned. “And here I thought you didn’t like me at all, Counselor.”

Kenna couldn’t understand why she wouldn’t have found this man charming. True, he seemed to be a few years younger than she was, but not enough to make any awkward difference. She had a feeling his sarcastic sense of humor was very much like her own, and she owed him more than she could repay for rescuing her and standing by her through this whole, tortuous ordeal. She tried to match his smile. “Tell me again why we’re supposed to be enemies? I hurt you, didn’t I? Hurt someone you care about. Oh, God, I didn’t sue you, did I?”

“No. You didn’t sue me.” He reached over to pluck the surgical cap off her head and let her hair fall around her face. “According to the doctor, I’d better not fill in the blanks. He said that in order for your memory to recover you need to figure out the missing details in your brain for yourself.”

That wasn’t all Dr. McBride had cautioned her about. “If it comes back at all.”

“You want to try again?”

“Try what?”

The detective pulled out his phone to show her a picture of a man wearing a black sweatshirt hoodie and blue jeans. "Do you recognize this man?"

Kenna studied the image for a few seconds. "Did he do this to me?"

"I can't say."

"Because you don't know? Or because you want me to tell you who he is."

Keir's firm mouth eased into a grin. "Can you identify this guy?"

She looked again. Even if she could remember the attack, there was little to identify in the picture. The man stood in the shadows behind a parked car, beneath a harsh circle of light from a street lamp creating shadows that rendered his face a black void that reminded her of the Grim Reaper.

"No. I don't know him." Not even the clothes looked familiar. She tucked the loose hair behind her ears. "What if I never remember what happened to me? How good a detective are you? Can KCPD solve a crime like that? I may not remember clients and faces, but I remember my books and law school and what it takes to make a good case. I can't imagine getting a conviction if the victim herself isn't a reliable witness. Any decent defense attorney would fry me in court."

Keir's eyes darkened to an unreadable midnight blue, and the grin disappeared. She'd struck a nerve there. Something to do with *shredding his case* again, she imagined. A fist squeezed around Kenna's heart. She didn't want whatever had happened between them in the past to ruin this…what? Friendship? Attraction? Maybe she was the only one imagining a connection between them. What if he was just a good cop following through on an investigation and she could have been any citizen he'd taken an oath to protect? Maybe she was more addled in the head than she knew and she couldn't tell the difference between being kind and caring.

Kenna dropped her feet to the floor and stood, reaching for Keir when he turned away. "What did I just say? I reminded you of something. What did I do to you?"

His cell phone vibrated, creating an audible buzz in the silence of the room while she waited for him to answer.

"Keir?"

But an explanation wasn't coming. Keir read the summons on the screen as it buzzed again. "The doc said I couldn't use my phone in here, but I need to take this."

An instinctive response to ask a different question—to get him to open up about something else before she steered the conversation back to what she really wanted to know—kicked in. "Who's calling you before dawn?"

"My partner. I asked him to do a wider search grid around the alley where I found you, see if he could find a primary crime scene or at least where you parked your car. He's searching to find the guy I showed you, too."

"He's a person of interest, isn't he?"

"I spotted him in the general vicinity where I found you. Don't know if he was sizing up a mark, if he was watching the alley to see if anyone noticed you or if he just had nothing better to do on a Friday night. I'd sure like to talk to him." The phone buzzed impatiently, and Keir backed toward the door. "I'll be out in the lobby."

Manipulating the conversation to get to the answer

she needed was starting to feel like second nature to her. Had she possessed this stubborn streak before the attack? "Tell me why you called me the Terminator earlier. It didn't sound like a compliment."

"I'll ask up front about getting you some clothes, too, since the CSI took your suit and shoe to the lab."

This conversation wasn't done. Kenna walked right up to him and fingered the lapel of his gray tweed jacket. She rubbed her thumb over the crimson smear staining the nubby material. "You'd better ask about a change of clothes for you, too. You've got blood on your jacket. My blood."

"I'm coming back." The gap—both literal and figurative—widened between them as he pulled the material from her fingers. Then he put the phone to his ear and turned away. "Hey, buddy. What's up?"

Kenna hugged her arms around her weary body and watched the door close behind him. Keir had managed to be supportive and evasive at the same time. "Run, you clever boy."

Clever boy. Where had that phrase come from? While she'd seen glimpses of a boyish charm, there was certainly nothing immature about Keir Watson. Not in his stature, his tone or his demeanor.

"Clever boy," she muttered the words again, mentally chasing the blip of a memory that floated through her head. "It's from a TV show." She watched TV. She had a hobby. "Blue box. British accents." One lightbulb, however dim, finally turned on inside her head. *"Dr. Who."*

She seemed to be in pretty good shape, so she wasn't a full-blown couch potato. Who did she watch it with? Family? Friends? A significant other? Why hadn't whoever she watched that show with come to see her at the hospital? Okay, sure, there was that whole thing with the missing phone and purse and relying on the police to track down where she lived and worked—but wasn't someone missing her? Alarmed that it was five in the morning and she hadn't come home?

Or was someone at home the danger she needed to fear? The person who'd gotten so angry that he or she had tried to kill her? How should she handle this? What was her next step? How was she supposed to know who to trust?

"Take a breath," she warned herself before panic reclaimed her.

Kenna hugged her arms around the thin cotton of her gown and glanced around the room, looking for answers. Looking for someone to talk to. Looking for a friend or sympathetic doctor or polite detective or anyone who could keep this helpless, lonely feeling from seeping in as surely as the air-conditioned chill that dotted her skin with goose bumps.

She had a feeling she wasn't used to relying on others to take care of her. Kenna eyed the soiled remains from treating her injuries that the nurse had wheeled into the corner. She wasn't used to being weak like this, forced to put her trust in people she didn't know. Had she put her trust in the wrong person, making herself a sitting duck who'd had no clue she was about to be attacked?

Fear crawled across her skin as the knowledge she would have to trust someone to help her through this sank in. Where was home? How was she supposed to get there? What was she supposed to do with herself the next morning? And the day after that?

Her gaze drifted over to the ER room's metal door. She'd put her trust in Keir Watson tonight. Not that he'd left her much choice. He'd allowed her a token argument, then had swept her up into his arms, bundled her into his car and driven her here. But she could have asked him to leave the treatment room at any time, and she hadn't. She wanted him with her.

Crazy as it seemed, Kenna knew Keir better than anyone else in her life. Once she'd come to and realized her brain had turned into Swiss cheese, it felt as if her whole life had reset. There was the time before the assault where her memory was riddled with empty spaces and vague shadows, and there was the time after—when she'd stumbled into Keir Watson's arms. He was the person she'd known the longest in the part of her life she was more certain of. And his abrupt departure to chat with his partner left her feeling about as vulnerable and confused and alone as she'd been when she first woke up with her cheek in a puddle of her own blood on the cold, gritty concrete.

Chapter Three

A sharp rap at the exam room door rescued Kenna from the maddening examination of her thoughts. She turned as quickly as the ball bearings inside her skull would allow and smiled, eager to apologize for showing Keir Watson anything but gratitude. "You came back."

"I haven't been anywhere yet."

Not Keir. Not a familiar face. Her smile quickly flat-lined and she backed her hip against the examination table as an older man with neatly trimmed hair that held more salt than pepper in it dropped what looked like a carry-on bag on the chair inside the door.

"Kenna, dear. Look at you. How horrible. Does it hurt?" He swallowed her up in a hug and planted a chaste kiss on her numb lips, giving Kenna the chance to do little more than wedge her hands between them and gasp in protest. "Of course it hurts. When I heard you'd been attacked..."

Kenna straight-armed him out of her personal space, pushing the older man back to get a better look at his face, hoping for a ping of recognition as he rattled on.

"...I paged the doctor. Pulled him out of a room down the hall and explained who I was so I could get a report." He squeezed her shoulders, threatening to hug her again. "He said you could have died."

"I'm sorry. I...?" Once again, it was disadvantage Kenna. *Something kick in. Please.*

The older man's eyebrows, as thick and wild as his hair was neatly cut, arched above his brown eyes like two fuzzy caterpillars. "You've forgotten me. The doctor said you had gaps in your memory—that you didn't even remember what happened to you." He covered her hand, capturing it against the front of the cashmere sweater he wore. "I'm your emergency contact. I'm the one who faxed your medical history to the hospital. It's me. Hellie."

What kind of silly name was that for a man? She tried to place the face, thinking those bushy eyebrows that so desperately needed a trim should look familiar. His skin was perfectly tanned, from too much time spent either on a golf course or in a pricey salon. And his teeth were unnaturally white. He was barely taller than she was in her bare feet, although he seemed reasonably fit for a man his age. "Hellie?" She repeated the odd name.

"Good grief, my dear, I've known you for fifteen years." Known her? How well? "Here. I'll prove it." He reached into the pocket of his pressed khaki slacks to pull out his billfold. "Here's my license, along with a picture of us with your mother and father."

"No. Wait." Kenna put a hand on his wrist to stop him. If Dr. McBride had talked to him about her condition, this man must have shown proof of a connection to her. The doctor had said she needed her memories to return to her naturally, that she needed to discover for herself what she knew and what she'd forgotten, or else she'd never be able to trust her own judgment again. "Let me figure it out."

The pungent scent of cigar smoke clinging to his clothes sparked a glimmer of recognition. He wasn't wearing a wedding ring, and she'd already noticed she wasn't, either. Not even an indentation from where one might have been stolen. Good. She hadn't forgotten a husband. But she had forgotten whatever relationship she shared with this man who thought he had the right to kiss her. Although it hadn't been much of a kiss. But perhaps the lack of any toe-curling response and spark of recognition had more to do with the anesthetic and swelling around her mouth rather than any innate repulsion. Still, she seriously hoped she could rule out boyfriend as a possibility.

The polished loafers and expensive leisure clothes reminded her of wealth. She'd been wearing a designer suit and one Jimmy Choo heel when Keir brought her to St. Luke's. So she had money, too. She was an attorney. She worked in a law firm. No, she was one of the owners of a law firm—an inheritance bestowed upon her by her father and earned through her own hard work. Bushy Brows was a partner. She pictured the letterhead on the stationery at an office desk—Kleinschmidt, Drexler, Parker and Bond—and understanding fell into place. He'd kissed her before, and she hadn't appreciated it then, either. "Helmut. You're Helmut Bond."

"Of course I am. I'd be surprised if you could forget old Hellie." Smiling, he went back to the doorway to pick up the bag. "I brought your overnight bag and insurance information and have already filled out the paperwork for you. I stashed your mail in here, too."

The man might be older, but he wasn't what she'd call old. He showed no lack of confidence, and clearly had money. Was this the kind of man she dated? She was feeling nothing like that little sting of awareness she'd felt when Keir held her hand. Was Helmut Bond supposed to mean more to her than a business associate?

Hellie set the bag on the examination table beside her. He pulled out a folder filled with papers and a sheaf of forms on a clipboard from the hospital. "These just need your signature. I took the liberty of canceling the forms you filled out earlier. These will be processed through insurance before you're billed."

Kenna took the pen he handed her, clutching it in her left hand while she fingered through the stack of letters and legal briefs bearing her name. Although she felt vaguely resentful that he had the presumption to make those business decisions for her, she supposed she had little choice about trusting that he had her best interests at heart.

Hellie tapped the form he wanted her to sign. "Are you sure you're okay? You remember how to write your name, don't you?"

"Sorry." Kenna switched the pen to her right hand and skimmed through the insurance form to make sure she wasn't agreeing to anything she shouldn't before signing her name on the bottom line.

Hellie returned the pen to the shirt pocket beneath his sweater. "Are these holes in your memory going to be permanent?"

"I don't know." She opened the file and pulled out a letter with the firm's letterhead and a space at the bottom awaiting her signature above her typed name.

Images of a group of people sitting around a boardroom table flickered in her brain, and the names on the stationery began to match up with faces. A stout older man with snowy white hair—Arthur Kleinschmidt. Her father's friend and a founding partner. Hellie—regaling everyone with a story. He enjoyed being the center of attention. Stan Drexler, only a couple of years older than Kenna, sat beside her. His gaunt face and receding hairline accentuated his pointy nose, reminding her of a rat. Yes, she was remembering having that amusing observation during the weekly staff meeting. She could see the faces of the other junior partners and personal assistants who sat at the table and moved through the lushly appointed room, although some of their names escaped her.

But that meeting had been when? Last week? Last month? Couldn't she be certain of anything more recent? Like yesterday and the events leading up to the assault?

"Do you remember what happened to you last night?" her visitor asked, frowning. "Did you give the police a description? Are we going to be able to arrest the SOB and prosecute him?"

She shook her head and pulled an envelope from the file, hoping that something else here would trigger a memory. "My body says that I was in a struggle of some kind. Unfortunately, I don't remember anything about it."

"Oh, Kenna." Hellie's gaze traveled with unabashed pity over the wounds on her face. But when he reached out to touch one, she turned away to open the envelope and pull out the letter inside. "I'm so sorry. Amnesia on top of being cut up like this? Will you have scars?"

Kenna's fingers flew to the stiches and glue as she clutched the folded paper to her chest. She hadn't even thought about disfigurement. Wasn't the memory loss enough of a burden to bear?

"It's a good thing you got Dr. Colbern off that murder charge. Maybe he can repay you with a little plastic surgery." Hellie chuckled at the inside joke Kenna didn't get. "Oh, come on. Andrew Colbern? Cosmetic surgeon? His wife accused him of hiring someone to have her killed? You proved the woman wrong, of course. Made the firm a tidy sum of money."

Of course? She'd defended this Dr. Colbern? Did she make a habit of defending would-be murderers? According to a few of Keir's comments, he thought the doctor was guilty. Yet she'd gotten Colbern off. That sort of history could go a long way toward explaining why a cop like Keir Watson might consider her an enemy.

Curious to ask those questions of Keir and confirm her suspicion, Kenna set aside the papers and unzipped the overnight bag. She dug through underwear, running shoes and yoga pants inside. But as soon as she'd located the cosmetics bag and pulled out a compact, she hesitated. Clutching the small bag to her chest, she turned to face Helmut. But it wasn't the fear of looking at her reflection that gave her pause, or even his crude remark about needing a plastic surgeon. Why would a coworker be her emergency contact? Didn't she have a family? Personal friends? A boyfriend? Why had she chosen to rely on this man? Because, frankly, he wouldn't be her first choice for a confidant if this uncomfortable meeting had been their first. "How do you have access to my personal things? Are we…?"

Hellie laughed. "You and me? Oh, honey, no. It's not for lack of trying, though. After my divorce, I thought maybe the two of us could hook up..." His good humor faded. "You don't remember that, either? We've served as each other's escorts to several fund-raising events. But when I suggested we could be something more, you turned me down flat."

She had? Did he hold that against her? This guy didn't seem particularly heartbroken.

"No matter how many laughs we've shared over the years, how much we have in common, you said, as partners in the same law firm—competing for the same promotions, high-profile cases and so on—that it wasn't a smart move for your career plan to see each other socially. I've accepted that and moved on. And your decision has paid off. Once Arthur retires, it'll be you or me who takes over as senior partner. Stan hasn't brought in the big clients and built his reputation the way you and I have."

Arthur? Stan? From the board meeting. Right. "And we're not seeing anyone else?" she asked.

"I've been dating Carol on and off."

"Carol?"

"Yes, she's your..." His voice trailed off and his lips curved into a pitying smile.

"My what?" A sister? Friend?

"I don't suppose you remember her, either."

Kenna shook her head.

"You said not to tell you."

"Hellie."

"Your executive assistant. Carol Ashton. Petite brunette? Shapely. Snarky. Superefficient? You're a stronger man than I am." He laughed at his male-female ribbing. "You've always been about the work and putting that first. But I need someone in my life. You don't complicate your goals with distracting relationships. I admire that about you."

She'd let the workaholic allusion, and the fact that she apparently defended criminals and had no personal life to speak of, slide for a moment. There was a more pressing clarification she still needed here. "So you can go to my house in the middle of the night and pack my things and greet me with a kiss because… we're old friends?"

How much of a player was Helmut Bond? Had she ever succumbed to his dubious charms?

"You did get a hard whack in the head, didn't you?" Hellie put one hand on her bag. "I picked this up at the office. Carol had those files stacked with the messages and mail on your desk. You always keep a bag packed in your closet in case you work late or are running straight to the gym. Your passport was in the safe there, so I pulled that for ID. Once the call to the firm's answering service was forwarded to me, I gathered the information I thought you'd need and came right to the hospital. We share the same insurance provider, of course."

"I see." She might as well ask him to confirm a few other suspicions. "I don't have any brothers and sisters, and both my parents are dead—Kenneth and…?"

"Gloria. Yes, they're both gone." Hellie cupped a hand around her shoulder again. She waited expectantly for him to continue, hearing the seconds ticking loudly from his watch near her ear. "You're worrying me. Do I need to call a specialist for you? We have several psychiatric consultants on retainer with the firm.

I could arrange for one of them to meet with you to go through hypnosis or memory exercises with you. We'd have to keep it hush-hush—out of the media so no one can question any of your recent or upcoming casework and claim incompetence and start filing appeals. I can draft a press release stating you're taking a leave of absence for your physical health after the assault. But I don't like seeing you like this."

Right. Being represented by an attorney who could be so easily distracted by the ticking of a watch, and who hadn't even remembered her own name a few hours earlier, would be bad for business. Appearing in court with her brains jumbled up like this wouldn't inspire a lot of confidence for the firm's clients. According to this man, those were liabilities that would have concerned her before the attack. But right now all she wanted was to understand who she was and what had happened to her.

"Kenna." Hellie's arms slid around her again. "Let me call someone. There are other cosmetic surgeons, other psychiatrists. If you're worried about a possible scandal, I can take you someplace outside Kansas City. I'll handle it personally."

Kenna shrugged off his tobacco-scented touch and stepped away before she realized the door was open and Keir Watson was standing there. His jacket was pulled back and his hand rested on the butt of the gun strapped to his belt. A frown deepened the angles on his face. How much of that conversation had he overheard? Had he heard the bit about her defending a man accused of murder? Or just the part about her so-called friend here claiming she needed a shrink?

As soon as she made eye contact over Hellie's shoulder, the detective pulled his hand off his weapon and strode into the room. "Dr. McBride said you had a visitor. For a second, I thought maybe Hoodie Guy..."

Was he worried her attacker had tracked her down to finish what he'd started? "I'm okay."

"Sure you are." Keir held out his hand, and Kenna deliberated for all of a nanosecond before she instinctively reached out to take it and let him pull her away from Hellie to stand beside him. "She's been through a lot tonight, sir. Maybe you should take a step back and give her time to process everything that's happened in the past few hours before you send her off to a psychiatrist and hire a spin doctor to protect your firm."

"Who are you?" Hellie's eyebrows met in an expression that was suddenly as serious as she'd expect any cutthroat attorney's to be. His gaze dropped to where she clung to Keir's hand. "This isn't a private room, son, but I can make it one."

Son? Kenna pointed a finger at Bushy Brows. "You're out of line. You owe this man an apology."

But Keir Watson didn't need her to defend him. He released her hand and took a step toward Helmut Bond. He held up his badge. "Keir Watson, KCPD. I drove Ms. Parker to the ER. I'm the one who called your office because that was the only lead I had to track down someone who knew her personally."

"Yes, of course. Thank you for calling, Officer."

"It's Detective. And you are...?"

"Helmut Bond. Ms. Parker's legal representative and friend. Thank you for your service to the community, *Detective*." He emphasized Keir's rank as though granting that concession of respect left a sour taste in his mouth. "But your presence here is no longer needed.

I'll be driving Kenna home as soon as the doctor dismisses her."

Garrulous? Self-important? Allegedly dating her assistant *and* playing touchy-feely with her? Kenna had had enough. "Thank you for bringing my things, Hellie, but—"

"*I'm* driving Ms. Parker home," Keir announced.

Heat flushed the side of her face that wasn't numb from the anesthetic. "You are?" Kenna was momentarily confused by the relief surging through her, yet she seized the offer without question or apology. "I mean, he is," she stated with a little more compunction. "I feel safer with a police escort. You understand."

"Kenna, in your condition, you're hardly competent to decide who—"

"I can make my own decisions, thank you," Kenna snapped. Hellie might be a well-meaning friend, but these verbal jabs about her mental state were starting to rankle. "Detective Watson knows more about the investigation into the attempt on my life than anyone. I feel safe with him. I want him to take a look around my place and make sure everything is secure."

Despite the hard feelings he seemed to have when he'd left the room, Keir didn't have any problem following her lead and backing her up now. "I also want to confirm that it's not the primary crime scene."

"Couldn't you do that in the morning?" Hellie suggested. His brown eyes lingered on her, even though he addressed them both. "Later this morning, that is. Kenna's estate is protected by the same security company and alarm system all of our firm's partners use. If there was a break-in at her home, believe me, the police would already know about it. Give her time to get some rest and freshen up."

"Do you really think freshening up is what I'm worried about right now?" she asked.

"I'm just saying the assault didn't happen at the Parker mansion."

Was he telling her to reassure her or to force her to remember? Kenna crossed her arms around her middle, suddenly feeling very aware that the only shield she had was her hospital gown, a pair of panties and whatever attitude she could muster. She didn't have the truth on her side, because she didn't know it. And she seemed to be particularly vulnerable to every barb and innuendo Hellie uttered.

Keir might have picked up on her hesitation. Or maybe this was a testosterone thing and he simply was refusing to lose an argument to the other man. "What if her attacker disabled the alarms and security? What if it was someone she knew and she let him in? What if it was you?"

"You're walking a fine line between investigating a case and slander, Detective." Helmut Bond certainly wasn't backing down from the position of authority he claimed to have in her life. "If you want to find out the facts, do so. Do the job you're paid to do. But leave Kenna out of it."

"He'll leave me out of nothing." The backbone she'd been searching for surfaced from the cloud of fear and frustration she'd been battling all night. Kenna linked her arm through Hellie's and guided him toward the door, winging this conversation based on the clues she'd gathered from everything the man had told her since barging into the room. "You know that I'm a driven woman. I don't wait for answers to fall into my lap. I take action. Keir is in a better position than anyone to help me with that."

"I would think you'd want a friend to rely on instead of some stranger."

"I know who I want. Detective Watson."

"At least you're sounding more like the woman I know." Helmut patted her hand where it rested on his arm.

He squeezed his fingers around hers, and she couldn't help comparing his light, smooth caress to the firm, calloused grip of Keir Watson's hand.

"Very well. I suppose it is a practical solution. What about your casework coming up next week? Anything you'd like me to tell Arthur and Stan? Anything you want Carol to put together for you?"

"It's the weekend." Between Keir and the doctor, she'd answered enough questions earlier to know she had that much right. "I'm allowed to take a couple of days off."

"You not work on the weekend?" Hellie shook his head as he opened the door. "Now I've seen everything. I thought you had a deposition on Monday to prepare for. Colbern's wife has threatened to file a civil suit against our client and the firm for emotional damages, and Arthur has asked me to step in and join the team. And though I don't really think she stands a chance of succeeding, we're on Judge Livingston's docket Thursday to go through preliminary motions. Plus, since you're the one who was working with Colbern, I'm counting on you taking that meeting with me to go over what role the firm will play when he faces the medical ethics board. I'll represent the firm's interests, of course, since he's threatened to sue, but—"

"I had my brains bashed in, Hellie. The doctor said half an inch in either of two directions and I'd be dead." More eager than ever to get rid of him, Kenna nudged him into the hallway. "I'll see how I feel Monday morning and call the office if I need to postpone or have someone else cover my appointments."

"But—"

"But nothing. I can't even think of who Judge Livingston is right now, much less what motions you're talking about. I don't remember Andrew Colbern or his wife or my assistant. And if you need me to manage your cases for you, you'll just have to wait."

His expression hardened and Kenna realized they had more of an audience than the detective watching them from inside the exam room. Did she always sound like such a harpy when she got upset? Was her impatience with Hellie a by-product of injury and fatigue? Whatever filter she'd had on her emotional impulses must have bled out with the gash behind her ear. Her nostrils flared with a deep breath and she lowered her tone to a more civil pitch and nodded to the nurse who'd helped her earlier.

Once the other woman's concerned expression eased, and she moved on down the hallway, Kenna looked to Hellie. "I'm sorry. I don't mean to snap at you. I'm not feeling like myself right now. The doctor said I'd need a few days for the swelling and headache to recede. I need to evaluate my recovery before I return to work."

Appeased by her apology, Hellie smiled. "Of course. Take whatever time you need. I just wanted you to know how valuable you are to the firm, and not worry for one moment that we don't need a woman like you at Kleinschmidt, Drexler." A woman like her? Was that a compliment or some kind of sexist remark? "My teasing about work is just the kind of tough love pep talk I'd expect from you if our situations were reversed."

She'd trade tough love for losing this headache and a little bit of TLC right about now. "Thank you for coming. Now if you don't mind, I'd like a little privacy so I can change out of this lovely hospital gown."

Kenna turned her head aside when he leaned in to give her a kiss. Was this uncomfortable feeling Hellie gave her the subconscious part of her brain trying to give her some kind of warning? Or was it simply having something come at her face, the same way she'd reacted to the syringe, that made her flinch? After a momentary hesitation, he pulled away. "I'll be in touch."

He was heading toward the lobby when Kenna reentered the examination room. She closed the door behind her and leaned against it with a weary sigh before crossing to the exam table to gather her things. "Thanks for rescuing me again. I thought he'd never leave."

"Told you I'm keeping tabs, Counselor." Keir turned to face the table with her while she packed up the papers Hellie had brought. "Although it sounded as though you could handle him yourself if you needed to."

The burst of indignant energy she'd shown Hellie seemed to ebb with every inhale of Keir's warm, musky scent. If calming reassurance was a commodity, this man could make a fortune selling it. Feeling herself relax a little, Kenna picked up the folded letter she'd wadded in her fist and opened it to make sure she hadn't damaged an important document. Several flattened, desiccated rose petals fell out and fluttered to her feet. She looked at the parchment-colored paper, flipped it over and a vague sense of unease quickened her pulse. She had no idea why, other than this was a really weird thing to receive in the mail. There was only one symbol typed on the entire page—a capital *O* in the top left-hand corner of the paper. The rest of it was just as blank as the important parts of her memory were. "What do you suppose that means?"

"Someone's printer ran out of ink?"

"The sender wouldn't notice the page was blank before stuffing it into the envelope?"

Keir knelt at her bare toes and gathered up the petals to drop them into her hand. "Secret admirer? Maybe that's just a piece of scrap paper to contain these, and the roses are the message."

"Why would I be sentimental about dead things?" There was certainly nothing about the once red petals that had shriveled and faded with age that sparked any kind of warm feeling inside her. "I suppose these meant something to me before the attack."

Keir picked up the envelope so they both could look at it. It had been addressed to her at work and stamped with a Kansas City postmark, although there was no return address.

"The sender definitely wants to remain anonymous." Keir opened the flap for her to drop the scentless petals inside. "Did Bond bring this to you?"

Kenna nodded, stuffing the wrinkled paper inside,

as well. “Everything was in the bag he brought. It all came from my office.”

“Do you mind if I catch up to him and ask him about it? Maybe find out where he was tonight?”

She tilted her gaze to meet his, hearing the suspicion behind his question. “Hellie’s a friend—maybe a little pompous and annoying—but he didn’t do this to me.”

“How do you know he’s a friend? You’re just going to take his word for it? The guy took his own sweet time in getting here. Made a couple of tacky comments that weren’t as funny as he thought. Asked a lot of questions, too—like he might be checking to see how much you remember.”

Keir’s fingers closed around her arm, and she wondered at the urge to turn into the warmth seeping through the thin cotton of her gown.

“How do you know he didn’t hurt you? Do you remember the face of your attacker? Was he wearing a mask? Anything about his build? His ethnicity? Whether it was even a man?”

The sensation of warmth quickly dissipated as she shrugged away from his touch. As much as she appreciated his honesty, the reminder that she hadn’t been able to give him any of those details rattled her. Maybe this blind faith in Keir Watson, this feeling that she knew him better than anyone else now, was a false comfort. “How do I know *you* didn’t do this to me, Detective? You said we were enemies. Maybe sending me what’s left of a dead rose after cutting me up is your idea of a joke.”

Instead of taking offense at standing her ground, the way Helmut Bond had, Keir grinned. “Now you’re being smart. Stay that way.” He lightly pinched her chin between his thumb and forefinger before heading out the door. "And I really am driving you home, so don't get any ideas about calling a cab and sneaking out of here. I'll be outside in the hallway chatting up *Hellie* for a few minutes. Then I'll bring the car around and meet you at the lobby exit when you're ready."

Nodding, Kenna closed the door behind him and crossed to her bag to pull out her clothes. It took her only a few minutes to put on the workout pants, tank top and jacket, and slip into her running shoes. It took a bit longer to carefully pull a comb through her hair without aggravating her injuries and dab on some copper gloss over her tingling lips.

With her papers and toiletries packed in the bag, she looked around the ER room one last time to make sure she had everything. Ready to leave this nightmare behind her, she hurried out into the hallway, only slowing her steps once she reached the lobby. She didn't have to worry much about curious stares because most of the people sitting or pacing among the pods of furniture had their own illnesses and loved ones to worry about. When she didn't see Keir anywhere, conversing with Helmut Bond or waiting out front in his black muscle car, Kenna perched on the edge of an empty chair near the front doors to wait.

Since she had no idea where he'd parked after dropping her off at the ER doors, she didn't know how long it would take him to walk to his car and come back for her. But the clock over the reception desk had already ticked away five minutes. Maybe Keir had gotten into another argument with Hellie. Maybe he wasn't coming back for her. Maybe putting her trust in the younger detective was the stupidest thing she'd ever done.

A nervous sense of abandonment tried to take hold, filling her shattered brain with fear and doubt. Determined not to give in to the debilitating feeling, Kenna squirmed in her chair, slowly turning her head to study the other patients and family members waiting in the lobby area. For the sun to not even be up yet, there were a surprising number of people waiting to be seen or to hear news of a loved one. Fortunately, no one seemed to notice her growing agitation—not the children putting together a puzzle with their grandmother and chatting about baby names, not the elderly couple holding hands while they both tried to read magazines, not the teenager dozing in a chair beside his texting buddy or the man on his cell phone pacing in front of the windows.

All of these people had connections to someone. All of them were absorbed in their own private worlds, oblivious of everyone else in the hospital. Kenna was the only one spying on anyone else's troubles, the only one curious enough to…

A chill rippled down her spine as if someone had blown a soft breath against the back of her neck.

She wasn't the only one watching.

Kenna spun around, immediately squeezing her eyes shut against the vertigo slamming through her skull. Several seconds passed before she dared to open her eyes. Had Keir pulled up out front? She didn't see any black cars beneath the canopy outside the hospital doors. Holding her palm against her throbbing temple, she stood and slowly surveyed the lobby. Was that…?

An afterimage of a man standing at the edge of the hallway to the ER treatment rooms imprinted itself on her brain. A faceless man in jeans and a black hoodie. Standing there. Watching her.

She blinked her eyes to focus them again, only there was no hoodie. No man, period. She glanced around the lobby again. The teenagers were both wearing hooded sweatshirts, one blue, one black. But they couldn't be in two places at once. Was she confusing them with the man she'd seen? Or imagining the picture from Keir's phone? Was her vision as addled as the rest of her brain?

Not willing to add hallucinations to the rest of the symptoms she had to deal with, Kenna hugged her bag beneath her arm and crossed the lobby to the hallway. She saw no one like the man she'd imagined here, only nurses hurrying about their business and an orderly pushing a patient in a wheelchair off the elevator. Needing confirmation one way or the other as to what she'd seen or hadn't seen, she walked down the hallway, glancing inside open doors, catching a glimpse of the empty elevator closing, wondering if the man she'd seen had stepped into a room or stairwell and shut the door behind him.

Kenna paused at the room where she'd been treated. The door stood ajar. Surely not… It would be too much…

Taking a deep breath and steeling herself for the unexpected, she pushed open the door.

Empty. Thank God. Her lungs deflated on an exhale of relief.

Until she saw Dr. McBride's work cart. The stainless steel tray had been moved across the room. And though the trash from bandage kits, hair bonnet and the saline bottle remained, someone had knocked the bloody gauze that had been there only minutes earlier onto the floor. No. There was only one lonely strip of soiled gauze lying there. The rest was missing. She checked the trash. She checked beneath the examination table.

Kenna's breathing grew shallow. Her pulse pounded against every wound on her head. This wasn't right. Something wasn't right. She doubted that any orderly had been in to clean—he would still be in here working if he hadn't cleared away everything.

Who would steal a souvenir of her blood and pain?

Who wanted that piece of her?

Who was the hooded man? "What do you want from me?"

Kenna turned and smacked into a solid chest. Hands clamped around her shoulders and a gasp of fear stuck in her throat. She twisted.

"Kenna?"

She shoved against the trap. "Let go of me!"

"Kenna." Strong arms tightened around her. "You're shaking. What's wrong?"

She couldn't catch her breath. She couldn't think. But she could feel. Strength and warmth. She could smell. Musky and familiar. Keir. Instinct guided her arms beneath his jacket and around his waist. She pressed her face against the warm column of his neck.

Keir shifted his hold on her, sliding one hand up beneath her hair to palm the nape of her neck, and whispered against her ear, "You need to talk to me. Right now."

"I saw him. The man in the hood. The man in your picture. He was here."

Chapter Four

Keir was in trouble. He hadn't been to bed in twenty-four hours, and had endured one hell of a day at work and an emotional roller coaster of a night at the hospital. He needed a shave, some food and a serious attitude adjustment—but he didn't care. As he pulled his car into an empty lane of the highway to skirt the beginnings of morning rush-hour traffic, he tried to figure out when and how his well-ordered world had subtly shifted into this dangerous, uncharted territory. He had the why nailed down already. Scrubbing at the weary muscles at the back of his neck, he glanced over to the woman dozing in the seat across from him.

Kenna Parker was the reason why.

She was the reason he'd given up a good night's sleep, the reason he was calling in favors to get intel on an investigation that wasn't officially his, the reason he was speeding across town to take her home when he could just as easily have called a cab or even a squad car for her.

She'd torn apart the murder-for-hire case he'd put together that should have been a slam dunk, guaranteeing that he'd be having a conversation with the major case squad's lead detective Monday morning to find out how she'd bested him in a courtroom. Nobody bested him. He'd turned success into an art form. He always had a plan B or a plan C if something went south on him. He won bets and had his pick of women and solved cases with a cool blend of resourcefulness, wits and determination that had rarely failed him.

Playing savior to Kenna Parker just didn't make sense.

He wasn't supposed to like the woman who defended some of the worst criminals he and the rest of KCPD tried to put away. And yeah, it still grated on his ego that he hadn't been able to get a conviction on Andrew Colbern. Yet there was something fascinating about Kenna outside the courtroom. She was confident and self-sufficient in many ways, yet surprisingly vulnerable in others. Maybe it was just the blow to the head and slice-and-dice some pervert had done to her face that had revealed that vulnerability to him. But she seemed at such a disadvantage to egomaniacs like Hellie Bond who wanted to dictate her choices, to the perp who'd attacked her so viciously and who could, quite possibly, come back to finish the job and to that creeper who'd shown up twice now and vanished without a trace, despite a sweep of the neighborhood and hospital.

He wanted to believe that the photo he'd shown Kenna had created the power of suggestion in her scrambled brain to misidentify one of the two teenagers in the lobby who matched Hoodie Guy's description. But she was certain the boys had been on the sofa the entire time she glimpsed the man watching her and had tried to track him on her own. She was adamant not only that the man had been spying on her, but that he'd stolen a gross souvenir from her time in the ER. What kind of sicko wanted to keep the blood of his victim? This was looking more and more like some kind of obsession, because Keir imagined her attacker had kept her shoe and purse and whatever personal belongings she'd had on her at the time of the attack, too.

She couldn't be imagining the threat lurking in the shadows around her. He'd seen Hoodie Guy, too. And he wasn't about to accept it as coincidence that a man matching that description had now shown up at two locations where Kenna was. And until she regained her memory or they could find some other way to identify her attacker, every person she met was a potential enemy.

Keir didn't like those kinds of odds in a fight. Nor could he deny her sense of humor and keen intelligence that had helped her cope with it all.

Kenna was as clever and complex as Tammy had been vacuous and transparent. He'd gotten a little rush from their verbal sparring matches. And what was with his straying gaze when it should be firmly fixed on the road? Kenna Parker had legs that went on for miles, with long, lean curves emphasized by the clingy yoga pants and zippered workout jacket she wore. At the hospital, she'd held on to him as if her life depended on it, and his body had waked at the contact. His fingers craved the smooth silk of her skin. His nose sought out the cool, citrusy scent of her hair. Their bodies fit together like two pieces of a puzzle. He'd held on as long as she'd needed him to, and then for a few seconds longer because he needed to hold her. Even now his heart hammered a little harder in his chest as he remembered the imprint of her in his arms.

"You're tired, Watson," he warned himself, inhaling a deep breath and dragging his focus back to the highway. Keir glanced at the GPS on the dashboard, and busied his mind with estimating how much longer it would be until they reached the Parker Estate off State Line Drive.

He wasn't supposed to feel compassion for Kenna Parker. He wasn't supposed to have his hormones buzzing with awareness about the color of her eyes or the clinging grip of her hand or those sexy, muscular legs stretched out beneath the dashboard of his Dodge Charger.

Yep. He was so in trouble.

"You're not falling asleep on me, are you, Detective?" a softly articulate voice asked.

Kenna's eyes lit like silver with the glow from the dashboard lights. Somehow he'd missed her studying him between those long blond lashes. Right. He'd been enjoying the view farther down and fooling himself into thinking that there was something real happening between them. Conceding how distracted he was, Keir flexed his fingers around the steering wheel. "It's been a long night."

She pushed herself up straighter in her seat and adjusted her seat belt. "I'd offer to drive, but—"

"No license, no insurance card, no idea of where we're heading?"

Her concern over dangerous driving fatigue seemed to ease with the teasing repartee. "Well, I know we're in Kansas City."

"Lucky guess."

She smiled at that, then winced just as quickly. When she touched her fingertips to the line of stitches along her jaw, he suspected the anesthesia the doctor had used on her was wearing off. She had to be in discomfort if not outright pain.

He was on the verge of asking if they needed to stop for aspirin or ice packs when she leaned forward and pointed out his window to the pink haze on the horizon. "And I know we're heading south because that's the sun coming up."

"Okay, so you *do* remember a thing or two."

"I remind you that I have partial amnesia, not a case of the stupids."

It was Keir's turn to relax his concern. "No, ma'am."

"Ma'am?" She groaned. "That makes me feel old. My passport says I'm only thirty-eight. How old are you?"

He liked the *only* distinction she put on her age. "Thirty-three. And a half," he added, just to get a rise out of her.

Kenna laughed and swatted him on the shoulder. "That's terrible, Junior. Are you always this obnoxious?"

"Pretty much."

"Well, it works for you." The laughter faded as another mile passed and she leaned back against the headrest. "Why do I get the feeling my house is way out of your way? Hellie gave me the entry codes for the gate and front door, told me how to reset them once we're inside. But what if the codes don't work or you discover something suspicious? Your late night is going to turn into a long day and I've already taken advantage of your kindness and sense of duty and…"

Was she thinking about how long they'd stood in

each other's arms at the hospital, too? "We've had this discussion. Driving you home is not a problem."

She rolled her head to face him and winked. "Must have forgotten that."

Keir shook his head, grinning at her ability to handle all this with humor and class. "Now who's obnoxious?" The distinctive growl of her stomach rumbling triggered a gnawing echo inside his own belly. "Hungry?"

"I think I had a dinner meeting scheduled last night. But I don't know if I ever made it to the meeting, or if I ate anything. I couldn't even think about food in the hospital." She flattened her hand over her noisy stomach. "I'd kill for a cup of coffee, at least. Maybe we could stop at a coffee shop before we get to my house?"

Trouble reared its head again and Keir didn't resist. He needed a distraction, and so did she.

"I've got a better idea. Time for a detour." Keir eyed the cars and semitrucks behind him and pulled over three lanes to catch the next exit.

"What are you up to?" she asked.

Once he'd circled around into slower traffic, he pulled out his phone and punched in one of his favorite numbers. "I'm starving. You need caffeine." Keir had loved his mother, his sister, Sophie Collins and one other woman in his life. When the woman who had raised him and still kept house for his father and grandfather answered the phone, he couldn't help smiling. "Hey. How's my favorite girl in the whole wide world?"

"Keir?" He'd always loved Millie Leighter's laugh. "What are you up to this morning?"

"Millie, my love. Have you got a pot of coffee going already?"

Across the seat, Kenna whispered, "You're inviting me to breakfast with your girlfriend?"

"Not exactly." He turned his attention back to Millie. "I'm just coming off an all-nighter, woman, and I'm hungry for your home cookin'. I've got a guest with me, too. Is that all right?"

"Is it Hudson?" From the moment Keir had first introduced them, Millie seemed to think his bachelor partner needed a little mothering and fattening up. The fact that Hud ate up all the attention only added to her infatuation with the man.

"Not this time." He laughed. "But I'm sure he'd take a rain check."

"You know there's always room at this table for you and your friends. The more the merrier. But I warn you, your oldest brother came home late last night to hash something out with your father. And Seamus is in a cantankerous mood this morning. I don't think his physical therapy went well."

Curious, that Duff had spent the night at the house where they'd grown up instead of in his own apartment. And when wasn't his grandfather at odds with someone or something anymore? "I'll risk it. See you in a few minutes."

It didn't occur to Keir to ask Kenna if she was up for meeting a good part of his family until he'd pulled into the driveway behind Duff's truck and was escorting her up the stairs to the brick porch. "I hope this is okay. The Watsons can get a little boisterous when there's more than one of us in the room, but I promise we're a casual kind of bunch. The food will fill you up and you won't find a better cup of coffee anywhere."

Kenna finger-combed her hair over the injuries on her face and nodded. "I'm sold."

He caught her hand before she lowered it and offered a squeeze of reassurance. "You don't have to hide those. Dad raised three boys and a tomboy—we're used to seeing stitches and war wounds."

Her fingers tightened around his. "Thanks. But that's not exactly what I'm nervous about. I haven't met any of them before, have I?"

"Not that I know of."

"Good. Then I'm starting with a clean slate. I may not make the best first impression, but at least they don't know any more about me than I do them."

A level playing field wasn't too much for a woman with amnesia to ask for, he supposed. But he couldn't imagine her not impressing anyone with her tall, confident posture and those beautiful, starlit eyes. He squeezed her hand one more time before releasing her to open the storm door. "You'll be fine."

He knocked on the inside door, triggering the excited barking of a dog, before pushing it open and inviting Kenna inside.

A dark brown dog, the size of a small tank, skidded around the corner on the wood floor and collided with Kenna's foot. "Oh. Hello."

"Look out," Keir warned. The dog righted herself, then rose on her haunches to meet the new visitor. "Ruby, down. Sorry about that."

Kenna pushed the Lab mix down into a sit position and held her fist to the dog's nose for sniffing and licking, making an instant friend. "That's okay. What is she? A chocolate Lab?"

"She's something all right. Dad rescued her from the

Humane Society. Ruby's half Lab, half mystery beast and half spoiled rotten."

"That's one and a half dogs." Correctly assessing that this was no kind of guard dog, Kenna scratched around the big galoot's furry ears. "Pretty impressive pedigree, Miss Ruby."

Duff Watson sauntered out of the living room, eating a cinnamon roll that smelled as if it was still warm from the oven, and Ruby immediately changed allegiance to the human with the food. "Look what the cat dragged in."

Millie hollered from the kitchen at the back of the sprawling two-story Colonial. "Thomas Watson, Jr., don't you be dropping crumbs in my clean house. And do not feed that dog."

"You're in trouble, big guy," Keir teased. "She used your real name."

Duff popped the last of the roll into his mouth and held up ten fingers to show empty hands. "What's she talking about? I didn't take any food out of the kitchen." He eyed Kenna, lingering a moment on her face before turning back to Keir. "You brought company."

"This is Kenna Parker. My oldest brother, Duff."

"I know who you are." After wiping his fingers on the front of his chest-hugging T-shirt, Duff extended his hand to Kenna. "Nice to meet you." Then he seemed to quickly dismiss her as he backed away toward the kitchen. "Millie baked fresh rolls this morning, baby bro. First come, first served." He patted his thigh for the dog to follow him. "Come on, mutt."

Once Duff and Ruby had turned the corner into the kitchen, Kenna leaned over and whispered, "I thought you said none of your family knew me."

"Yeah." Keir scraped his fingers over the stubble on his jaw. "Maybe I didn't think this through. Even if you haven't met, they know you by name and reputation. Duff's a cop, too. My grandpa is retired KCPD and Dad works as an investigative consultant for the department."

"I see. And I'm Enemy Number One to every Kansas City cop?"

Not every cop.

"Son." Keir didn't get to respond as his father came down the stairs. This time of the morning, before he'd been on his bum leg for too long, his limp was barely noticeable. "Millie said you'd called." He pulled Keir in for a hug before stepping back to shake Kenna's hand. "I'm Thomas Watson. Welcome."

"Thank you. I hope I'm not imposing, sir."

"Thomas," he corrected with a smile, then invited them to follow him down the hallway to the kitchen. "We've got a full house this morning. Saturday usually means a big breakfast around here, which means one or more of the offspring tends to show up. Come on in and I'll introduce you to everyone." He nodded to the silver-haired woman stirring eggs on the big, six-burner stove. "Good morning, Millie. Coffee ready?"

"Of course." She turned off the burner and wiped her hands on her blue apron that read If You Can't Stand the Heat, Get Out of the Kitchen and reached for Keir. He willingly wrapped her plump figure up in a hug. "There's my favorite boy."

Duff came up behind her. "I thought I was your favorite."

"I saw you share that piece of bacon with the dog, so you're on my naughty list. Now go sit down before you eat us out of house and home, and I'll put the food on the table so we can eat like civilized people."

"Yes, ma'am." Duff planted a kiss on Millie's cheek and reached around her to steal another strip of bacon.

Duff was twice the older woman's size, but she swatted his hand and shooed him out into the dining area before turning to Keir again. She reached up to cup his unshaven cheek. "Where's my handsome boy? You're scruffy this morning. You look like you haven't slept a wink."

"I haven't. Spent the night in the ER with Kenna."

Millie smoothed his wrinkled lapels, and her smile faded. "What's this? Blood?"

"Relax, it's not mine."

But in Millie's mind this was an emergency and she would handle it. She patted the crimson marks before pushing the jacket off his shoulders. "Take this off and let me spot-clean it before the stains set."

"Millie—"

"Come on, now. I insist."

"All right." Keir shrugged out of the jacket and handed it to the older woman. But as soon as she stepped toward the sink, he helped himself to a strip of bacon, too.

"Oh, you."

He grinned when she shooed him away from the counter, too.

"Your big brother is a bad influence on you. I need Niall here to keep the peace."

Keir had a feeling the middle Watson son wouldn't be interested in refereeing his brothers' misbehavior anytime soon. He grinned at the thought of his quiet, brainy brother, a medical examiner with the crime lab who'd been occupied the past few months learning a whole new set of skills as father and husband-to-be. Who'd have thought that Dr. Niall would be the first Watson brother to be getting married? Keir had always thought that Niall had the emotional range of a lamppost. But after saving his sweet, feisty neighbor and the baby boy she fostered from a ruthless killer, Niall hadn't just fallen—he'd fallen hard for Lucy McKane. Thank goodness he'd been smart enough to propose. Keir had a feeling there weren't two people on the planet who needed each other more than Niall and Lucy did.

Yep. Keir might have the moves with the ladies. But Niall had the luck. If Keir didn't like Lucy so much himself, he'd be jealous. "Niall is probably up to his eyeballs in diapers and wedding plans."

Millie folded the jacket over the crook of her elbow and clapped her hands together. "That reminds me, I promised Lucy and Niall that I'd be over to their place to babysit Tommy later this morning while they go to the mall and start registering for wedding gifts. So we'd better get this meal on the table." She reached for Kenna's hand even before introductions were made. "Where are my manners? You must be Keir's friend Kenna. How are you feeling, dear?"

"I've had better nights." She matched the older woman's smile. "But my mood is picking up already. It smells wonderful in here."

"I'm Millie. I run this household."

"I can see that. Thank you for adding one more. May I help you carry food to the table?"

"Nonsense. After a trip through the ER? You need to sit down and relax." Millie poured a mug of coffee and pushed it into Kenna's hands as if she thought their guest could use a little mothering, too. She set the platter full of bacon in Keir's hands and nudged him toward the kitchen island and the dining area beyond. "Cream and sugar's on the table. Grab the eggs and take Kenna in there and introduce her to your grandfather while I take this to the laundry room."

"Yes, ma'am." Keir led Kenna into the dining area and set the platter and bowl of scrambled eggs on one end of the long oak table. "Good morning, Jane. Grandpa." He nodded to the nurse in green scrubs with a short brown ponytail helping his white-haired grandfather reach his chair with his walker. It was good to see the family patriarch on his feet and moving, albeit slowly, under his own power. Up until a few weeks ago, he'd still been relying on a wheelchair after the brain damage from being shot had resulted in a massive stroke that had paralyzed his entire left side. Keir circled behind Kenna to pull out a chair for his grandfather and help him position himself while the nurse steadied the walker. "Kenna, this is Jane Boyle, Grandpa's live-in nurse. And this handsome old fart is Seamus Watson."

His grandfather groaned at the introduction and angled his rheumy blue gaze up at Keir while the two women exchanged a polite greeting.

Kenna nodded. "How do you do, Mr. Watson?"

"Say-moof," Grandpa insisted, his half-limp mouth curving into a shadow of his once robust smile. Despite his somewhat labored breathing from the exertion of walking to the table from his room at the back of the house, he planted himself securely beside his chair and held on to Keir's arm while he extended a hand to Kenna.

Without batting an eye at his slurred articulation or questioning what he was trying to say, Kenna quickly set down her coffee and reached out to take his hand between both of hers. "Seamus." She frowned at the scar that bisected the buzz cut of white hair along the side of his head. "Looks like you and I both have some battle scars."

Seamus's blue eyes crinkled and he released her to point a bony finger at her. "You pwettier."

Even in his fragile condition, the man could flirt. Kenna responded by tucking a feathered lock of hair behind her ear and returning the older man's crooked smile—either feeling more comfortable exposing her wounds now or putting them on display in a silent show of compassion for the injuries his grandfather couldn't hide. Keir felt an unexpected twist of appreciation and admiration in his gut, and found his hand sliding to the small of Kenna's back and lingering as he guided her into the seat next to Seamus.

The more time he spent with Kenna, the harder it was to remember just how resentful of her he'd been twenty-four hours earlier. But then, that was the Terminator with her smug confidence and razor-sharp intellect who'd burned him in court. This Kenna Parker was softer, warmer and dangerously attractive to Keir's bored libido.

When the rest of the food arrived, Keir realized his fingers were still splayed against the warmth of her back, and he quickly pulled his hand away to take his seat. Maybe some food in his empty stomach would send energy to his weary brain and clarify his wandering thoughts. He was probably confusing compassion, or maybe even gratitude at the way Kenna was engaging his grandfather this morning, with attraction. This was not a *thing* happening between them. He was a cop helping an injured woman, performing his sworn duty, doing what was necessary to safeguard a victim and stay with her long enough to hopefully come up with some sort of lead on the investigation into her attack. A cop and a criminal defense attorney? It wasn't like there was any real chance of a relationship happening between them anyway.

Once they were all seated, Thomas said grace and then Keir focused on filling his belly with Millie's home cooking and catching up on all the family news, mostly about his brother Niall's pending nuptials and adoption of the baby his fiancée, Lucy, was the legal guardian for. Despite the lively chatter, and Duff's moaning and groaning about being measured for another monkey suit and tie, Keir was aware of Jane Boyle being curiously quiet.

The thirtysomething nurse was probably about Kenna's age, although she didn't seem eager to elaborate on any of the polite questions Kenna asked in an effort to get acquainted. In between helping Seamus use a spoon for his eggs and encouraging him to pick up the bacon with his less dominant hand, Jane seemed to be disengaged this morning. She answered politely when spoken to but then drifted away into her thoughts and picked at her plate. And more than once, she pulled her cell phone from the pocket of her scrub jacket and checked it beneath the edge of the table.

Keir glanced down to the head of the table. His father had noticed Jane's withdrawal from the conversation, too. In fact, judging by the scowl lining his expression, Thomas Watson was downright irritated with the nurse. Had the two butted heads again over who was in charge of caring for Seamus and overseeing his rehabilitation? Or was something else creating tension here at the Watson household?

Keir's self-reproach and his speculation about his father were both put on hold when Millie pushed her chair away from the table. "I need to get going. Since you boys are home, I'm putting you in charge of the dishes."

"Yes, ma'am," Keir and Duff chimed in together.

"And I hung your jacket in the laundry room. Don't forget it."

"No, ma'am."

While Millie scuttled down the hallway to her room, the brothers fell into their old routine of clearing the table, just as they had done growing up. Keir encouraged Kenna to relax and stay put. There weren't that many pans and dishes to rinse and load into the dishwasher.

But when Jane Boyle excused herself to go upstairs to her room to make a phone call, Thomas got up and left the table abruptly. "I'll help."

"We've got this, Dad," Keir assured him.

But the point wasn't up for discussion. Thomas carried his plate and coffee mug to the kitchen sink. But just as quickly as he'd gotten up, he switched mental gears and grabbed his jacket off one of the pegs at the back door into the garage. "You boys finish up. I have errands to run. Is anyone parked behind me?"

Without waiting for their answers, the door closed behind him. The garage door opened and a truck engine started before Keir heard his father drive away. "What was that all about?"

Duff had watched his father stride out the door, too. "I'm not sure. But things have been tense since I got here last night." He rinsed out his milk glass and loaded it into the dishwasher. "Maybe he's just frustrated about the lack of progress on the church shooting. I know it's hard on him to see Grandpa like that. He's called in every marker he has to get some answers."

Keir handed the last glass to Duff. "He'd tell us if he found out something, wouldn't he? I mean, it's not like when Mom died and we were just kids. I know at the time he sugarcoated the true details about her murder. But we're all grown-ups now. We deal with this kind of stuff every day."

Duff dried his hands on a towel while Keir started the dishwasher. "I probably didn't help, dumping on him like I did last night."

"About what?"

"Work stuff." Duff glanced around to make sure the others were out of earshot before he nodded toward the foyer. "Meet me out there."

Keir grabbed his suit jacket from the laundry and followed Duff out to the foyer. "What's up?"

"I'm the one who should ask 'What's up?'" Duff unzipped the gym bag he'd set on the front hall table and pulled out his shoulder holster and badge. "Isn't Kenna Parker the mouthpiece who made you look like a dumb-ass on the Colbern—"

"Yes," Keir cut him off, bristling. Although he wasn't sure if he was taking offense at his brother pointing out how he'd screwed up, or at him bad-mouthing the woman who wasn't as cold and ruthless as half the department—including him—had pegged her to be. He draped the jacket over the banister and started unrolling the long sleeves of his shirt. "I'm doing my job. I found her wandering in an alley near the Shamrock Bar sometime after she was assaulted last night. The perp dumped her off there. She doesn't remember the attack at all."

"That's rough. Somebody did a real number on her." Duff slipped the straps of his holster over each shoulder and adjusted the gun beneath his arm. "Any leads?"

"Nothing useful. I'm taking point on the case for now, until somebody tells me differently. Hud's helping with the legwork." Keir shrugged into his jacket, straightening his open collar over the damp lapel. "Right now I just need to keep an eye on her."

"For medical reasons? Legal ones? Or have you got something else going on with her?"

"She's got no family to take care of her. And her emergency contact who showed up at the hospital was a self-centered prick. I wasn't sending her home with him. For all I know, he's the one who assaulted her."

Duff clipped his badge onto his belt and pulled his worn leather jacket from beneath the bag. "You got a bad vibe on this guy?"

"He was asking an awful lot of questions about what happened. And not one of them was, 'How are you feeling?' He has access to the security system at her house and told her she needed a shrink and a plastic surgeon."

"That's cold."

No kidding. "Maybe there's some professional jealousy. He's as good a suspect as anyone right now. Besides Hoodie Guy."

"Hoodie Guy?"

Keir pulled up the picture on his phone to show his brother. "He was close to the dump site and at the hospital."

"I don't see any gang colors. The neighborhood around the Shamrock is open territory anyway. Too many cops hanging out." Duff shook his head and Keir pocketed the phone. "A woman like Kenna Parker could have a lot of enemies."

"Tell me about it. It'd be nice to know where to start, though."

Duff pulled his jacket on and zipped the bag shut. "You need anything, you've got my number. I might answer."

Keir grinned at the ribbing, knowing either of his brothers, sister or father would be there in a heartbeat if he said he needed help. But he was still curious about the question Duff had dodged earlier. "What did you have to come over here to talk to Dad about?"

"I'm gearing up to do some undercover work. There's an outside shot it's related to the church shooting."

A bolt of energy shot through Keir's blood. "How so? Why didn't you or Dad say anything sooner?"

"Like I said, it's a long shot. The ATF and state police have been running down some leads on how illegal arms are getting into the city."

"Like the Mauser rifle and Glock nine mil our perp used."

Duff nodded. "They were looking for volunteers who know the area, and I was first in line. If I can find out who's selling the guns—"

"Then maybe you can find out the bastard they sold them to."

"I might be off the grid for a while. But I wanted to come up with a plan on how I could keep tabs on Grandpa's recovery and if KCPD gets any new leads on the shooting."

"Anything I can help with?"

"I'd like to use you, Liv and Niall as couriers. Dad will fill you in on the contact plan we figured out." Duff looked down the hallway toward the kitchen, as if their father were still there. "Keep an eye on him, too. Dad's worried I'm going to let things get too personal because I'm chasing down a lead on the shooting. You know what happened the last time I had a personal stake in an undercover op."

His brother had nearly died on that particular assignment. "You're smarter now, right?"

Duff grunted at the question that was both a teasing jab and an expression of concern. "I'd like to think so. But if there's a chance I can get a name on our shooter, I have to do this."

Although he hated the idea of his big brother putting himself in that kind of danger, Keir agreed. He'd do the same if he was in a position to do so. "Don't worry about things at this end. We'll keep pressing for answers on Grandpa. Let us know if you find out anything. Be safe."

"You know I'm too tough to take down."

"I know." Keir extended his hand. "Watch your back anyway."

Duff pulled him in for a hug, then pushed him away, glancing back toward the kitchen. "Watch yours. I don't know if a high-powered attorney who defends bad guys with more money than you or I will ever make is someone you want to get involved with."

"I'm not involved."

"Dude, you brought her home for breakfast. You're involved."

Chapter Five

"Sorry to keep you waiting." Kenna pulled open the passenger door on Keir's black Charger and dropped into the front seat before he could get out and open the door for her. She could tell she'd startled him. He'd been so intent on studying the image on his phone that he hadn't heard her leaving the house. "Are you looking at the man with the hood again?" she asked, nodding to the picture.

"No. It's the man who shot Grandpa."

With that bald pronouncement, the reprieve of relative normalcy she'd enjoyed for the past hour with the Watsons faded. "Did you find him?"

"I wish." Keir handed her his phone. "Duff and I were discussing the progress on the investigation—or lack thereof. This guy was no amateur. There was no DNA on any of the shell casings, and he didn't leave any other trace behind. All we know so far are the two types of weapons he used—an M-98 Mauser and a Glock handgun. KCPD has combed through a list of legal owners without anyone suspicious popping."

"What about illegal weapons?" She knew the sale of unregistered guns was a thriving business, and not every gun owner bothered to get a license.

"Duff thinks he might have a lead on that. But getting the information won't be easy. And if he can't track down the supplier, I'm afraid we'll have to wait until one of the weapons is used in another crime. Then we could at least match ballistics."

"I can see why you're having a hard time identifying a suspect. Is this your only photo?"

"It's the best one. And that's with enhancement from the crime lab." He reached over to swipe the screen back to the image of the man he'd seen lurking in the neighborhood where Keir had found her. "I sent Hoodie Guy to the lab, too, to work their magic. Even if we can't see his face, they can determine his height and see if there are any identifiers on his clothing. I don't know that he's the perp who hurt you, but I'd sure like to talk to him."

More comfortable thinking like a defense attorney than a victim who couldn't identify or discard a potential suspect, Kenna swiped her finger across the phone screen to take another look at the man who'd shot Seamus. Even if KCPD made an arrest, they'd need a lot more evidence than this photograph to convict him or even get the DA to take the case. She studied the slightly blurred image of a man in a black ski mask, wearing gloves and a long black coat. There was a handgun strapped to his waist beside a big, shiny, silver and brass belt buckle that reflected the light streaming through the stained glass windows. She touched her fingertip to the indistinct rectangle of shiny metal with something that looked like a star engraved on it, which he proudly wore as if he was some kind of rodeo champion. But there was nothing heroic about the image. He held his rifle to his shoulder like a well-trained sniper and was firing down from the balcony of a church.

Kenna's breakfast curdled in her stomach as she imagined how helpless everyone in the sanctuary below must have felt. "This guy looks like he knows what he's doing. You're lucky there weren't more casualties."

Keir shook his head as she returned the phone with the disturbing images. "I don't think it was luck. A guy with that kind of weaponry who could enter the church full of cops without being detected, and then escape as if he'd vanished into thin air? I think he did exactly what he came to do."

"Shoot your grandfather?" She looked out to the welcoming gray facade of the Watson family home, thinking how comfortable she'd been spending time there. "It's easier to believe someone would try to kill me than to harm one hair on that sweet, charming man's head."

"Hey." He started the engine before turning to her and winking a handsome blue eye. "I'd like to keep everyone in my city in one piece, if you don't mind."

Kenna knew at least half her mouth was smiling. "Thanks. But I read the newspaper reports. There were several injuries at the shooting. Why do you think he was targeting Seamus?"

"The other injuries were from shrapnel—all minor. One lady twisted her ankle and the organist had a heart attack." Interesting clarification. Keir continued, "The guy didn't hit anyone else, and I don't believe he was a lousy shot. Maybe he was targeting our family—upsetting Liv's wedding, making each of us question every case we've worked, every criminal we've put behind bars—sending some kind of message we don't yet understand. If somebody wanted to hurt us, he certainly hit us where it would do the most emotional damage by going after an eighty-year-old man."

She hadn't helped the family's self-doubts by apparently destroying Keir's most recent case. Instead of apologizing for something she couldn't remember, Kenna focused on trying to help. "Seamus told me a little bit about the shooting. He said he doesn't remember being shot or anything that happened until he woke up in the hospital after surgery. But he told me all about your sister Olivia's wedding—how she wore your mother's veil, how you and your brothers were acting up at the altar before the ceremony started, how he knew from the sounds that the first shots came from a rifle." The older gentleman had seemed adamant about sharing what he remembered, as though he was worried he might forget the details the way she had. "Seamus has lots of time on his hands now, and has been doing a lot of reading. He was wondering if you or one of your brothers or sister could pull his case files so he could read through them instead of newspapers and books."

Keir's blue eyes narrowed. "He said all that to you? Were you interrogating him?"

Refusing to take offense, Kenna pulled her seat belt over her shoulder and fastened it. "No. I listened. If you don't rush him, he can articulate well enough to be understood. I could tell it became an exertion for him, but he seemed determined to carry on a conversation…until Jane came downstairs and said he needed to rest." As she settled more comfortably in her seat, Kenna thought about the pretty, if slightly unsociable, nurse. "Do you know what was bothering her? At first

I thought it was me—that Jane thought I was expecting her to take care of me, too, or that I'd ask for free medical advice. But then I realized it wasn't resentment that had her so distracted, but concern. It was like she was expecting a call that wasn't coming—or she'd gotten a text about something that upset her."

"No clue. But you've got a good eye for details. I wanted to ask Dad about it, but he wasn't in the mood to talk."

"Maybe he's worried about her. He had a hard time keeping his eyes off her at breakfast."

"No way." Keir dismissed her idea with a shake of his head as he shifted the car into Reverse. "He was probably just avoiding an argument, since we had company. He and Jane have rubbed each other the wrong way since he first hired her—Dad's used to being in charge, and she's not used to taking orders. But Grandpa has made good strides in his recovery with her, so I think Dad tolerates her for his sake."

Kenna leaned forward to study the rays of muted sunlight poking through the low-hanging clouds as they headed east. "About Seamus..." This probably wasn't any of her business, but she wasn't one to retreat, apparently. There must be something in her personality or legal training that refused to let a subject drop until she got the answer she needed. "He was serious about wanting to take an active role in the investigation. He mentioned it three different times."

"Grandpa was a desk sergeant for most of his career. He didn't work that many investigations. He's been retired almost twenty years. I don't know who'd still have a grudge against him."

Kenna was only repeating Seamus's request, standing up for the stubborn octogenarian the way she hoped she stood up for her clients. "I think he'd appreciate whatever records you could pull for him. He wants to feel useful, like he's competent enough to help find answers for himself."

Having made her point, she sat back, turning to watch the houses and tall sweet gum trees in this older residential neighborhood pass by. Fatigue and the achy aftermath of her injuries were quickly sapping the mental boost she'd gotten from her visit with Keir's family. She was heading home to a place she couldn't remember and back to that abyss of amnesia where she wasn't sure who she knew, much less who she was supposed to trust. "I can sure relate."

Kenna startled when a warm hand wrapped around hers. She turned back to study Keir's fingers lacing together with hers, resting on the center console. He'd been a solid rock she could cling to when he held her at the hospital. But she liked this, too. It felt like such a high school thing for two grown-ups to do, but she loved the way their hands fit together, the way Keir's warmth seeped through her skin and heated the blood that seemed to rush to the place where they touched. Keir's grasp was a tangible connection to another human being, an anchor to a certain reality, while the people whose faces drifted through her addled brain seemed like ghostly shadows and vague threats she couldn't be sure were real or imagined.

"We'll find out who did this to you," he promised. "I'm going to find out who hurt both you and Grandpa."

As closely knit as everyone at the Watson house seemed to be, she had no doubt that none of them would rest until they found justice for Seamus and knew for certain their family was safe from any future threat. But Kenna wasn't holding her breath that she'd find that same kind of unflinching support from anyone at her house. Or that she could count on this kind of support from Keir for much longer. She wasn't part of his life. He was the Good Samaritan who'd rescued her. And once he'd seen her safely home, he'd go back to his family and his work, and she'd go back to the people and places that she'd forgotten, and get on with her own life.

Still, she held on to the grounding, reassuring contact of Keir's hand for as long as he was willing.

Kenna was relieved to discover that she remembered the black wrought-iron fence and the redbrick facade of the family estate as they pulled up. He'd already circled the block once, ensuring that there was no one loitering in a parked car nearby, and no hooded stranger standing among the shadows, watching for her return.

The guard shack beside the gate was empty and locked up. Keir called the number from the Weiss Security decal glued to one of the windows and put it on speaker so she could hear the conversation. They confirmed that, although Max Weiss's company electronically monitored security at the estate, the company didn't provide guards for onsite security unless specifically requested by a client. The last time any of their people had been there—beyond routine maintenance visits—was for a fund-raising event Kenna had hosted on behalf of the firm…nearly two years earlier.

Wow. Wasn't she the social butterfly? Not. Based on Helmut Bond's comments and that call, it was looking more and more like she had no personal life. Unless snubbing Hellie's attempts to date her had bruised his ego enough to want some kind of retribution. Otherwise, logic seemed to indicate that she should be concentrating on work and client issues to see who had a motive to kill her.

Keir ended the call and tucked his phone back into his pocket before entering the key code into the security pad beside the gate. He waited for the gates to slide open and shifted the car into Drive again. "Weiss has a good reputation in town. Maybe you should consider hiring one of his bodyguards until we find out who did this. At least keep someone on the premises to monitor any activity."

"You're not volunteering for the job?" The words were out of her mouth before she realized how teasing could sound like an anxious plea. The gates closed behind them with an ominous clank and Kenna jumped in her seat. Suddenly, she felt trapped, as if something or someone was closing in on her. She tried to mentally shake off the vague instinct—or was it a memory?—with little success. Maybe she hadn't been teasing, after all. She leaned back against the headrest, taking the nervous hitch out of her tone. "I'm getting used to having you around."

"These past twenty-four hours have been… interesting."

"Said the master of understatement." Kenna matched his knowing grin and relaxed a little more. Apparently, she'd been very good at being alone before the assault. She'd find a way to be good at it again.

Like the other mansions in this old-money neighborhood, the size of the two-story home with painted white columns and a black iron chandelier hanging over the front door seemed a little pretentious. Still, she loved the tall locust and pine trees, with trunks so thick she wouldn't be able to hug her arms halfway around one. There were spots of color, too, that caught her eye and made the yard feel much more inviting than the house itself. The long driveway that wound up the hill to the house was lined with hedges of spirea bushes that were budding with white and pink flowers.

The colorful splash of tiger eyes, begonias and other annuals potted in two concrete urns on either side of the front door added a touch of warmth to the cold red-brick. "This was my parents' house. We moved here when the firm became a success. My mother had all those spirea bushes planted. I remember them hosting big parties here when I was growing up."

"Do you remember being here yesterday?"

"No." She was remembering a more distant past. She shivered at the possibility that she would never be able to fill that most important blank spot of her memory.

"If things seem familiar, at least you can trust that I've brought you to the right place." Keir slowed his car in the circle drive at the front of the house, but instead of stopping, he pressed on the accelerator. "Hold on."

"The code Hellie gave me opens the front door," she reminded him.

But his blue eyes had narrowed and he was pulling back the front of his jacket and hooking it behind the holster of his gun. Keir was unbuckled before he shifted the Charger into Park in front of the three-car garage on the south side of the house and opened his door. "If everything's locked up tight, why isn't the garage?" The third door stood wide-open. She'd been looking at flowers, thinking about her mother and worrying about being alone, while he spotted a potential break-in. "Stay put. I want to check this out."

"Don't..." Her heart thundered in her chest as a forgotten fear tried to take hold. The fact that he pulled his gun and was cradling it between both hands was reason enough to wonder if he'd just discovered the scene of her attack, reason enough to be concerned about the wary cop entering the open bay without proper sight lines or backup, reason enough to find the locks on the Charger's door and secure herself inside. "Be careful," she whispered when he crept around the corner into the garage and disappeared.

Several seconds ticked by, a minute perhaps, and Kenna found herself staring at the clock on the dashboard. It was one fifteen. "One. Time is running out," she murmured, repeating the echo of a memory she couldn't quite hold on to. "There's a deadline."

What deadline? What did the number one mean? What couldn't she remember?

Kenna combed her fingers into her hair and cupped her scalp, as if she could stem the flow of memories seeping out of her head. Without Keir here to ground her, she was quickly spiraling into confusion and despair. She shifted her gaze back to the open garage door. "Hurry back, Detective."

What was he finding? Evidence of a struggle? A horrid shrine to her injuries, decorated with streamers of bloody gauze? A perp lying in wait? Finally, Keir reappeared at the open door. Alive. Unharmed. Six feet of broad shoulders and piercing blue eyes and shielding strength. Kenna released a pent-up breath, silently chastising her wandering thoughts and ping-ponging emotions. But she didn't waste any time scrambling out of the car when he holstered his gun and waved her over to join him.

"I found your car," he announced.

"My car?" Shivering at the cooler temperature inside the shaded garage, or maybe the frissons of anxiety still firing through her system, she hugged her arms around her middle. "It's here?"

"I don't think it ever left." He pointed to the cream-colored Lexus trimmed with gold parked in the first bay. Its shiny surface and luxury appointments were a stark contrast to the paint-chipped pickup with mud and gravel caked around the tires and wheel wells parked in the open bay behind her. "You don't own this truck, do you?"

"I don't think so."

Crinkling her nose at the dank smell of churned-up soil, Kenna circled around the truck to the potting bench and workstation at the back of the garage while Keir pulled out his phone and called someone to say he wanted to run a plate number. "Your car is clean—no signs of blood or a struggle of any kind—so I think we can rule out a carjacking."

Eliminating what couldn't have happened was some kind of answer, wasn't it?

What else could the open garage and dirty truck tell them? She ran her fingers along the brightly painted ceramic pots and bags of potting soil and fertilizer stacked on the workbench. She traced the outlines drawn around the tools hanging from the Peg-Board above the bench. Something seemed familiar here among the hand shovels, rakes and pruning shears. A long, thin shape drawn in magic marker indicated a spade had once hung here. But the skinny shovel was missing. Was that significant? Was her brain trying to recall something important? Or was she just remembering her late mother's penchant for beautiful flowers and an award-winning garden that had helped turn this imposing mansion into a home? "Look how neat this work space is compared to that truck that's been off-roading. They don't belong to the same person, do they?"

"It's not registered to you," Keir confirmed, disconnecting the call and joining her between the truck and the bench. "The truck belongs to a professional landscaping company. Probably someone you hired. I don't like that whoever parked it here left the garage door open, though. There's a locked door between here and the main house. I already made sure it was secure, but still… Kenna? Where are you going?"

Her nose had picked up another scent, more pungent than the earthy dampness of the fresh mud clinging to the truck. "Do you smell that?"

"Kenna, wait."

As soon as she opened the door that led to the backyard, a gray wisp of smoke curled around her, triggering a silent alarm inside her. The trail of smoke on the early afternoon breeze was easy to follow. Was the house on fire? Jogging over the flagstone path, she darted through an open gate and followed a vine-covered arbor up to the slate-tiled patio at the back of the house. She spotted the fire that was more smoke than flame burning in a round fire pit at the corner of the patio. A few feet beyond that she saw a wheelbarrow with the missing spade and the backside of a man in a dark green shirt and muddy jeans bent over the four-foot-high brick wall that surrounded the outdoor space. He held a bucket of white paint in one hand and a large brush in the other.

"Hey, you. Sir."

The man swiped another streak of whitewash over the bricks, then wiped away part of it with a rag to let some of the bricks show through with a pinkish color. He dipped the brush into the paint again, oblivious of her approach.

"Hey!"

He startled when she raised her voice, slopping paint on the slate at his feet. He muttered a curse and set the brush in the bucket to pull a second rag from his pocket and kneel to wipe up the spill. But he didn't turn or acknowledge her as she walked up behind him.

"I'm talking to you. Who are you? What are you doing on my property?"

"Kenna, stop." A firm hand clamped around her upper arm and pulled her back a step.

"I can handle—"

But Keir's broad shoulder was suddenly wedged between her and the intruder. "I'm Detective Watson, KCPD. Sir, I need you to identify yourself."

The workman was shorter than Keir, so she didn't get a look at his face even when he stood. But she wanted to see his face, see if she recognized him as staff or a friend or maybe something terrifying. Minding Keir's cautionary stance, she shifted half a step and peered around his arm.

Not that it did her any good. The man tilted his downturned gaze to hers, but nothing about his dark eyes or the perspiration-dotted points of skin in his receding hairline seemed familiar. Maybe she'd gotten whacked on the particular part of the brain that remembered faces. That particular blank spot in her memory was worse than inconvenient.

Kenna gave her head a slight shake and swallowed a curse of her own as the man pulled a set of earbuds from his ears and let the wires dangle around his neck. "I'm Marv Bennett. Marvin. Boy, you two sure gave me a fright. I didn't know anyone else was here."

"Do you have ID on you, Marvin?" Keir asked, putting away his badge.

"Ms. Parker knows me."

She jerked her gaze up to look at him again. His face was as unrecognizable as the man beneath the shadowed hood.

"You won't vouch for me?" The man sounded surprised.

"Your ID," Keir insisted.

Since looking at the stranger working in her backyard hadn't triggered anything helpful, Kenna walked over to the fire pit. Her eyes watered at the smoking chemicals, thorny bits of stalks and charred leaves tossed in the pile of ashes. Her mind instantly went back to the letter filled with dried rose petals. Did she have a thing for roses? Were they a secret message that she and a lover she couldn't remember shared? What did that little twisting in her gut mean as she watched the plants swell and pop and then shrivel with the heat? Or was this just an unfortunate coincidence?

Kenna blinked her eyes and turned away to see the man pulling a wallet out of his pocket and showing his driver's license to Keir. There was a logo on his coveralls, but she couldn't read it from this distance. He kept his face slightly averted, in deference to the man with the badge, she supposed. "You're burning my rosebushes?"

Seeming more eager to talk to her than to the cop asking him about the truck in the garage, Marvin Bennett angled his ruddy face toward her. "I thought you'd tossed those in there. Found 'em when I came in this morning. Looked like somebody lit a fire in there, but with all the rain it didn't catch. That's why I added the kerosene." His mouth eased into a gap-toothed smile. "I figured you got impatient and started the project without me."

"What project?"

The smile faded. He twirled his finger in the air, indicating the plants around him. "Pulling out these old rosebushes. The ones we're replacing around the patio wall. You know we struggled with leaf blight last year."

She'd dug up the flowers and started this fire? When? Like the potting bench in the garage, the ruined flowers *did* seem to have some significance to her. But her stomach was queasy at the sight of the smoking plants. Was it sadness over losing something that had been so important to her mother? Was she sensing something beyond the reach of her current cognitive abilities? Or was she simply irritated that the man in charge of her garden didn't seem to be very competent, and she'd had to do his job for him? Kenna thumbed over her shoulder. "There's still some green in them. They're not going to burn."

"I could have told you that. I would have chopped 'em up and composted them. But you're the one who said you didn't want to risk the bacteria spreading to other plants."

She'd talked to this man before? His posture shifted when she didn't respond.

"Two days ago? Remember? You said you wanted this taken care of as soon as possible, but I warned you the ground was too wet to plant the new roses because we wouldn't have the proper drainage. Now, I hear your mama had a legendary green thumb, but I think you need to listen to me. That's what you hired me for, isn't it?" He tried to move around Keir, but her rescuer put out his hand to block the gardener from moving any closer to her.

Looking vaguely offended, Marvin stuffed his wallet back into his pocket and retreated a step. "You didn't call the cops on me, did you? Were the fumes getting to you? I didn't mean to bother you, ma'am. And I'd have called to tell you I was coming, but I didn't think you'd be here today."

Kenna closed her fingers around the sleeve of Keir's jacket to remove the blockade and stepped up beside him, appreciating his effort to protect her, but needing answers almost more than she needed to feel safe. She tucked her hair behind her ears, deciding which question she wanted to start with. But the gardener's mouth rounded with a soft whistle before she could speak. "Oh, wow. Ms. Parker, what happened to you? Are you okay?"

For a while there, she'd forgotten the damage done to her face. Hating that others could be so distracted by her unfortunate appearance, she quickly feathered her long bangs back over her cheek and forehead. "Why didn't you think I'd be at home?"

"You always go into the office on Saturday mornings. When you said you wanted the project handled

ASAP, I just assumed that as soon as the rain let up a bit, I could…" The man stared at her face long enough that she ended up averting her own gaze to the pattern of light gray and charcoal threads running through the shoulder of Keir's jacket. "I can come back another time to finish up. I wanted to get those new rosebushes planted before the soil got too muddy. Weatherman says we're supposed to get more rain tonight and tomorrow. You sure got a lot of stitches. Were you in a car accident?"

Kenna hugged her arms around her middle and turned her face completely away from his curious concern, feeling her breath lock up in her chest at the wave of helpless self-consciousness sweeping through her.

But Keir's smooth, authoritative voice took up the interrogation she couldn't continue. "How long have you been here today, Mr. Bennett?"

"Since eight thirty."

"If that's your truck, you must have seen Ms. Parker's car in the garage. Why didn't you think anyone was at home?"

"Yeah, I thought that was weird, but, well, the house was dark—shades were drawn on most of the windows. I've been here all morning and nobody said boo to me. Ms. Parker almost always comes out to talk about the garden if she's in. You know how she likes to be in charge."

Kenna's chin came up at what almost sounded like an insult. But Bennett chuckled and lowered his voice to a whisper. "Besides, it isn't my business to be too curious about where a pretty lady spends her nights. I'm sure she spends them with you, of course," he added hastily, as if the thought that she or Keir might be offended came a few words too late. "I didn't mean to imply anything."

Keir wasn't laughing. He didn't correct the man's assumption about spending the night together, either. "How long have you worked at the Parker Estate?"

"Couple of years. That's how long I've worked for Riley Greenscapes, at any rate. I guess they've been mowing the grass and taking care of the yard here a lot longer than that." A defensive note crept into his tone as the questions kept coming. "Hey, I'm not asking for overtime because it's Saturday. As long as I put in my hours and I'm not disturbing the household, I've got permission to be here. We have a contract to do regular upkeep of the yard and garden."

That didn't make sense. The suspicious attorney in Kenna found a strength the depleted woman couldn't seem to hold on to. She peeked around Keir's shoulder to look directly at the gardener. "Then why are you painting?"

Marvin shifted on his feet with an embarrassed chuckle. "Well, um, no offense, ma'am, but when you pulled out the old bushes, some of the ground must have settled behind it. I guess the roots and weathering over the years dislodged the mortar holding it together. This section here was all tumbled down when I came here this morning. I didn't want you to hold me responsible, so I put it back as best I could and replaced the dirt, but I couldn't get the bricks to all line up like before, and some of the red was peeking through. Thought if I painted it, you wouldn't notice the difference. I found the paint and brush out in the garage. Like I said, ma'am, I didn't even know you were here. I'll put out the fire if that's bothering you."

He picked up the shovel, scooped up a spade of dirt from the wheelbarrow and tossed it onto the smoking yard waste. "And I'll get that wall finished right away."

"Your repairs look fine." When had she worked in the garden? Was it a hobby of hers? An homage to her late mother? Or was she such a tyrant that she'd attempt to complete the job herself if the hired help couldn't get it right? Kenna's headache seemed to be coming back. She rubbed at her temple. "Have you seen or heard anyone on the property or in the house?"

He tossed another shovel of dirt onto the dying flames. "I just told you I hadn't."

"You didn't see a man wearing a black hoodie?"

"No. Why?"

Keir didn't bother to explain. "How did you get onto the grounds if no one was here to let you in?"

Marvin stabbed the spade into the dirt in the wheelbarrow and rested his elbow on top of the handle before turning. "Am I in some kind of trouble?"

"How did you get in?" Kenna repeated.

"I've got the company's passkey to get through the gate and into the garage." He reached inside his green uniform shirt and pulled a lanyard with a key card from around his neck. "It's not like I'm here casing the joint, wanting to rob it. I'm doing more than I'm supposed to here. I've never had one complaint from a customer about using my passkey privileges, I swear. You can check with my boss, Mr. Riley."

"We will," Kenna and Keir chimed in together.

Less and less surprised to find out how well their drive complemented each other's, Kenna looked up. The faint shadows beneath Keir's eyes and the day-old beard stubble added a tough edge to his chiseled features and indolent grin. She had a feeling it hadn't been an easy task to discredit him on the witness stand—Keir Watson was intelligent and observant, dedicated to uncovering the truth and protective of the people he represented—traits she believed she shared. She liked teaming up with him a lot more than she imagined she'd enjoyed facing off against him in court. Her heart beat a little faster in her chest when he winked a silent message of support at her, and she wondered if she'd ever felt this inexplicable burst of excitement, this empowering sense of feeding off someone's intellect and energy, with another man in the life she'd forgotten.

Marvin interrupted her speculation before she could come up with an answer. "Ma'am, is everything all right? You never did say how you got hurt. You don't think I had something to do with it, do you?"

Kenna's nostrils flared with a deep breath of the damp air upwind of the fire pit. Hormonal rushes aside, she was exhausted. She needed to be in better shape, both physically and mentally, to pursue this investigation any further today. And while she hadn't been entirely satisfied with the gardener's answers, she had a feeling that the man would only grow more defensive if she and Keir kept pushing.

Apparently, Keir agreed. "I'm just doing my job, sir—talking to anyone who might have seen something."

"Seen something? Are you saying she got mugged?" he asked Keir. "Some kind of home invasion? In *this* neighborhood? Should I not be here by myself?"

"I think you're perfectly safe, Mr. Bennett," Keir assured him. "However, do you think you could come back Monday to finish this job? Ms. Parker really needs her rest."

"Well, as long as I don't get blamed for the job not being done." The gardener wiped his forehead with the back of one of his work gloves. His brown eyes were focused squarely on her when his face reappeared. "I didn't mean to upset you, ma'am. If it isn't raining too hard, Monday will be just fine. You're not going to file a complaint with my boss, are you?"

"No." She dredged up half a smile. Of course he'd be worried about his job after being grilled by a cop and an attorney, and then being asked to leave. "I appreciate your flexibility. Thank you."

While Marvin tossed more dirt into the fire pit, Keir's hand slid to the small of her back, turning her toward the double French doors lining the patio. He nodded to the keypad. "Can you get inside from here?"

"We'll find out." Kenna pulled the paper from Hellie out of her jacket pocket and punched in the code. Nine-six-four-two-one. The glass door unlocked, but her fingers hovered over the keys without pushing the door open. "One isn't the right number."

"Sure it is. It's open… Kenna?"

She looked up into the narrowed focus of Keir's blue eyes.

"That's what you said when you stumbled out of the alley last night."

"I did?"

"Yes. You couldn't tell me what it meant then. Are you remembering something now? If *one* is wrong, then what's the right number?"

Dozens of numbers cycled through her brain—big numbers, small numbers, numbers in every type of graphic she could imagine. A chalk drawing. A neon sign. Markings on a plastic syringe. The time on a digital clock, ticking away. She tried to latch on to one of those numbers, tried to make all the counting stop, tried to make sense of any of it. "I don't know. I keep feeling like I'm on a deadline, like I'm going to miss something important if I don't remember it. But then…" She shook her head. "There's nothing there."

"A one o'clock appointment? A trial that starts on the first of the month?"

"I don't know!" she snapped, more irritated with herself at not having an answer than at Keir for prodding her with questions. She drew in a calming breath and repeated in a more civil tone, "I don't know."

Besides, the phrase that kept playing in her head was that one was the *wrong* number. So neither of Keir's suggestions could be the answer.

When she turned her gaze back to tell him so, she saw that they still had an audience. A very interested audience standing there with a brush and pail of white paint in his hands. "Mr. Bennett. I thought we'd dismissed you."

He set the paint and brush inside the wheelbarrow before answering, "I was worried, ma'am. You sure you're all right?"

No. I'm frightened out of my mind and afraid I'm completely losing it. But out loud, she answered, "I'm fine."

The warmth of Keir's hand moved across her back. "You go on in. I'll get rid of him. I want to scout out the grounds, make sure no one snuck in by some other route. It'll be a while before I come back. Lock up behind me."

He leaned in and gently pressed a kiss beside the stitches at her temple. Kenna gasped, though whether it was surprise at the tender contact or the chill she felt when he pulled his hand away, she couldn't tell. She couldn't ask about that reassuring little kiss, either. She tilted her gaze to briefly meet the deep blue of his eyes, but Keir was turning away as if sharing that kind of intimacy with her was his right, and as normal and natural an occurrence between them as breathing.

He strode across the patio to the gardener. "Bennett, you're coming with me."

Chapter Six

Overwhelming fatigue rushed in as Kenna locked the door and rested her forehead against a cool pane of glass. She watched the two men disappear from sight along the path back to the garage and still she couldn't bring herself to move.

The only part of her body that seemed alert were the nerve endings still dancing with a newly discovered delight where Keir's mouth had caressed her. Tiny strands of her hair had caught in the coffee-brown stubble of Keir's beard and she'd felt a dozen ticklish little tugs across her scalp as he moved his lips over her skin. She could recall each individual sensation as if it were happening to her at this very moment and savored it. She could recall just as clearly the heat of Keir's arms closing around her, absorbing her panic and filling her with comfort and strength. Even now her body warmed at the memory of his fingers gently caressing the nape of her neck and sifting into her hair, and her small breasts rubbing against the harder planes of his chest as she pulled herself closer. She remembered breathing in his spicy masculine scent from the skin beneath his shirt collar.

Kenna's gaze wondered over to the freshly turned

earth and potted roses lined up and ready to be planted along the top of the patio wall. Every detail about Keir Watson was tattooed on her brain. But why couldn't she remember the conversation she'd had with Marvin Bennett? Why couldn't she remember dinner or who she'd met or why she'd gone out yesterday in the first place? Why were faces from the distant past so much clearer than the friends and business associates and staff she must have interacted with over the past twenty-four hours or so? Was her brain truly as bruised and battered as her face? Or was Dr. McBride right, and she was subconsciously trying to shield herself from a memory so shocking and horrible that she'd never remember anything pertaining to the attack?

And how vital was it for her to start recalling those details? She couldn't help thinking that giving her amnesia and a new look hadn't been her attacker's goal. Would she even know she was in danger if he or she came back to finish the job until it was too late?

And why had Keir Watson kissed her? Did she look like she was on her last leg and he'd felt sorry for her? Was he making a point to Marvin Bennett that the lady of the house was protected? And why did she keep trying to imagine what that kiss would have felt like on her lips? It seemed as if answers to the important questions weren't coming this afternoon.

Pushing away from the door, Kenna noticed the skin print she'd left on the glass and pulled the sleeve of her jacket down over her hand to wipe it clean. "Hmm."

As beautiful and inviting as the wide patio with the tall oaks, colorful flowers and rock paths beyond might be, she apparently didn't take the time to enjoy them as she should. There wasn't another mark on the wall of windows and doors, inside or out, no fingerprint on any of the knobs. Didn't she or anyone else ever go out and sit in the sun or walk the shady paths? Did she ever prop a door open to let a cooling spring breeze into the house? What a waste.

Turning into the carpeted entertainment area, with a wall of built-in cabinets, a fireplace and a flat-screen TV above the mantel, she strolled through the long room to the marble-topped island and pristine white kitchen on the other side. Maybe she didn't cook, either. There wasn't a mark on any of the stainless appliances, and the only thing adorning the countertop besides a display of lemons and oranges was a handwritten note beneath the cordless phone on the wall.

Kenna scanned the note about weekend meals left in the fridge by someone named Renata and waited for a familiar image to form in her brain. Nothing. Agitation stirred in her blood as she set the note down and moved on to reacquaint herself with her house. Pushing open a swinging door, she entered a formal dining room with twelve chairs around a long cherry wood table. Beyond that, she passed through a squared-off archway into the marble-tiled foyer.

Here there was a fresh-cut bouquet in a tall crystal vase on a side table beneath a mirror. Opposite that hung a large painting of the mansion, when it had been draped with red, white and blue bunting for a patriotic holiday. She peeked into a study with a desk surrounded by floor-to-ceiling shelves filled with books.

"My father's office," she murmured out loud, remembering the tall windows and leather couches. A second door revealed her mother's office—with lighter-colored woodwork and paint, the shelves filled with gardening and decorating books instead of legal tomes. The other rooms on the first floor were set up for entertaining but were so spotlessly preserved she wondered if the reception a year and a half earlier that Weiss Security had mentioned when Keir called them was the last time she'd had guests in the house. Either that or she'd hired a wicked-good cleaning staff. Maybe that Renata who'd left salads and a casserole for her was Superwoman.

"I live in a museum," she murmured, thinking the house was as cold and sterile and empty as the Watson home had been filled with noise and love and living. What kind of person chose this sort of life? Was she really the workaholic Helmut Bond had claimed? Maybe that was why no one had come looking for her in the hospital besides an associate from the firm who'd had to be paged by an answering service. The more she discovered about her life, the less she was liking the woman she'd been.

She heard the growling noise of a diesel engine starting up. Marvin Bennett was probably driving away. Soon, Keir would follow, and she'd be all alone in this well-appointed mausoleum.

That unsettling thought made her breath lock up in her chest. This house seemed to indicate that she was very experienced at being alone. The idea should have given her comfort. If she was alone, she wouldn't have to worry about the disadvantage of not knowing someone on sight. She wouldn't have to be afraid of failing to recognize her attacker. But *alone* sounded very… lonely right now. Kenna tilted her gaze up the central, polished walnut staircase with a runner of Oriental wool. "Maybe I live upstairs."

But the bedrooms and baths up there were just as spotless. Clean. Beautiful, like live-screen captures from a home decorating magazine, but stagnant, cold. Kenna found the room she thought was hers, a fact confirmed by the business suits, dresses and shoes stored in the walk-in closet. A chest of drawers revealed just how finicky she was at sorting her jewelry and lingerie by color and design. Dressy stuff up top—more casual at the bottom.

"This is nuts," she said out loud. How boring, regimented, guarded and uptight could one woman be? Was all this perfection some sort of defense strategy? Had she felt some other aspect of her life was beyond her control? She didn't think her parents had been harsh taskmasters. Beyond remembering the high expectations they'd had for her, she recalled long conversations at the dining room table and numerous trips they'd taken together. Had something happened more recently that had made her go all scary control freak on the place she called home?

In the bottom drawer she found several colorful items that had been folded up for so long, the clothes had creases in them. She pulled out a pair of cotton lounge pants in royal blue. They were decorated with old-style London police boxes printed in a bright turquoise color. Kenna smiled and hugged the pants to her chest, feeling a twinge of relief. Somewhere along the line, she'd had a sense of fun. She had a kitschy obsession with British television.

Why wasn't she fun anymore?

Why was she so alone?

Who had done this to her? Or perhaps a better question to ask was why had she done this to herself?

Rebelling at the stringent restraint that seemed to have dictated her life before the attack, Kenna tossed the pants onto the four-poster bed and pawed at the comforter, freeing the pillows and blanket underneath and raking them together into a pile in the middle of the bed. "That's better."

Slightly breathless, and secretly satisfied at the hint of anarchy in her overly organized world, she went into the small bedroom next to her own that had been converted into a home office, complete with barrister cases, a couch and a treadmill desk set up in front of another TV. If work was her thing, maybe she'd find something here that would make her feel more at home than the rest of the mansion had. Kenna opened the drapes and sat at the traditional Chippendale-style desk near the window.

Other than a pewter tankard filled with ink pens and mechanical pencils, there was nothing but a framed photograph of her and her parents sitting on one side of the blotter, and a cordless telephone propped up in its cradle on the other. The red light was blinking on the answering machine, drawing her attention to the numeral 5, indicating the number of messages recorded on the machine. She snorted a wry laugh. "Maybe that's the right number." Wondering if she'd recognize any of the voices or names, Kenna pushed Play.

She opened drawers and searched through the contents of her desk while a woman identifying herself as Carol came on the line. Remembering the name Helmut Bond had mentioned, Kenna tried to put a face to her assistant's friendly voice. "Hey, Kenna. You weren't answering your cell, so I thought I'd leave a message on your landline. I'm guessing you're already at your meeting with your friend Barbara Jean." Barbara Jean?

Kenna pulled out the yellow legal pad she found in the main drawer and jotted down the name. *Barbara Jean?* Was that who she'd met for dinner? Had she ever made it to that meeting?

"Just wanted to remind you that I'm leaving early today for my class reunion, but I've got the correspondence typed up and ready for you to sign on your desk, along with the files you requested on those old cases. I also wanted to give you a heads-up. Congrats on winning that case this morning, but I've already fielded a wild, surprisingly colorful call from Devon Colbern, Dr. Colbern's wife. Pretty sure the woman was drunk. I saved it in case you need a recording for evidence."

"Evidence?" Kenna whispered out loud while the message continued.

"In polite terms, she's not thrilled with the outcome of the trial and holds you personally responsible for everything that's wrong in her life." Kenna's assistant laughed. "There's a message from Andrew Colbern that isn't much better. Instead of being grateful that you kept him out of prison, he's worried about what the divorce and civil suit is going to cost him. He said you should have found a better way to clear him of charges than to blame the police for not doing their job."

Kenna's stomach was twisting into knots. That was why Keir considered her an enemy. Was blaming the police—apparently Keir, in particular—the only way she'd been able to defend Ddr. Colbern? Just how many people hated her, blamed her, had a reason to want to hurt her? Did she like these people she represented? Did she really believe in their innocence and thought she was serving justice? Or was she just all about winning her case and making money? That reputation could certainly earn her plenty of enemies.

"Anyway, that's it," Carol finished. "Have a good weekend. See you Monday."

After a beep, the second message began to play. But there was nothing recorded but a few seconds of silence before there was a hang-up and the recorder beeped again. Probably just an automated call or a misdial.

Kenna ignored most of the third message as Hellie's voice came on the line. Goodness, the man loved the sound of his own voice. While Carol's message must have come yesterday afternoon before her attack and the trip to the hospital, Helmut Bond wished her a good morning and was following up to make sure she'd made it home safely. If she needed anything, she was to call him. He'd be there in a heartbeat. Better yet, why didn't she come stay at his house so he could take care of her? Kenna frowned. What would Carol have to say about her boyfriend inviting another woman over while she was away at her reunion? Yet, if they were a couple, why hadn't Hellie gone to the reunion with her?

But while he poured out two-faced platitudes, Kenna's attention was fixed on the legal pad.

"What is that?" She turned her pencil onto its side and shaded over the indentations that had been left from a page that had been torn away. The echo of an earlier message soon emerged. *"Talk to Arthur? BED file."*

Talk to the senior partner about what? When had she jotted this note? What bed? Whose bed? Why would she talk to Arthur Kleinschmidt about a bed? She'd written the letters in all caps, so maybe they were an abbreviation or acronym.

Kenna opened other drawers, looking for any file or flash drive labeled *BED*, in case it meant something significant. She looked for some kind of address book, too, hoping to find a last name for the Barbara Jean friend she was supposed to meet. About the only thing she did find was a wall calendar folded up in the bottom drawer. It was a souvenir from what she supposed was her insurance agent. But neither the company nor the agent was named Barbara or had the initials BED. With no success here at the main desk, she got up and went to the treadmill to boot up the laptop sitting there.

She clicked on various icons. No BED file here, either, but she did find a folder labeled Contacts and opened it to scroll through the names of what must be clients and business consultants. She found phone numbers for members of the firm and her assistant, Carol. But, of course, they were listed by their last names, so she scrolled through each one line by line, searching for anyone named Barbara. An unhappy message from Andrew Colbern played like white noise in the background while she let the cursor hover over someone named B. J. Webster. There had been other *B* names. Could one of them be the Barbara Jean she was supposed to meet? And how smart was it to call up someone she couldn't remember out of the blue and ask if she knew Kenna Parker? She'd sound crazy, for sure, and might possibly be tipping off her attacker, or the person who'd set her up to be killed.

Until she could decide the wisest course of action, Kenna shut down the laptop and moved on to inspect the barrister cases. Everything inside was as annoyingly organized and neatly arranged as the items in her bedroom had been.

Everything, that is, except for stack of envelopes wedged beneath a law dictionary. Kenna opened the glass door and lifted the heavy book to pull out the odd packet of letters.

After another beep, the last message played. It was another automated call. Kenna turned the envelopes, tied together with a wrinkled ribbon, over in her hand and gasped.

Feeling an uncomfortable suspicion licking at her pulse, she carried them to the treadmill table and untied the ribbon. The stationery was familiar, an identical match to the plain beige envelope she'd opened at the hospital. Suspicion grew into apprehension, kicking her heart rate up a notch as she leafed through the stack. The postmarks were all from Kansas City, each dated seven days apart. Each had been sent to her office, and not one had a return address.

Swallowing hard to keep the tension in her gut from rising into her throat, she opened the oldest envelope and pulled out the letter inside. She unfolded it. Three brittle rose petals fell out. A brief message was typed across the top. *Your DEADline is in 147 days.* "Deadline? What deadline?"

If this was a reminder for a journal article or legal brief she had to write, why keep it hidden away? Why would she ever write herself a letter like this instead of making a notation on her calendar or phone? Did she have 147 days to get the house ready to sell or lose twenty pounds or enter some kind of competition? Maybe the rose petals meant she planned to enter a flower show?

She opened the second envelope. There were only a few words typed there, too, and more petals. *You have 140 days until your DEADline.*

The third one was similar. A piece of paper holding the remnants of a faded, dried-out rose. A terse message was typed across the top: *133 days left.*

The next one mentioned the number *126.* The next, *119.* Then *112.*

Kenna stopped reading.

The letter that Hellie had delivered this morning at the hospital—the symbol on it wasn't the letter *O.* It was a zero.

These letters were some kind of terrifying countdown.

Kenna snatched her fingers away as if the paper had cut her.

These weren't souvenirs from any lover. She dashed back to the desk and pulled out the calendar to check the dates. She opened the calendar on top of the desk and recoiled. Every date had been marked through with an *X.* From the date when the first letter had arrived until yesterday. She'd been counting down the numbers, too. Today's date had been circled half a dozen times. Today was the deadline. Today was zero.

And then she realized that the last message was still playing. Only, it wasn't silence at all. Someone was breathing on the long recording. The caller inhaled a stuttering breath from time to time, fighting to control exertion. Or emotion. Someone was there, listening, waiting for her to pick up.

Kenna slowly turned toward the disturbing wheeze of breath on the recording. She was in trouble. All this meant something. The calls. The missing BED file and meeting with the mysterious Barbara Jean. These haunting, terrifying letters. Someone had been threatening her for months before the attack. Had she been afraid before the assault? Because she was damn certain she was afraid now.

The creepy breathing faded away into a growly whisper of noise until the voice finally spoke. "Your time's up. The deadline is today. I'm so sorry about yesterday. It wasn't supposed to happen like that. But I'll see you tonight."

Stone-cold dread filled her veins. The breathing grew more ragged again, as if the anticipation of meeting her excited the caller. Kenna hugged her arms across her chest and backed away from the cruel taunt. Dead. Line. "He's coming back to kill me. Tonight."

Another telephone rang in the background. She heard a muffled curse and a hasty scramble before the recording suddenly went dead.

How could a phone ring when the caller was already on the line? None of this made any sense. And she desperately needed something to make sense.

A sharp rap of sound startled her. Kenna screamed as the noise dragged her from her miasmic thoughts. Shaking inside her skin as her pounding pulse tried to regulate itself, she glanced around the office, fighting to orient herself in the here and now.

"Kenna!" She heard pounding at the front door. A blessedly familiar voice shouted, "Kenna? It's Keir. Open up or I'm breaking in."

Before he knocked a third time, Kenna bolted out of the room. "Keir?" She ran down the stairs, hurriedly punched in the security code and swung open the door. "Keir!"

She saw shoulders and a gun before an arm snaked around her waist and KCPD Detective Keir Watson dragged her away from the open door. "You screamed."

"I did?"

"Yes." He shut the door behind him and twisted the dead bolt. He was still pulling her with him as he peeked into the dining room and her father's office. "Is somebody here? Baby, what's wrong?"

"Don't call me baby. I'm not two years—"

"Then tell me what's wrong!"

Kenna instinctively recoiled from the harsh command.

Keir released her and raised his hand in apology. "Ah, hell. With no sleep I've got no filter in me. I'm—"

He started to apologize, but she waved his softer tone aside and cut the distance between them. "No. You're right." Bracing her palms against his chest, she looked straight into those questioning blue eyes. She was still too panicked to be very polite herself. "Don't be nice to me right now. I need you to be a cop." Her fingers fisted in the front of his jacket and she pulled him to the stairs. "It's a countdown."

"What's a countdown?"

"Just come with me. I need you to see this. I need you to hear. Please."

When he nodded, she released him and hurried up the stairs. Keir followed, right on her heels. "Counselor, you're scaring me."

"Join the club." She led him past her bedroom to her office. "In here."

Keir grabbed her wrist and pulled her back so he could enter first. After a quick survey, he holstered his gun and crossed to the scattered letters and pile of rose petals on the treadmill desk. "Explain to me exactly what happened."

Assuming he considered it safe enough for her to enter, Kenna cued up the fifth message on the answering machine and started talking.

"The numbers. They're a countdown." She talked about the spotless house and the mysterious Barbara Jean and BED file, the weekly letters she'd stashed away and the caller who seemed to think she ought to be dead. Bursts of angry frustration and soul-deep fear peppered her rambling words. "One is the wrong number because I was supposed to have one day left. Today is day zero. Today is when he planned to attack me. I think he's coming to kill me."

"Who?"

"I don't know." She slapped at the calendar on her desk. "Clearly I was keeping track long before the attack. Someone was stalking me." She applauded Keir's muttered curse when he listened to the vile message. "I think that's why everything is so freaking perfect in this house. Because that's something I can control. It's a classic response for dealing with abuse or a stalker. And I don't have the injuries to indicate abuse—Dr. McBride looked at my medical records and—"

"Did you report it to the police?"

"I don't remember." She hugged her arms around her waist. "Would it have done any good? Aren't I the enemy?" Keir's gaze had fixed on her, following her as she paced across the room. "Someone has been threatening me, and maybe...maybe I wasn't scared enough for him. I'm too stubborn and independent..." But even her emotional rant was running out of steam. She was breathing hard as she stopped in front of him to meet those blue eyes. "My parents raised me to be that way. And I work in a tough field, a man's world, and… and…" Kenna swayed with exhaustion and fell silent.

"Can I be nice to you now?" Keir's voice was deep-pitched, calm.

All she could do was nod. He turned her into his arms and led her into the hallway, away from the grim secrets of her home office.

Once he'd put some distance between her and the collection of threats, he stopped and let her lean back against the wall to rest. "It's a good thing you're such a strong woman. I can't imagine anyone else still standing after all you've been through." His tone was as gently hypnotic as the stroke of his fingers through her hair. And then his hand stopped, cupping the side of her neck and jaw. She didn't realize how chilled she still was until she felt the warmth of his palm seeping into her skin. She didn't know how much she needed to see the honest desire darkening his eyes. "Don't sue me for this."

Keir leaned in and pressed a soft, chaste kiss against her lips. He lingered for a moment, long enough for Kenna to reach up and wind her fingers around his wrist. They stood like that for several seconds, lips gently touching, warming each other. She felt the strength of his pulse beating beneath her thumb, felt her own pulse leaping against the heat of his hand.

When he pulled away, Kenna felt bereft. Keir's chest expanded in a deep sigh that matched her own. His gazed dropped to the quivering pout of her lips. With no trace of anesthetic to numb them, she'd felt every moment of that kiss. She felt how cold they were now without his touch. And then his feet parted slightly, his fingers tightening against the sensitive nape of her neck.

A hand at her back pulled her body into his, imprinting her with a hard chest and belt buckle and even a badge against her belly. Kenna tilted her chin, her lips already parting as Keir closed his mouth over hers.

As tender and sweet as that first kiss had been, this one was hungry and bold.

Kenna tasted coffee and salty bacon on the tongue that speared between her lips and danced against hers. Keir's mouth was a heady mix of demand and request, daring forays and soothing retreats. He was careful of the stitches close to one side of her mouth, but took his sweet time exploring the rest. Kenna's pulse pounded in her ears. The shock that had chilled her body melted away, and a different sort of adrenaline poured like honey into her veins. She needed this contact, this realness, and drank in everything he offered as if it was her life's blood she needed to survive.

She stretched her body against his, reaching up to cup his jaw between her hands. She felt the rasp of his day-old beard tickling her palms and fingertips and sensitized lips. There was a needy moan and a satisfied catch of breath, although she couldn't be sure if the sounds were Keir's or hers or belonged to them both. A very feminine response tingled in the tips of her breasts as he walked her back against the wall, his chest rubbing against hers, his muscular thighs crowding her own.

The kiss blotted out every fear, every doubt, leaving only this moment, this man, filling her head. This scorching connection they shared had been an inevitable spark between flint and steel, waiting to be struck from the moment he'd first swept her up in his arms and carried her to his car. Keir Watson looked like sin and danger all rolled up into a tailored suit. He matched her verbal sorties zing for zing, and grounded her in a world that was safe and secure. And the man could flat-out kiss a woman like he meant business.

Kenna was as mindless with passion as she'd been with panic a few minutes earlier by the time Keir angled his hips away from hers and eased some space between them. She still clung to the sandpapery angles of his jaw as he rested his forehead against hers. His mouth hovered above hers, his warm, panting breaths caressing her kiss-stung lips.

"So that got out of hand." He braced his hands against the wall on either side of her head as if he couldn't risk touching her right now. He studied the marks on her forehead, cheek and jaw and, a moment later, brushed her hair aside to study them more closely. But she sensed concern rather than any kind of repulsion in his curious perusal. "You're a strong woman, Kenna Parker. But in some ways you're as fragile as glass. I didn't hurt you, did I?"

Kenna looked up into eyes of deep, rich blue. "Not a bit." She eased her grip on his face and pulled her arms down between them. She curled her fingers into the nubby wool of his jacket, feeling slightly saner as she sagged against his chest. "You're a good kisser, Detective."

"So are you, Counselor." A deep sigh stirred the crown of her hair and he straightened, folding his arms protectively around her. "Believe me, so are you."

He must have felt her breath steadying, sensed some of her strength returning after a few moments, because he tipped his head back from hers, rubbing his hands up and down her arms. "I'd like to say that was unexpected, but—"

"You just never expected it to happen with me."

"Honestly?"

"Always."

"No." Thankfully, the man didn't mince words or speak in riddles, giving her one more reason to trust him. "I don't want to be enemies anymore. But I know we're going to face off in a courtroom again one day, and we're going to try to prove each other wrong. You're going to piss me off by being such a damn good attorney, and I'm going to side with KCPD against you every time."

Kenna nodded, hating to agree. "There are a lot of reasons why you and I wouldn't work. A lot of potential conflict down the line. A lot of gossip behind our backs, maybe some unfriendly accusations."

His hands stopped their soothing massage and came to rest on her shoulders. "This isn't the time to try to figure all that out." He pressed a kiss to her temple and pulled away altogether. "Time to get to work." He strolled back to her office and punched in a number on his phone. "I'm calling the lab. We're analyzing everything."

A bit of the panic returned as he walked away. When he moved on down the hall toward the stairs, she hurried after him. "Keir?"

He stopped at her bedroom door and flipped on the lights to peek inside. "Don't worry. I'm not going anywhere."

He checked the closet and en suite and locks on the windows. Kenna waited in the doorway until he moved on to inspect the next room. Even though he was talking on the phone, she followed him, reasoning out the practicalities of why he needed to go as rationally as she would argue salient points in front of a judge. "But you should leave. You have a life. I'm just this crazy woman who stumbled into your arms, and you've been too kind to walk away. There are other cops in this city who are willing to help me, right? They can't all hate the *Terminator* so much that they wouldn't do their best by me." She couldn't help noticing the weary shadows beneath his eyes as he faced her in the doorway and ended the call. "You haven't slept. Your family needs you."

"I'm the first officer on the scene, so I have to call this in, no matter what. It'd be a hundred percent more efficient if I'm the one to report our observations and suspicions instead of you having to go through everything that's happened all over again with someone new." He pocketed his phone before pulling back the front of his jacket and splaying his hands at his waist. "Do you want me to stay?"

Kenna imagined a clock slowly ticking off the beats in her head as she debated between what was smart and what felt right. What was a little pride or worry over losing her independence in the face of mind-numbing fear and loneliness? She offered him a wry smile. "Desperately."

An answering grin appeared on his sexy mouth and he held out his hand to her. Kenna laced her fingers together with his and he took her with him as he secured the rest of the upstairs rooms. Then they headed downstairs and he repeated the security sweep on the lower floor and basement.

Keir was still holding her hand after the team from the crime lab had taken pictures and packed up the evidence from her office and left. Kenna was dead on her feet, but she insisted that she be kept in the loop on any information the police found. Her fingers were still linked to Keir's as his partner, Hud Kramer, gave them a rundown on the information they'd been able to assess thus far.

The short, stocky detective with wavy brown hair pulled a notepad from the pocket of his blue chambray shirt and opened it. "We dumped the LUDs on Ms. Parker's phone. The first unidentified call came from a disposable cell at about three p.m. yesterday. We assume that call came in before the assault—maybe he was verifying your location—that you were en route to your meeting. Maybe that's what prompted you to leave your home and its security system in the first place—you thought you were going to put a stop to the harassment. You've gotten a call from that number every day this week, different times of the day and night. But we can't trace it."

Keir leaned his hip on the stool beside the one where she sat at the kitchen island. "What about that last call? That had to come after the attack. You're not telling me there are two different perverts out there, getting their rocks off at Kenna's expense."

Hud hesitated. He glanced from his partner to Kenna and back to Keir.

Kenna didn't need any soft sell of the facts. She needed answers. "Where did the last call come from?"

"The number is registered…to you."

"How is that possible?" she asked.

Keir stood, muttering a curse as if he already knew the answer. “The perp took her purse.”

Hud nodded. “Whoever that is…he called from your cell phone.”

Chapter Seven

Keir walked with his brother Niall around the outside of the Parker mansion, checking that the house, garage and yard were secure. Even though the driveway and buildings were well lit, the two men carried flashlights. The clouds rolling in overhead blocked out the moon and stars, leaving plenty of shadows between the iron fence and house where an intruder could hide.

Kenna and Niall's fiancée, Lucy McKane, were inside, getting better acquainted, cleaning up after the enchilada casserole they'd shared for dinner and watching over Tommy, the foster baby Niall and Lucy were adopting after their autumn wedding. The couple had brought over a bag with a change of clothes, toiletries and his phone charger so Keir wouldn't have to leave the estate just yet. Going on thirty-eight hours without sleep, Keir felt better about having another set of eyes on the premises for a while. Niall wasn't much of a conversationalist, and when Kenna had politely asked about their wedding plans, he jumped at the chance to join his younger brother as Keir suggested he wanted to make sure everything was secure before the storm hit.

The two men had made their way back to the slate-tiled patio before Niall, a medical examiner with the

KCPD Crime Lab, finally spoke about something other than the weather and Keir's security concerns. "Do you think they're still talking about wedding showers and bachelorette parties in there?"

Keir grinned. "Are you all planned out?"

Niall turned his light into the trees out back while Keir walked around the patio furniture to circle the perimeter of the painted brick wall. "I suggested an elopement, but Lucy has never had the chance to be part of a big family event before. She's so excited about including all of us, I didn't want to disappoint her."

"She's hard to say no to, isn't she?"

Fortunately, Lucy was as outgoing as Niall was introverted. Keir couldn't think of any two people who complemented each other more. She brought him out of his esoteric shell, and he grounded her in a sense of security and belonging the woman had never known.

"I've tried," Niall admitted, adjusting his glasses to peer into the darkness beyond the flower garden. "It's not a statistical impossibility, but on this project it has been particularly difficult." He swung his flashlight over to Keir. "By the way, I don't know what you and Duff are planning, but there are to be no strippers at my bachelor party."

Keir laughed out loud. "Is that coming from you or Lucy?"

"Lucy and the victims on my autopsy table are the only women I ever want to see naked." Niall raked his fingers through his hair. "That didn't come out right. Of course I never want to see Lucy on my table."

Keir laughed and gave his brother a teasing punch on the arm. "It's a good thing that woman loves you. I don't know how you'd ever catch anyone else."

Niall peered down at him through his glasses, giving him that stop-being-a-wiseass look, before deftly changing the topic. "So you're staying the night with Kenna? Aren't you supposed to be off the clock this weekend?"

"Yes. And yes." Keir expected some kind of teasing or curious follow-up question about letting things get too personal. Duff or Millie or someone had no doubt filled his brother in about bringing Kenna to the house where they'd grown up, making it clear to someone with even half of Niall's intellect that he'd turned an off-duty rescue into a 24/7 investigation and bodyguard commitment.

But teasing wasn't Niall's way. "Good. With a head injury like she has, it's a good idea that someone stays with her."

"Not to mention the guy who wants her dead may come back tonight to finish the job."

"True. Or maybe that countdown is all about making her *think* he's coming tonight. That would be a pretty terrifying way to get in her head."

From everything Keir had observed, the perp had done an exemplary job of that. But Kenna was stronger than the creep could ever imagine, and he couldn't imagine her allowing that fear to defeat her.

Their lights converged on the wall Marvin Bennett had been painting earlier that day. The top three rows of bricks were bulging out like a potbellied stove as the ground settled behind them. Keir touched one with his fingertips first to make sure the paint had dried; then he handed his flashlight to Niall. "Here. Hold this."

He tried to push the bowing wall in with his hip, and when it barely budged he bent down and put his shoulder into it. Niall set the flashlights on top of the wall and added his strength to the effort. But he pulled away when it became clear it wasn't going to be an easy fix and vaulted over the top of the retaining wall. He knelt between the roses waiting to be planted and put his brain to work instead, scraping aside some of the loose dirt and shining his light down behind the wall. Catching on to what his brother was doing, Keir removed a few of the loose bricks to see if this was a simple repair they could take care of so Kenna wouldn't worry about it, or if she'd need to call a professional.

Niall eyed the potted roses on either side of him. They all had double containers from the nursery, so he picked one up and pulled off the extra plastic pot to use it as a makeshift shovel. A minute later he stopped digging and sat back on his heels. "That's good ol' Missouri clay down there at the bottom under the potting soil. With all this rain, the water's gotten behind the wall and expanded it into a solid mass. You'll have to dig that out with something stronger than a plastic pot."

But Keir was less interested in his brother's soil assessment than he was in the dark red smear staining the underside of the brick he held in his hand. "Hey, Niall. What do you make of this?"

Niall jumped down to the patio and shone his light on the faded whitewash. "Looks organic. It's not rust-colored enough to be the clay. Look at the corner where it's chipped away. I'd say it's blood."

"That's what I thought." An uncomfortable scenario was forming in Keir's head. This brick had been turned upside down and freshly painted. How long had that stain been there before the gardener had covered it up with his botched repair? Keir turned to look inside the house. The first-floor rooms on this side of the house were all lit up, and he could see through to the kitchen where Lucy was pouring a mug of coffee while Kenna sat at the island, playing with the baby in his jump seat on top of the counter. The two women seemed to be enjoying their conversation. Keir turned away from their laughter and looked up at his brother. "Is it Kenna's?"

"There's no way to tell unless I analyze it. It could belong to the mason who built the wall, or any worker or guest. Could even be from an animal." Niall took the brick to study it at another angle. "The sample looks degraded. It's been out in the elements. But brick is porous enough that it could absorb the serums. Possibly, there's a purer sample deeper inside, beneath the paint."

Niall started to hand it to him, but Keir pushed it back into his brother's hands. "Can you take that to the lab and analyze it?"

Niall glanced inside the house, too. "You think this is Kenna's blood?"

"I think I haven't found the original crime scene yet. She was in a fight somewhere. Why not here? This is as good a lead as anything I've uncovered so far."

Niall nodded. "If she was cut here, too, there should be more blood. Directional splatter from the knife or scalpel or whatever instrument was used."

"If the perp had time to dump Kenna downtown, then he'd have the place to himself and plenty of time to clean up." He tilted his gaze to the overcast sky. "And Mother Nature hasn't exactly been kind to crime scenes."

"I'll grab my kit from the car and bag the brick. I'll get some luminol and my ultraviolet light to see if I can pick up anything else out here." He hesitated a moment before leaving. "You know, even if this is her blood, it could have been left by an earlier injury. Could I take a look at her head wound? See if it's consistent with striking the wall?"

"We can ask. I imagine she'll say yes. She's as anxious to find answers as I am."

"We need to get Tommy home and put him to bed. But I can drop him off with Lucy and head out to the lab tonight."

Keir extended his hand to his brother. "Thanks. I'll owe you one."

"No, you won't." Niall hooked his thumb around Keir's and shared the bros' handshake. "You were there for me when Tommy's birth father tried to kill Lucy. I figure I still owe *you*."

TWO HOURS HAD passed since Niall and his new family left the estate and Keir locked it down tight. Kenna had given Keir his pick of guest rooms upstairs and he'd settled into the one across from hers. It hadn't taken him long to unpack, but he'd indulged a few extra minutes in the shower. The hot water and shave had gone a long way to unkinking his weary muscles and washing away the grit of the day.

Before he turned in, he pulled a pair of jeans on over his briefs and padded across the hall in his bare feet. He nudged open the door to Kenna's room to see for himself one last time that she was safe before he turned in. The room was pitch-dark except for the sliver of light from the hallway, but it fell over the top of her four-poster bed and he could see that there was no blond head of hair resting on either pillow.

Feeling a twinge of alarm, he pushed the door wide-open to verify that she wasn't sitting in a chair with a book or in the adjoining bathroom. No light under the bathroom door. That didn't necessarily mean…

And then he heard voices downstairs. A man's voice mostly. "Ah, hell."

Had that creep called Kenna again? Was someone here? Was he making good on his zero-hour threat?

Keir dashed back into his room to get his gun and raced down the staircase toward the muffled conversation. Front door locked. Lights off. He'd given himself fifteen stupid minutes to clean up and feel halfway human again, and that was all the time it had taken for someone to get into… He burst into the kitchen to find it empty. A light was on over the stove. "Kenna?"

He saw her sitting in the middle of the family room in front of a big-screen TV. That and the lamp on one end table provided the only light in the room. Keir's alarm quickly fizzled into annoyance when he realized the voices he'd heard were coming from the television. Kenna held a mug in her hand and was reading something on the computer screen in her lap.

"Everything okay down here?" he asked, wondering what had her so mesmerized on that computer that she hadn't answered when he called out to her. Just to appease his own peace of mind and let the adrenaline that had charged through him earlier run its course, he crossed behind her to check the back doors to the patio. All secure.

He spared a few moments to study the flashes of lightning in the clouds whipping through the night sky. A storm was coming. Breathing normally again, he tucked his Glock into the back waistband of his jeans and came back to the tan sectional sofa. Kenna sat cross-legged in the middle. She'd wrapped a cream-colored afghan around her shoulders and had her laptop computer open on the knees of her royal blue pajama pants.

"I brewed a new pot of coffee." She finally spoke, pointing toward the kitchen without taking her eyes off the words scrolling across the computer screen. "Changed it over to decaf if you want some."

Keir considered pouring himself a cup of the fragrant brew, but he wanted an explanation first. He crossed his arms over his chest and waited for her to look up. "Is there some reason not answering and scaring me seemed like a good idea? Is everything okay?"

She closed out the page she was reading and glanced up. Her silvery eyes widened with surprise. "You're half naked—you shaved." She took her time gazing her fill of his shoulders and chest before she turned away. He'd never realized how a woman's hungry look could be such a turn-on. Instead of acting on the desire arcing between them, however, she dialed the intimacy back a notch and opted for the clever banter thing they shared. "That's a good look on you." She thrust her long legs out from beneath the cover and scooted forward to set down her drink and grab the remote from the coffee table. "Did I wake you? Sometimes the sound effects get a little loud."

"I was getting ready to turn in when I realized you hadn't gone to bed."

"I needed to do a little work." She pointed the remote at the television and turned down the volume several notches until the characters running around on-screen were barely whispering. "I turned that on for background noise. Besides, if tonight is the deadline, and he's coming for me—"

"You don't want him to take you by surprise. That's what I'm here for." Keir moved to the far side of the table to face her. Even in the flickering light from the television, he could see the bruises on her pale skin and the fatigue lining her eyes. "Why haven't you passed out yet? Dr. McBride and my brother both said sleep would be good for you."

She tucked a swath of damp, straight hair behind her ear and tilted those moonlit eyes up to his. "I don't know how long I was out the last time I lost consciousness. Long enough for the man who did this to think I was dead and haul me downtown and leave me in a filthy alley. Maybe I'm afraid the next time I go to sleep I'll never wake up again."

Keir plucked the computer off her lap, moving it beyond the grasping hands that tried to take it back. "And maybe you're too much of a workaholic." He sat down beside her and pulled the laptop onto his thighs. "What are you working on?"

"I'm reading through old case files. My personal notes on them, anyway. I'm assuming copies of the actual paperwork, trial transcripts and so on are kept at the Kleinschmidt, Drexler offices."

While Keir skimmed over the icons on her screen, Kenna picked up the steaming mug of decaf and cradled it between her hands. "I'm a horrible person. Look at that list of people I've defended. Andrew Colbern. The Rose Red Rapist. Jericho Meade's nephew."

A community leader who'd rather commit murder than pay for a divorce, a serial rapist and a mobster wannabe who'd made a bid to take over his uncle's criminal empire. Two of the three had been convicted, but Brian Elliott was serving at least forty-two years with consecutive sentences, and Austin Meade was serving a life term instead of facing the death penalty, thanks to Kenna.

Her pale gaze stared at the fireplace beneath the television, and Keir wondered what dark place her thoughts had wondered to. *A horrible person* seemed like a pretty harsh condemnation for a woman he was quickly growing to care about. He even felt a pinch of guilt at the *Terminator* nickname he'd once tossed so casually around the precinct offices. "Maybe you're doing a service to Kansas City."

She blew a snort of derision across her coffee. "Yeah, right. If you can afford her, Kenna Parker will defend anybody."

Keir scrubbed his fingers over the smooth skin of his jaw, thinking how he wanted to say this. "We need good criminal defense attorneys. You make sure those trials are fair so that when we put the perpetrators away in prison, they stay there. No one can argue an appeal and get them back on the streets because you've already given them the best defense possible."

She set the mug down and turned to him. "That's a pretty speech, Detective. You almost make me sound like one of the good guys."

"It's the truth." The more he thought about it, the more Keir believed what he was saying. He just hadn't bothered to see the whole picture of what a trial looked like before now. "Think of it this way, when I arrest a perp, I want him to go away because the department proved he committed a crime and that he deserves to be locked up. I don't want to win because you're lousy at your job—I want the guy to know we did our job right and we nailed him."

She pulled the afghan more tightly around her shoulders. "Maybe I should become a victim's advocate. The police would like me better, and I'd certainly be able to relate to my clients now. I wonder how much pro bono work I used to do. It might be good for my conscience, if not my tough-chick image, to do more pro bono work on the victims' behalves."

"You representing the little guys? Wow. It's something to consider. But only if it's what you want to do."

She sank back into the sofa beside him. "I don't know what I want."

"That's because you haven't slept in two days."

"I wonder if I used to know—in my life before I forgot faces and days and…"

The wistful despair in her voice pricked at something tender and protective inside Keir. He needed to hold her. He needed to do something to help her or he was going to have to go for a very long run in the rain. But what did a woman he'd only known for a couple of days need from him? He lifted the computer off his lap. "Everything saved?"

She nodded and he shut it down and set it on the coffee table. When he leaned back, his heavier weight shifted the cushion and she tilted toward him. Her shoulder bumped his. And when she rested her cheek against him and breathed a heavy sigh, he didn't mind that he'd booked it down the stairs, fearing the worst, and she hadn't responded to his shouts. Her hand drifted over to rest on his knee and they watched the muted show together for a few minutes before Kenna curled her legs up on the cushion beside her. Keir stretched his arm across the back of the couch and she snuggled up against his chest. Nope. With that clean, citrusy scent of her shampoo filling his nose and the heat of her long, lithe body warming his side, Keir didn't mind, at all.

Thunder rumbled outside, rattling the windowpanes on the patio doors. Kenna shifted, resting her back against him and pulling his arm down over her stomach like a second blanket to watch the first drops of rain fall. He tried not to notice how his forearm was tucked beneath her breasts. Maybe it was all the electricity in the air outside that made his skin tingle, but even through the crocheted afghan and cotton knit of her pajama top, the small, pert mounds teased the hair on his arm with every inhale of breath.

The first wave of gentle rain quickly passed. Then sheets of water poured down, drumming with a growing fury against the slate and glass as the wind picked up. A streak of lightning forked out of the sky, followed a second later by an answering crack of thunder. "Your brother must have worked out there for an hour."

Keir's nostrils flared with a frustrated sigh. "And the only useful trace he found was the blood on the brick."

"But he thinks the shape of the wound at the back of my skull is consistent with hitting the sharp corner on that wall. Do you think out there—right outside my own home—is where I was attacked?" Her breasts swelled with a deep breath against his forearm. "That means my attacker was someone I know—someone I thought was a friend, or someone I was meeting because of work. I wouldn't let a stranger through the gate, would I?"

"I doubt it."

"Do you think Niall will find an answer that can help me?"

"He may be able to determine that you hit your head on the brick, but between all the rain and Marv Bennett's handiwork, any other evidence we might have found out there is probably nonexistent." He tried to concentrate on the conversation, but she kept toying with his fingers until he splayed them out. She slipped her fingers between his and he gently closed his grip around hers, hoping she found comfort, assurance and the unique connection they shared in this simple contact the way he did. "We probably won't even be able to prove it was anything more than an accident that you hit your head."

"I didn't trip and fall and get these hash marks on my face."

"You haven't sent those letters or made those phone calls, either. But a good attorney would want us to prove cause and effect. And right now we can't prove that the harassment and your injuries are related."

"Really?" She squeezed her hand around his in a gentle reprimand. "You're throwing the attorney card at me?"

"No. I don't want there to be any doubts." And then he whispered a vow. "I want the guy who hurt you to know we nailed him."

He pressed a kiss to the crown of her hair and wrapped the other arm around her. He turned, scooting his back against the pillows. He lifted her onto his lap, stretching his legs out beneath hers on the long couch. Just as their hands fit so perfectly together, just as their mouths had meshed in those kisses upstairs, Kenna fit his body as if hers had been made for him.

Their toes touched as their legs tangled together. Her bottom nestled against his groin. Her long, lithe back leaned back against his chest, and her head rested on his shoulder, allowing him to simply turn his cheek to rub it against the softness of her hair.

His body was reacting to this quiet intimacy. Something deeper inside—something protective, something hopeful, something warning him of what he could have—what he could lose—was reacting, too. Another woman, another time, another circumstance, and he might have acted on the arousal simmering in his veins and swelling between his thighs. But right now there was no other woman, there was no other time that mattered. He'd loved and lost a woman before because he'd taken too long to admit what he felt. But in the short span of time he'd known Kenna Parker—really known her—he was more certain that this was something serious than in the two years he'd been with Sophie. Maybe the difference was being a young buck hungry to establish himself as a success outside his older brothers' shadows—and being a mature man who'd seen enough of the ugly side of life to know that if he wasn't comfortable in his own skin, then he'd never be happy anywhere.

But that was a lot of thinking, a lot of feeling and wanting and fearing, to make a smart decision right now. So Keir ignored the messages his body and heart were sending and stuck to the conversation about his investigation. "I'm just pointing out that we haven't gathered all the evidence we need to make a case yet. The jerk who did this to you still has the advantage of anonymity—unless that blood somehow turns out to be his. Even then he'd have to be in a database somewhere to be identified."

"What if I have to spend the rest of my life wondering if I know that face? What if I pass him on the street or meet him in the courtroom or at a cocktail party, and never even know I'm looking my attacker in the eye? My coworkers? My clients? The people who work for me? What if I think he's a friend and I blithely follow him out of a room, and he pulls a knife to finish what he started? I'll never see the threat until it's too late. If I never remember what happened, he'll always have the advantage over me." The moan in her chest was almost a cry of sorrow. "I can't imagine how I'm ever going to resolve those kinds of trust issues with people."

She squirmed in his lap at the disquieting thought and Keir hugged his arms more securely around her, pressing his lips into her fragrant hair. "Do you trust me?"

After a moment, she nodded, stirring her hair against his mouth and releasing that heady fragrance. "I think so. As much as I can anyone right now."

"Then trust me when I tell you that I'm not going to leave you until this guy is caught and behind bars."

With that vow, she pushed his arms away and scooted onto the edge of the sofa so she could turn and face him. "You have to go back to work on Monday. You can't promise me twenty-four/seven. Even if the storm or you being here keeps him away tonight, he'll try again. And chances are you won't be here. What if it takes days to identify him? Or months? Years? What if I never—"

He caught her face between his hands, carefully

avoiding the marks on her cheek and jaw. "He's never going to hurt you again, Kenna. I promise you that."

Gray eyes locked on to his, searching, deciding. And just as he thought she was going to nod or say she had that much faith in him, or even argue that he was being unrealistic, she pulled away, spinning toward the coffee table. "Wait a minute. The BED file. That's not the name of the file. It's the name of the person."

Keir tried to keep up with the abrupt change in topic. "You know someone named Bed?"

She picked up her laptop. "Initials. *Brian Elliott*. There's no *D* in his name, but I did defend him. Maybe it means *Brian Elliott Defense*. I don't remember his face, but I remember the trial. The newspapers nicknamed him the Rose Red Rapist because he left a rose with each of his victims. Could the rose petals have something to do with me representing him? He always claimed he was innocent."

Keir pressed the top of the laptop back down when she opened it. "He was caught in the act, attempting to rape a woman he'd abducted. She's now married to the cop who rescued her. They both made extremely reliable witnesses."

"Yes, well, the man's delusional and completely sociopathic. He doesn't have to really be innocent to be upset that I didn't get him off at his trial."

"The man is in prison." Keir moved the laptop back to the table and pulled his phone from the front pocket of his jeans. "I can call and confirm it if you want. But I'd have gotten a department-wide alert if he'd escaped. Elliott didn't do this to you."

"Has he made phone calls? Had any visitors?" She touched his wrist as if he kept that kind of information on his phone. "The man is a billionaire. He has plenty of assets to hire someone to do his dirty work for him."

"I'll request the communication logs from Jefferson City. They'll fax them to the department tomorrow." Keir pulled up his contacts and scrolled through to find a number for the prison office. The assistant warden wouldn't be there, but he could leave a message requesting the information. "I'd have to get a court order to look into his finances."

"I need to see that BED file." If Keir was exhausted, he knew that Kenna had to be running on fumes. Still, while he placed the call, she jumped up and hurried to the phone in the kitchen. He watched her pick up the receiver, but pause with her finger on the keypad. Frustration at obviously forgetting the number she wanted to call was evident in the sag of her shoulders. But the woman was nothing if not stubbornly resilient. She replaced the phone in its cradle and pulled open a drawer to retrieve the phone book. She muttered out loud as she flipped through the pages. "It's probably at work. I can call Hellie to borrow his keys or let me in until I get my set replaced. I know we keep hard copies of completed cases on file. I need to see a list of Elliott's known contacts." Keir ended his call and followed her to the kitchen. "Maybe a witness who testified against him or one of his surviving victims—"

"Kenna." He closed the phone book and pushed it to the back of the counter. When she started to protest, he cupped the uninjured side of her beautiful face and brushed the long damp bangs away from the wounds on the other side. "It's midnight. People are sleeping. You should be, too. You need to rest. And heal. Elliott's not going anywhere. You can call Bond in the morning and I'll drive you into the city to your office."

"It's midnight?"

"Yeah. The deadline's passed."

She nodded, then shook her head. "Just because nothing happened doesn't mean…"

He feathered the heavy silk of her hair between his fingers and tucked it behind her ear, letting his hand linger against the warm pulse at the side of her neck. In one moment he was soothing her manic energy; in the next, he was dipping his head and claiming her mouth in a sweetly drugging kiss. Even as he tasted the soft, full curve of her lower lip, even as he teased the seam of her mouth with his tongue and she welcomed him into her warm, decadent heat, he sensed her energy flagging. Her hands settled at his waist, singeing his bare skin, igniting the impulse to pull her onto her toes and bury his tongue inside her mouth, to bury himself inside her body and surround himself with her heat.

But this wasn't the time to give in to the passion that sparked inside him. The hour was late, the woman was exhausted and the danger was still out there, lurking, stalking, waiting for the opportunity to strike again. With a reluctant groan, Keir pulled his mouth from hers. He planted one more soothing kiss on her lips, another in her hair. Then he pulled her into his arms and cradled her head against his shoulder. Her arms snaked around his waist and she relaxed against him with a contented sigh.

"I'll be with you while you sleep," he promised. "And I'll make sure you wake up in the morning."

"That'll be another one I owe you, Detective." Her lips tickled his skin as she spoke.

He squeezed his eyes shut at the unintended caress and tried not to notice the tips of her breasts beading against the plane of his chest or the way her fingers splayed across his spine. He hoped she didn't hear the hitch in his breathing when she adjusted her stance to snuggle closer, inadvertently stroking across his own sensitive flesh and coaxing his nipples to proud attention. "Told you, I'm keeping tabs."

"Send me the bill." She tried to give the teasing right back, but her mouth opened in a big yawn that blew a whisper of warm breath across the hollow of his throat. And yeah, that touch triggered a little crazy inside him, too. But what surprised him more was the almost painful grasp of tender heat squeezing around his heart.

And that was the impulse he acted on.

"Come on." He reached down to hook a hand behind her knees and swung her up into his arms. "No more brilliant ideas or arguing with me tonight, okay? We can catch the bad guys tomorrow."

She wound her arms around his neck. "Promise?"

"You're like a dog with a bone." He wasn't sure if that was a kiss or a smile he felt against his throat, but he'd treasure either one. Keir carried Kenna back to the couch and tucked her in with the afghan. He picked up the remote and pushed the volume up again before settling into the cushions beside her. "Now tell me all about this time-traveling doctor and why you're so fascinated with him."

"Well, if you had a Scottish accent, you'd remind me a little of..."

Her voice trailed away and she was gone. Relieved to see her finally succumb to much-needed sleep, Keir turned off the television. He pulled his gun from the back of his jeans and slid it beneath the end pillow. Then he stretched his legs out beneath her on the sofa, draped the afghan over them both and, while the storm outside thundered around them, surrendered to sleep.

Chapter Eight

"Thank you, Hellie."

Helmut Bond met Kenna at the curb with an umbrella as she climbed out of Keir's car in front of the high-rise building housing the Kleinschmidt, Drexler law offices in downtown Kansas City. With his arm circling her back, the older man held the umbrella over their heads and dashed inside the main lobby of the building, leaving Keir to drive on down the street to find a parking place as if he were nothing more than a chauffeur to her.

She'd survived a 147-day countdown to a dire threat that she suspected had happened one day early for some unknown reason. But the fact that the presumably connected assault was out of sync with her stalker's meticulous timeline, and the fact that she was still alive, made her believe the danger wasn't over by any stretch of the imagination. Until she could either remember her attacker or piece together enough circumstantial evidence to identify him, she wouldn't be able to shake the fear that must have plagued her every waking thought for the past four and a half months.

"I was coming in anyway this afternoon to meet with a client."

"A client? On a Sunday?"

"He was free. I was free. He said he'd be in the city, so I gave him a call." Hellie stopped on the mat inside the door and shook the excess water off the umbrella and the shoulders of his trench coat. "I was hoping for a break in the weather, though."

Kenna wiped at the spots of rain on the sleeves of her navy blue geometric-print sweater set and the knees of her skinny jeans. A few moments later, Keir shoved open the glass door behind them and joined them. He straightened the collar of his black KCPD jacket that he'd turned up against the curtain of rain falling outside and shook the water out of his hair, spraying both Kenna and Hellie.

Kenna smiled at the boyish disarray of sleek dark hair spiking out in a dozen different directions, but Hellie wiped a spot off his cheek and grunted. "I see the police department is still offering you protection."

Irritated with Hellie's condescending tone, and simply because she wanted to touch it, she reached up and combed her fingers through Keir's short, wet hair, smoothing it back into place. *That's right, Hellie. Keir Watson means a whole lot more to me than just the hired help.* "Yes, Detective Watson has been taking very good care of me."

Keir winked as if he understood the point she was making for the other attorney's benefit. Hellie must have observed the personal interaction, too, because his tone didn't change. "I'm glad to know my tax dollars are being put to good use. Shall we?"

Keir wrapped his hand around Kenna's and gestured toward the bank of elevators. "By all means, Mr. Bond. Lead on."

Once inside the first elevator, Hellie pushed the button for the fifth floor. "I must say you're looking better than you did a couple of nights ago at the hospital. You actually have some color in your face—and I don't mean the bruises." He chuckled at his own joke.

"Getting a good night's sleep helped."

She squeezed her fingers around Keir's, silently thanking him for the gift of serenity he'd given her last night. Being held so securely in his arms, surrounded by his heat, was the only thing that had allowed her to drop her guard, shut off her brain and finally relax enough to sleep. The rest had been healing and rejuvenating for her spirit and energy, although waking up with a firm arousal wedged against her thigh and a warm hand cupped possessively over the curve of her bottom had stirred up a very different sort of energy inside her—one that still hummed with a sensual awareness of the man holding her hand.

As tender, protective and compassionate as he'd been with her over the past two days, she suspected that Keir Watson would be a skilled and generous lover. And she'd been half tempted to run her fingers over all that warm, firm skin that stretched tautly over his shoulders and chest, and initiate a kiss to test her theory about just how good they could be together. But when he'd caught her staring her fill of his interestingly handsome face, Keir caught her hips between his hands and lifted her away from the evidence of his desire to set her on the cushions beside him. "Sorry about that. Not exactly stellar timing for that sort of thing, is it?"

His blue eyes danced with a rakish twinkle and her addled, wishful brain heard, *"Oh, what I couldn't do with you for a couple of hours."*

But her ears heard an imminently more practical "Ready to get to work?" before he caught her lips in a good-morning kiss. Then he was standing up, searching the kitchen for fresh coffee and telling her to shower and get dressed while he dug up something for brunch.

As she watched the numbers above the elevator door light up with each floor, Kenna wondered if she'd ever be able to look at a progression of numerals without this wary jump in her pulse again. Or maybe it was the spicy scent of the detective beside her who was making her heart beat a little faster. Had she ever been this attracted to a man before the attack? There were no photographs of any man other than her father on display at the house, no silly little mementos tucked away in any well-organized drawer that could be a sentimental souvenir and certainly no engagement ring box or heart-shaped pendant to indicate evidence of a serious relationship.

Even with amnesia blanking names and faces, wouldn't she remember feeling this deliciously sexy awareness if she'd ever experienced it before? This soul-mate sensation of meeting a personality of equal drive, wit and intelligence? This feeling of being in love?

Love?

The elevator stopped with an abrupt jolt on the fifth floor. Or maybe that jolt was her brain admitting the word *love* and mulling over the possibility of what, exactly, she felt for the detective standing beside her. Kenna pulled her hand from Keir's and hugged her arms around her middle. Gratitude? Certainly. Attraction? Couldn't help herself. But love? How could a mature, sensible woman fall in love in the space of a couple of days?

The obvious answer was that she'd crashed her brain against a brick wall and wasn't thinking sensibly. The less obvious answer was that she was confusing love with something else. And though she wasn't naive enough to think that Keir didn't find her equally attractive, having an overly developed sense of responsibility for a victim and wanting to share a roll on the couch didn't mean he was getting a relationship kind of serious feeling about her, too.

The elevator opened across from a bank of glass doors with a Kleinschmidt, Drexler, Parker and Bond logo plaque up on the wall behind the receptionist's counter inside. Maybe Hellie saw the fact that she'd released Keir's hand as an opening to get a little more personal with her. He unlocked the door and, palming the small of her back, led her across the plush gray carpet to the tall white counter. He hooked his dripping umbrella over the edge of the reception counter and shrugged off his tan raincoat. "Do you remember where your office is?"

Kenna took a moment to look around. Familiar images started to drop into place—the neutral color scheme of the centrally located reception area, the long hallways leading in opposite directions. "Partners' offices are to the left—paralegals and storage rooms to the right." She pointed to the left. "I'm down there."

Hellie took her arm. "Come this way first."

Although Keir used a few extra seconds to scan both hallways, he quickly followed her and Hellie around the counter through the door marked Boardroom. The long room looked the way she remembered from that past board meeting. The heavy walnut table and leather rolling chairs looked familiar, as did the bookshelves and a bar sink complete with coffee cups and liquor glasses. Kenna walked to the row of windows looking out over the city street. Rivulets of rain streaked the tinted glass, giving the buildings across the street and the cars below a gray, gloomy look in the middle of the afternoon. There must be some kind of convention going on at Bartle Hall or a matinee concert at the Folly Theater nearby to account for the bumper-to-bumper parking along each sidewalk and the row of cars lining up to pull into the parking garage kitty-corner from the building.

"Here you are." Kenna turned past Keir unzipping his jacket in the doorway to Hellie pulling something from the safe he'd opened at the far end of the room. He jingled a ring of keys in his hand, and Kenna moved away from the windows to retrieve them. "Arthur ordered spare sets made to award the newbies when they make junior partner. I don't think he'd mind if you kept these until you can get all your keys replaced. What about your car keys—will you be able to get around?"

"I had a spare set at home." She'd found keys for the house, too, that she could use if the security codes didn't work, or she forgot the numbers, and had given a set to Keir.

Hellie pressed the keys into her hand, folding her fingers around them and holding on until she lifted her questioning gaze to his. "What about replacing your driver's license and other cards that were in your purse?"

"I've already called and put a stop on my credit

cards. Replacements are in the mail, and I'll be visiting the DMV tomorrow to get my license replaced."

One bushy eyebrow climbed higher on his forehead as he leaned in to whisper, "With Detective Watson?"

Kenna pulled her hand away and glanced over at Keir, who hadn't missed a word of her conversation with Hellie. "I don't know," she answered honestly, remembering Keir's promise to keep her safe until her attacker was found. Although she longed to believe he'd stay with her indefinitely, realistically she knew the man had to return to work. And she doubted she'd be a welcome addition hanging out with his team at precinct headquarters. She was going to have to hire a bodyguard or learn how to face the frightening blanks of her life on her own. Neither option could quell the sudden discomfort that tightened her chest.

"I'd be happy to take you," Hellie offered. He cupped his hands over her shoulders, and she had the feeling he was offering more than a ride to the DMV. "Just say the word and I'm yours."

Not gonna happen. Pasting a smile on her face, Kenna shrugged off his touch and headed for the door. "I'll let you know. Right now I need to track down some information for the police. Thanks again for your help, Hellie."

"Please tell me I don't have to like that guy," Keir said a few moments later as he draped his jacket on the back of a chair over an air vent in Kenna's office while she sat down at her desk and reacquainted herself with her work space.

"I'm pretty sure I don't like him," Kenna admitted, booting up her desktop computer. "I have a feeling I merely tolerate him because he was a friend of my father's—and we have to work together. Those eyebrows of his are a little scary. They remind me of two—"

"Fuzzy caterpillars?"

Kenna laughed, and the tension she'd been feeling, analyzing her feelings for him and thinking about how lost she was going to feel when they had to go their separate ways, receded to a manageable level that she could ignore. Meanwhile, she opened drawers until she found an address book. Keir stood and looked over her shoulder while she thumbed through the pages for the *W*'s. Finally. *Barbara Jean Webster. Hulston Hall.* "That's at a law school." A loud, energetic laugh echoed through her memories and Kenna snapped her fingers. "She's an old friend of mine. We went through law school together."

Keir pulled his notepad from the back pocket of his jeans and perched his hip on the corner of the desk. "Call her. Put it on speaker."

Kenna dialed the number and waited for her friend to answer. "Barbara Jean?"

"Hey, Kenna." Barbara Jean sounded breathless, as if she was in the middle of a workout. "It's good to hear your voice. I heard that you got mugged Friday night. I didn't know if you were up for visitors or I'd have stopped by."

"You heard I was attacked? It wasn't in the news."

Barbara Jean shouted a boy's name and something about tracking mud through the house before she returned to the phone. "The legal community is a small world. I heard it from a friend of a friend. Don't know the details, of course. How are you feeling?"

Kenna could remember dark hair now, and two equally dark-haired children, as she began to place her friend in her life. "I'm a little beat up around the edges."

"I hope the police catch the creep."

"Well, that's the reason I'm calling." Although she still couldn't recall her friend's face, the fast-talking, bighearted personality was feeling more and more familiar. "The police are investigating, and I'm a little foggy on the details leading up to the assault. Can you remind me why we were meeting and where?"

"Honey, are you okay?"

"I will be if you can answer a few questions."

Barbara Jean seemed to be wrestling galoshes off children's feet, but she didn't hesitate to respond. "We were meeting for coffee after you wrapped things up at the courthouse. As to why? You tell me. I was hoping maybe you were coming to me to finally file a sexual harassment lawsuit against your buddy Hellie. Boy, does that man have a problem with keeping his hands to himself! I felt like I had to shower off after that New Year's Eve party at the Drexlers'. It didn't make any difference telling him I had a husband."

"Did I mention a lawsuit?"

"No. Mostly you vented about dealing with too much stress and living under a microscope with Mr. Kleinschmidt dangling that promotion in front of you—how everyone at the firm was scrutinizing your work on the Colbern case."

The squeal of children's voices startled Kenna but quickly faded into silence as Barbara Jean sent them out to the kitchen for snacks.

"You know, when I heard about the mugging, my first thought was that Hellie had done something to you. I wouldn't put it past him if it meant getting you out of the running for senior partner. The man's an idiot. Of course, you made that police detective look like an idiot, too."

Kenna shot Keir an apologetic look. But if he'd gotten a new dent on his ego, he didn't show it. Instead, he gestured for her to keep asking questions and went back to jotting his notes. "And we had coffee at…?"

"Balthazar's."

Keir jotted a message on his notepad and showed it to her. *When did you leave Balthazar's?*

"Hey, do you remember about what time I left the coffee shop?"

Barbara Jean sounded as if she'd finally caught her breath. "That's an odd question."

"I couldn't remember the exact time." She couldn't remember meeting her friend at all. But she could recall sharing an apartment with Barbara Jean in Columbia, Missouri—and making coffee and red licorice runs when they'd been up late studying for exams. "The detective here says it could help if I retrace my steps leading up to the attack."

"Let's see. You left Balthazar's at almost straight-up three o'clock. I had to get home to meet the kids when the bus dropped them off after school—and you said you had a five o'clock, and you were going home to get changed."

"I went home?"

Where she'd fought with someone and clobbered her head on the patio wall.

"That's what you told me."

"Did I say who I was meeting?"

"No. But I gather it was a man. Why else would you go home to get gussied up? Although you were already wearing one of your power suits and a pair of those knock-'em-dead high heels." Barbara Jean hissed an apologetic sigh. "Sorry. Poor choice of words."

A *"Don't worry"* died on her lips when the significance of what her friend had said registered. Kenna leaned toward the phone. "Do you remember what suit I was wearing? What heels?"

"The police want to know what you wore to coffee with me?"

"It could be important."

"Um, let's see. Oh, sure. It was your kick-ass-in-court suit—the tan Armani—and the Jimmy Choos you splurged on down on the Plaza." Barbara Jean scoffed. "You know, the ones with the mile-high heels? Like you need to be any taller."

Kenna remembered her clothes being bagged up in the hospital several hours after the assault. She reached over to squeeze Keir's knee. "I never changed my clothes. That's what I was wearing when I was attacked."

Keir nodded. "That narrows the timeline considerably."

"Between three and five o'clock."

"What's that?" Barbara Jean asked, thinking Kenna had been talking to her.

Keir scrawled a question on his notepad and she read the message. *Rose petals?*

"Barbara Jean? This will sound strange, too, but..." Keir's hand settled over hers where it fisted on the desk. She turned her palm up to meet his. She could do this. "Did I mention anything about roses? Or about someone stalking me?"

Barbara Jean gasped. "Oh, honey. Is that what happened to you? No. I wish I'd known. Maybe I could have helped. You just said you needed to get away and have a normal conversation with someone you could trust. You did seem to be wound up pretty tight. I figured it was the stress of the trial, but I guess this stalker creep was weighing on your mind. Knowing you, you probably thought you could handle the situation yourself. You should have said something."

Keir closed his notepad, indicating he'd gotten the information he needed. "Thanks, Barbara Jean. I appreciate the help."

"Anytime, my friend. And hey, whenever you want to leave the good ol' boys' network and go into a partnership with Walter and me, just say the word. We'll take good care of you. I know you're loyal to Kleinschmidt, Drexler because your dad was a founding partner, but if the old guy promotes Hellie ahead of you, I'd jump ship."

"I'll think about it. Thanks." Kenna disconnected the call with a wistful smile. So there were two people in this world she trusted without question. Barbara Jean Webster and the man sitting beside her, who maybe didn't have much reason to trust *her*.

She pulled her hand from beneath Keir's. "Still dislike Hellie?" She tried to make the question sound like a teasing gibe, but the reality of her getting Colbern acquitted at Keir's expense made the joke fall flat. "If Arthur had assigned him instead of me, you might have won your case."

He stood and pulled her to her feet beside him. "Don't you go soft on me now, Counselor. You beat me, fair and square. I didn't like it. I still don't. But that just means that next time I appear in court, I'm going to up my game and put together a case that not even the great Kenna Parker can tear apart."

She arched an eyebrow and tilted her skeptical gaze to his. "The great Kenna Parker?"

"Too much?"

She squeezed her thumb and forefinger together and smiled. "Li'l bit."

He traced the curve of her lip with his fingertip. "That's better. Besides, friend or foe, I'd rather look at your legs than Hellie's bushy eyebrows any day."

Although her lip still tingled from the touch of Keir's finger, she knew they were here for business, not flirty reassurances. She nodded toward the phone. "Chatting with Barbara Jean helped. I never got the chance to change my clothes that night. I never made my five o'clock."

"I think you did."

Of course. "Whoever I had that appointment with—"

"Is the man who tried to kill you."

The stitches at the base of her skull throbbed with the dire realization. "That's why no one called to see why I never showed up for dinner." She pointed to the appointment calendar she'd pulled up on her computer screen. Except for the court appearance in the morning, and the initials *B.J.* at three o'clock, the square for Friday was blank. "Why didn't I write down who I was meeting? Clearly, it wasn't work related or my assistant would have posted it."

"Maybe that's exactly what the meeting was about—work." Kenna frowned, needing more of an explanation. "I just heard your friend rattle off a lot of complaints about Helmut Bond. Sexual harassment?

Good ol' boys' network? Vying for the same promotion? If he sees you as a threat—that's motive. Being a longtime family friend, you'd be comfortable inviting him to your house. You'd probably try to reason out the conflict with him before you took any kind of legal action." Keir shrugged. "Or maybe you did threaten legal action and that set him off. He's certainly kept an eye on you since the attack. He could be trying to see if you remember him being there."

Personal aversions aside, Kenna hated to think that someone her father had mentored could get angry enough to hurt her like this. There had to be another answer. "What about the phone calls and letters? All that happened before the attack—before I would have confronted Hellie. Those are detailed, planned actions, meant to frighten and intimidate me." She swept her hand in front of her face. "This is impulse, not a patient, calculated terror campaign. Helmut Bond is glib and annoying, not violent."

"Unless something you said or did at that meeting triggered the rage he's been holding in check."

Kenna overlapped the front edges of the cotton cardigan she wore, hugging herself against the chill that shivered through her body. "Then we've still got a lousy case, Detective. I have no idea what I said or did, much less who I said or did it to."

Keir rubbed his hands up and down her arms, trying to instill in her the warmth and confidence she couldn't find. His voice was a hushed, intimate whisper of encouragement. "If you won't consider your buddy Bond, then we'll go find more suspects. If we can't have eyewitness testimonies, then let's dig up all the circumstantial evidence we can find and put together a list of persons of interest who might have motive to hurt you."

Kenna knew what he was asking. "The BED file. Brian Elliott. The Rose Red Rapist."

Keir crossed to the door and opened it. "We know he didn't send the letters with the rose petals, because they'd be marked with a prison stamp. And he didn't make those calls, because the prison would have a record of them."

"And he couldn't be the man in the hoodie watching me, because he's locked up in Jefferson City."

"But he could easily hire someone to do the work for him."

Steeling her shoulders on a resigned breath, Kenna grabbed her keys and moved into the hallway ahead of him, preceding him down the long hallway to the file storage room. "Technically, he's still my client, so I won't be able to show you the file."

"Are any of the contacts, victims or witnesses in his file your clients?"

"No."

"I've got that list of everybody who's visited Elliott in the past three months. While you're reading files, I'll start making phone calls. All I need are names, and then I can do the legwork to check alibis and criminal histories and find out who has a grudge against you."

Kenna was sorely afraid of just how long that list might be.

Nearly half an hour later, Kenna was hugging an armload of file folders to her chest when she and Keir left the storage room. "I feel like I'm back in law school," she said, waiting for Keir to lock the door behind him before heading to the boardroom, where they could spread out at the conference table. "Toting around case files I have to memorize for Professor Owenson's class."

"Are you sure you don't want me to carry those for you?"

"It's a conflict of interest for a police officer—"

"What's he doing here?" Kenna stopped short when the compact, blond-haired man who'd been conversing with Hellie at the reception counter charged down the hallway to meet her. The accusing finger he'd pointed at Keir swung toward her. "Conspiring with the enemy?"

The man was middle-aged, angry and completely unfamiliar to her. "Excuse me?"

"Kenna?" Keir stepped up beside her to make the introduction. "This is Andrew Colbern."

Shock drew her back half a step as she sorted through her memories for an earlier consultation that would make the sneering expression spark a recognition in her. She looked over at Keir, knowing this man's trial was a point of conflict between them. But the only hint that this unexpected meeting might have poked that sore point was for Keir to shift his posture, splaying his fingers at his waist, possibly reminding the other man that he wore a gun, or maybe just relaxing his stance to show the other man he wasn't intimidated by him.

"There's no way he's attending this meeting," Colbern announced, either uncaring or unaware of Keir subtly nudging his shoulder in front of Kenna. "He's the cop who tricked me into saying I wanted to have Devon killed."

Hellie placed a hand on Colbern's arm. "Andrew,

as your attorney, I advise you not to say anything in front of Detective Watson."

Kenna was having a hard time getting up to speed on this conversation. But she knew a manipulation when she saw one. She looked past Dr. Colbern to Hellie. "You set up this meeting as soon as I hung up after asking you to let me into the office. You know I'm not ready to deal with clients."

"Somebody better be," Colbern warned. "I want to know what you're going to do to get this stain off my reputation. Do you know how many of my patients have canceled appointments since I was arrested? Devon has a lot of social contacts, and I know that witch is spreading lies about me."

Keir's voice remained calm. "You're talking about a PR campaign, Colbern, not legal action. That's not Ms. Parker's area of expertise."

"Why are you even talking to me, Watson? How is this any of your business?"

"Kenna Parker is my business."

Colbern's blue-eyed gaze darted between Kenna and Keir. "Oh, so it's like that, is it?"

"Dr. Colbern is *our* client," Hellie emphasized, steering the conversation away from Keir. "I wanted to reassure him that we're ready to move forward to block his wife's civil suit."

"But we're not. *I'm* not," Kenna reminded him.

"But we will be," Hellie insisted. His brown eyes narrowed with a silent message she didn't care to read. "I have a plan of action mapped out. I just need you to confer—add your two cents, as it were."

"Two cents? Ha." Andrew Colbern's snort was filled

with bitterness. "With what this firm is costing me, I ought to be getting a lot more advice than that."

Kenna wasn't sure if her gut was telling her to be leery of Dr. Colbern or Hellie. But she knew she didn't want to deal with either man's attitude right now. "I'm sorry, gentlemen." She lifted the files she carried. "But I'm in the middle of a project. Doctor, why don't you call my assistant tomorrow and make an appointment for later in the week?"

"Don't bother, Andrew."

Kenna read the flush of temper brewing beneath Hellie's tan cheeks.

"I have my car downstairs. What do you say to an early dinner, and you and I can discuss your wife's threats there?"

"Let's just reschedule when Kenna's available." The doctor shook his head, eyeing Keir. "I may not like the company she keeps, but I think we need her input on how we're going to move forward against Devon. This afternoon was a waste of my time."

"Very well." Hellie fixed that bright white smile on his face, but the door was already closing on Andrew Colbern's emphatic exit. "I'll call you."

Kenna was suddenly very tired. Maybe she'd overtaxed her energy level too soon after being in the hospital. And maybe this was the kind of stress she'd wanted to talk to Barbara Jean about. Perhaps she did need to consider her friend's offer to work for a smaller firm.

"How dare you embarrass me like that in front of a client?" Hellie seized Kenna by the shoulders, shaking loose two of the folders she carried. "Bringing your boy toy to work—"

"Hey, pal." Keir snatched Hellie by the wrist and

twisted his arm behind his back, earning a grunt of pain as he pulled him away from Kenna. "You don't threaten the lady."

Surprised by both Hellie's outburst and Keir's swift response, Kenna stooped down to retrieve the folders from the floor. "It was presumptuous of you to arrange a meeting without informing me, Hellie. Are you so worried you can't win a case without me on the team? Or that you're going to lose a client?"

"I'm not worried about anything." Hellie shrugged off Keir's hold as soon as the younger man loosened his grip. "Except maybe your choice in men." He grabbed his umbrella and raincoat off the reception counter where he'd left a puddle of water on the carpet beneath and strode toward the door. "I thought I knew you, that I could count on you the way I counted on your father. But you've changed. Don't call me for any more favors until you've come to your senses."

Once the elevator door had closed behind Hellie, Keir turned back to Kenna. "Do you still believe that conniver couldn't snap and lose his temper?"

Chapter Nine

Kenna's growling stomach startled her awake. Her chin slipped off her hand and she was painfully aware of the throbbing in her wrist after bending it back at the unnatural angle to support her head. It took a few seconds to orient herself to her surroundings. Folders and paperwork stacked in various piles across the long conference table. Rain pattering at the window. Grinning man watching her from the end of the table.

"Please tell me I wasn't drooling."

Keir set down his phone and the ink pen he'd been using. "Nothing significant."

She tossed a wad of paper at him. "Very funny."

He caught it and tossed it right back before checking the time. "We've been at this for three hours, and Dr. McBride said you should take it easy for a while. Ready to call it a day?"

"Did we find any viable suspects?"

"A few." He picked up the legal pad he'd borrowed to record notes from the phone calls he'd made and thumbed through several pages of yellow paper to reveal all the names he'd been able to cross off from the lists they'd generated. "Between Hud and me and my sister, Liv, we're narrowing it down. The women Brian

Elliott preyed on whom we've been able to reach thus far have solid alibis for three to five p.m. on Friday, so we can rule them out as your attacker."

"Do you really think a woman could do this to me?"

"If she subdued you somehow—drugged you, or a blitz attack. We shouldn't automatically rule out the possibility." He read the first names on the page where he'd stopped. "April King. She was working her shift at Truman Medical Center." He picked up the pen and scratched through her name. "Tabitha and Ezekiel Rule—the victim and her husband—were involved in a fender bender out near Lenexa. State Patrol has them on the scene for several hours." He scratched those names out, too. "Genie D'Angelo—committed suicide two years after Elliott sexually assaulted her."

"How horrible." When he scratched out the last young woman's name, Kenna's heart twisted with guilt. It was difficult to uphold the law and ensure due process for everyone when faced with a loss like that. "What about the family members or friends who blame me for defending the man who hurt their loved ones? Does anyone stand out there?"

"That's a bigger list. But we'll keep hitting the Rose Red Rapist angle, since you seemed suspicious of Brian Elliott before your amnesia." Keir flipped the legal pad back to its first page and stood. "By the way, I went with my gut and checked out Hellie Bond's alibi. He was more than happy to tell me how wrong I am. But it's sketchy at best. He claims he went for a drive in the country. Alone. Said his girl left town and he was missing her."

"You're so determined it's him." Kenna rolled her chair away from the table and pushed to her feet. Could someone she saw nearly every day of her life, someone her father had trusted, someone who claimed he cared for her, really be so insecure or vindictive that he'd spend months trying to drive her crazy or leave her scarred for life? "I would have thought Andrew Colbern resented me more than Hellie ever could. Until today. Maybe he does have motive to send me rose petals to remind me of my biggest and most unpopular case—to make me paranoid and second-guess every choice I make—to put me off my game just when Arthur is about to name one of us senior partner." She picked up one of the files and straightened the papers before closing it. "Maybe there's someone in every file here who wants me to crack up or bow out of the human race or simply fail at getting the things I want."

Keir placed his hand on top of the folders Kenna was stacking to return to the storage room. "Do you want to be a senior partner?"

Kenna honestly didn't know the answer to that question anymore. "I thought I was breaking through some kind of glass ceiling, making a statement for women, and I was proud of that. I felt I deserved the promotion and worked hard to bring in big-money clients. I wanted it because that's what my father always envisioned for me, and I loved the idea of honoring his legacy."

"If you want it, go for it. And don't let Helmut Bond or whoever this bastard is stop you from being who you want to be. He's one man, and he doesn't get to win. If your dream changes and you want something else, you'll be a success at that, too, because that's who you are. The Kenna I've gotten to know doesn't settle for halfway or second best. I can't imagine any father not being proud of that legacy." He gestured to the remaining folders strewn across the table. "And don't forget that there are good people in these files you've helped, too. Maybe their names don't make headlines like a billionaire with a sexual depravity. But they're there. Innocent people who needed a champion to represent them. Not everybody in these files wants to hurt you. You may have more friends out there than you think."

Heartened by the rallying show of support, empowered in a way that only this man seemed to manage, Kenna threw her arms around Keir's neck and hugged him tight. She turned her lips to the collar of his white button-down shirt and kissed the warm beat of his pulse. "Thank you."

He wrapped his arms around her, pulling her into his ample heat and sealing the embrace.

"I don't know if you're always like this, or if you're only like this with me at this moment, but you said what I needed to hear. I think that I'm a strong woman. But you make me stronger. Be sure to add that to the list of things I owe you for."

Kenna kissed the corner of his firm mouth. With an eager moan, Keir curved his mouth over hers to accept and deepen the invitation. Sliding her fingers into his hair, Kenna had every intention of taking up where every other potent kiss between them had left off. But another noisy grumble in her stomach vibrated between them. With a sound that was half laugh and half sigh of regret, Keir pulled his lips from hers. He rested his forehead against hers and looked down into her eyes. "One day, woman, we're going to finish this."

His voice was raw and deep, and the promise behind it left her embarrassingly weak in the knees. "I'm going to hold you to that promise."

He pressed a warm, ticklish kiss to the end of her nose, then pulled away entirely. "In the meantime, I'd better feed you."

"Are you going to treat me to some of Millie's cooking again?"

Keir pulled his jacket off the back of his chair and shrugged into it. "I'd be just as happy to go to your place and heat up that leftover casserole."

"Why don't we swing past Balthazar's and get a couple of cups of java to go on the way?" she suggested. "We could ask a few questions of any staff or customers who might have seen someone following me Friday afternoon."

"You're relentless. Did anyone ever tell you you'd make one heck of a cop?"

"Never."

He laughed out loud and that made her smile. This man made her feel like teasing and laughing and smiling again, instead of hiding in her big, empty house and maintaining rigid control over every aspect of her life.

"All right. Balthazar's it is." He kissed her temple, then circled around the table and out the door. "Gather up what you need. We can read through the rest of these at the house. I'll go bring the car around so you don't get soaked. Lock up and meet me down at the front door."

Moving with a lighter step than she had had all day, Kenna quickly gathered up the folders that were ready to be refiled and locked them in the storage room. She grabbed a tote bag from her office closet and hurried back to the boardroom to pack Keir's notes and the remaining case files.

As she was closing one of the files she'd kept on her defense of Austin Meade—a former crime boss's nephew, who'd been more of an embarrassment than a success in the defunct family business—a sheet of white paper caught her eye. It wasn't a transcript of a deposition or a handwritten note. It wasn't a photograph. A little tremor of apprehension shivered through her as she reached for the blank page and pulled it out. If there was one rose petal… Only, it wasn't a plain sheet of paper, after all. Kenna's relief blossomed into curiosity when she saw the small pencil drawing of a geometric figure, hastily drawn in the top left corner.

She remembered this image.

But how? From where?

Although it was basically a rectangular shape, the edges were scalloped and there were several caret-shaped marks drawn in the blank space around the design inside the rectangle. Two lines swooshed toward a small circle that sat off-center, and was surrounded by eight points of a star. "It's a spur. A spur off a cowboy boot."

She didn't know any cowboys, did she? What did the symbol mean?

Knowing that Keir would be coming for her soon, she went to the bank of windows to look out. Groups of people were hurrying down the sidewalk, and traffic was backing up in the street. The event at Bartle Hall or one of the theaters must have let out. And with the rain still coming down and people eager to get into dry cars and go home, no one seemed particularly anxious to let anyone else merge into traffic. She wanted to show the drawing to Keir. She wanted to see if it struck a familiar chord with him, too. But she couldn't see the black Charger anywhere. He probably had to drive around the block to get to the front of the building.

Eager to show him her discovery, Kenna locked up the offices and rode the elevator down to the first floor. She waited inside the lobby doors, amused by the people hurrying by with their raincoats and umbrellas, and those without protection from the elements hurrying by even faster. She was keeping one eye out for Keir and mentally scanning through her Swiss cheese brain for the significance of the spur to fall into place when she gradually became aware that not everyone was rushing through the rain.

There was one person standing perfectly still. One person watching. Watching her.

Her heart beating a stitch faster, her chest expanding and contracting with quicker breaths, she scanned both sides of the street, up and down the block, until she zeroed in on the absence of movement. There. Lurking in the shadows at the entrance to the parking garage across the street.

The faceless man in the black hoodie.

Her lips parted to take a deeper breath as an urgent sense of being singled out for some evil purpose fluttered through her pulse. Kenna recoiled a step from the shadowed face that was still there each time a pedestrian walked past or a car drove by. She was afraid. She was so damn tired of being afraid. She needed to make it stop.

He doesn't get to win.

Keir's vehement words resonated in her head, tamping down the fear. All this guy did was show up where she was, and watch. She'd seen him twice now. And he'd probably been there a third time when Keir spotted him near the alley where he'd found her. Maybe Hoodie Guy had followed her more often and she just hadn't noticed. His strength was in the shadows, in his anonymity. Well, she could take that advantage away with one simple task. She was a strong woman. She took action. She wasn't giving this faceless stranger the chance to terrorize her again.

"I think it's time the two of us meet." And this time, she wouldn't forget his face.

Looping the tote bag over her neck and shoulder, Kenna pushed open the door and stepped outside. Rain slapped her in the face and she squinted her eyes against the onslaught. The guy wasn't moving. Maybe she could use the crowd and traffic to her advantage and get close enough to see beneath the hood before he realized she was there. That was all she had to do. She didn't have to confront him. She just needed to see his face.

When a group of schoolchildren and parents jostled past, she turned and walked with them, ducking behind a parked van as soon as she reached it. She peeked around the taillight of the van and saw Hoodie Guy slowly moving his head back and forth. Good. He'd lost sight of her. For once, she had the advantage.

When he turned his scan away from her, she darted between stopped and slow-moving cars until she reached his side of the street. Blending in was a little trickier here, since she was moving against the flow of pedestrians leaving the theater in the next block. Just a little closer. *Look this direction.* Kenna reached the entrance to the garage and paused. The rain had soaked through her hair and was running down her scalp and beading in her eyelashes. He was on the other side of this concrete archway, just a few yards away. She'd never be closer to the truth.

But the fear was sinking its talons into her again. She should have thought this through better. She should have waited for Keir. She should get her stupid cell phone replaced so she could call her protector and tell him what she was doing. But what if Hoodie Guy was on the move and she lost him? What if he was already gone?

"Just count to three and poke your head around the corner," she murmured, steeling her resolve. "That's all you have to do. One. Two."

"Looking for me, Kenna?"

She heard the toneless whisper the same moment a gloved hand closed around her shoulder and she screamed a startled yelp and jerked away from his grasp. Kenna spun around the concrete arch to face him. "Where…?"

She heard breathless laughter. Heavy boots on concrete.

"Ma'am?" She yelped a second time at the touch of another hand on the wet sleeve of her sweater. But this time she looked up into the apologetic face of a tall, lanky cowboy. "Sorry. Are you all right?"

A Good Samaritan. Not the terror that lived in the fringes of her mind every single day of her life. "Do you have a phone on you?"

"Sure do." Water ran off the brim of his hat when he nodded. He pulled a cell phone from a pocket inside his corduroy jacket.

"I need you to call the police." The sound of heavy

footsteps was fading. Hoodie Guy was getting away. Again. "There's a man following me. He just accosted me. Black hoodie. Ski mask. Blue jeans. Give them this address."

"Okay. Do you want to wait with my wife…? Ma'am?"

Kenna hoped the cowboy took directions well, because she wasn't coming back to repeat them. She ran all the way up the ramp to the next half level where she could hear the garage's metal infrastructure ringing with the heavy tromp of the man's thick-soled boots. She was slightly breathless herself by the time she spotted him at the far end, running with a bit of a limp down the center of the aisle. She crouched near the trunks of cars as she gave chase. "Hey, you! Why are you following me?"

He disappeared up the ramp to the next floor. Ignoring the burning in her lungs, she ran to the base of the ramp. She saw his torso, legs and work boots though the crisscrossed steel railings attached to the open interior edge of each parking level. Still no face.

"Did you do this to me?" No answer. "What do you want? How did I ever hurt you? Why don't you talk to me like a man would?"

Kenna raced toward the ramp until she realized he'd stopped running. Through the railing she saw him brace his gloved hands on his knees and lean forward as a deep cough shook his body and he fought to catch his breath. Creeping back toward his position on the half level below him, Kenna moved toward the railing, thinking she could peer up between the bars and get a look at his face. If he'd turn just a fraction of an inch, she could finally fill one empty spot in her memory. She panted through her open mouth, breathing silently, hiding her approach. He was holding his side now, his breath wheezing like rales in his chest. Was the man older? Injured? Out of shape? All three?

Then he seemed to catch his breath and hold it as he turned. Kenna watched the hood, waiting for his face to appear. She was so crushed to see the ski mask hiding his features that she nearly missed his hand coming around at the same time. But a glint of the garage's yellowish lights reflected off a long steel blade. He laughed as he thrust the knife toward her and slashed it through the air. Once. Twice. Thrice as he mimicked slashing her throat.

Kenna jerked back as if the blade had actually cut her.

Her hands flew to her neck and the man laughed until another coughing fit took hold. "Oh, yeah," he rasped. "Now you're scared. That's how I like it."

In the moment she blinked, he'd vanished around the next concrete post. She heard a horn honking and a screech of tires spinning over pavement in the distance. "Kenna!"

Red-and-blue lights flashed in her peripheral vision as she ran to the railing and shook the metal like the bars of a jail cell. "You coward! I'm going to rip that mask right off your face! Talk to me!"

Was that why she'd blanked out any memory of her attacker's face? Because there'd been no face for her to remember?

"Kenna!"

The swirling lights were blinding now as her eyes filled with tears of emotional exhaustion. A car slammed on its brakes and skidded to a halt behind her. The man was long gone. So was her hope. There were only two ways this whole nightmare was going to end. Either she'd have some kind of nervous breakdown or she'd be dead.

"You single-minded, stubborn..."

Kenna was still clinging to the railing with a white-knuckled grip when Keir ran up behind her.

"Are you hurt?"

She shook her head. The man in the hoodie hadn't harmed her, not physically, at least.

She was aware of how heavy her clothes were with the rain and how she squished the puddles inside her tennis shoes when she wiggled her toes. She was aware of Keir's hands cupping either side of her neck, then sliding up and down her arms. Each touch was an urgent brand that warmed her, then quickly dissipated and left a chill in its place when he pulled away.

"Woman, you're like ice."

Kenna stared at the drops of water dripping from his dark hair onto his white shirt as he shrugged off his jacket and wrapped it around her shoulders.

"What were you thinking? *I* chase the bad guys. *You* defend them."

Wow. That was a painfully awkward reminder of what her life had distilled down to these past few days. She pushed from his grasp, swiping away the tears before too many of them spilled over.

"Ah, hell, baby, I'm sorry. I wasn't thinking." He caught a tear with the pad of his thumb and flicked it away before pulling her into his arms. "You scared me. I saw you take off after that perp by yourself, getting farther and farther away from me. And all the damn traffic—I couldn't get through until I put up my siren."

Keir was as soaked to the skin as she was, but his body exuded a warmth and vitality she couldn't seem to generate.

"Didn't you see the knife? He got you alone once before and look at what he did to you. Look how he hurt you. I can't let him hurt you again." He leaned back to pinch her chin between his thumb and forefinger and tilt her face up to his. "I need you to say something right now or I'm taking you to the hospital."

Kenna braced her palm against his chest, seeking the solid beat of his heart and willing hers to answer with that same kind of strength. "I was thinking I could put an end to this nightmare if I could see his face. I thought it would help me remember."

By now there were other red-and-blue lights filling the parking garage like the thick mist hanging in the air. Keir walked her around the front of his car, waving aside offers from uniformed officers to call for an ambulance and directing them to post a search perimeter to find any trace of the man who'd threatened her. "Did you see him? Did you remember anything?"

A long, thin knife blade slashing at her face. But nothing useful.

"He wore a mask. And he hates me. He enjoys doing this to me."

Keir muttered a curse and opened the passenger side door. "Get in the car. You're wet clean through. The last thing I need is for you to get sick."

Kenna tightened her grip on his shirt. She didn't want to move. She didn't want to lose contact with him.

"Please, babe." He shook his head. "I mean Counselor. Kenna." He'd go back to calling her Ms. Parker or the Terminator if she didn't get into the car in the next few seconds.

Right. He needed her to be strong, too. She could dig down deep and find a way to keep it together for him.

"I'll be okay, Keir." She sat on the edge of the seat, facing him, still holding on to that fistful of his shirt, and prayed it was a promise she could keep. He reached past her to crank the heater up to high, then knelt in front of her, just as he had two nights ago when he rescued her from that alley.

He pried her fingers from the wet cotton and captured both her hands between his, rubbing some warmth into them. "I need to work this, Kenna. I need to leave you for a few minutes, but I have to know you'll be safe. I called Hud and alerted my major crime unit. I've got a whole team of officers here and a citywide BOLO for anyone matching Hoodie Guy's description. But somebody needs to run the show until the senior officer gets here."

"I love that you called in the cavalry for me, but you won't find him." This guy was too good at blending in. "He probably had a change of clothes stashed somewhere in the garage, or the hoodie and jeans were masking whatever he's wearing now, and he walked out with them in a backpack or briefcase."

"I have a feeling you're right. But I have to try." He threaded his fingers into her wet hair and lifted it away from her face. "You'll have to replace those bandages so your stitches don't get wet."

"I'll take care of it."

He still wasn't convinced it was all right to leave her. She reached out and captured his jaw between her hands and leaned over to kiss him. It was tender, potent, brief. She pulled back a few inches and whispered, "You can call me babe or baby if you want. If it makes you feel better. But only you, and not in front of your friends. Now go. Do your job. You're good at it, you know."

"I'm gonna get this guy, babe."

Nodding, Kenna pulled her legs into the car. Keir waited for her to lock the doors before he strode off to join a group of officers. She watched him direct them to various assignments. They each nodded and moved to do his bidding.

While KCPD worked to get some kind of clue on Hoodie Guy's identity or whereabouts, Kenna needed something else to concentrate on while she waited for answers. But it was hard to put together any kind of strategic plan when her memory was riddled with holes and the evidence that could help her defeat her stalker was practically nonexistent.

But the heaviness of the bag in her lap reminded her she had other cases she could be working on. She pulled the strap of the tote bag off over her head and retrieved the file with the odd drawing. The papers inside were soft with moisture and trying to stick. She carefully pulled them apart and held the pages in front of the vent to dry. She studied the drawing from different angles, certain she'd seen that image before, but not quite able to place it. Maybe if she read more about the case itself, something would click.

Twenty minutes later, when Keir climbed in behind the wheel of his car, she thought she had her answer. But she needed to verify one thing before it became an admissible fact.

"Nothing yet." He turned off his warning lights and

pulled the magnetic beacon off the roof of his car. "We think he made it to the south stairwell, changed his clothes somewhere along the way and disappeared into the crowd outside. We found some boot prints on the stairs that could be his, but we found a lot of shoe prints in the gravel and mud there. A good lawyer would argue it's impossible to make a definitive match."

Kenna knew the last comment was a wry joke for her benefit, but her only response was, "I need to see your phone."

Other than a curious narrowing of his eyes, he didn't question the request. He pulled the phone out of his pocket and handed it to her. "Who's your provider? We can stop at the phone store and have them transfer your contacts to a new device."

"Tomorrow, maybe." She tapped the camera icon and opened his pictures. "I just need to see… Here. At least I can find the answer to something. I think this is a match."

"What's a match?"

"I may not be able to solve my problems, but I think I can help with one of yours." She put the phone in his open palm and held the drawing up beside it. "Look."

"This is Grandpa's shooter. I hardly think your assault is connected."

"No." She reached over to enlarge the image of the man who'd put a bullet in Seamus Watson and pointed to the silver and brass rectangle at the center of the screen. "But this guy *is* connected to one of my case files."

"Son of a…" Keir looked over at Kenna, then back at the two images. He saw the same thing she had seen.

"That drawing was made by a witness in a murder

investigation four years ago. A professional hit. He said the killer was wearing a belt buckle that looked like that." She showed him the name on the folder where she'd found the drawing. "The Austin Meade trial. He was up on several charges, including a murder for hire to eliminate the owner of an auto repair business who wouldn't sell the building and land to him."

"KCPD put the Meade family out of business years ago."

"Well, apparently they didn't catch this guy. In Meade's deposition he tried to bargain with some information but couldn't give a name. He said the deal was made by contacting the hit man through an unlisted number and asking for a Gin Rickey."

"Like the drink?"

Kenna nodded. She tucked the paper back in the folder and put it away in the tote bag at her feet. While studying the details of the drawing, she'd had a thought that was as disquieting as not knowing the identity of her faceless attacker. "Do the notch marks on the buckle mean what I think they do?"

"Probably." Keir's tone was grim. "The number of jobs he's completed."

"I know it not a complete answer, but—"

"It gives me something to go on. I can look up similar incidents, maybe even talk to Meade in prison." He swiped the picture away and pulled up his contacts to text a message to his father and brothers. "I'll let them know we might have a break in the case."

"There's a general physical description of him in the file, too. I'll type it up for you and include it with a copy of the drawing. It looks like a unique work of art, not something that was mass-produced. You could track down artists and retailers who might sell metal-work like that, too."

Keir sent his messages and set his phone in the console between them. He reached across to capture her hand and pull it to his lips for a kiss. "Thank you."

Kenna knew right then that the two of them would never be enemies again. It gladdened her heart to the point of bursting and warmed the chill from her body. She wasn't a horrible person who defended the bad guys—she helped the good guys, too. And if she believed that forty-eight hours was long enough to really get to know someone—what his deepest needs, fears and beliefs were—and fall in love, she would have admitted that, too.

"YEAH, DAD." KEIR was loading the dishwasher in Kenna's kitchen while he updated his father on the forward movement on the investigation into Seamus's shooting. "Liv is pulling rap sheets on any known hit men in the area. Niall is going through lab records to see if the belt buckle showed up as evidence in any other cases. And before he leaves town, Duff is putting out feelers on the street to see if anyone knows how to contact this Gin Rickey guy now."

"Sounds like you're on top of things. And you informed the detectives officially assigned to the case?"

"Yes, sir." Although, admittedly, that had been an afterthought once he'd gotten word to his family. He added detergent to the machine and started the wash cycle before taking one more walk around the downstairs to secure the doors and windows before turning in himself.

"And Kenna? How is she doing? Your grandfather

asked when she'd be coming by the house again. I think he's sweet on her."

Keir grinned. The old man had good taste. "I sent her upstairs to get some sleep." He checked the back doors and patio outside. Doors locked. Security lights on. The wind was picking up dirt and debris and flinging it against the glass panes as the next wave of thunderstorms rolled in. The overcast sky blotted out any moonlight, shrouding the mansion in darkness and making the hour seem even later than it was. "I'll be heading up myself when we're done. It's been a long day."

"Son. If you love this one, don't let her get away."

"I have to save her first, Dad. Then I'll start thinking about how real these feelings are."

"You know, when I was fresh out of college, fulfilling my ROTC commitment, I was excited about going off to see the world for six years. I was going to sow a lot of wild oats and live a grand adventure until I came back home and went to work for the department."

Keir paused in the foyer at his father's deep sigh.

"My first post was in the UK and I met your mother the second day I was there. I didn't need to be an intelligence officer to know I'd found the one. The third day I told her so and she said she already knew. So much for waiting until the time was right to settle down."

Keir loved hearing these stories about his parents before he was born, but he understood the underlying parental advice being offered, as well. "Dad, I didn't call to talk about my love life."

"I know. Maybe I'm just thinking about your mom tonight. She died on a stormy night like this."

Keir felt a pang of melancholy as he recalled the beautiful woman with the lilting Irish accent.

"You know we lost her way too soon. Makes me glad I didn't waste any time sowin' those oats and not being with her."

"I'm glad you didn't, either."

"Love you, son."

"Love you, too, Dad." Keir disconnected the call and pulled up the tail of his untucked shirt to stuff the phone into his jeans.

He smiled at the memories of his mother playing in the tree house with him, and sitting in her lap as she read him a bedtime story. He grinned as he checked the lock on the front door and peeked through the side windows to make sure the security lights were shining through the trees along the curving driveway down to the gate. He remembered the time-outs alone in his room his mother had given him when he didn't mind her rules. For a social kid, it was a dire punishment for the few minutes it lasted. And to be denied one of his mother's pastries with hand-whipped cream because he'd "borrowed" Liv's dollhouse and painted it with camouflage to be a base for his action figures? Yeah. He missed his mom tonight, too.

Keir shut off the foyer light and headed up the stairs. How many memories had been stolen from Kenna? Although she seemed to have a better recollection of the distant past than of more recent events, she must feel violated to have something as personal as a memory stolen from her.

He reached the landing and turned to see a light shining through Kenna's open door. What aversion did that woman have to sleeping? He wondered if she'd developed a taste for sleeping with a long, warm body nestled against her as quickly as he had last night. Picking up the fresh scent of the citrusy shampoo she used, he knocked and walked into her bedroom. "Kenna?"

He found her inside her closet, staring at the rows of shoes displayed on the shelves of a floor-to-ceiling rack. "What happened to my other shoe?"

She'd showered and was wearing those funny blue pajama pants again. Her damp hair was a shade darker, like sweet latte, and it was making little wet spots above the swell of each breast on her turquoise T-shirt. The marks on her face had been cleaned and were open to the air, highlighting her classic bone structure like badges of honor. She was barefoot like he was, and Keir's heart constricted at the regal beauty that couldn't be compromised by stitches or *Dr. Who* pants.

"Find the shoe, find the man." She stopped counting off sexy heels and running shoes and turned to face him. "He has it, doesn't he—some weird kind of souvenir or trophy like the notches in that killer's belt buckle?"

Keir splayed his hands at his waist, glad he'd untucked his shirt earlier so the long tails masked the way other parts of his body were reacting to her cool brand of smart, sexy strength. "Speaking of belt buckles—that lead you gave me has given my family hope they haven't felt in months." He thought of all the times he'd teased her about tabulating what she owed him. "I'd say we're even now, Counselor."

Kenna turned the light out in the closet and joined him in the room that was now lit only by the lamp beside her four-poster bed. "Not by a long shot."

"I'm the one keeping tabs and I say we're even. The debt is settled. I say thank you, and you say you're welcome." She walked right up to him, stopping close enough that he could dip his head and kiss her without moving. So he did. "Thank you."

She wound his arms around his waist and hugged her body around his. "Thank *you*."

So much for keeping secrets hidden from her.

"You are one stubborn woman. You can't just say you're welcome?" Her breath shuddered against his chest and he realized she was crying. Gut check. Embarrassing himself didn't matter. "Hey." He leaned back against her arms so he could see the redness rimming those moonlit eyes. He slicked her hair off her face and tucked it behind her ears, catching each tear that ran onto her cheek with his thumbs and stroking it away. "I never expected to see tears on you. Twice in one day now? They kind of freaked me out this afternoon. I thought you were crashing on me."

She blinked several times to stop the flow and gave a good sniffle before resting her cheek against the pad of his shoulder.

"What's going through that jumbled-up head of yours?"

"I've been thinking how, even though you mean well, you can't really stay with me until all this is settled. You'll have to go to work, and I will, too, eventually."

Her fingers wandering lazily up and down his spine weren't helping him quell the desire thrumming through his blood.

"I don't know how I would have gotten through this

weekend without you. And when tomorrow comes, I think I'm really going to miss you."

"The thought of this guy getting to you again makes me crazy," he admitted. He didn't want her to be afraid for her safety. "If I can't physically be with you, I'll make sure someone I trust is. My partner, Hud, will help. Or my brothers or sister. Even Dad. He's the smartest cop I ever knew. He's still got the goods to keep an eye on you."

"No. I mean, I'm going to miss *you.*" When she pulled back, the tears were gone. But there was still a hint of sadness in her eyes. "There are a lot of differences between us, Detective. I'm an older woman. Money—I know guys can be funny if a woman earns more than he does. You come from a big family and I have empty rooms. The different sides of the courtroom we each represent."

"Look, I was an idiot for holding that against you. You were doing your job, just like I was doing mine. You might still be the Terminator, but I say it with nothing but respect now."

"I know that." Those mesmerizing fingers moved to the placket of his shirt and started tracing lines up and down his chest. "But we've only known each other for what—three days? Besides this investigation, what reason do you really have to be with me?"

"This." His body couldn't take it anymore. Didn't she understand what she was doing to him? He caught her face between his hands and claimed her mouth in a hungry kiss. Her lips parted and he took full advantage of the wanton heat inside, inviting her tongue to dance with his, nipping at her bottom lip, then soothing the pliant curve with the stroke of his tongue. Her lips chased after his when he finally pulled away. He felt the pulse in her throat thumping beneath his fingertips, and her breath came in stuttered gasps that brushed the sweet pearls of her breasts against his own heaving chest.

"This *thing* happening between us doesn't have anything to do with the investigation. I don't need three days or three weeks or three years to know how much I want to be with you. I don't understand it. And maybe it's not the smartest move I've ever made with a woman. But you and I... There's something here I want to explore. Maybe physically, you're not up for much more yet, but..." The woman was smiling. Keir's fingers tunneled into her hair, but maybe he should be backing off. "What? What are you thinking?"

"That even if three days is all I ever have—I've been lucky to spend them with you."

"One. You are having a nice, long life, Counselor. Two. I'm glad I spent them with you, too. And—"

"Three." She backed him up against one of the bedposts and kissed him.

Then things got real. Fast. Kenna unbuttoned his shirt and pushed it off his shoulders. He caught the hem of her shirt and swept it off over her head. When they were chest to chest, skin to skin, he reversed positions and pinned her against the bedpost. He only abandoned her mouth to bend down to worship her breasts. He loved the tight little buds and drew them into his mouth, loving the gasps and throaty moans each touch elicited. Then Keir went down on his knees, pulling her knit bottoms down inch by inch, introducing his lips to each new stretch of soft, taut skin until he felt the goose bumps beading beneath every grasp of his hand. He tasted the crease between each hip and thigh, teased the blond thatch in between. Finally, her pants were on the floor and he was feasting his way down every quivering, incredible inch of those long, glorious legs.

"Keir… Keir…" Her fingers clutched at his hair with needy abandon. "I don't think I can stand any more."

"Patience, baby, patience." He kissed the dimple beside her knee and started to work his way back up. "I want this to be good for both of us."

The fingers in his hair were more urgent now. She was shaking. "No. Standing. I can't…"

Ah, hell. Keir pushed to his feet and picked her up. He set her on the bed, fighting to calm his deep, ragged breaths and ignore the arousal straining painfully against his zipper. Worry and a cold shower would soon put things into proper perspective again. "I'm sorry, baby." He folded the bedspread over her naked body and lay down beside her, gathering Kenna and the bulky cover into his arms. "You haven't been out of the hospital very long. Does anything hurt? You should have told me you weren't up for this. We'll stop."

"It only hurts that you're thinking about stopping." She pushed at the cover, pushed at his arms. He didn't fight when she pushed him onto his back and straddled his hips. "I meant my knees were about to buckle from what you were doing to me, and I didn't want to embarrass myself and wind up flat on the floor, and then you'd worry if I was hurt and you'd stop, and I—"

Keir sat up, catching her bottom and keeping her squarely in his lap when she would have tumbled. "You're sure? Because I want this."

Her fingers dropped to the snap of his jeans. "Me, too."

Keir pulled his wallet from his back pocket before his jeans and shorts wound up on the floor and his gun ended up on the bedside table. He bit his lip as Kenna rolled the condom over his manhood. And when he couldn't stand another bold touch, he moved on top of her, marveling at the utter perfection of how their bodies fit together. "You are the only thing on my to-do list tonight."

He stopped up her answering laugh with a kiss and pushed inside her. There were no more words, no more teasing. She wrapped those long, glorious legs around him and they rocked together in a decadent rhythm until she cried out his name and arched against him. Keir groaned with the power of his own release before falling down onto the bed beside her. He reached down to find her hand and laced their fingers together.

Yeah. Perfection.

Chapter Ten

Kenna woke with a delicious ache that had nothing to do with her injuries and everything to do with the two rounds of bliss she'd shared with the naked man sprawled out asleep in her bed with little more than a sheet draped over his hips.

She wasn't sure if the noise of the storm had waked her, or if the wishes that flitted through her dreams had demanded she make some conscious decisions about her life. Keir Watson was as kind and considerate as he was skilled and passionate. He made her think, made her laugh, made her feel cherished and safe. So she'd gotten up to visit the bathroom, then slipped back into her pajamas and curled up with a blanket in the window seat to watch the storm illuminate the night with pulses of lightning and the rain streak and chill the glass.

Kenna wasn't precisely sure what kind of life she'd lived before the attack. But the glimpses she'd seen of fear and control and loneliness didn't seem like the kind of life she wanted to live anymore. She wanted nights like this. She wanted to defend good people and help them find the justice they deserved. She wanted happiness.

She wanted love.

A bolt of lightning forked down to the earth and the answering thunder rumbled in waves for several seconds after.

"Should I be worried?"

Kenna turned to the hushed seduction of Keir's voice and smiled. He sat on the edge of the bed and smiled back before pulling on his shorts and jeans. He picked his shirt up off the floor and shrugged it over his broad shoulders as he crossed the room. She tilted her face to his and he leaned down to give her a kiss.

"Just thinking some deep thoughts."

He sat down beside her, resting his hand with a casual possession on her thigh. "Okay, now I am worried. Want to share?"

Lightning flashed.

"I was thinking about something you said this afternoon—about being successful at whatever I wanted—"

The answering explosion of thunder rattled the window, startling her.

A second later, all the yard lights went out.

Keir leaped to his feet. "The storm didn't do that."

With the pitch-darkness outside, he hurried to the bed to turn on the lamp. Nothing. "Electricity's out."

Mother Nature lit up the earth with a trio of lightning bursts, filling her backyard with fleeting moments of daylight. In the third flash, she saw him. Standing among the trees, his faceless mask angled up toward her window. "Keir!"

Kenna scrambled off the window seat as Hoodie Guy vanished into the darkness.

She ran to Keir's side as he hung up the bedside phone.

"He's cut the landline, too." He tucked his gun into

the waistband of his jeans, snatched up the spare keys to the house and pushed his cell phone into her hands before running out the door.

Kenna dropped the blanket and hurried down the stairs behind him.

"Call 9-1-1. Give them my name and this address and tell Dispatch that an officer needs assistance."

He punched in the security code and threw open the front door. Kenna grabbed his arm, trying to stop him. "You're going out there?"

But he was already slipping out of her grip. "He's not coming in here. Lock up behind me. I've got my own key. Don't let anyone else in."

"Keir?"

He charged down the steps and circled the house to catch the intruder by surprise. She caught a glimpse of his white shirt near the garage at the next flash of lightning. And then he was gone. Swallowed up by the rain and darkness. Kenna locked the door and felt her way through the dining room to the kitchen. She called 9-1-1 and remained on the line as the dispatcher asked. Then she pulled a butcher knife from the drawer beside the stove and crouched down behind the island, praying that Keir would be the one to find her.

"AH, HELL." KEIR SAW the truck parked on the far side of the garage and finally knew the answer.

He swiped the rain from his face and darted through the dark garage. Muddy work boots. The same kind of boots that had left the tracks at the parking garage. Free passkey onto the estate anytime he wanted. Hoodie Guy didn't need to get into the house when the boss lady came out to talk to him every time he worked in the yard. Keir still didn't know the why. But Marvin Bennett was done terrorizing Kenna.

He wished he could risk using a flashlight to follow the muddy tracks over the flagstones into the trees in the backyard before the rain washed them away. But he couldn't risk giving away his position to a man who was more familiar with these surroundings than Keir was.

The gardener hadn't been covering up Kenna's gardening mistake that day they found him rebuilding the brick wall. He'd been covering up his own crime scene. Painting over Kenna's blood where she'd either fallen or been shoved against the bricks. He'd probably tried to burn some other kind of evidence in the fire pit, like rosebushes that had been crushed or broken in a struggle. Bennett was a damn cool customer, being surprised by a cop and the woman he was obsessed with—the woman he thought he'd killed—and going on like some kind of idiot who barely knew his way around a flowerpot. He'd kept his wits about him the night before, too, moving Kenna's body to that downtown alley. When Keir first saw Bennett in disguise, he'd probably been watching the alley to see if anyone discovered her body.

Had Kenna figured out who'd been sending her rose petals and making those disturbing calls? Had she made an accusation? Caught him doing something suspicious? Had she simply given the gardener one order too many and he'd snapped?

Whether the murder attempt itself was planned or accidental, stalking Kenna for weeks leading up to the attack—seeing her often enough that he could watch and enjoy his handiwork as she grew angry and paranoid, helpless and afraid—meant Bennett had a game plan here. It might have started as a quest for vengeance or a sick obsession. But Bennett was here tonight to end the game. He'd already gotten one taste of Kenna's blood. And clearly, he was here for more.

Keir stopped beside the shelter of a giant locust tree. He silenced his breathing, listening for any sounds of movement in the noisy storm. He wondered if Kenna had placed the call for backup and how long it would take other cops to get here. She might not have that kind of time. He needed to confront Bennett and take him out himself.

Just as Keir opened his mouth to shout Bennett's name, lightning flashed in the sky overhead, silhouetting branches and leaves and the shovel swinging at his head. Keir tried to dodge the blow. The shovel glanced off his temple but smacked his head into the tree's unyielding trunk. Pain jolted through his skull. Lightning danced across his vision and he crumpled to the ground.

Keir's last thoughts were of Marvin Bennett rifling through Keir's pockets for his keys, picking up his gun and running toward the house, and the knowledge he hadn't told Kenna he loved her.

KENNA WAS SHAKING so badly that she'd been forced to set the cell phone on the floor beside her so she wouldn't drop it and make a noise that would give her hiding place away. Instead, she clung to the handle of the knife with both hands and prayed she'd never have to use it.

When she heard the key turning in the lock of the patio door, the breath she'd been holding rushed out in a noisy huff and she set the knife on top of the island and pulled herself to her feet. But the man in the black hoodie was locking the door behind him. The faceless mask was pure terror as he crossed the long room, and Kenna was suddenly as cold as the marble countertop.

"Hello, Kenna," he rasped in that toneless voice. Lightning fluttered like a strobe light behind him, silhouetting his familiar shape and giving her a glimpse of the gun he pointed at her. It was Keir's weapon. "I'm afraid Lover Boy isn't here to rescue you anymore."

"What have you done to him?"

She lunged for the knife, but he fired off a wide shot that hit the cabinet behind her and she froze, raising her hands. "Now, be a good girl and toss that knife over here."

After she did what he said, he unzipped his jacket and shoved the hood off his head. He slipped the butcher knife through his belt next to the long sheath with the knife he'd used against her earlier. Shrinking back against the opposite counter, she felt her foot come down on Keir's phone and she wondered if the dispatcher could hear what was happening and rush an ambulance and the entire police force here before she and Keir died.

When he pulled off the ski mask, Kenna gasped and collapsed against the counter. "Oh, my God." How long had this creep been right under her nose? How many conversations had they shared? How many times had she patted him on the back or shaken his hand? *He doesn't get to win.* Tears burned her eyes as she thought of Keir lying wounded or dead outside. She pulled herself up straight and articulated the name for the woman listening in. "Marvin Bennett."

She nudged the phone under the lip of the cabinet as he reached the island and circled toward her. "It's just you and me and the task I wanted to finish last night. I've enjoyed seeing you afraid. Watching how you tried to control your fear by controlling everything else in your life. I wanted you to suffer the way she did."

"The way who did?"

"Genie. My daughter."

Kenna backed toward the dining room door, wondering if she could get through it before he fired off another shot. "I didn't know you had a daughter."

"She killed herself six years ago. Two years after she'd been raped."

"Raped?" Kenna halted. This was about Brian Elliott.

"The Rose Red Rapist. Your biggest case. You made headlines—and a fortune defending that scum who ruined my daughter's life."

"Genie D'Angelo." She remembered the name from the case file she'd read. "Genie is your daughter?"

"Was. That's an important distinction, Kenna. You're the one who likes to get every detail right."

"I'm so sorry, Marvin. I didn't know."

"Move away from that door." He pointed the gun at her and gestured for her to walk toward the sectional sofa. When she didn't immediately respond, he snagged her by the elbow and dragged her there. "D'Angelo was her married name. But her marriage couldn't survive what that bastard Elliott had done to her. She wouldn't let her husband touch her. She barely let me—her own father—comfort her. Every day was a misery for her after the rape. She went into a depression. She slashed her wrists once. I found her and got her to the hospital. But I didn't know about the pills. I couldn't save her from the pills."

"You blame me for her death."

"No." He threw her onto the couch and she tried to scramble away, but he caught her by the ankle and dragged her back to press his knee into her gut and lean over her. He drew the tip of the gun across the stitches on her jaw. "I blame you for Brian Elliott still being alive."

Kenna could barely catch her breath to speak. "I was just doing my job. I never condoned anything he did. Every person in this country deserves a fair trial—"

He back-handed her across the face and she felt the cut on her cheek split open.

"You defended him! You kept him from the lethal injection he deserved."

"Rape isn't a capital offense. But he's probably going to die in prison before he's ever released—"

"Shut up! He shouldn't be living any kind of life. And it's all your fault." He dipped his gloved fingers in the blood on her cheek and drew an *X* over her heart. "I wanted you to suffer the way Genie did. Elliott violated her in so many ways, and then had the gall to leave a rose on her beaten body? She hated roses after that. I'm a gardener. I raise beautiful flowers. But she couldn't even look at them."

"So you sent me roses." Her fingers clenched in the sofa cushions, seeking a weapon to defend herself from the man who surely intended to kill her.

"I wanted to cut you—the way she cut herself."

Cut. The answer was staring her right in the face. Yes, a gun was being pointed to her heart, but her hands were free and that butcher knife was within her reach.

"When you came to me on Friday and said you wanted me to rip out all the rosebushes and plant hydrangeas, I lost my temper. They're supposed to be there to remind you of my daughter. They're supposed to remind you of that horrible man you defended. The roses were there to haunt you and make you suffer the way my little girl did. So I pulled my knife out to stop you. We fought. And when I cracked your head open and saw all that blood, I thought I'd killed you." His face twisted up as if he was about to cry. "You ruined everything. You weren't supposed to die until last night. I had to get you out of here and reset the stage for your death. But then that stupid cop was here, and I couldn't. But I've taken care of him. He won't stop me now."

Keir. Kenna's heart squeezed in her chest. What had this lunatic done to him? Kenna wanted to make sure there would be justice for the man she loved. She wanted the dispatcher to hear everything. "Why last night? What was so important about your deadline?"

"Because of Genie. This is all for my daughter. This is justice. I wanted you to know just how many days you had left to live. I wanted you to die on the same date my Genie did."

"I didn't know it was you, Marvin. I couldn't remember your face or what happened. I still don't. You could have walked away a free man."

"Forgetting's not good enough. My Genie could never forget her suffering." He pressed the gun into her breast, pinning her as he unhooked the sheath on his belt. "That's no better than Elliott's punishment. You don't get to forget, either."

Another flash of lightning lit up the night sky, giving her a glimpse of Keir Watson at her patio door, swinging a shovel at the wall of glass.

Thunder shook the house as the panes of glass splintered and crashed. Marvin raised the gun and Kenna reached for the knife on his belt.

"Bennett!" Keir shouted.

The blast of the gunshot deafened her ears and the ejected casing hit her arm, singeing her skin. Her fingers fell short of snatching the blade and she heard the feral roar of Keir charging across the room.

"Let her go!"

Instead of obeying Keir's order, Marvin hauled her up off the couch and pulled her in front of him to use as a shield. She saw the blood staining the shoulder of Keir's mud-stained shirt and would have cried out. But Marvin squeezed his forearm around her throat and ground the gun barrel into her temple.

Keir halted a few feet away and dropped the shovel he carried and raised his hands to placate her abductor. "No one has to die here, Bennett."

"She does." Kenna fingered the knife butting against her hip but couldn't get it to budge. "I want you to watch her die, too."

"I'm not going to let you do it."

"Better idea." Marvin pointed the gun toward Keir. "I'll kill you first. That'll make her suffer more."

"No!" Kenna got a grip of the knife and yanked it from Marvin's belt, slicing a cut across his shirt and belly as she pulled it out.

Marvin cursed as he pulled the trigger, firing a wild shot. Startled by pain, he loosened his hold on her.

"Get down!" Keir yelled, charging toward Marvin. Kenna dove for the floor as Keir sailed over the couch and tackled Marvin. The gun flew from his hand and got knocked beneath the coffee table. The two men fought, grunting and cursing. Marvin punched at Keir's wound and Keir lost his grip on Marvin's neck.

"Look out!" Kenna warned when she saw Marvin's fingers find the gun and close around it. "Gun!"

Marvin turned the gun on Keir. But Keir had armed himself, too.

Before Marvin could fire, Keir rammed the knife straight into the old man's heart.

Marvin's hand dropped to the floor and Keir pried his gun from the dead man's grasp. He stood up slowly, hearing the wail of sirens through the noise of the storm.

His shoulder was throbbing where he'd been shot, he had a rotten headache and he'd cut his left heel on the broken glass near the door. But nothing was going to stop him from catching Kenna when she ran to him and wound her arms around his neck. "Keir. Oh, Keir. I thought…I thought he'd killed you."

He wanted to stab Bennett again when he saw the blood oozing down her cheek and marking her shirt. "You okay, baby?"

"I'm fine."

That was all he needed to hear. He slipped his good arm around her waist and walked her away from the dead body. They ended up in the darkened foyer, where he opened the front door. Then he sat on the stairs where the approaching police would see him and pulled Kenna into his lap.

"You've been shot. And what's this scrape on your head? I can't believe it's finally over. How am I ever going to repay you?"

He set his gun on the step beside him and tunneled his fingers into her beautiful hair. "Just listen to me for a minute without interrupting. I need to say this. You need to know this right now, before all those other cops come pouring in here, before we make our statements, before we get whisked away in an ambulance to the hospital. Will you do that?"

He could tell it was killing her to keep her mouth shut, but she nodded.

"I love you, Kenna Parker. It may not make any sense for it to happen this fast or for two people who are so different to make a relationship work." She opened her mouth to argue, but he pressed his thumb against her lips. "You promised."

She clamped her mouth shut.

"I've done this all backward with you. I was carrying you in my arms before we were even properly introduced. I want to kiss you every day of my life and argue with you and make love to you and laugh with you—and I don't even know when your birthday is or what your favorite color might be. I want to ask you out on a date and get to know you and see if the age and money make any kind of difference. But I know they won't. Because we belong together. And I hope that when we get out in the real world and get a regular night's sleep and crazy men aren't out to hurt you… You may never remember the night of your attack, but I will never forget the seventy-two hours that followed."

He'd run out of words. But he hoped he'd said enough. He couldn't have risked waiting a moment longer to spill his heart.

When he pulled his thumb away, she smiled. "Do I get to talk now?"

He nodded.

"I love you, too. I love the idea of kissing you every day and arguing with you—hopefully, not too often. I want to make love to you and laugh with you. My birthday is March tenth, my favorite color is the blue of your beautiful eyes and if you ever want to ask me out on a date, I'll say yes. But..."

Keir was grinning all the way down to his heart. "You're arguing already?"

"You don't think this time we've spent together qualifies as a first date? We haven't been separated since I stumbled out of that alley. If you take away the stalker and the amnesia, the rest of it was a lot of special. I loved spending that time with you."

"Then we finally agree about something." He slipped his arm around her and, cautious of each other's injuries, leaned in for a kiss. "Best. Date. Ever."

Epilogue

The unhappy man opened the newspaper to the page where the ink was smeared because he'd looked at the picture and read the announcement so many times before. He handed it across the desk to the younger man sitting in the leather chair drinking a glass of *his* finest gin. "Niall Watson's engagement announcement. They're planning a fall wedding."

The other man set down the glass and picked up the paper to read the details. "Well, ain't that sweet? They're gettin' married on the old man's birthday."

"It isn't sweet, and it isn't acceptable." The unhappy man pulled a gun and silencer from the top drawer of his desk while the man he'd hired amused himself by reading the announcement out loud.

"Oh, that's rich. They're even going to do it at the same church."

"Yes. I'm sure it's some kind of testament to the Watson family's will to survive and succeed despite the tragedy of Olivia's wedding."

The other man set down the newspaper, picking up on the disgust in his tone. "You said you didn't want dead bodies—that a clean kill was too good for them—

even though I said it was a mistake. You wanted chaos and suffering. I did what you paid me to do."

"That's not good enough. Not anymore." His blood was boiling with rage at the injustice of it all. They'd forgotten her. Thomas Watson had stolen Mary from him and she'd been murdered and forgotten. But stroking the trigger of the gun beneath the desk was the only outward expression of his roiling emotions. "Shooting the old man was supposed to destroy them. But they're going on with their lives as if nothing happened. They're happier than ever."

"I can finish the old man if you want. In his condition, it wouldn't be hard."

"You had your chance." The unhappy man raised the weapon and shot his guest twice in the chest. He set down the gun and pulled a pocketknife from his trousers as he walked around the desk. He tipped the slumped man back in his chair and cut the fancy buckle off his belt. He fingered the notches carved into the silver, then slid the buckle into his own pocket, along with the knife. "This will be the trophy for *my* kill."

He picked up the glass and finished off the drink in one long swallow. Then he returned to his seat and placed a phone call. "I have a situation I need you to clean up for me. I'll pay your usual fee." He started to hang up but put the phone back to his ear. "Do you have anyone inside KCPD you can trust?"

"Does this have anything to do with the situation I'm cleaning up?"

"No. I need some information."

"I know someone who owes me a favor."

"Good. I want to meet with him tomorrow."

* * * * *

Look for the next thrilling installment
in USA TODAY *bestselling author*
Julie Miller's suspenseful series
THE PRECINCT: BACHELORS IN BLUE,
coming in 2017!

Look for it wherever
Mills & Boon Intrigue books are sold.

He brushed his fingers along the sides of the collar, the hot flutter of Erin's pulse beneath his fingertips sending a jolt of awareness through him.

The contrast of her silken flesh with the unyielding metal collar made her seem all the more fragile and out of place here—like finding a lily blooming in the middle of a minefield.

"Can you cut it off?" she asked.

"I don't think we can risk it," he said. "It looks as if there are wires embedded in the metal and running all the way around. My guess is if we sever one of those the bomb would go off."

She swallowed hard, her eyes as big and dark as a terrified deer's. "What are we going to do?"

He looked away, at the lab equipment arranged neatly on the workbench, at the sparse furnishings and barred windows of the place that had been his prison for the past twelve months. "We need to get out of here," he said.

PHD PROTECTOR

BY
CINDI MYERS

First Published in Great Britain 2016
By Mills & Boon, an imprint of HarperCollins*Publishers*
1 London Bridge Street, London, SE1 9GF

ISBN: 978-0-263-91925-7

46-1216

Our policy is to use papers that are natural, renewable and recyclable products and made from wood grown in sustainable forests. The logging and manufacturing processes conform to the legal environmental regulations of the country of origin.

Printed and bound in Spain
by CPI, Barcelona

Cindi Myers is the author of more than fifty novels. When she's not crafting new romance plots, she enjoys skiing, gardening, cooking, crafting and daydreaming. A lover of small-town life, she lives with her husband and two spoiled dogs in the Colorado mountains.

For Vicki and Mike

Chapter One

What's the worst thing you would do to protect the ones you love? Would you lie—steal—even kill?

It was a question from a party game, the kind you played over beers with a bunch of buddies, the answers all alcohol-fueled machismo, backed by the knowledge that you would never really have to make those kinds of choices.

Mark Renfro had had to choose. To protect his daughter, his innocent only child, he had lied too many times to count, and though he hadn't stolen or killed—yet—he had joined with a group of men who were working to kill thousands, maybe even millions of people. They called themselves Patriots, but he knew they were terrorists. They had murdered his wife, and if Mark didn't do what they wanted, they would kill his daughter, Mandy, as well.

He closed his eyes and rested his forehead against the cool metal of the laboratory hood. Formulas scrolled across his closed eyelids like a particularly boring and technical movie, the complex and intricate calculations of energy transfer and nuclear fusion, pages from textbooks he had read long ago and committed to memory, fragments of scientific papers he had written or read, and columns of computations that lodged in his brain the way phone numbers or the memory of a wonderful meal might take up residence in the brains of others. His photographic memory for all those numbers and calculations had allowed him to breeze though his undergraduate and graduate education and excel at the research that had propelled him to fame and even a little fortune.

All of that worthless, with his wife dead and his daughter far away from him. Amanda had been four when he had last seen her. She'd be five now—a huge chunk of her life he would never get back.

The door to the cabin that had been Mark's prison for over a year burst open, but Mark didn't even jump. The people who held him here were fond of such scare tactics as bursting in unannounced, but he was numb to that all now. "Renfro!" The man Mark knew as Cantrell had a big, booming voice. He was always on the verge of shouting. "We brought you a surprise."

A muffled cry, like that of a wounded animal, made Mark whip around to face Cantrell. But instead of the dog or deer or some other nonhuman victim he had expected to see, he came face-to-face with a furious woman. Her hazel eyes burned with rage and hatred, and the tangle of auburn hair that fell in front of her face couldn't obscure the high cheekbones, patrician nose and delicately pointed chin. She was young—midtwenties, he guessed, with a taut, athletic frame, every muscle straining against the man who held her, a baby-faced goon named Scofield. They had taped her mouth and bound her arms behind her, but still she struggled. So far her efforts had earned her a purpling bruise on one cheek and a torn sleeve on her denim jacket.

Mark half rose from his stool, an old, almost forgotten rage burning deep in his chest. "What do you think you're doing?" he demanded.

"The boss figured you needed some help to speed things along." Cantrell nodded and Scofield shoved the woman forward. She stumbled into Mark and he had to brace his legs and wrap his arms around her to keep them both from crashing into the lab table. "She's your new assistant."

Both men laughed, as if this was the best joke they had heard all year, then they retreated, the locks clicking into place behind them.

Mark still held the woman, though they were both steady on their feet now. It had been so long since he had touched another person, longer still since he had felt a woman's soft, lithe body beneath his hands. She was almost as tall as he was, with small, firm breasts and gently curved hips, and she smelled like flowers and soap and a world very far away from this remote mountain cabin.

She wrenched away from him and stumbled back, staring at him with eyes filled with hatred. He got the feeling she had no more of an idea why she was here than he did. "Turn around and I'll untie your hands," he said. "But you have to promise not to strangle me when I do."

Her eyes made no such promise, but she turned and presented her hands to him. He clipped through the plastic ties with the pair of nail scissors—all his captors would allow him in terms of sharp objects. Though his kidnappers had provided him with a laboratory full of the most up-to-date equipment, they had been very careful to exclude anything that might be used as a weapon.

Ironic, considering the purpose of the laboratory itself.

He pocketed the nail scissors and the woman brought her hands to the front and rubbed them, wincing, then picked at the corners of the tape on her mouth.

"Trust me, the best way is to just rip it off," he said. "It still hurts, but you get it over with quickly."

She hesitated, then did as he suggested and jerked at the silver rectangle of duct tape. "Ah!" she cried out, followed by a string of eloquent curses.

He retreated to his stool in front of the lab bench, fighting the urge to smile. She wouldn't get the joke, wouldn't understand how good it was to hear someone else express the sentiments that had filled his mind for months now. "I'm Mark Renfro," he said. "Who are you?"

"I'm not your assistant," she said, her voice low and rough. Sexy.

She went back to rubbing her wrists, the movement plumping the cleavage at the scoop neck of her T-shirt. Mark felt a stirring below the belt, his libido rising from the dead, startling him. He had thought himself past such feelings, that part of him burned away by grief and the hopelessness of his situation.

"I didn't request an assistant," he said. "That must have been Cantrell's idea. Or someone higher up the chain of command. I'm sorry they dragged you into this, but I had nothing to do with it."

"You work for them." She moved closer, scanning the array of scientific equipment on the table. "You're their scientist." The disgust in her voice and on her face showed just what she thought of a man who would do such a thing.

"There's a difference between being a slave and an employee. I didn't have any more say about being here than you did." He glanced at her. "Maybe less. You still haven't told me your name."

"Erin. Erin Daniels."

It didn't ring a bell.

"You don't have any idea who I am, do you?" she asked.

He shook his head. "Should I?"

"I don't know. But I would hate for anyone to associate me with this scum." She began to move about the one-room cabin, taking in the double bedstead in the corner where Mark slept, the open door beside it that led to the single, windowless bathroom, the three-burner gas range and round-topped refrigerator and chipped porcelain sink on the other side of the room, and the table and two chairs that provided the only other seating, aside from the laboratory stool he currently occupied. Her intelligent eyes scanned, assessed and moved on. She tried the sash on the larger of the cabin's two windows.

"They're screwed shut from the outside," he said. "And there's reinforced wire over the glass. If you broke a pane, all you would accomplish would be to let in the cold." He had endured a freezing month right after they took him, when he had tried to cut out one of the panes of glass, in hopes of fashioning a weapon. The glass had shattered and Mark had shivered for weeks before he had persuaded Cantrell that the low temperatures were detrimental to his lab work, and his captors had repaired the pane.

"There must be some way out of here," Erin said, moving to the back door.

"The doors are locked and dead bolted from the outside, plus there's an armed guard out there at all times. The floor is a concrete slab. The gas is shut off, so the stove doesn't work. They bring in food, unless I'm being punished for something, then I don't eat." They had kept him on short rations for a week after the glass-breaking incident.

"If there's no gas, how do you heat this place?" she asked. "It's in the forties out there today, but it feels fine in here."

"There's electric heat," he said, pointing to the baseboard heating unit along the side wall. "A solar panel charges a battery for that. If the sun doesn't shine for a few days then too bad. I had better learn to like working in the cold." He had spent whole days in bed under the covers in the middle of last winter—he didn't want to think about going through that again.

"How long have you been here?" Her expression was guarded.

"What month is this?" He had tried to keep track at first, then gave up. What did it matter? His captors weren't going to let him leave here alive.

"January," she said. "Today is the ninth."

"Then I've been here fourteen months," he said. The weight of all those months rested on his chest like a concrete block. Crushing.

Erin sank into a chair at the table. "Why?" she asked. "What are you doing here?"

He wanted to say "as little as possible" but he could

never be sure the guards weren't listening. He suspected Cantrell or his bosses had the place bugged. She might even be a plant, sent to learn his intentions, though her anger felt very real. Maybe his captors' paranoia was rubbing off on him. "First, tell me your story," he said. "How did you end up here? Are you a scientist?"

"No. I'm a teacher." She straightened a little, as if one of her students might be watching. "I teach math to seventh and eighth graders in Idaho Falls, Idaho."

"Then what are you doing in the middle of nowhere in western Colorado? Do you know anything about the men who brought you here?" What had she done to end up on the wrong side of a group of terrorists like the Patriots?

"Oh, I know about them all right." Her expression grew even more grim. "Their leader is my stepfather."

ERIN KNEW SHE had succeeded in shocking Mark Renfro. Frankly, he had shocked her, too. She had heard so much in the past weeks about the famous scientist who was going to help Duane Braeswood and his group of deranged thugs bring the world to its knees. She had expected him to be like them—a hardened, arrogant braggart whose cruelty showed in knotted muscles and cold expressions. She had been prepared to have to fight him—possibly to the death—to prove she wanted no part of his "mission."

Instead, she had found a thin, weary-looking man in a dirty lab coat, with despair weighting his eyes and slumping his shoulders. He might have been handsome once, before deprivation and grief and whatever other emotions had etched lines at the corners of his eyes and mouth and drained the life from his expression. "You're Braeswood's daughter?" he asked.

"Stepdaughter." At least she didn't have to claim any of that madman's DNA ran through her veins.

Mark sighed and let his hands rest loosely in his lap. "Maybe you'd better start at the beginning," he said.

The beginning. *Once upon a time there was a girl named Erin, who had everything she wanted. Then her father died and her mother made some very poor choices.*

"My mother met a man online when I was twelve," she said. "My father had died two years before, of liver cancer. She moved back to Idaho to be closer to her family and started hanging out on a survivalist message board. Who knows why?"

"And she met Duane Braeswood through these survivalists?" He nodded. "I guess his ranting might appeal to the more radical factions in that group."

"Do you want me to tell the story or not?"

He looked sheepish. "Sorry. I haven't had anyone to talk to in a while, so I'm rusty at conversation. I won't interrupt again."

She hugged her arms over her chest. "Mom didn't meet Duane on the message board. She met a guy named Amos or Abe or something like that and they dated for a while. She started going to meet ups and gatherings with him and at one of those she met Duane Braeswood." Just remembering the way Duane had come into their lives and taken over made her sick to her stomach. "Among that bunch, he was already a big celebrity. Maybe Mom was flattered by his attention, or impressed by the way he threw money around. Maybe she was just lonely. I don't know."

"Ah, Duane." Mark said the name the way he might have referred to a notoriously badly behaved public figure.

"Yeah. My mother's second husband." Erin gave him a hard look, ignoring the sympathy in his expression. Maybe he was just a good actor. "Obviously, you know him well."

"No. I've only seen him a few times. He reminds me of a televangelist. One who prefers camo to shiny suits. Though his charm is lost on me, I can see he has a kind of creepy charisma."

"Exactly." She rubbed her arms. "He gave me the creeps from day one, but my mom fell for it. Next thing I knew, she had married him and we moved to this big house with a bunch of other like-minded people, sort of a commune for survivalist types. At first I thought we were just going to stock up on dried food and hunt our own meat and that kind of stuff. I was a kid who wanted to fit in and I thought it might even be fun." Looking back she could see how pathetic she had been, wanting love and approval from her stand-in dad, playing right into his manipulative hands. "As I got older, I figured out he had a more sinister plan."

"The government needs fixing and he's the man to do it," Mark said drily.

She nodded. "He tried to recruit me as one of his loyal followers, but I balked."

"I'm guessing that didn't make you very popular," Mark said.

"I told my mom he was a terrorist, plain and simple. We had a big fight about it. She just couldn't see it." The memory of her mother's rejection still stung. "The day after I graduated high school I left the compound and swore to my mom I wouldn't see her again until she came to her senses and got out of there, too."

Her stomach still knotted when she remembered that day. She had walked out, sure the next time she saw Helen Daniels Braeswood she would be either dead or on the news, arrested for her involvement with some plot of Duane's.

"That must have been tough," Mark said.

"Yeah, well, we didn't speak for four years. Then she called, out of the blue one day, to tell me Duane and the others had left her and moved to Colorado. She sounded worn-out. She asked if she could come stay with me awhile. I was thrilled. I moved her into the house I was renting in Idaho Falls and after a few weeks she was a new woman. She was the mom I had known and loved before. She still refused to admit that Duane was evil. She called him 'misguided but sincere.' She said she had loved him very much but that she was determined to get over him."

Erin fell silent again, remembering all the hope she had had in those months.

"What happened?" Mark prompted after a moment.

"She stayed with me about eighteen months. I thought everything was great. Then one day I came home and found her bags all packed. She said she had had a call from Duane. He had been injured in an accident and he needed her. They were still legally married, so she was going back to him. I went a little crazy. I screamed and yelled and threatened to call the police. She was perfectly calm through the whole thing. She told me one day I would be in love and I would understand. Then she got in a taxi and left."

"How did that lead to you ending up here?" Mark asked.

"I'm getting to that." She took a deep breath, steadying herself. "About six weeks ago, I got a call, from a man who identified himself as Duane's personal assistant. He said he thought I would want to know that my mom was very ill. In fact, she was dying of cancer. She was in hospice and didn't have long and had been asking to see me. He gave me the address he said was for the hospice and suggested I might like to visit her before it was too late." She covered her eyes with her hand, fighting back tears—of grief and rage and shame.

"Did you see her?" Mark asked, his voice gentle.

"She wasn't even sick! It was a trick, to get me to a place where Duane's men could grab me. He showed up, too. He was in a wheelchair, with an oxygen tank. He'd clearly been messed up somehow, but that didn't seem to lessen the power he had over everyone around him. He told me I needed to be punished for upsetting my mother so much, and that he had a job I could do to make up for all the trouble I had caused."

"And his men brought you here."

"First they took me to a fishing camp somewhere in the area, and we stayed there for a few days. I guess they were waiting for some signal from Duane or the stars to align or something. Then they took me to a house in Denver. I stayed there for weeks, in a locked room with the windows blacked out." She glanced around the cabin. "At least this isn't as bad as that."

"Do you know why I'm here?" Mark asked. "What it is that you're supposed to assist me with?"

"Duane always referred to you as his scientist," she said. "A genius he had working for him, I assume on one of his crackpot schemes. What is it this time? A truth serum? Some potion that allows him to see in the dark? A new weapon?"

Mark shifted on his stool and cleared his throat. "You don't know what kind of scientist I am, do you?"

"Duane just told me you were a scientist, and you obviously have some kind of laboratory here."

"I'm a nuclear physicist. Duane Braeswood is holding me prisoner so I can build him a bomb. A nuclear bomb."

Chapter Two

Erin's lovely face reflected all the emotions that had battered at Mark the first time he heard the terrorist leader's plans for him—shock, outrage and finally puzzlement. She glanced around the cabin, with its sparse furnishings and makeshift lab. "How—?"

He didn't let her finish the sentence, but sprang up, grabbed her hand and pulled her toward the refrigerator. "Let me fix you some lunch," he said. "There's cold cuts and stuff in the refrigerator."

She struggled to free herself from his grip, but he held her firmly, pulled open the refrigerator door and leaned in, tugging her alongside him. "We have to be careful what we say," he said, keeping his voice low. "I think the place is bugged."

Her expression tightened and he braced himself for her to dismiss him as a nut. After so many months alone, maybe he was losing it, letting the paranoia take over. But her gaze remained level and she nodded. "That would be just like Duane," she said. "He doesn't trust anyone or take anything for granted."

Mark released her hand and pretended to look through the packages of ham, turkey and cheese on the shelf. "I spend all my time pretending to do the impossible," he mumbled. "Your stepfather wants a nuclear bomb that can be carried around in an oversize suitcase or a backpack, but there's no way that can be done. Certainly not by one man in a facility like this."

"But you've convinced him you can do it." She sounded both horrified and fascinated by the prospect. "Why?"

"As long as I keep working for him, my daughter lives." He grabbed a package of ham and another of cheese and moved away from the refrigerator, back to the table. "There's bread in the cupboard over the sink," he said.

She hesitated, then grabbed the bread and followed him. "You have a daughter?" She kept her voice low, just above a whisper.

"Mandy is five. She was four the last time I saw her."

"Where is she?" Erin's voice rose. "Duane isn't holding her prisoner, too?"

"No, she's safe. She lives with her aunt." At least, he prayed that was still true. Mandy had been with his wife's sister the day Mark left on the hiking trip from which he had never returned. He and Christy had both designated Claire as their chosen guardian for Mandy in their wills, so he had assumed his daughter had stayed with Claire after his disappearance.

"What happened to her mother?" Erin asked.

"She died two months before Duane brought me here." He glanced up from spreading mayonnaise on a slice of bread. "Officially, it was ruled a one-car accident, but someone tampered with her car, I know.

Duane wanted to send me a message about the consequences of not cooperating with him."

Sympathy darkened Erin's eyes. "I heard rumors about that kind of thing when I lived with him," she said. "I wanted to believe they weren't true. That no one would be that cruel and manipulative."

"Oh, this is true." When Christy had died, grief and rage at the man responsible consumed him. All these months later, he felt only numb.

"But how did you meet Duane in the first place?" she asked. "You don't strike me as the prepper type."

"No, I'm not. I had never even heard of Duane Braeswood when he stopped by my office at the University of Colorado one morning about eighteen months ago. He presented himself as a businessman who was interested in providing a grant for research. I was naive enough to be flattered." How many times over the past year had he wished he had had the sense to see through the madman's ruse and refuse to ever speak to him?

"And once he had snared you, he wouldn't let go." She nodded. "He's done it before. He identifies something he wants and then uses whatever means possible to get it."

"At first, he tried to sell me on the scientific advantages of working for him—a private laboratory with top equipment, an endless supply of resources, eventual fame and fortune, and a key role in his new world order." He grimaced. "When that didn't sway me, he turned to threats. I didn't believe him. I thought he was a crackpot but harmless. I found out too late that he was anything but."

"I'm sorry about your wife," Erin said, all the hardness gone from her voice.

"Thank you." He swallowed, regaining his composure. "When he threatened my daughter next, I knew I didn't have any choice but to cooperate."

"So now you're trying to do the impossible."

"I'm the best—or one of the best—nuclear physicists in the country." He raised his voice for the benefit of anyone who might be listening in. "The organization supplies me with anything I need, from high-grade uranium ore to the most sophisticated equipment. It's only a matter of time." He met her eyes, letting her know he was lying through his teeth.

"And I'm supposed to help you." She stared down at her completed sandwich. "I don't know the first thing about nuclear physics."

"You're a math teacher. That should come in handy. You can help me with my calculations."

She looked around the cabin again. "You don't have a computer?"

He shook his head.

"And I don't see any books. Don't you need reference materials? Formulas?"

He tapped the side of his head. "It's all in here." He almost laughed at the skepticism that was so plain on her face. "No, really. I have a photographic memory. I've memorized all the textbooks and formulas and manuals. Once I read something, I remember it. Some of my colleagues thought I was a freak, but it made me the perfect candidate for Duane's little project." Finding out how thoroughly the Patriots' leader had vetted him had made Mark feel even more vulnerable and helpless, as if there was nowhere to hide from Duane's reach.

"I thought photographic memories were something people made up for movies and books," she said.

"No, it's a real phenomenon. Something to do with how the person's brain is wired. There may even be a genetic component in this case. My mother had perfect pitch. My twin brother never forgets a face."

"You have a twin?"

"Yes. Luke is an FBI agent. He's part of a special task force composed of people like him—super-recognizers who never forget a face."

"An FB—" She shook her head. "Then Duane is an idiot—and I don't care who hears me say that."

"Duane believes he's untouchable," Mark said. And maybe he was. The man had managed to get away with murder—literally—for a while now. "I know Luke is looking for me," he continued. "But Duane is hunting him, too. He's made it known he'll pay a big bonus to anyone who kills a Fed."

"He bragged about it to me, too."

He studied her, wishing he could decipher people as easily as he could chemical formulas. Was she telling the truth about how she had ended up here, or was this merely one more way for Braeswood and his bunch to mess with Mark's mind? "Why did he send you here, really?" he asked, leaning toward her. "I don't need an assistant for this project. Are you here to spy on me? Will you report back to him everything I've said?" He ought to be afraid of those consequences, but after all this time trapped here with no way out he would welcome a bullet to end it all.

"You really think I would work for people like

them? That I could believe in their sick plots or condone anything they do?" She shoved the sandwich away and glared at him, cheeks flushed, eyes blazing.

"Accusing me isn't the same as denial," he pointed out.

"No! I don't want anything to do with those monsters. And I don't want anything to do with you." She stalked away and sat on the end of the unmade bed, her back to him.

Even from across the room, he imagined the heat of her anger washing over him. He welcomed the warmth, the intensity of the emotion, the *life* in her. For so long now—before they had even brought him here, since Christy's death—he had felt cold and hollow inside, more robot than man. Only his daughter had been able to stir him, her tiny breath able to coax sparks from the few coals of life left inside him.

Then she was gone and the fire had died altogether. He had gone through the motions of living, but had felt nothing.

Now Erin was here, all fiery anger and glowing life, making him remember things—hatred and hunger and sex. Somehow being near a woman, after so many months with only the company of other men, reminded him of his own humanity. He wasn't dead after all, but he didn't know if that knowledge was good or bad. Living meant feeling—risking and caring and hurting. All things he had told himself he couldn't afford to do again.

ERIN ENVIED MARK'S COMPOSURE. She couldn't sit still, agitation driving her to pace. She had lived with fear for so long it was part of her makeup now, like the color of her hair or the shape of her face. Even years after she had left the family compound she continued to look over her shoulder, expecting her stepfather to make good on all the threats he had hurled at her when she'd walked away from him. Duane had a need to control situations and people. If you thwarted him, you could expect to be punished.

He had bided his time, but he had finally exacted his revenge, though she still wasn't sure of his final plans for her. She kept expecting his thugs to come back for her—to tie her up again and tell her there had been a change of plans, that this remote cabin wasn't her real destination. This place was too bizarre, even for Duane. Did he really believe he could build a nuclear bomb in a place like this? With a scientist who didn't even bother to look at a book?

She risked a glance at Mark, who had returned to work at the lab table. He wore goggles and a mask and was working with his hands in heavy gloves, manipulating something inside a large glass box. Maybe the protective gear was because the material in that box was radioactive. She wrapped her arms around her shoulders to ward off a sudden chill.

She couldn't figure Mark out. The story he had told her—about his wife and little girl—was horrifying. She was pretty sure Duane had killed other people, so why not Mark's wife? But how could Mark be so calm about his situation? She had spent every waking moment for the last six weeks trying to figure out how to escape from her captors. She had almost succeeded twice—she still winced, remembering the beatings she'd received when she had been caught. But Duane hadn't let them kill her or rape her or otherwise harm her. She had thought he drew the line there out of consideration for her mother, but now she wondered if it was because he had other plans for her. Plans that included the enigmatic Mark Renfro.

Her stomach growled. The sandwich she had made earlier still sat on the kitchen counter, so she retrieved it and took it to the table to eat. Mark glanced up from his work. "They usually bring dinner by now," he said. "Since they haven't, we may have to make do with cold cuts."

She shrugged. She didn't want to talk to him, didn't want to get any closer to him, but curiosity—and maybe loneliness—weakened her resolve. "What are you doing?" she asked.

"I'm using a solvent to extract pure uranium from powdered ore," he said. "The process takes a couple of days, but there's a lot of high-grade ore in this area. I think that's why Duane was interested in the property in the first place. Some things I've overheard make me think he hasn't owned the place long—that he acquired it specifically for this purpose. The remote location suits his purposes well, too."

"I still don't understand how you convinced Duane you could make a bomb out here," she said. "He's insane, but he isn't stupid."

He removed his hands from the box, pulled down the mask and pushed up the goggles and faced her. "I didn't convince him of anything. He decided it could be done and chose me to do it."

"But what made him think it was even possible?" she asked. "Don't you need, I don't know, a particle accelerator or something like that?"

He chuckled. "Actually, in the 1960s, three physics students working in a small laboratory were able to design a functional bomb. The United States government paid them to make the attempt. They wanted to see if it was possible for a few people with a limited amount of knowledge and not a lot of sophisticated equipment—a situation that might crop up in an underdeveloped country, for example—to make a nuclear weapon. Turned out they could. The government called it the Nth Country Experiment. You can read about it online if you're interested. And in 1994 a teenage Eagle Scout built a nuclear reactor in his backyard, using materials he found around the house."

"So you really could build a bomb?" The idea made her skin crawl.

"I'm sure I could, given enough time and the right materials." He scrawled something on a piece of paper and passed it over to her. *In case anyone is listening, building a bomb isn't the problem. Building one small enough for one person to carry around inconspicuously is.*

She nodded and crumpled the paper, holding it tight in her clenched fist. "I still don't see how I can help you."

"Perhaps you're merely here to boost my morale."

She narrowed her eyes. "Don't get any ideas."

He frowned. "I only meant that having someone to talk to is a nice change."

Right. Maybe she had grown too accustomed to the company of Duane's goons who, despite their boss's orders not to lay a hand on her, spent plenty of time leering and making lewd remarks. "How have you kept from going crazy, alone here for so many months?" she asked.

"I try not to think about it too much," he said. "And I focus on the work." He turned back to the lab equipment.

She stared at his back for a long while, then stood and walked to the window. He could focus on work all he wanted, but she was going to focus on finding a way out of here.

In different circumstances, she might have enjoyed the view out this window. The cabin sat on a slight rise at the edge of a valley. Feathery junipers and piñon pines dotted the rocky ground amid a thick blanket of snow. A few hundred yards beyond the cabin the land fell away in a steep precipice. Across from this gorge rose red rock mountains, the peaks cloaked in white, the setting sun painting the sky in brilliant pinks and golds. How ironic that such a peaceful-seeming place could be the source of potentially great destruction.

A cloud of white off in the distance, moving in their direction, caught her attention. "I think someone's coming," she said.

Mark was by her side within seconds. "That looks like Duane's entourage," he said, as three black Humvees slowly made their way up the narrow, rutted track. A guard who must have been seated on the other side of the door rose and walked to the edge of the narrow porch, an automatic rifle cradled in his arms. When the vehicles stopped in front of the cabin, the guard snapped off a salute.

Erin didn't even realize she had backed away from the window until she bumped into Mark. He rested one hand on her shoulder, steadying her, and she fought the urge to lean into him. She didn't even know the man, and didn't fully trust him, yet she felt safer with him than with any of those on the other side of the door.

Men piled out of the first and third vehicles, all dressed in camo and bristling with weapons. One man unpacked a wheelchair and set it up next to the middle vehicle, while another man opened the back door of this Hummer, leaned in and lifted out Duane Braeswood.

Mark sucked in his breath. "Is that really Duane?" he asked. "What happened to him?"

Instead of camo, Duane wore a black suit and turtleneck. His thin body was twisted and hunched, and tubes trailed from his nostrils to an oxygen tank that one of his goons hooked to the back of the wheelchair.

"You didn't know?" She had been shocked, too, the first time she saw this sick, diminished version of her stepfather. But he was diminished in physical stature only. His spirit had struck her as stronger than ever.

"I haven't seen him in almost a year," Mark said.

"Don't let his appearance fool you. He isn't weak." Despite his disability, the man in the wheelchair radiated power, with every man out there focused on him.

The group headed for the cabin, two of the men lifting the wheelchair, with Duane in it, onto the porch. Mark pulled Erin into the middle of the room as locks snicked and the door opened.

She forced herself to look at her stepfather, to meet the blue eyes that burned feverishly in his withered face. "Erin, dear." The sound of her name on his lips made her flinch. "Your mother sends her greetings."

She bit back a curse, aware of the guards looming on either side of him. She had found out the hard way what they thought of any slur on the man they viewed almost as a religious figure. "How is my mother?" she asked, because she wanted desperately to know, though she knew Duane would tell her the truth only if it suited him.

"Helen is fine." He rolled his chair toward the lab. "Renfro!" The strident voice seemed incongruous coming from such a weakened frame. "What progress have you made?"

Mark walked to the workbench, unhurried, his hands in the pockets of his lab coat, the picture of the singularly focused genius who couldn't be bothered to worry about anything outside of his work. "I've almost perfected the refining process," he said. "And I'm accumulating the quantity of uranium I'll need for the project."

"You need to finish within a week," Duane said.

Mark's expression didn't change. If anything, he looked even more bored, eyes hooded, his expression guarded. "I can't promise that. The process takes as long as it takes. I can't change physical laws."

Erin didn't see any signal from Duane, but he must have given one. Without warning, two men seized her arms, while a third forced her head back.

"Leave her alone!" Mark shouted, all semblance of boredom vanished, but the fourth guard held him back.

Erin tried to struggle, terrified her captors intended to cut her throat. But the two men who held her remained immobile, impervious to her kicks and shouts. A third man wrapped something hard and cold around her throat. She heard a click, and all three men suddenly released her.

"I wouldn't make any sudden movements if I were

you, Erin." Duane's voice had its usual smooth cadence. "The mechanism in your new necklace is fairly sensitive."

The three goons stepped back and Erin grabbed at her throat, grasping the thick metal collar now fastened there. The edges chafed her skin and the weight of it dragged at her. "What have you done to me?" she demanded.

"You're wearing an explosive device," Duane said, as calmly as if he had been commenting on the weather. "It has a timer, and is set to go off exactly one week from today." He turned to Mark. "You deliver the product as promised by then and we will remove the collar."

"Why such a hurry now?" Mark asked. "You've waited all these months, why not a few more to make sure things are done correctly?"

"I'm done with waiting." Duane's voice was strident, his face red with strain. "You will have the device for me in a week."

"And if I don't?"

"Then the bomb goes off and you both die."

Chapter Three

Mark stared at the man in the wheelchair. The eyes that looked back at him were as cold and untroubled as a mountain lake. Erin had been right—whatever physical ailment had reduced Duane to a husk of his former self, it hadn't diminished his madness. A man with eyes like that might very well kill his own stepdaughter just to make a point. But delivering what Duane wanted within a week—or even within a year—was impossible. Mark chose his words carefully, wary of upsetting his kidnapper more. "Mr. Braeswood, building a…an apparatus such as you require isn't like baking a cake. I can't just throw a bunch of ingredients together and come up with a viable product. I need time and—"

"You've had time," Braeswood snapped. "If I don't have what I want in one week, you both die."

And even if I could deliver your bomb, we would still die, Mark thought. Duane wouldn't leave any witnesses to his plans. "You're asking for the impossible," he said.

"You'll have your bomb. Next week!" Despite the constricting collar Erin turned her head to face Braeswood. "Mark is being a typical scientist—overly cautious. He was telling me earlier that he's almost ready to assemble it. With both of us working together I know we can meet your deadline."

"Erin." Mark sent her a warning look.

Her gaze burned into him, pleading with him to go along with her lie. Her terror swamped him. Maybe he would feel the same if he had a bomb at his throat. "Sure," he said, dropping his gaze to the floor. "There's still some work I need to do…with the plutonium catalyst ratios." There was no such thing, but Mark had learned that Braeswood appreciated it when he threw around scientific jargon.

"Excellent." Braeswood's voice sounded much stronger than he looked. Floorboards creaked as he turned his chair and rolled back to the door. "I'll see you next week, then."

"You can't just leave me like this!" Erin's voice rose, on the edge of panic.

"So impatient." Braeswood regarded her coolly. "You were that way as a child, too, never content to wait for a reward, no matter how hard I tried to teach you. I would have hoped that maturity would have curbed that unfortunate character trait, but I see it has not. This should be a good lesson for you." He nodded to his henchmen and one opened the door while two others hoisted the chair.

The locks snapped into place again after the door closed behind the entourage. Car doors slammed, engines growled and the pop of tires on gravel gradually faded away.

Erin sank into one of the kitchen chairs, as if her legs would no longer support her, her hands clutching the collar. "I can't believe this is happening," she moaned.

Mark's hands knotted into fists and his heart hammered, emotion rocking him back on his heels. He recognized rage—something he hadn't felt, something he hadn't allowed himself to feel, in months. The intensity of the feelings caught him off guard. He was furious with Braeswood and his men, but also with himself. Why hadn't he done something to stop them? Why hadn't he protected Erin? And what was he going to do to help her now? He may have given up on life, but she deserved to live.

He pulled his hands from his pockets and moved to her side. "Can I take a look at the collar?" he asked.

She dropped her hands to her lap and looked up at him. "Do you know anything about disarming bombs?"

"Not a thing, unfortunately." He studied the collar, which was gold colored—plated, he imagined, with platinum or aluminum or some other sturdier alloy beneath. About three inches wide, it fastened at the back with a locking mechanism similar to a seat belt, the halves fitting tightly together. The explosive device sat front and center, the size of a pack of playing cards, comprised of wires and button batteries and a glob of yellowish plastic he suspected was the explosive. Who had made this horrible yet ingenious device for Duane? Did he have a combination jeweler-explosives expert in the ranks of his followers? Or was he holding another man prisoner, compelling him by threat or force to do Duane's malevolent bidding?

Mark brushed his fingers along the sides of the collar, the hot flutter of Erin's pulse beneath his fingertips sending a jolt of awareness through him. The contrast of her silken flesh with the unyielding metal made her seem all the more fragile and out of place here—like finding a lily blooming in the middle of a minefield.

"Can you cut it off?" she asked.

"I don't think we can risk it," he said. "It looks as if there are wires embedded in the metal and running all the way around. My guess is if we sever one of those the bomb would go off."

She swallowed hard, her eyes as big and dark as a terrified deer's. "What are we going to do?"

He looked away, at the lab equipment arranged neatly on the workbench, at the sparse furnishings and barred windows of the place that had been his prison for the past fourteen months. "We need to get out of here," he said. "We need to get you to someplace with people who know how to disarm something like this." The FBI had experts who could deal with this kind of thing. If he could get to Luke, his brother would know what to do.

"How are we going to get away?" she asked.

If he knew that, he would have left months ago. Escaping from the cabin might not even be the most difficult challenge. Once they were free, they would have to cross miles of wilderness in freezing weather before they could even reach a road, or a telephone they could use to summon help. "I don't know." He dropped into the chair across from her. "I tried everything I could think of when I first got here. I was always caught." Caught and punished. He closed his eyes. He understood now that it wasn't merely confinement that wore down prisoners—it was the utter helplessness, the loss of control over even the simplest aspects of life.

"How many guards are there?" she asked.

"Two at a time—one on the front door and one on the back. They work eight-hour shifts, so that means six men a day, plus two others that rotate in and out when one of the others needs to take a day off. They're armed with semiautomatic rifles and unlike the men in books and movies, they don't fall asleep or get distracted." He had spent many hours in the early days of his captivity studying his guards and trying to learn their patterns and spot any weaknesses. Unfortunately, he hadn't identified any of the latter.

"So Duane has eight men stationed somewhere near here, but only two of them are up here at a time," she said. "There are two of us now. That evens the odds." She sounded stronger, and some of the color had returned to her face.

"Except we're not armed," he said. "And where do we go when we do get out of here? We're miles from any major road, we don't have a map and, in case you haven't noticed, there's snow out there."

"I'd rather freeze to death in the mountains than sit here waiting to be blown up."

Until she showed up, Mark would have opted for sitting. Truth was, he had given up months ago. Without his wife, without his daughter or his work, he had nothing to live for. But Erin was young. Not that much younger than him in terms of years, but she was so full of life. She had every reason to avoid death.

"Why is Duane doing all this now?" he asked. "Why lure you back to him after years away? Why demand a bomb in a week after I've been working on it over a year? He hasn't shown any sign of impatience with the project before now."

"Maybe he's tired of paying for all the man power needed to keep you up here," she said.

"He hasn't balked at paying the money before. Has something happened to make him worried about finances?"

She shook her head. "Duane's grandfather was some kind of robber baron who made a killing in insurance in the twenties. Apparently, even the Depression didn't touch his fortune. His father parlayed those millions into billions with a string of tech companies. Duane apparently inherited their knack for business and invested in everything from highways to high tech to fund his more nefarious activities—the actual source of the money all neatly hidden in various shell companies and shadow corporations. Add to that the donations he receives from people who support his cause and he's got an endless supply of bucks. All this—" she swept her hand around the lab "—probably only qualifies as a footnote on a spreadsheet somewhere."

"If it's not money, what else is driving him?" Mark asked. "Has something happened on the world scene to make him think now is the best time to strike? I haven't heard a news report in the last year, so we could be ruled by Martians right now and I wouldn't know it." He'd been like a castaway on a deserted island. He had told himself he didn't miss knowing what was going on in the rest of the world, but now that Erin was with him, he fought the urge to bombard her with questions: *Who was president of Russia these days? What was the dollar worth? What was the hot-*

test tech gadget? Who was hosting the next Olympic Games? Who'd won the World Series?

But he had held back, and now, with that horrible collar around her neck, didn't seem the time to worry about trivialities.

"There's nothing much new in the world situation that would have set him off," she said. "Though maybe his accident has him thinking about his mortality, and that's given him this sense of urgency."

"What kind of accident?" Mark asked. "I'll admit I was shocked by his appearance this afternoon—I haven't seen him in months. I thought maybe he had cancer or something."

"I'm not sure what is wrong with him, but I don't think it's cancer," she said. "I only heard bits and pieces of the story from my mom or from things people said when they didn't know I was listening. It's something to do with the FBI—he was injured when they tried to capture him or something like that. It's one of the reasons he hates them so much."

"Did you overhear anything else interesting, about Duane or his plans?"

"There was some rumor about a power struggle between Duane and his second in command, a man named Roland Chambers. He lived with us for a while when I was a teenager and he practically worshipped Duane, so I don't know how much truth there was to the rumors that he was trying to take over after Duane was injured. But Roland was killed last month, so Duane doesn't have to worry about him anymore."

"So no money problems, no political upheaval and no rival." Mark ticked off the possible reasons for Duane's sudden change of plans. "Maybe you're right and it is a mortality thing. I guess it doesn't matter why he's putting the pressure on us, only that he is."

"We've got to find a way out of here," she said.

"If you think of a plan, I'll try it."

She surprised him once more by leaning over and gripping his hand. "We'll think of something," she said.

Her conviction both stunned and moved him. A wave of emotion—regret, longing, even hope—welled up in him, so strong he had to look away for fear of betraying his weakness. Five hours ago he had been contemplating ways to end his life. Now, thanks to Erin, he was desperate to hang on to all the time he had left—to not only survive, but to live.

THE COLLAR WASN'T tight enough to choke her, Erin reminded herself, fighting the panic that lurked at the very edge of consciousness. But the thick metal band felt like Duane's hands around her throat, threatening to squeeze the life from her.

Mark had returned to his workbench, bending over his experiments as if the previous hour hadn't happened. She supposed his work was his escape, the way some people lost themselves in television shows or books. But she had no escape, only a hyperawareness of the weight around her throat and the fear that a wrong move could set off the bomb that would tear her to pieces. She had lived with fear so long she thought she had grown accustomed to it, but Duane had found a way to ratchet up the terror until it was almost unbearable.

She replayed every conversation she had had with him since she had returned to his sphere of influence—not so much conversations as arguments and debates, often exchanged at top volume while her mother hovered nearby, a diminutive referee prepared to throw herself between the opponents should they come to blows.

Erin's refusal to follow Duane's dictates or believe in his worldview had always annoyed and even angered her stepfather. As a teen, his attitude had only egged her on. As an adult, she saw a hatred she hadn't noticed before, lurking beneath the surface ranting. Maybe this whole charade with the kidnapping and the collar was an elaborate revenge plot. Maybe she was the primary target of Duane's latest ultimatum, not Mark and his bomb-building assignment. He was collateral damage incurred along the way.

Engrossed in his work, Mark didn't even seem aware she was in the room. She studied him, determined to distract herself from thinking any more about the collar. He was a fairly tall man—over six feet, his frame lanky beneath the loose-fitting lab coat. His dark hair just touched his collar, the cut uneven, as if he had done it himself with the pair of nail scissors. The thought of him struggling to remain well-groomed despite the direness of his situation touched her.

He had probably shaved this morning, but now dark stubble shadowed his jaw, sharpening his features and making him look less like a scientist and more like an outlaw, or a fugitive on the run.

She wanted to be on the run, but the wire mesh on the windows and the guards at the doors blocked their escape. She studied the ceiling. If they could find a way to climb up onto the roof, could they jump off and flee before the guards noticed? But the cabin didn't appear to have an attic, and she doubted they had tools capable of sawing through the metal roofing. The concrete beneath the floor meant tunneling wasn't an option.

She sighed and closed her eyes, determined not to give in to the tears that threatened.

"It's getting dark."

Mark's voice startled her. She opened her eyes, surprised to note the landscape around the cabin was no longer visible through the windows.

"Darkness comes early at this elevation, this time of year," Mark said. "Are you hungry? You should try to eat." He moved from the workbench to the refrigerator and began pulling out cold cuts. "I'll make sandwiches."

"I couldn't eat," she said, but he kept assembling bread and ham and cheese.

He set a sandwich and a bottle of water in front of her and took the chair across from her. She stared at the food and shook her head. "I couldn't."

He looked down at his own plate, then pushed it away. "Yeah. I don't have much of an appetite, either. Maybe we should just call it a night. The batteries drain pretty fast once the sun goes down, so I've gotten in the habit of retiring early. Maybe in the morning we'll think with clearer heads."

She looked at the double bed with its tangle of sheets and blankets. "I don't think I could sleep," she said.

"Take the bed," he said. "I'll stretch out on the floor."

"That's ridiculous. I won't take your bed."

His expression grew stubborn. “Call me old-fashioned, but I’m not going to rest in comfort while you try to make do on the floor.”

“Then we’ll share the bed.” She looked him in the eye, striving for a calm she didn’t feel. “We’re adults. We can do that. Under the circumstances, it’s ridiculous to be prudish about something like this. There’s only one bed and two of us, so we should make the best of it.”

“All right. Suit yourself.” He stood and returned their leftovers to the refrigerator, then removed the lab coat and draped it over the stool at his workbench.

Erin blinked. The baggy coat had hid the outline of his body. Beneath it he wore a blue flannel shirt that stretched across lean but muscular shoulders, and canvas hiking pants that hugged a narrow waist and decidedly attractive backside.

He turned and caught her staring at him. “Is something wrong?” he asked.

She shook her head, fighting to hold back a blush. “I was just…lost in thought.” The thought that there was more to the depressed scientist than she had first surmised.

They moved to the bed. The metal frame was shoved into the corner. “I’ll take the outside,” she said, not wanting to be trapped between him and the wall.

“All right.” He removed his shoes, then, still wearing his pants and shirt, slid under the covers and rolled over to face the wall, his back to her.

She sat on the side of the bed and slipped out of her own shoes, then switched off the lamp and lay back on top of the blankets. The metal collar rubbed against the underside of her chin and she tried not to think of the possibility that she might roll over in sleep and put pressure on the wrong wire or something…

She closed her eyes and tried to focus on her breathing—eight slow counts in, eight slow counts out. A friend who taught yoga had assured her that this was a surefire technique for releasing tension and falling asleep.

On the first count of eight Mark shifted, the movement rocking the bed and banishing all thoughts of achieving calm. The heat of him caressed her skin and she sensed the shape of him only inches from her, the jut of his shoulders, the long line of his spine, the length of his legs. The memory of him brushing his fingertips along her throat made her heart speed up and her breath catch. Not because she could ever be attracted to a man like Mark Renfro—a man still in mourning for his dead wife and lost child, a man whose eyes held a despair that tore at her. She was reacting this way only because it had been a long time since she had slept with a man. A long time since she had lived in the same house with anyone else. She had avoided close relationships, fearful of exposing anyone else to Duane's manipulations and hate. Duane controlled people by threatening those they loved, as he had done with Mark. Avoiding love protected other people, but it was also a way of protecting herself.

But that kind of life was lonely, and clearly, Erin was paying for that now. She told herself simple human contact, not sexual attraction, had set her heart pounding and her skin heating over Mark's proximity.

She took a cue from him and rolled over to put her back to him, clinging to the side of the bed and trying to ignore the weight of the bomb collar against her throat. She closed her eyes and allowed the tears to wet her lashes and slide down her cheeks as she prayed for sleep to take her.

MARK LAY AWAKE deep into the night, stretched out rigid on the mattress, the events of the day playing and replaying behind his closed eyelids. The sudden appearance of Erin, followed by Duane's visit and his homicidal ultimatum, unsettled him more than he would have thought possible, like a trumpet blast disrupting the white noise of the lab, or a slash of vivid crimson across a black-and-white photo.

When sleep finally pulled him under, he dreamed restless, confusing vignettes: he was at a birthday party for four-year-old Mandy, Christy leaning forward, cheeks puffed out, helping her daughter blow out the candles on the cake. He saw Christy in the kitchen, long blond hair partially covered by a pink bandanna, a smudge of flour on one cheek, brows drawn together in fierce concentration as she studied the directions in a cookbook.

Then Christy was in bed beside him, the thin straps of her nightgown slipping off her shoulders, a warm smile deepening the dimple in one cheek as she pulled him to her. She was so incredibly warm and soft, skin as fine as silk as he glided his hands over her shoulders, turning her around and pulling her back tight against him, the curve of her bottom snugged against the hard length of his arousal.

He cupped her breast, the beaded nipple nuzzling into his palm. She murmured and shifted, then made a sound of alarm and jerked away.

Mark stared into a pair of wide feminine eyes—

not blue like Christy's, but the gold-green hazel of the forest floor. Erin's eyes, filled with accusations and questions.

Chapter Four

Erin had surfaced from a stupor of exhaustion to luxurious warmth—the warmth of a firm male body pressed to hers, strong hands caressing her. She smiled, and snugged into the heat of him, this dream man whose fingers played across her skin as if she was precious to him. She gave a purr of satisfaction as he cupped her breast, a glow building within her. Yes. How long had it been since she had felt so aroused—so cherished?

The question intruded into the fantasy, demanding an answer, summoning reality. Opening her eyes, she stared at the lab equipment on a counter across from her, shadowed in the dim light of early dawn filtering through the mesh-covered windows of the cabin. Emotions tumbled over her like falling debris—confusion, anger, fear—topped off by the knowledge that whoever had his hands on her and his body against her, it wasn't a lover, because she hadn't had one of those in a long time.

Fear lanced through her as she pulled out of his grasp and rolled onto her back to stare into the troubled face of Mark Renfro. "I'm sorry." He held up his hands, like a robber caught reaching into the till. "I didn't mean… I was dreaming… I'm sorry."

She did a quick check as her initial panic receded—they were both still dressed, nothing out of place. Mark looked so horrified she had to believe him. After all, she had been dreaming, too, and the dream hadn't been at all unpleasant. "It's okay." She managed a smile. "Nothing really happened. I guess this just proves you're human."

He rose up on one elbow and wiped his hand over his face. "Nothing like this has ever happened to me before."

"I think we could both say that about pretty much everything these days." She sat up and hugged her knees to her chest. "Must have been a nice dream, huh?"

The room had lightened enough to show the flush of color on his cheeks that made him look much younger and quite endearing. "It's okay," she said again. "The mind is a funny thing. The subconscious can throw up the oddest stuff when you least expect it."

He sat up also, then leaned over and pulled a small transistor radio from beneath the bed and switched it on. The white noise of static surrounded them. "I read once that was one way to make it tougher for a hidden microphone to pick up conversation." He shrugged. "I don't know if it's true or not, but it doesn't hurt to be careful."

"Where did you get that?" she asked.

"I found it under the bed after I had been here a couple of weeks. I guess whoever owned the cabin before left it behind." He leaned back against the iron bedstead. "I don't suppose your subconscious has come up with a way to get us out of here?"

She touched the collar at her neck, the metal smooth and heavy and deadly. Then she glanced at the array of lab equipment. "There must be something there we can use as a weapon," she said. "I mean, you're supposed to be building a bomb. So you must have some dangerous stuff."

"Radioactive material is potentially deadly," he said. "But by itself it doesn't kill or disable instantly, like a bullet or a knife. If we threatened the guards with a chunk of radioactive rock, they would just shoot us."

"What else have you got? Chemicals?"

"I have some solvents, a couple of acids—"

"That's it." She leaned toward him. "Throw acid on someone and you could certainly disable them."

"But they have to get close enough for you to be sure you don't miss," he said. "You might take out one guard that way, but not both of them."

She mulled over this problem. "I could create a distraction. Something they would both have to respond to. You could douse them with acid and we could make a run for it."

He didn't automatically dismiss the plan, which she considered a positive sign. "What kind of distraction?"

"I don't know. It would have to be something that would bring them inside. What about a fire? Or a minor explosion in the lab?"

"I tried that the second week I was here. One of them stuck his head in and told me if I burned the place down with me in it, I would save them all a lot of trouble. I ruined my only sweater putting out the blaze."

"I could scream rape."

He shook his head. "From what I've seen of this bunch, they'd either want to watch or participate."

She cringed. "Right. Bad idea." She rubbed a finger under the collar. "If I told them something was wrong with this, they would probably want to keep their distance." She looked around the cabin. "What do they care about in here?"

"Nothing," he said. "The only time they set foot inside is to bring food, and then one of them keeps his gun on me while the other one sets the bags on the table. The whole process takes about three minutes."

"So you've been practically living in solitary confinement." No wonder he was depressed.

"I would rather be by myself than have anything to do with people like them," he said. "Killers who justify what they do with a pretense of saving the country from itself."

"So we'll have to make our move when they bring the food," she said. "When do they usually bring it?"

"Midafternoon. I thought they were making a delivery when they brought you."

"Do they come every day?"

"No. Three or four times a week."

"Next time they come we won't make our move, but we'll watch and see if we can spot any weak points. Have you ever seen any other women up here?"

"Never."

"I've seen a few hanging around Duane's compound—a few wives and girlfriends of the men who follow him. Maybe a few of the women are followers, too. But there's never any female muscle. That runs counter to all those old-fashioned values they like to espouse."

"What are you getting at?" he asked.

"These guys aren't around women a lot," she said. "They don't know how to handle them."

"They don't have any problem killing women," he said, and she wondered if he was thinking of his dead wife.

Her stomach knotted. "I don't intend to let them kill me if I can help it. But I was thinking if I got a little hysterical it might throw them off balance long enough for you to douse them with the acid."

"That's a lot of *if*s."

"The alternative is sitting here and waiting to be blown up. I would rather take the risk."

"And what happens after that?" he asked. "After we get outside? I don't even know where we are. Do you?"

"No. But there is a road leading up here, and if we head down the mountain and keep walking, we're bound to eventually reach a house or a highway or someone who can help us." She angled her body toward him. "We can gather supplies to take with us—food and water and blankets. When we get to a phone we can call your brother the FBI agent."

"The guards will come after us. It won't be as simple as walking away from here."

"If we disable both guards on duty, we'll have a head start. I'll admit it won't be easy, but if we don't at least try it, we'll die for sure."

He let out a long breath. "You're right." His eyes met hers, a strength in them she hadn't seen before. "We'll do it."

ERIN'S DETERMINATION TO escape kindled a fire in Mark. He felt like a man awakening after a long sleep, dormant emotions coming to life once more. Last night's erotic dream was just one more sign of his reawakening. When he had first come to the cabin, he had fought, but weeks of isolation and torture and no success from his efforts had left him listless and numb. The sight of the beautiful woman sentenced to death by the bomb around her throat hit him like an injection of adrenaline.

"I did an inventory of the lab equipment and supplies," he told Erin as they ate lunch—the last of the sandwich fixings—that afternoon. She had spent the morning looking out the windows, not speaking. Maybe the direness of their situation was sinking in.

"How do you replenish your supplies?" she asked. She lifted the top slice of bread on her turkey sandwich and frowned at the grayish meat inside.

"I make a list and give it to the guard who delivers the food." Mark bit into his own sandwich. After his first weeks here he had learned to eat when food was offered, since he could never be sure when the next meal would arrive. "I'm pretty well stocked right now, but I need more nitric acid. I use it to process the plutonium." Any chemist would recognize this as a gross oversimplification of what he did, but the guards didn't strike him as chemistry majors.

"So you think they'll bring more food this afternoon?" she asked.

"I hope so. We need more food since there are two of us now."

"It must be pretty boring for the guards," she said. "I've been watching them all morning and they just walk around the cabin all day. What do they do when it snows, or at night?"

"There's someone on guard all the time," he said. "Sometimes they build a fire in winter, and they have a trailer parked nearby, where they can take turns warming up."

He could almost read her thoughts. She was thinking if they could get out of here at a time when only one guard was outside, they would have a better chance of getting away.

"They keep the doors locked from the outside," he reminded her.

She nodded, still thoughtful.

The crunch of tires on ice alerted them to new arrivals. "This might be our dinner," he said, standing.

She stood also, and together they faced the door. A car door slammed, locks turned and the door swung open to reveal a guard Mark had named Tank—a thick-muscled, broad-shouldered guy with a shaved head, a gold front tooth and a permanent scowl. The floor shook as he strode toward them, two plastic grocery bags looped over one hand, the other balled into a fist at his side.

A second guard—a wiry black man with a thin mustache—positioned himself by the door, a semiautomatic rifle held across his chest. He glanced at Mark, then his gaze fixed on Erin and one corner of his mouth lifted in a sneer. She moved a little closer to Mark, her breath shallow, skin pale. He wanted to put out a hand to steady her, maybe squeeze her shoulder to reassure her, but doing anything to draw attention to her felt like the wrong move.

Tank set the grocery bags on the table, the cans and

bottles inside rattling. At this point, he usually turned and shuffled out, but this afternoon was different. He moved toward Erin, who shrank back.

"I'm supposed to check your collar," he said, and took hold of her arm, dragging her toward him.

She stood rigid, jaw clamped shut, as he ran one thick finger under the edge of the metal collar. The other hand slid down her arm to cup her breast. "Yeah," he murmured. "Nice."

"Get your hands off of me," she warned.

"Now, sugar, seeing as how you're going to be here awhile, we might as well be friendly." He squeezed, and Erin brought her knee up toward his crotch, but he blocked the move and twisted her arm around her back, hard enough that she let out a cry.

Mark launched himself at the thug, landing a knuckle-bruising blow that sent blood spurting from Tank's nose. Howling, the guard released Erin and swung the butt of his rifle against the side of Mark's head. Mark staggered back, his vision blurring. Erin's screams mingled with the pounding of his pulse and the animal growl that rose from Tank. Mark fell backward over one of the kitchen chairs and tried to regain his balance as Tank lunged toward him. He scanned the area for a weapon and grabbed for the chair, swinging it up to block a second blow from the rifle. Then the barrel of the weapon zeroed in on him, stalling his heart in his chest as he stared death in the face.

Chapter Five

"No!" Erin's scream tore through the noise of their struggle. "Don't be an idiot." She lunged toward the biggest thug, held back by the black guard, who wrapped his arms around her and lifted her off the ground as if she weighed no more than a pet dog. She kicked and flailed anyway, desperate to keep the other man from hurting Mark. "If you kill him before he finishes the bomb, Duane Braeswood will make sure you suffer," she shouted.

The big thug hesitated, and Mark staggered to his feet. He swayed, blood trailing down the side of his face, but he managed to glare at the guard, who snarled, but lowered the rifle. Then the thug turned and stalked to the door. The black guard shoved Erin toward Mark and seconds later the front door slammed behind them and the locks slid back into place.

"You're bleeding." She rushed to Mark, her fingers fluttering over the broken bruise on the side of his head, fearful of hurting him more if she touched him. But when he swayed alarmingly, she gripped him by the arm and led him to the bed. "Stay here and I'll get something to clean you up."

He opened his mouth as if to protest, then closed his eyes and said nothing. She hurried to the sink and ran cold water over a clean dishrag, keeping one eye on him in case he toppled over. The guard had hit him so hard she had been afraid at first that he'd been killed.

But he opened his eyes when she returned to his side, and sucked in his breath when she dabbed at the wound with the wet rag. "Sorry," she said, "but I need to clean up this blood. You've got a nasty bruise, and it broke the skin."

"At least I'm not dead," he said. "If you hadn't said that about Duane and the bomb, I probably would be."

"You shouldn't have punched him." Her hand tightened on his shoulder as she continued dabbing at the blood. Now that her initial terror had faded, she felt light-headed and shaky. "You didn't ask for me to come here and it's not your responsibility to defend me."

"I wasn't going to stand by and let him maul you." Mark turned his head to meet her gaze. "I didn't ask for you to come here, but I'm glad you're here."

The sad, defeated look had left his eyes, replaced with such strength and vitality she might have thought she was with a different man altogether. She lost track of everything in the heat of that gaze and for that split second, he wasn't hurt, she wasn't wearing a bomb around her neck, they weren't trapped and this whole nightmare had never happened. They were a man and a woman making a connection.

But under the circumstances, that kind of moment couldn't last. The situation was too dire, their need to get away too urgent. She squeezed his shoulder again, then dropped her hand. Her voice trembled only a little as she changed the subject. "Did you notice?" she asked. "The one who grabbed me after you hit the big guy left the door unguarded. We might be able to use that information."

"I don't think we can risk trying the same moves again." He touched the wound on the side of his head and winced. "Next time they might kill me. They might kill both of us."

"No, we can't risk it. But that tells us that under the right circumstances, the man on the door will abandon his post." She stood. "Let's see what they brought us to eat."

The two plastic grocery bags the guard had carried in had tipped over and spilled their contents across the table: canned soup and fruit, sliced cheese and cheap lunch meat, a partially smashed loaf of bread, toaster pastries, instant coffee, crackers, corn chips, canned ravioli and a box of chocolate cupcakes. Mark picked up the cupcakes. "This is new," he said. "They never bring anything sweet."

Erin stared at the cupcakes, heart pounding. It was just a stupid box of cupcakes, but still…

"What's wrong?" Mark asked. "You look like you're going to faint." He put a steadying hand on her arm.

She shook her head, trying to clear the fog. "It's silly."

"But you think you know why the cupcakes are here this time?"

She swallowed, trying to keep her composure. "They're my favorite. When I was a kid, my mom would buy them as a special treat for my lunches.

And even as an adult, she would keep them around for me." Erin swallowed tears at the memory of sitting at the kitchen table after school, peeling back the thick chocolate frosting with the white squiggle through the center to reveal the cream-filled chocolate cake beneath, while her mother sat across from her, sipping coffee and asking about her day. "Mom must have persuaded Duane to include them in the delivery for us. Either that, or it's his sick way of reminding me that he knows all about me." She turned away, fighting to regain control of her emotions.

Mark said nothing for a long moment, either because he didn't know what to say, or because he wanted to give her time to recover. When she turned to face him again, he had his hands in his pockets, his eyes fixed on her with a look of cautious sympathy. He cleared his throat. "If you're hungry, I can fix us some supper."

"Not yet. How are you feeling?"

"I've got a killer headache, but I'll live."

She leaned forward to look into his eyes, trying to remember the signs of a concussion from the first aid course she had taken prior to her first year of teaching. Something about uneven pupils—Mark's pupils looked okay. Maybe more than a little okay—dark and clear, set in the center of irises the color of a deep Alpine lake. They dilated a little now, and his breath caught, just as hers became more shallow. Her gaze shifted to his lips—well shaped and smooth, lips that looked as if they would know how to kiss a woman. She leaned toward him, wondering what he would think if she kissed him right now. Would he write it off as her reaction to the tension of the last hour?

Could she blame their situation for the attraction she felt for him now?

He shifted and a bottle of mustard toppled and rolled toward the edge of the table. He deftly caught it and she used the moment to step back and collect herself. "I was checking to see if your pupils were the same size," she said. "If they're not, it's a sign of concussion."

"I guess I have a harder head than I thought."

The cupcake box pulled her thoughts back toward home. Suddenly, she wanted to talk about what had happened to her, as if talking would help make things more clear. "My mother was there—when I arrived at Duane's house," she said. "But she wasn't sick. If anything, she looked better than she had in years. She had gone along with the whole plan to lie and tell me she was dying. She said she thought it was the only way she would get to see me again. Duane told her he needed my help with a project and she believed him. She even told me it would be good for me to go with him, so I could see how important his work was."

"She probably doesn't know about the exact nature of the project," Mark said. "Maybe he even told her he was developing something beneficial."

Did he really believe that, or was he only trying to make her feel better? "There's no way she could not know about the people he's killed, the destruction he's caused," Erin said. "He doesn't try to keep it a secret. I heard him brag more than once about attacks he had masterminded."

"She couldn't know about that bomb he strapped on you," Mark said.

Erin touched the metal collar, her fingers ice-cold.

"I hope she doesn't know." Her mind refused to accept that her mother would ever condone someone hurting her. "Duane would have hid that. At least, I hope he did."

"She obviously sees a different picture of Duane than we do," Mark said.

Erin sat and began lining up the canned goods in a row. "In her case, I guess love really is blind." But how could love—something that was supposed to be good—distort a person's vision so much?

Mark sat in the chair at the end of the table adjacent to her. "I think in the best relationships, each partner gives the other something they need. Maybe Duane gives your mom something she needs—security or devotion or something."

"What did your wife give you?" Erin asked. The better she got to know Mark, the more curious she was about the woman he mourned. "If it doesn't bother you too much to talk about her."

"When we met, she was a teaching assistant at the University of Colorado, where I was doing research. I spent most of my time in the lab, my head full of hypotheses and proofs, facts and figures. She was much more carefree and creative. Spontaneous and warm and so many things that I wasn't. Being with her made me feel anchored in the real world, the one outside my lab."

"And what do you think you gave her?"

His smile made Erin think he had been out of practice at forming the expression, as it came out more of a grimace. "I gave her a home and a child and security—all things she wanted but had never had. She lost both of her parents right out of high school and had been on her own ever since. I was a tenured professor with a good salary and a nice home in Boulder. I know that's what attracted her to me."

He made their relationship sound so…mercenary. "Are you saying you married for practical reasons?"

"Oh, I think Christy grew to truly love me. We didn't have a great, burning romance, but I never expected that. I was thirty-three when we met and pretty much married to my job. Having a wife and then a family made me happier than I would have thought possible. Christy got pregnant right away after we married and I thought my life was set."

Maybe the relationship he described wasn't so unusual. People came together for all sorts of reasons and formed a team that benefited them both. It was a simpler—and safer—plan than the kind of consuming love that had led her mother and other women like her to destroy their lives following a madman.

"So you were happy, then Duane came along and ruined everything," she said. "He specializes in that."

"I think he likes deciding the fates of others."

"Yes, he does." She rested her chin in her hands. "I'm always trying to figure out why people behave the way they do."

"It's the mathematician in you," he said. "Numbers obey logic, whereas people don't."

"I guess. Duane's parents died when he was very young, did you know that? I wonder sometimes if this is his way of maintaining control—or maybe exacting revenge on everyone who ever hurt him."

"Or maybe he's just nuts. People don't always act according to scientific principle."

She finished lining up the cans. "We'd better save

most of this to take with us when we get out of here," she said. "We don't know how many days it will take us to reach help." She slid the cans of fruit, ravioli and soup over to one side. "I can stow them in a pillowcase."

"Better take a can opener and some utensils," he said. "There's matches on the shelf next to the sink."

"We'll need all our extra clothes and blankets," she said. "Do you have a coat?"

"I have an old ski jacket I was wearing when they snatched me. I'm more concerned about you. That denim jacket of yours isn't nearly warm enough for the kind of nighttime cold we're liable to experience in these mountains. It can get close to zero at these elevations this time of year."

"I can wear layers underneath it, and cut a hole in a blanket and wear it like a poncho," she said.

He nodded. "Moving around and keeping blood flowing to the hands and feet are most critical. We can't weigh ourselves down too heavily." He moved aside half the cans. "Our best bet will be to cover as much ground as possible, as quickly as possible. Stay off the roads, but parallel them when we can. Navigate using landmarks so we don't travel in circles. Try to avoid cliffs, box canyons and other choke points where we would have to backtrack."

She stared at him. "How does a man who spent most of his time in a lab know so much about backcountry travel?"

"I never said I spent all my time in the lab. I hiked a lot, too. Solo trips into the backcountry, mostly. I was on a trip like that when Duane's men kidnapped me and brought me here."

"They ambushed you in the middle of nowhere?"

"They were waiting at the trailhead when my brother dropped me off. After he left, they followed me up the trail and attacked me. They knocked me out and when I awoke I was tied up in a cave somewhere in the mountains."

"No offense, but why go to so much trouble to get you?" she asked. "There must be a lot of scientists who do what you do, including some who would buy in to Duane's crazy plan to reform the government by destroying it."

Mark rubbed his hand over his eyes. "I've thought about that a lot. I think it's because I wrote an article on the future of nuclear technology for a popular magazine. It got a lot of buzz on the internet. In the article I noted that nuclear weapons had shrunk in size over the years and that some people thought a so-called suitcase nuke was within reach. I was much more interested in the technical possibilities for nuclear power generation, but Duane and people of his ilk latched on to the few comments I made about weapons. Duane decided I must know more than I'd let on in my paper. Apparently, once he gets an idea in his head, he refuses to let it go."

"Yes, he is obsessive," she said. "I heard rumors about other people he kidnapped because he decided they—or their loved ones—could be useful to him."

"How are you useful to him?" Mark asked.

"I'm not. I don't know why he brought me here, except that he hates the way I've always defied him and this is his way of punishing me." She put a hand to the collar.

"I think you're here to influence me," Mark said.

"How can I influence you? We're strangers."

"You're a beautiful young woman. If I don't give Duane what he wants by the deadline he set, you die. No decent human being could be unaffected by that kind of threat."

"I'm not convinced everyone would be so motivated by the threat of a stranger's death."

"Except you're not a stranger to me now. We've made a connection. You're the person who made me feel alive—feel human again—after so many months of isolation."

She looked away. What could she say to that? Except that she felt a connection to him, as well. In some ways, they were very much alike. While he'd been forced to live alone in this remote mountain hideaway, she had kept herself apart from the people around her, afraid her connection with Duane Braeswood might lead to them being harmed.

But she didn't have to protect Mark from that part of her life. In a little over twenty-four hours, he had forced her to lower a barrier she hadn't even realized she had built around herself.

"The only thing that kept me going before now was the thought of keeping my daughter safe," he said. "Maybe they sensed that motivation was weakening the longer I went with no word from her. I don't even know for sure if she's all right."

Erin took his hand, needing the contact as much for herself as to comfort him. "When we get out of here you can find her again. Your brother and the FBI will bring down Duane and you won't have to worry anymore."

He squeezed her hand, holding on tightly. "That's

the new goal. We just have to figure out how to make it happen."

"The next time they bring food," she said, "we'll be ready with the acid."

"It may be a while. In the past when they were angry with me about something, they let me go hungry for a few days as punishment."

"There's a special place in hell for people like them." She reluctantly released his hand and stood. "We might as well eat what they brought."

They settled on a dinner of canned ravioli and applesauce, and ate in silence. As Mark cleared the table she said, her voice low, "When we were talking earlier, I forgot all about the possibility that the guards might be listening to us. Do you really think they have this place bugged?"

He piled their dishes in the sink and ran water over them. "I don't know. I was probably being a little paranoid—a side effect of what has essentially been solitary confinement for over a year. After all, since I've been here by myself, what would they hear? I don't think we really have anything to worry about."

She stood and stretched. "What is it about doing nothing all day that's so exhausting?" she asked, and stifled a yawn.

"The tension gets to you. That, and the fact that there's nothing else to do after dark but sleep. Most days I spend an hour or two working out. It fills the time and I tell myself it's good to keep in shape."

She remembered the feel of his body against hers. He had definitely kept in shape. She glanced toward the bed, and the memory of waking in his arms this morning was so real she could almost feel the warmth of his fingers. "Speaking of sleeping—my offer still stands to bed down on the floor."

He shut off the water and began sponging plates. "That isn't necessary. We can share the bed again. You don't have anything to fear from me."

She wasn't worried about him—not really. But her own strong attraction to him unsettled her. She couldn't say what she might do if he wrapped his arms around her in the darkness again.

Maybe he mistook her silence for disagreement. He dried his hands and turned to face her. "Look, we're both adults," he said. "I don't know about your past relationships, but it's been a long time since I slept with a woman. You're beautiful and I like you and yes, I'm attracted to you. But I'm not going to do anything you don't want."

The look in his eyes sent heat curling through her and she struggled to keep her voice even. "I haven't been involved with anyone in a long time," she said. "And yes, I am attracted to you, too. But I don't think, under the circumstances, that acting on that attraction would be a good idea."

"No, it wouldn't." He crossed his arms over his chest. He had rolled up the sleeves of his shirt and the corded muscles of his forearms stood out. "So are you okay with sharing a bed?"

"Sure." Though she doubted she would get much sleep with him so near.

She helped him finish the dishes, the light outside fading away as they did so. He lit the oil lamp in the center of the table and left the box of matches beside it, then gestured toward the bathroom. "You can go first."

She debated taking a shower, but no telling what water would do to the collar, so she settled for a sponge bath, then brushed her teeth and resigned herself to sleeping in her clothes for a second night. Mark was waiting when she emerged from the bathroom, and slipped in behind her. She removed her shoes and slid under the covers and lay staring at the ceiling until he returned. He blew out the lamp and slid under the blanket beside her.

Though their bodies didn't touch, the heat of him seeped into her, and the subtle scent of him surrounded her—a mixture of shaving cream and lab reagents and male that left her longing to inch toward him. She shifted, trying—and failing—to get comfortable.

"I know it's hard, but try to sleep," he said. "Everything is that much more difficult if you're exhausted."

"They don't ever come in here at night, do they? The guards?" The thought of one of those creeps watching her while she slept made her skin crawl.

"They haven't before. I'm a pretty light sleeper, so I think I'd know."

"Yeah, but I wasn't here before," she said.

"Good point." He slid his arm around her. "I won't let them do anything to you. I promise."

She let herself relax against him. After a moment she moved closer and rested her head on his shoulder. "Is this all right?"

His arm tightened around her. "It's more than all right. Now try to get some sleep."

She felt safe in Mark's arms—safe enough to drift into the most restful sleep she had had in weeks. She was deep in slumber, surrounded by darkness and the warmth and strength of Mark's body against hers, when the blare of a light and a man's shout roused her.

"Get up!" someone ordered.

She shielded her eyes with her hand and tried to see who was speaking. "What?"

"Mr. Braeswood has ordered you moved," the intruder said. "Now get going."

Chapter Six

Heart slamming against her chest, Erin gaped at the three men with guns who had burst into the cabin. An icy breeze swept through the open door behind them, fluttering papers on the workbench and raising goose bumps on her bare arms.

"What are you talking about?" Mark's voice was sharp, and much more alert than she felt.

"You're moving." The beefy guy who had fought with Mark earlier prodded him with the butt of the rifle. "Get up and get dressed to go."

Erin scrambled from the bed before the guard could focus on her, and began pulling on clothes, layering a sweater and her jacket over the T-shirt and jeans she had worn to bed, then shoving her feet into her boots.

Mark dressed, too, also pulling on his coat. The blond guard and the wiry black man who had accompanied him earlier kept watch over them while a third guard lit an oil lamp and began packing the items on the workbench into a cardboard box that had once held vodka. The lamplight reflected off the blond peach fuzz of this younger guard, whose acne-scarred face made him look as if he was scarcely out of his teens.

As Erin came more awake, her fear increased. If she and Mark were being moved, maybe it was to a more secure location. They might be separated. Or maybe Duane's men planned to take them out into the wilderness and shoot them. She had heard rumors once that this was the way he had dealt with one of his followers who had done something to displease him. She caught Mark's eye, trying to telegraph her panic.

His gaze locked to hers and he gave an almost imperceptible nod. A clatter from the workbench made him jerk his head in that direction. "Hey!" His shout made her jump. "What do you think you're doing?"

Before either guard could react, Mark had crossed the room and grabbed the arm of the man who was packing up the lab supplies. "This equipment is delicate and in some cases dangerous," he snapped. "Break anything and you jeopardize everything I've been working on—everything Mr. Braeswood ordered me to do." He yanked the box from the man's hands. "Let me take care of this. You and one of the other men see to that trunk." He indicated the silver metal trunk beneath the bench. "Don't jostle it, and whatever you do, don't drop it. It's the key element in this entire project."

Erin stared at the box, a chill shuddering through her. She hadn't noticed it before. Was it really that dangerous?

The guard stepped back and eyed the trunk warily. "What's in it?" he asked.

Mark focused on rearranging items in the box. "Do you know why I'm here?" he asked.

The guard furrowed his brow. "You're building some sort of secret weapon?"

"A nuclear bomb." He turned to face the guard, one hand on the box beside him. He nodded to the trunk. "I'm almost finished. I won't be to blame if you screw this up."

"Quit wasting time and get moving," the blond guard, who had moved closer to Erin, said.

The young man with Mark shrugged, slung his rifle across his back and bent to pick up the trunk. He grunted and managed to lift it a few inches.

"Get someone to help you!" Mark's voice was sharp with annoyance. "Didn't you hear anything I just said?"

The door was still open, letting in a bitter cold. Erin grabbed the blanket from the bed and wrapped it around her shoulders, though some of the chill that engulfed her came from inside her. What had happened to the calm, stoic man she had come to know? This version of Mark was a crazed mad scientist, exactly the kind of man who would build a nuclear weapon for a maniac. And what was really in that trunk? Had he actually been building Duane's bomb, despite his denials to her?

"Trey, you help move the box." The blond guard indicated the black man, who had positioned himself by the door. "Don't waste any more time."

Trey moved forward to help the younger man with the trunk. The two of them hefted it and shuffled toward the exit. Mark began packing more items from the workbench into the box and the blond guard positioned himself between the two prisoners, his rifle cradled in his arms.

Time, which had been moving forward too quickly up to this point, seemed to slow down as the men with the trunk stepped through the door and onto the porch. The thud of their booted feet on the wooden steps echoed in the middle-of-the-night stillness. The lamp sputtered and Erin pulled the blanket more tightly around her. Mark stood beside the laboratory bench, his hand wrapped around a tall glass beaker. The blond man took a step toward the bench, blocking Erin's view of Mark. She glanced back toward the open door.

"Run!" The command had her moving toward the door before the meaning of the word had fully registered. The blond screamed, an animal howl of rage, and she turned to see him with his hands over his eyes, liquid dripping down his face, the rifle on the floor, almost at her feet. He shouted curses as Mark hurled a now-empty glass beaker at him, then grabbed Erin's hand and dragged her toward the door. She pulled away and scooped up the rifle, then raced with him out onto the front porch.

MARK PAUSED AT the top of the steps, trying to get his bearings. In front of him and a little to the left, light spilled from the open back hatch of a black Humvee, where the other two guards struggled to shove the heavy trunk inside. One of them looked up and shouted, jolting Mark into action once more. Pulling Erin along behind him, he raced past the vehicle and down the rutted track that led away from the cabin.

The thunder of gunfire shattered the night stillness, and shards of rock pelted the legs of his hiking pants. Erin screamed, and he held on to her more tightly. They stumbled along in the dim light of a quarter moon. Bright white patches glowed amid the rocks and he realized with a start that it had snowed recently.

The rev of an engine behind them told him the guards had started the Hummer. "We can't outrun a vehicle," Erin sobbed.

"No. But a vehicle—even a Hummer—can't drive cross-country here." He yanked her off the road and they stumbled and slid down a slope of loose rock. They wove in and out among stunted piñon and junipers, and clusters of boulders like crouching giants silvered in the moonlight.

"I have to stop." Erin pulled him back against one of these boulder formations, her breath coming in ragged gasps.

"Are you okay?" He moved closer to study her face in the moonlight. Her hair was a wild tumble around her face, and the blanket flapped behind her like a cape.

She nodded and swallowed. "Just winded. And scared. What about you?"

"The same." He took a deep breath. "I kept expecting a bullet to slam into my back at any minute."

She clutched his shoulder, fingers digging in hard. "What was that all about back there?" she asked. "All that rage over the lab equipment and the trunk?"

"I wanted to catch them off guard. I've been so passive these past few months, that's what they expect from me. I thought if I stunned them enough, they would agree to do as I asked. After all, they're men who are used to obeying commands."

"You certainly startled me." She still looked wary. "What was really in that trunk?"

"Exactly what I told them—a nuclear bomb. Or

rather, something that looks like a nuclear bomb, minus the fuel or the means of detonation. I built it months ago as a decoy, in case Duane ever pressed me for results. I figured I could show him the trunk and he would believe I had been making a good-faith effort. It's not the suitcase nuke he wanted, but any serious reading on the subject would tell him he was asking the impossible. I wanted to placate him with something that at least looked probable, even if it wasn't the real thing."

"Why would you try to placate someone like him?" she asked, with surprising vehemence.

"Because I would do anything to get away from him and get back to my daughter, or at least to keep him away from her, including acting as if I was as dedicated to his crackpot cause as he is."

Her shoulders sagged. "I'm sorry," she whispered. "I'm so angry at Duane I forget that I'm not the only one he's hurt."

"I don't blame you for being suspicious," Mark said. "After all, you don't really know me."

"No. But I want to trust you. I want to believe you're a man who can be trusted."

Before he could respond to this confession, or even process it, she pushed away from the rock. "We should be going," she said. "They'll be coming after us."

He glanced over his shoulder, but heard no sounds of pursuit. Maybe the guards were being stealthy, but he didn't think they would be at that point yet. "It will be morning before they can see well enough to track us," he said. "We need to use that time to get as far away from the cabin as possible."

"I don't know if I can keep up," she said. "I can't

see where I'm going and I keep stumbling on the rock. Maybe we should split up so I won't slow you down."

"No way," he said. "If not for you, I wouldn't have worked up the nerve to try to get away." He squeezed her arm. "You're doing great. Bringing that blanket was a good idea." They would need all the warmth they could get. Already his fingers were numb and aching.

"I got something better than a blanket," she said.

When she pulled the rifle from beneath the blanket, he could have kissed her.

And then he was kissing her, anxiety and relief and pent-up need driving him to pull her tightly against him and press his lips to hers. She shivered slightly and he stilled, unwilling to move away, but knowing he would if she protested or pushed at him.

Then all the stiffness went out of her and she melted against him, her arms sliding beneath his coat and encircling him, her mouth slanting against his, lips parting slightly so that he tasted her heady sweetness.

He had forgotten how wonderful a woman could feel, how soft and strong, delicate yet powerful, every feminine part of her designed to remind him of what it meant to be a man. She shaped her body to his, and he slid his thigh between hers, her sigh of delight warming him as no fire could.

He slid his hand to her side and knocked the rifle that hung from her shoulder, startling them both. Looking flustered, she jerked away. "I… I didn't mean for that to happen," she stammered. "I just…"

"It's okay." He busied himself zipping up the ski jacket, as if he could somehow keep in the memory of her hands on him. "It happened. It's okay." More than okay.

"We'd better get going," she said. She looked to her left and right—anywhere but at him. "Which way?"

He started to apologize, but he wasn't sorry about the kiss. For now, he'd follow her lead in pretending it had never happened. "We can try to parallel the road as much as possible, but that may not be feasible all the time," he said. He glanced overhead. "How much do you know about navigating by the stars?"

"About as much as I know about nuclear physics," she said. "What about you?"

"Nothing," he admitted.

"I was hoping it was a secret hobby of yours," she said. "Along with gourmet cooking with wild foods and erecting palatial wilderness shelters."

"Sorry to disappoint." He smiled, even though he doubted she could see much of his expression in the dark. He felt so much lighter and freer out here in the open, even though they were far from out of danger. He put his hand on the rifle. "Let me carry this."

She relinquished the weapon. "Do you know how to use it?" she asked.

"I do." And he would, if necessary. He took her hand. "We'll stick close to the road for now," he said. "We should be able to hear anyone coming."

Even walking in the roadway, the going was tough. The twin ruts in the snow were barely visible in the pale moonlight, strewn with loose rock in others. The cold was numbing, slicing through his clothes as if they were made of paper. Even with the blanket wrapped over her thin jacket, Erin must be freezing. They picked their way across an icy stream, then fought to keep their balance on a steep pitch. "I wish I had grabbed a flashlight, too," she said.

"It would be too risky to use it," he said. "I did palm the box of matches while I was pretending to pack the items from the workbench. They're in my pocket, but we ought to save them for starting a fire when we get somewhere safe to do so."

"You sound so confident," she said. "I'm completely out of my element here."

"In the morning we should be able to get our bearings and come up with a plan," he said. "All we have to do until then is focus on staying alive."

"Hiding from crazed killers, not freezing to death and not falling off a cliff. Piece of cake."

"Well, when you put it that—" He broke off the words, tensed. "Did you hear that?"

They listened to the distant growl that grew louder. "It's a vehicle," she said. "Headed this way."

The roar grew much louder as the bright, blue-white beams of headlights swept around the corner. Mark pulled her to the side of the road, where they crouched behind a rock outcropping, out of range, for the moment, of those searching beams. "We've got to get out of here," she said, her voice trembling.

He stared toward the approaching headlights. Behind them, a third beam swept the sides of the road—probably a handheld spotlight. In daylight, he might have a chance of taking out the driver, and maybe one of the other men, but he would never be able to shoot three of them before one disabled him, and probably Erin, as well. With the bright lights blinding him, he didn't have a chance.

"This way," he said, He pulled her around the

outcropping of rock, feeling his way along a narrow ledge. By the time the vehicle crawled past them, they were well behind the screen of rock.

Erin sagged against him as the sound of the engine faded. "Thank God. I was sure they were going to see us."

"They didn't see us." Not this time. They still had an hour or more before daylight to make their way down this mountain toward safety. It wouldn't be easy, but maybe they were past the worst of it now.

Then the ground gave way beneath them and they were sliding and falling, careening down a steep slope, Erin's scream echoing in his ear as she was torn from his grasp.

Chapter Seven

Erin clawed at the ground as she slid over it, rocks and chunks of ice tearing at her skin and catching at her clothes. She bounced and skidded down the slope, grappling for purchase and finding none. She felt, rather than saw, Mark hurtle past her, and realized she was screaming, her throat raw, the sound echoing off the rocks around them.

Then, as suddenly as she had started moving, she stopped, something bulky and soft cushioning the blow of her landing. Somehow, she had landed on Mark. He wrapped his arms around her. “Are you okay?” he asked.

Hearing his voice, knowing he was all right, made her all but sob with relief. “I think so. You?”

“A lot of bruises, but I’m okay.” He sat up, bringing her with him. “I still have the rifle.”

“I lost the blanket,” she said. She peered up the slope, but could make out nothing but lighter and darker gray smudges of rock. “What happened?”

“I think the ledge gave way. We’re lucky we didn’t fall farther.” He stood and helped her to her feet. They had come to rest in a dry wash, choked with rock and shrubby trees. The air smelled of fresh pine and damp earth. Though the sky was beginning to lighten, she could no longer see the road from here. The knowledge of how close they had come to death shook her. "We could have been killed," she said. She touched the collar at her neck — it could have gone off. She swayed, unsteady at the thought.

"We weren't." His voice was strong. "We just have to stay alert. We won't take unnecessary chances, but we won't be so cautious we miss our best opportunity to get out of here."

"Do you think the guards heard us?" she asked.

He glanced overhead, back the way they had come. "I think if they had, we'd know it by now. The snow swallows up a lot of sound. For now, we had better stay put until daylight, when we can see where we're going. We need to get back up to the road and we can't do that in the dark."

She hugged her arms across her chest and shifted from foot to foot. "It feels colder down here. Maybe I'm in shock." Her feet ached with cold, and her fingers and face were numb.

"Canyons like this trap the cold." He picked up a branch that had probably been broken in their fall. "Let's build a fire. That will warm us up."

"Do you think that's safe?"

"We can shelter it under the overhang of the cliff, where it will be harder to see from above. As long as we keep the blaze small, it should be all right. We need to warm up before we go on."

"Good idea." She moved alongside him, gathering kindling.

"Are you feeling okay?" he asked. "No dizziness or unsteadiness?"

"I'm okay." She picked up a large pinecone. "Maybe I just needed to move around." She would take his advice and not think about what had almost happened, and focus instead on what she wished would happen. She would envision warm rooms, hot food and people around her who weren't trying to kill her.

When they had gathered a double armload of kindling and larger pieces of wood, he cleared a space on the frozen ground and set about building a fire. He worked quickly, his hands deftly arranging the smaller sticks and larger pieces of wood. He lit a match and touched it to the mixture of pine needles and pocket lint he had piled beneath a pyramid of twigs. The flame caught and spread, licking at the sticks until they, too, were ablaze.

"You look like you've done this before," she said, moving to stand closer to the warmth, and thus to him.

"I always did my best thinking in the wilderness."

"What are your best thoughts now?"

He didn't answer right away, the snap of the fire the only sound. "I'm thinking that I'm glad I'm not doing this alone," he said after a moment.

The desolation in his voice pinched at her. She had endured only a few weeks of deprivation thanks to Duane. Mark had been the madman's pawn for fourteen months. "You've been alone too much lately," she said.

He sat back on his heels and stared into the fire, the shadows of the flames flickering across the planes and hollows of his face. It wasn't a classically handsome face, but his strong jaw and high forehead hinted at his strength and intelligence. "I'm not someone who tolerates the company of others well," he said. "Though I make exceptions for people I care about."

Was he saying he cared about her? She pushed the thought away. "Why do you think they decided to move us?"

"I want to hear your theory before I share mine."

"I wondered if they heard us talking about our plans to get away and decided to preempt them."

He nodded. "That's what I wondered, too. But it could have just as easily been part of Duane's original plan, to keep us off guard."

"Do you think they're still looking for us?" she asked. "I mean, maybe now that they have that trunk and what they think is a bomb, Duane will be happy and let us go."

"A man who will go to the kind of trouble and expense he has in order to carry out a plan he's concocted isn't going to just drop things," Mark said. "And he doesn't let people get away with crossing him, either."

"No." She ran a finger under the edge of the collar. "No, he doesn't." She was a prime example of what happened to people who crossed Duane. He never simply forgot about them and let them go. She lowered herself to the ground beside the fire. As her body thawed, her mind became less numb, too. "Can they do anything with the contents of that trunk?" she asked. "I mean, could they find another scientist or explosives expert to build them a real nuclear bomb?" Knowing the trunk even existed had come as a shock to her.

Mark sat on the ground beside her, and fed a larger stick to the blaze. "It's doubtful. Given more time and money and higher grade ore, it might happen, but Duane strikes me as a man who's running out of patience."

"I think you're right, and that worries me. He has a lot of resources, and from what I've seen, he doesn't mind throwing lots of money and man power at whatever goal he's after. What if he brings in dogs to track us? Or follows us with a helicopter?"

"He might do those things, but the fall could work in our favor. The searchers won't expect to find us down here. That could throw them off the track. We need to take advantage of whatever lead we've gained."

"It would help if we had the slightest idea where we are." She craned her head to scan the embankment they had slid down. Boulders the size of furniture and logs scattered like straw pocked the landscape.

"I'm pretty sure this drainage runs north-south." He pointed to the heavy growth of moss on the side of a tree near them. "Moss like this tends to grow on the north side of trees. The road ran that direction, too, so I think we're paralleling the road, but about fifty feet lower."

"So we keep following this and we'll get to wherever the road leads?" she asked.

"Maybe. Or we could end up in a box canyon that goes nowhere." He joined her in looking up the slope. "As I said before, I think we're going to have to climb back up there."

She swallowed. "And to think I left my mountain-climbing gear at home."

He caught her gaze and held it. "I'm glad you still have your sense of humor. Things could get pretty tough before we get out of here. But we're going to be tougher."

Right. Except that with him she felt more vulnerable than she had in years—since before Duane had come into her life and distorted everything she knew about love and trust. "Do you know what frightens me the most?" she asked.

"No, but I'm willing to listen if you want to tell me."

She stared into the coals that glowed orange amid the remnants of branches white with ash. "I'm terrified that I missed my chance to stop him," she said. "When I first left home I didn't tell anyone the things I knew—and the things I suspected—about Duane's activities, because I worried about what it would do to my mother. I thought if I kept quiet, she would be all right and I could forget all about him. When she came to live with me I suggested we go to the authorities, but the idea upset her so much I didn't pursue it. These last few weeks with him and his men—learning the extent of his madness and the lengths he will go to in order to carry out his twisted plans—I realize how much my silence has cost. What if he finds someone to arm that bomb and he kills hundreds, even thousands, of innocent people? How can I live with the knowledge that I could have stopped him, but when I had the chance I chose to do nothing?"

"You were afraid for yourself, but even more frightened for your mother," Mark said. "Believe me, I know how paralyzing that kind of fear can be. It's the same fear that kept me working in that cabin for months. Duane bought my silence with his threats to my daughter, but in the end the cost was much greater.

I lost my perspective and I almost lost my will to go on. You've given that back to me. Now I realize the only way I can protect Mandy is to fight back against the vision of the world that Duane wants to make a reality." He reached over and took her hand. "It helps me to know I'm not fighting alone. And I think we have an advantage over Duane."

"We're not insane. I suppose that helps."

A ghost of a smile flitted through his eyes before he sobered once more. "He thinks we're both passive, cowed by what he's done to us. He's guilty of one of the primary errors in scientific research—making a false assumption. He's expecting one result—for us to fail—and has an unconscious bias to pay more attention to any evidence that supports his assumption. We can take advantage of that and attack him when he's not expecting it."

Everything Mark said made perfect sense, and Erin found herself believing he might be right. But the reality of their situation—stranded in the middle of nowhere in bitter cold, with a bomb strapped around her neck—made it more difficult to visualize the success he seemed so sure was theirs. She took a deep breath. "I guess the first thing we need to do is get out of this ravine."

"Right." He glanced at the sky. Though low clouds obscured the sun, it was now light enough to see clearly. He stood and began to kick dirt onto the fire. "It won't be the easiest climb, but it's doable. We'll take it slow and choose the route carefully. You go first and I'll be right behind to catch you if you start to fall."

She helped him put out the fire and scatter the

ashes, even as she mourned the loss of warmth. As they worked, the cold was already seeping through her clothes, making her teeth chatter. They swept branches over the area and scattered gravel, trying to obscure any obvious signs that they had stopped here. Then Mark turned to survey the slope they had to climb. "It's a little less steep there, where that gravel has washed down." He traced a line in the air and she followed the direction he was pointing. "Those trees and bushes will give us hand- and footholds," he said. "And the overhang, just to the right, gives us some cover while we check things out up top."

"Right. Piece of cake." She rubbed her hands together. "You go that way and I'll find the elevator."

He chuckled and put a hand at her back. She liked the way it felt, his palm pressed to her spine, providing both guidance and reassurance. They stopped at the bottom of the area he had indicated, which didn't look any less steep to her. "Grab hold of that branch and put your foot on that tree root, then pull yourself up," he instructed.

Proceeding this way, with him directing her from behind, the climb wasn't so bad. She managed to push away the image of her falling and sending them both crashing back down, and focused on carefully placing each foot and using her hands to haul herself up. Before she had traveled too many feet she was panting and beginning to sweat, her earlier chill forgotten.

The trouble began about halfway up, when a narrow stream of cold water, perhaps from some underground spring, trickled down the bank, turning the soil in the area to slick mud. When Erin tried to plant her foot, it skidded from under her, and only her death grip on a spindly scrub oak kept her from hurtling back down the slope.

Mark was at her back once more. “Try digging your toe in and kicking in a step,” he said.

She did as he suggested and after three hard kicks was rewarded with a firmer foothold. She proceeded this way up the rest of the slope, until she came to rest under the sheltering overhang of a rock outcropping. She was winded, her hands aching from gripping the cold, slippery branches and rocks that had served as hand- and footholds. Her hands, face and clothing were streaked with a reddish mud that smelled slightly metallic and felt gritty against her skin.

Mark joined her beneath the rock overhang after a few minutes. He looked as disheveled and dirty as she felt, but a grin split his face. “I haven’t climbed like that in months,” he said. “It felt good.”

She couldn’t help but return the smile. “It does feel good.” She’d won a battle of sorts—against the steep slope and against her own fears. “What next?”

“Let’s wait here a bit and catch our breath and see if we hear anything alarming up there.”

But the only sounds to break the early morning stillness were the deep intake and exhalation of their own breaths, the trickle from the dripping spring, and the lonesome call of a dove.

“I think we’re okay.” Mark spoke in a whisper, his mouth close to her ear, his warm breath tickling her neck above the metal collar, sending a startling current of heat through her. “I’ll go first, then I can pull you up,” he said, shifting to move past her.

A tremble shot through her when his body brushed hers. She told herself it was simply the aftereffect of adrenaline from the climb, but the word *liar* came quickly on the heels of that thought. This strong, virile version of a man she was already attracted to stirred a more primitive desire deep within her. Mark Renfro might be an overly serious scientist, but right now he was a very sexy scientist.

She pressed her body against the cool earth and listened to the scrape of rock against his boots and the soft grunts of exertion he made as he swung onto the ledge from which they had fallen earlier. She didn't even realize she had been holding her breath until she heard his voice again and saw his hand reaching down for her. "All clear," he said. "Hold on tight and I'll pull you up."

Half climbing, half letting him lift her, she struggled onto the ledge and lay for a moment in the dirt, panting. He helped her to her feet and led the way along a narrow path that must have been made by animals. From time to time she caught a glimpse of the road, but the landscape around them remained silent. Maybe Duane's men had temporarily abandoned the search and were awaiting further instructions from their boss. Or maybe they had headed off in another direction.

All we need is a little more time, she thought. *As soon as we get to a phone, we'll be all right.*

They walked for the better part of an hour without speaking. The sun disappeared completely behind a bank of heavy clouds and the wind picked up, cutting through Erin's jacket and jeans. She hugged her arms across her chest and bowed against the wind, gritting her teeth to keep them from chattering. She ached with the cold, and stumbled once, almost colliding with Mark, who marched stoically along in front of her. He had to be almost as chilled as she was, but he showed no signs of it, walking confidently upright, the rifle slung across his chest. Knowing he was watching for any sign of trouble, she was able to relax a little. *Think warm thoughts*, she told herself. *Hot chocolate. Mulled wine. Chicken soup. Roaring fires and warm quilts. Naked bodies twined together beneath those quilts, in front of that fire...*

A shout broke the stillness—a man's voice, risen in alarm. Mark dived to the side of the trail, pulling her with him, even as gunfire raked the area where they had just stood. She pressed against him, trying to make herself as small as possible. "How did they find us so soon?" she whispered.

He shook his head, his hands gripping her shoulders, holding her tightly to him. "I don't know, but they aren't that close. The shots came from somewhere on the ridge to our left. He must have spotted us and fired from there."

"If you're trying to reassure me, it's not working. With that rifle, he doesn't have to be close in order to kill us."

"Point taken. But if we can keep from getting shot, we have a better chance of evading them at this distance. It will take them a while to get to this trail. By the time they do, we'll be gone."

"But he has us pinned down."

"Not necessarily. He may not have seen where we ended up."

"Don't make assumptions, Professor."

"Then let's perform a little experiment." Before she could object, he picked up a rock about the size of his fist, wound up and fired it out of their hiding place. It landed with a clatter fifty feet up the trail and bounced twice before coming to rest at the base of a tree. A split second later bullets thudded into the tree, sending splinters flying. Mark grinned.

"What are you so happy about?" she asked.

"He didn't fire at us. He didn't see where the rock came from. He was only reacting to the movement and sound. We can use that to our advantage."

"How?"

"We'll head that way." He pointed down the trail, back toward the cabin. "If we move slowly and keep to the cover of the trees, he shouldn't see us."

"But it's the wrong direction," she said.

"When they give up and start moving in another direction we can backtrack," he said. "Right now it's more important to get away from them than to stick to our goal."

He was right, of course, but that didn't make this knowledge any easier to accept. At this rate she'd be frozen or crippled by the time they reached safety. Better to swallow the bitter medicine and get on with it. "I'll follow you," she said.

He slipped through the narrow line of trees and shrubs between the road and their trail with the stealth of a cat burglar. She followed, trying to place her steps where he had placed his, trusting that his instincts were better than hers when it came to moving through the wilderness. She collided with his back when he stopped suddenly, frozen like a deer in the headlights. "What is it?" she whispered. "What's wrong?"

"This is where we fell before," he said. "The whole ledge collapsed, remember? There's no way to cross."

The feeling of falling was fresh enough to make her heart pound. She turned away. “Then we have to go back,” she said. Not waiting for him to answer, she moved forward, her steps more sure now, covering familiar territory. Whoever had been shooting at them up on the ridge had held his fire for several minutes now. She prayed he wasn’t training a pair of binoculars—or a rifle scope—on them right this minute, preparing to fire the bullet that would end this whole crazy game Duane had forced them to play.

Mark caught up with her. “Let me go first,” he said.

“No, I’ve got this.” She walked faster. Relying on Mark to always take the lead had been a mistake. She had to force herself past this paralyzing fear.

The first shots exploded above and behind them. Erin couldn’t hold back her scream, and terror propelled her forward. She ran blindly, branches lashing her face and arms, feet slipping on loose rock. She didn’t know if Mark followed, or even if their unseen pursuers fired more shots. Fear made her blind and deaf to anything but her own pounding heart and her need to get away.

She had no idea how long she had been running when she tripped and landed hard on her knees, rocks tearing her jeans and bloodying her hands. Sobbing, she slumped in the dirt, braced for the bullets she was sure would come.

Instead, strong arms embraced her, then lifted her and carried her deeper into the undergrowth. “Shh. It’s okay. You’re going to be okay.” He repeated the words over and over, a soothing mantra that eventually slowed her heart and beat back the wave of terror that had crowded out reason. When she was finally able to open her eyes and lift her head from his shoulder, she stared into eyes dark with concern. "What happened?" she asked.

"You panicked. It could have happened to anyone."

She sniffed. "I know I panicked. I mean, what happened to the man who was shooting at us?"

Mark shook his head. "I don't know. Maybe you outran his field of vision. Or he was too far away to clearly see what was happening. Or your guardian angel is working overtime."

"I'm sorry." She tried to pull away, but he held her gently but firmly to him. "My stupidity could have killed us both."

"You weren't stupid," he said. "You were scared. I know the difference."

"I don't know what came over me." She forced herself to meet his gaze. "You should have run while you had the chance."

"I'm not going to leave you." He shook her gently. "I know a little bit about post-traumatic stress," he said. "I think that's what you're suffering from."

"What are you talking about? I never fought in a war."

"But you did. You've been at war for years with Duane and your own conscience. That's bound to take a toll."

She rested her forehead against Mark's and closed her eyes once more. "I'm just so tired of being afraid all the time."

"I understand. I really do."

She believed he did. He had endured his own hell of wondering and waiting for the other shoe to drop, not knowing when Duane would tire of his games and decide to kill him, or his daughter. Of all the people in this world, Mark knew a little of what she had been through. For whatever reason, his newfound freedom had given him courage, while hers had allowed all the feelings she had been avoiding for too long to overwhelm her. But knowing he understood gave her strength, too.

"Maybe the worst is over," she said.

"Even if it's not, we'll get through this," he said. "Together."

As her shaking subsided and the panic receded, a new wave of unsettling sensations stole over her. Heat from his body warmed her. The brush of his muscular arm sent a tremor through her. The desire to be away from this place and this situation faded, replaced by a different longing that was just as fierce—to be even closer to him. His arms tightened around her and she met his gaze once more. Her heart felt too big for her chest as she recognized the same wanting in his eyes.

His gaze shifted to her mouth, and she lifted her chin, angling toward him. If he didn't kiss her right now she wouldn't be able to stand it. She slid one hand up to cup the back of his head, threading her fingers into his thick dark hair and urging him toward her.

He let out a sound that was half sigh, half groan, and covered her lips with his. The last bit of frost melted from her bones as he skillfully teased her mouth, the silk of his tongue and the roughness of his beard setting every nerve ending humming. She trailed her hand along his jaw, reveling in the masculine feel of his unshaved face. How had she ever mistaken him for a passive, even weak, academic?

The man in the lab coat had merely been a disguise for his true role of rugged outdoorsman.

They broke apart at last, both panting and dazed. "Lousy timing for this," he said, his voice rough. He glanced at the woods around them and the reality of the situation crashed over her once more. She moved out of his embrace and wrapped her arms around herself, though his warmth still enveloped her. "Yeah. Lousy timing." Running from killers wasn't the best time to give in to her attraction to this man. How much of her feelings were due to fear, and how much were genuine?

"You look cold," he said. "Why don't we build another fire and try to get warm?"

"The smoke could attract the wrong kind of attention," she said.

"We won't stay long," he said. "Just long enough to thaw the worst of the chill." He flexed his fingers. "I can't feel my hands anymore."

The prospect of warmth won out over her fear of discovery. "All right. A fire would be good."

He patted her shoulder. "You find some kindling and I'll get some bigger wood."

Keeping Mark within sight, she searched the ground for the dried twigs and pinecones they had used to build their fire earlier. Beneath the overhang of a leaning juniper she spotted a pile of shredded bark—perhaps a nest made by some kind of animal. In any case, the dry material would be the perfect fire starter.

She ducked under the branches and began to gather up the bark, folding up the hem of her shirt to form a carrying pouch. Nearby she could hear Mark walking around, getting the other fire materials ready. “I’ve found some great stuff here,” she said. “We can get the fire going quick.”

“There’s not going to be any fire,” said a deep voice behind her, and a beefy hand closed over her arm.

Chapter Eight

A woman's scream rose above the staccato report of gunfire, freezing Mark in his tracks. He dropped the armful of wood he had gathered and looked over his shoulder in the direction of the sound. Erin struggled with Cantrell beneath the branches of a leaning juniper, looking small and fragile in the big man's grasp. Mark turned to go to her, but bullets thudded into the trunk of a pine tree inches from his face, splinters and the sharp scent of pitch filling the air. He jolted forward, animal instinct driving him to flee as more gunfire erupted around him, so close he heard the whistle of bullets past his ears.

He ran until his lungs burned and pain stabbed his side. The gunfire had long since ceased, but he still imagined someone pursuing him. Ducking behind a many-branched juniper, he bent at the waist, hands on his knees, fighting for breath. His ragged breathing competed with the sigh of wind in the branches overhead as the only sounds in this part of the woods. If anyone still pursued him, they did so stealthily.

The memory of Erin struggling with Cantrell taunted him. Why hadn't he stayed and fought for her? He still had the rifle. If he had stopped and studied the situation more closely he might have found a way to help her, instead of fleeing like a coward.

Maybe a trained soldier wouldn't have run from someone firing at them, but he was only a scientist. The thought did nothing to assuage his guilt. Now that he was safe, he knew he had to go back. He wouldn't leave Erin alone to suffer whatever punishment those thugs dealt out.

Cantrell and the others wouldn't expect him to return. They thought of him as weak and passive. He had done exactly what they had expected of him: he had run away. They would believe themselves safe now, since he posed no threat.

He hefted the rifle and checked that there was a bullet in the chamber, ready to fire. He wished he had an extra magazine. The one he had was oversize, capable of holding thirty bullets, only two of which were missing. In a firefight he wouldn't last long, but if he had to fire off only a couple of rounds…

He didn't have to ask himself if he could kill another human being. To protect Erin, he would do what he had to. After all, Cantrell and the other guards wouldn't think twice about killing him. They had told him so many times.

He moved east, toward where he believed the road must be. After fifteen minutes of bushwhacking through thick undergrowth he reached the narrow track, where dirt and rocks showed through the snow. Then he headed back the way he had run. Cantrell and his companion must have parked on this road before pursuing Erin and Mark into the woods. They wouldn't expect him to be waiting for them when they returned to their vehicle.

He spotted the Hummer much sooner than he had expected, parked in the middle of the road like a hulking black beast. There was scarcely room on the cliff side to open the passenger door, while the driver had less than a foot of roadway to maneuver on before a steep drop-off. Mark paused fifty feet away, hiding in the underbrush along the side of the road, watching the Hummer, but in five minutes of waiting he saw no signs of life around it.

He approached cautiously, rifle at the ready. He tried the driver's door and found it unlocked, but the guards had taken the key with them and he saw nothing of interest on the seats or floorboards. He shut the door gently and turned his attention to the front left tire. Kneeling beside it, he fished the nail scissors from his pocket. They were old-fashioned and sturdy, the blades dull from use but coming together in a needle-sharp point. He grasped the handles and drove the point into the tire, using all his force and burying it all the way to the looped handles.

At first he feared the scissors weren't long enough to do any real damage, but then he heard the satisfying hiss of air escaping and the tire began to deflate.

He moved to the other front tire, intending to work his way around to all four tires, but a high-pitched keening stayed his hand. He jerked his head up in time to see movement in the undergrowth on the other side of the car. Scuttling like a crab, he retreated down the road and into the trees, positioning himself so that he was well concealed, but still had a clear view of the parked vehicle. Within seconds he caught a glint of auburn hair, and then Erin stumbled forward, Cantrell close behind her. The other guard—the young kid who had started packing the lab supplies at the cabin, flanked them on the left.

"Help! Someone help me!" Erin screamed.

Cantrell's slap snapped her head back and left a red imprint against her pale cheek. "Shut up!" he ordered. "Nobody can hear you out here anyway." He dragged her toward the car.

"What are you going to do with me?" she asked, her voice strained.

"Not what I'd like to do, that's for sure," Cantrell said.

The younger guard moved past them toward the vehicle. "We got a problem," he called back over his shoulder as he neared the Hummer.

"What is it?" Cantrell asked, still holding tight to Erin.

"Flat tire." The younger guard gestured toward the sagging front end. "We must have driven over a nail or something."

"Then get busy and change it."

The young man shrugged, then slung the rifle over one shoulder and walked around to the back of the vehicle and opened the hatch. While he retrieved the jack, lug wrench and spare tire, Cantrell pushed Erin down onto a log. "Sit," he ordered.

She sat, and glared up at him. Her face was deathly pale, except for the bright red imprint of Cantrell's hand. Mark studied the guard through the gun sight and wondered what his chances were of hitting the man from here. Then Cantrell moved to join his coworker at the rear of the Hummer. "We've got some rope back here somewhere," he said. "I'm going to tie her up before she can cause any more trouble." He glanced over at Erin again. "Don't even think about trying to run away. I won't hesitate to shoot you." He patted the stock of the rifle he held. "And I'm a really good shot."

The younger man carried the spare tire and other items to the front of the car and began to work on the flat while Cantrell continued to rummage in the rear of the vehicle. Now, while neither was close to Erin, would be Mark's best opportunity to surprise them without hurting her. With agonizing slowness, he crept closer, placing each foot with ultimate care in order to keep from making a sound.

He was less than ten yards from Cantrell when the guard straightened. "Found it," he said, holding up a coil of thin rope. "Now I'm going to deal with you."

He took a step toward Erin, but it was his last step. Mark fired and red bloomed in the man's chest. He stumbled backward, clutching at the wound, then dropped to his knees and pitched over in the snow. Mark swiveled toward the other guard, who gripped his weapon and looked around wide-eyed. Mark's shot caught him in the thigh, making him stagger. The young man dived off the road, into the ravine below.

Erin jumped up and looked around. "Over here!" Mark shouted, and motioned to her. She spotted him and started walking toward him, then running. He took her arm and urged her forward, adrenaline lending strength to his movements.

They ran wildly, not caring about the noise they made, crashing through the forest. They didn't stop until they reached a small clearing, where the bright sunlight streaming down seemed almost disconcerting after the darkness of the woodland. Mark stopped on the other side of the clearing and looked back. The woods were completely still, giving no indication of pursuit.

"Do you think they'll come after us?" she asked, sagging against a tree beside him, chest heaving as she gasped for breath.

"Not right away. I'm pretty sure the first guy I shot—Cantrell—is dead, and the other one is injured. The car is out of commission, at least until they change that tire. It will take a while for the young guy to regroup and get word to the others."

"They'll keep looking," she said.

"Yes." Mark turned to her. "Are you okay?"

"I don't know. I mean yes, I'm not hurt, and I'm still alive. That's something."

He touched the mark on her face, which was beginning to fade. "When he hit you, I wanted to make him pay. I never thought of myself as a killer, but..."

She grasped his wrist. "You're not a killer. You did what you had to do to save us. You know either one of them would have killed both of us without even blinking."

"You're right." But that didn't mean he wouldn't have nightmares about taking another life. "Come on." He straightened. "We have to keep moving. We still have a long way to go before we're safe."

"How far do you think?" she asked.

He didn't want to tell her they probably had many miles to go. She already looked to be on her last legs. "We'll probably be there by tomorrow," he said. "If we can keep paralleling the road."

"Tomorrow?" She seemed near tears.

"We'll find a safe place to spend the night," he said.

Right now, even more than food, they needed rest and a break from the constant stress. Maybe they could find a cave, or an old mine shaft. Anything to get out of the wind and try to let their bodies recover a little.

ERIN TRUDGED ALONG behind Mark, all her efforts focused on putting one foot in front of the other. As they moved through the woods, they tried to keep the road in sight, since it was the only sure way down the mountain. Every few minutes a shudder ran through her and she looked back over her shoulder, expecting to see one of Duane's men coming after her.

Maybe Mark was right and she was suffering from a kind of PTSD. Maybe that even explained why her mother insisted on staying with Duane. Erin didn't see how anyone could love a man who was so intent on destroying others. But what did she know about love? She had never been married, or even had a serious lover.

"What first attracted you to your wife?" she asked Mark.

He glanced at her, his surprise at the question evident. "What do you mean?"

"What was it about her that made you want to be with her?" she asked. "Out of all the female students and women you worked with that you encountered every day, what made her the one you wanted for your wife?"

"She was beautiful, and very different from me. And she pursued me." He stepped over a fallen branch. "I never would have worked up the nerve to ask her out first."

"Was that important—that she be different from

you?" Erin asked. "I always thought the things people had in common brought them together."

"I told you before—I'm not good at relationships. I'm too impatient with other people, too inward focused—selfish, really."

He hadn't been impatient with her. And he had risked his life to turn back and save her, not the act of a selfish man. "You're thoughtful and intelligent," she said. "You don't strike me as a man who acts rashly. That's not the same as being selfish."

"Christy wasn't like me. She was outgoing. Generous. She reveled in luxury. When we married she said my decorating style was 'dorm room aesthetic.' She turned our home into a warm retreat. I appreciated those things about her, even if I didn't always understand her."

Erin caught the wistful note in his voice. "I didn't mean to make you sad," she said. "I'm only trying to understand what brings a couple together. My mother always says she loves Duane, but I can't understand how that could be possible."

"People who knew me and my wife probably wondered what we were doing together," he said. "She could have had any man on campus that she wanted. For whatever reason, she chose me."

Maybe that was all love really was, Erin thought. Two people who needed each other. Mark had found a woman who overlooked his reticence and she had gained the home and security she craved. No wonder Erin had never had a serious relationship. She had spent most of her life learning to not need anyone.

"When we get out of here, I'm going to tell the police everything I know about Duane and his followers," she said. "Even if it means hurting my mother, I can't let him keep escalating his bizarre plans. Next time he might find a less ethical scientist to work for him."

"Yes. We have to make sure there's no next time."

"I won't let him capture me again, either," she said. "I couldn't bear it." The murderous look in the guard's eyes when he had slapped her would haunt her for a long time to come.

"We won't let him get to us again," Mark said. "I'll fight with everything I have to keep that from happening." He glanced at her. "But I really think the worst of our ordeal is over. We've got a big head start on the guards who were hunting us, and it's going to take them a while to regroup."

She wanted desperately to believe him, to believe they were almost safe again. She was about to say as much when something soft and wet hit her cheek. She wiped away the moisture. "I guess things can get worse after all," she said, then bit her bottom lip to keep from bursting into tears or hysterical laughter.

"What are you talking about?" Mark asked.

"It's snowing." She looked up, and the swirl of white looked like a lace curtain settling over them. "We don't have to worry about Duane and his men finding us. We're going to freeze to death first."

Chapter Nine

The snow fell wet and heavy, melting on their clothes and bare skin. The clouds had foretold a storm all morning, but knowing it was coming hadn't really prepared them for the onslaught. Mark shoved his hands in the pockets of his jacket and hunched his shoulders against the icy wind and damp flakes. Erin huddled against him, her teeth chattering. "This snow just might save us," he said. "The guards will have a harder time following us, and it will cover our tracks."

"They might have a harder time following, but we're going to have a harder time moving, too." She tilted her head back to look up at the gray sky, snowflakes drifting down over her.

"Come on." He put a hand to her back. "We'd better get moving. That will warm us up, too." Though already he could feel the damp chill settling in.

They kept to the edge of the road, pausing often to listen for the rumble of engines or nearby voices. But a deep, muffling silence had descended with the snow, which fell in a white curtain, already almost obscuring the road, and settling in clumps on the bushes and trees around them. "Do you remember how long you traveled on this road after you turned off the highway when they brought you here?" Mark asked.

"I think we were on a series of roads like this for a while," she said. "I remember a lot of bouncing around over rough ground and a lot of turns or curves. But I was blindfolded and disoriented, so I can't be sure. I thought they were taking me out in the wilderness to kill me, or to abandon me and leave me for dead."

The tremor in her voice made Mark tighten his hands into fists. If he did nothing else once he was free, he would see that Duane Braeswood paid for the suffering he had caused Erin and others like her.

"Did you ever hike in this area before?" she asked as they negotiated a narrow passage around a grouping of boulders.

"Nothing around here looks familiar," he said. "I think we're farther south than I ever ventured. Old mining claims like the one we were on are all over the place in that part of the state. People use them as summer retreats, but the roads don't get much use in the winter."

"Too bad for us. If we could flag down a tourist, they would probably have a cell phone we could use."

"Phones might not work up here," he said. "I haven't seen any cell towers and companies don't have much incentive to build them in an area with so few people."

"Then I'd settle for a ride in some tourist's car to a town with working phones and police."

"I guess it doesn't hurt to dream," he said.

They fell silent again, only the sounds of their breathing or the occasional shifting rocks beneath their feet disturbing the winter stillness. Had the guards stopped their search, or moved to another area? Or were they even now scanning with infrared scopes, looking for the moving outlines of heat amid the cold that would give away their position?

"We're going to have to risk walking on the road for a while," he said when they came to a section with a wall of rock on one side and a drop-off on the other. "We'll duck back into the woods as soon as we can."

She said nothing, but followed as he dropped down onto the road, discernible only as a flat, white track alongside the cliff, the dirt surface completely obscured by an ever-deepening carpet of white. They rounded a curve and something darted from the rocks ahead. Erin's hand tightened on his arm, then she relaxed. "That rabbit scared me half to death," she said.

He looked down at the rifle, which he had instinctively brought into firing position. "No one could blame us for being jumpy," he said. He scanned the area, trying to make out anything unusual in the whiteness. They moved forward again, though he kept both hands on the rifle, ready to fight for his life and hers.

Behind him, Erin stumbled. "What the…?"

He turned. "Are you all right?"

"I'm fine." She held up a round, red reflector on the end of a three-foot long rod. "I tripped over this. Why do you think it's up here?"

"Maybe it's marking a culvert or some other hazard." He moved toward her, scanning the area.

"I've seen these at the ends of people's driveways." She started to toss the marker aside, but he took it from her, his heart thudding at her words.

"I think that's exactly why this is here," he said.

"Marking a driveway leading to one of those mining claims I told you about." He scanned the roadside and spotted the opening in the trees. Only about eight feet across, the space was cleared of trees and brush and dipped down below the level of the road. "Come on." He took her arm and pulled her toward the drive.

She dug in and refused to move. "Where are we going?"

"If it is a claim, it might have a cabin," he said. "We need shelter to warm up, and they might have food, too."

"You just said the magic words. Let's go."

They stumbled down the steep, narrow track, snow falling hard enough now to obscure their vision and slow their progress. But at least the storm would cover their tracks. Mark had taken the reflector with him. If Duane's men didn't already know about this place, they weren't likely to find it now.

"I don't see any cabin," Erin said when they had traveled about a hundred yards. They were well below the level of the road now, out of sight of anyone passing by.

"This drive has to lead to something," he said. Maybe they would find only someone's campsite, or an old mine dump. But at this point, when he could no longer feel his fingers or feet, he would settle for any kind of temporary shelter. If they didn't get warm soon, they risked frostbite. And spending the night in this storm meant the real possibility of freezing to death.

They trudged on, the track gradually leveling out. Then he spotted the cabin ahead. Painted a dull green and almost obscured by trees as it was, he might have walked right past if he hadn't been so intent on searching for it. "Is that what I think it is?" Erin asked, stopping beside him.

"Let's go find out."

The cabin was even smaller than the one where he had been held prisoner, and looked much older, the paint dulled by weather and streaked with moss. Heavy wooden shutters covered the windows, and a stout padlock secured the door. They walked all around the building, but Mark couldn't see a way inside.

Erin hugged her arms across her chest and stamped her feet, visibly shivering. "Can we break in?" she asked.

"I could shoot off that lock, but the sound of gunfire carries a long way," he said. "It could lead Duane's men right to us."

"What about the windows?" She looked around them. "There must be some way to pry off those shutters."

He spotted a shed a short distance away. It proved to be a combination outhouse and woodshed. Far in the back, he found an ax, the blade red with rust. Hefting it, he returned to the cabin. "Stand back," he said. "I'm going to try to wedge the blade under one of the shutters."

He moved to the back of the house, so the damage wouldn't be visible to anyone approaching down the drive. He found a gap at one corner of a wooden barrier, inserted the blade and put all his weight into pulling back on the ax. The wood gave way with a groan he hoped was muffled by the storm. Working the blade along the edge, he managed to pry away the entire shutter.

Erin tried to shove up the window sash, but it refused to budge. “It’s stuck.”

He peered over her shoulder. “I think it’s nailed shut.” He pointed to the heads of large nails visible on the inside sill.

She muttered a curse and pounded her fist against the window. “I don’t want to steal anything, people,” she said. “I just want to get warm.”

Mark hefted the ax once more. “Stand back. I’m going to break the glass.”

The pane shattered into dozens of shards that glittered on the snow before the fast-falling flakes obscured them. Mark wrapped his hand in his jacket and knocked out the remaining shards, then reached in and managed to grab hold of the nail head. He pulled and the nail slid out. Erin stared. “How did you do that?”

“It was probably designed to come out so whoever lived here could open the window for ventilation,” he said. “Let me get the others.” The remaining nails also slid out with little protest. Mark turned back to Erin. “Come on. I’ll boost you inside, then I’ll climb in after you.”

THE CABIN SMELLED of dust and rodents. Erin tried not to think of all the mice—or worse—that might be living here as she moved away from the faint light streaming through the uncovered window, into the dark interior. She stumbled against something and felt along the back of a sofa, then turned to see Mark climb in after her. He was still carrying the ax, and leaned it against the wall beneath the window.

"We need to find a light," she said.

He lit a match, which illuminated grim surroundings—a sofa so faded the pattern of the upholstery was indiscernible, two wooden bunks along one side wall and a table and two chairs along the other wall. A two-burner camp stove and a metal bucket sat on the table and above that hung a wooden box with assorted canned goods, the labels worn and faded. Next to the canned goods sat a camping lantern. Mark crossed to this and lit it, the golden glow making Erin feel a little less desolate, if not any warmer.

A large, shallow box of sand occupied the middle of the room. Erin studied it. "Someone's idea of a cat box?" she asked.

"Probably for a woodstove." Mark pointed to a square of galvanized tin tacked to the ceiling. "That's probably covering where the stovepipe exited the room."

"Just our luck the stove is gone." She dragged one finger through the layer of dust on the table. "I don't think anyone has been here in a long time," she said.

"No. But that's something in our favor, I think." He slid the rifle from his shoulder and set it beside the ax beneath the window. "Let's find something to plug this broken pane."

She unearthed a towel from a box beside the bunks and he stuffed it in the broken window, blocking the draft, though the cabin remained cold. "I'm tempted to start chopping up chairs and build a fire anyway," she said.

He moved to the end of the bunks and pulled off a rolled-up sleeping bag. "Bundle up in this while I check out the canned goods," he said. "If there's propane for the camp stove, we can at least have something hot to eat."

She unzipped the sleeping bag and shook it out, grateful to see no signs of mice. Wrapping it around her, she settled on the sofa and watched as he sorted through the cans on the shelf above the table. "Beef stew, chili or chicken noodle soup?" he asked.

"Soup." She burrowed deeper into the sleeping bag, still shivering.

She closed her eyes, the sounds of him opening cans and shuffling pots lulling her not to sleep, but into a kind of frozen daze. The sleeping bag smelled of mildew and wood smoke, the scents transporting her to a long-ago camping trip with her mother and Duane. She had been fifteen, and had wanted to be anywhere but in the woods with a man she already despised. What her mother had promised would be a fun getaway turned out to be Duane's idea of survival training—sleeping on the ground in army surplus camping gear, cooking over a campfire and enduring daylong hikes that were more like forced marches.

When she had complained, he had threatened to leave her behind with only a compass and a sleeping bag to find her way home on her own. Her mother had watched, tight-lipped and wide-eyed, as Duane berated Erin, but the unexpected appearance of a trio of other hikers had prevented him from carrying out the threat, and Erin had reluctantly trailed after him all the way back to Duane's car.

"This should warm you up." Mark handed her a tray on which sat a bowl of fragrant soup and a steaming mug.

Erin balanced the tray on her lap and warmed her

hands around the mug, inhaling deeply of the rich aroma of the contents. "Chocolate." She almost sang the word, and grinned at him.

He settled beside her and dug into his own bowl of soup. "There's enough food and bottled water here that we could hold out for several days if we have to," he said.

"We'll have to leave eventually." She touched the collar at her neck. "We can't linger too long." Duane had said the bomb would go off in a week, which left, what—five days? So little time.

"We'll leave as soon as we can," he said. "But not until the storm is over. For now, we've got a safe place to spend the night and regroup."

They ate in silence until their bowls and cups were empty. Erin set her dishes on the floor beside the sofa and burrowed deeper into the sleeping bag. "I feel so much better," she said. "I don't know how much longer I could have gone on out there."

"You and me both." He carried their dishes to the table, then retrieved the sleeping bag from the second bunk and settled in beside her with it wrapped around him. Though many layers of cloth separated them, the position felt somehow intimate.

"About what happened earlier," she said. "That kiss..." The memory of his lips on hers had haunted her all day and she had to clear the air.

"I'm not going to apologize for that," he said. "My timing may have been lousy, but I'm not sorry it happened."

"I don't expect you to apologize," she said. "And I'm not sorry it happened, either. I just wondered why you kissed me."

"Does a man need a reason to kiss a woman he's attracted to?"

She shifted, as if simply changing position could somehow make her comfortable with this awkward conversation. "I meant, why are you attracted to me? Is it just because you've been alone so long? Or do I remind you of your wife?" Erin bit her bottom lip, dreading the answer to her question, but needing to know.

"Maybe part of it is because I've been alone awhile, but I like to think I'm a little more evolved than that. I'm not attracted to you simply because you're a woman. As for my wife—no, you don't remind me of her." He sounded almost angry.

"I didn't mean to upset you," she said.

"I'm only upset that you seem to think so little of yourself. That I couldn't be attracted to you just because you're you. It's not only that you're beautiful, but you're strong. I was ready to give up on my life, and you showed me I still have so much to live for."

She looked away. She didn't feel strong most of the time. Yes, she had endured a lot, but she hadn't really had a choice. And as for her looks, they hadn't brought her anything but attention she had never wanted.

He leaned over her and gently took her chin in his hand and turned her head until she was looking into his eyes. "It's my turn to ask you why you kissed me back."

"Because you're the first man I've met in a long time who I felt I could trust." She said the words before she could stop them, and the truth of them shook her.

"You thought I was working for Duane," he said. "You came into that cabin already hating me."

"You convinced me I was wrong."

"How did I do that?"

He had let her glimpse his vulnerability before he showed her his strength. But she didn't know how to say that without embarrassing them both. "You didn't take advantage of me when you could have. You stood up to Duane's thugs. And I believed your story. I've spent a lot of years seeing through lies, and I believe you've been telling the truth."

"Then why don't you believe me when I say I'm interested in you because you're you? I feel a connection to you I haven't felt with anyone for a very long time."

"I was afraid to believe you because I wanted so badly for it to be true."

He caressed her cheek. "What about our bad timing? We're not in the best circumstances for romance."

"If everyone waited for everything to be perfect before they began a relationship, a lot more people would be alone." She didn't want to be alone anymore—not when she had no idea how much time they might have left. She grabbed the front of his jacket and pulled him to her, crushing her mouth to his. For once she allowed herself to be greedy, taking what she wanted.

His fervor matched hers, two hungry exiles suddenly presented with a feast. Tongues tangled, lips twined, hands explored. She dragged down the zipper of his jacket and slid her hands beneath his sweatshirt, over the firm plane of his abdomen and the hard muscles of his chest. She brushed fingertips through the dusting of hair on his chest, delighting in the beautiful maleness of him.

He helped her out of her coat, then coaxed off her sweater. His lips traced the curve of her breasts, his tongue sliding silkily down the valley between them. Then he peeled aside the lace of her bra and drew the hard bead of her nipple into his mouth.

She gasped and arched against him, the pull of his mouth reaching all the way to her sex. She twined her fingers in his hair, holding him to her, then dragged his head up to kiss him once more. With one hand, she groped behind her for the clasp of her bra and released it.

His eyes followed her movements as she sent the lacy garment sailing over the back of the sofa. "I've heard that cuddling naked in a sleeping bag is a good way to keep from freezing to death," she said.

"I've heard that, too. But I don't think we're in danger of freezing to death."

"I don't know about that. I'm pretty cold." She pressed her naked chest against his, reveling in the warmth and the delicious contrast of hard to soft, rough to smooth.

He caressed her arm and kissed the top of her shoulder. "I have a confession," he said.

"Oh?"

"I've wanted to be naked with you since the day the guards threw you into that cabin with me."

"Mmm." She traced her tongue along his collarbone. "I wanted that, too. Well, maybe not right away. It took me a few hours."

"Then we have a lot of time to make up for," he said.

“I like the way you think.” She reached for the zipper of his pants, but he grabbed her wrist to stop her.

“I hate to be the one to point this out,” he said. “But there probably isn’t a condom within miles of this place.”

Knowing he had even thought of protection made her want him that much more. She racked her brain, rationalizing their situation. “We don’t have to worry about disease,” she said. “I’m healthy and I haven’t been in a relationship for a couple of years.”

He stroked her cheek. “Are the men where you live blind or crazy?”

She shook her head. “Neither. It was my choice.” Though she had been physically intimate with a few men over the years, she had never allowed any of them to get emotionally close, and she had always ended relationships after a few weeks or months. Anything more was too dangerous. She had never felt as connected to a man—or as safe—as she did with Mark now.

“I haven’t slept with a woman since my wife.” He wrapped a strand of Erin’s hair around his finger. “Are you on birth control?”

She pressed her forehead to his and sighed. “No such luck.”

The dance of his fingertips up her spine sent a flutter through her. “There are a lot of things we can do short of actual intercourse.” He cupped her breast and her breath quickened.

“I’m listening,” she whispered.

He kissed the tender spot beneath her jaw. “I want to be intimate with you in whatever way we can.”

She took hold of his zipper once more. "I want that, too."

A need to linger and savor replaced their earlier haste, as if they were both silently acknowledging that, no matter what the uncertain future brought, they would sear this interlude into their memories. They helped each other out of their clothes, then pressed their bodies together, naked beneath the sleeping bags.

"I'm warmer already," she said, and wrapped her legs around his hips, his erection nudging at her entrance, both teasing and thrilling her.

He trailed his hands down her back, then cupped her bottom, caressing, sending a shimmer of fresh arousal to her core. When he shifted his attention to the front of her thighs, she obliged by moving apart from him enough to allow his hands between them, his fingers tracing around her entrance, then delving in the folds above.

She arched into his palm as he slid one finger into her and began to stroke with his thumb, playing her like a skilled musician. When he lowered his mouth to her breast and began to suckle, she no longer felt tethered to the earth, instead soaring in a thrilling ride to unknown heights.

His hands and mouth coaxed sensations from her she had all but forgotten about—or never known. As she wrapped her arms around him, pulling him as close as possible, she battled the desire for this moment to never end, and her growing need for it to do so. When at last her climax crashed over her, his mouth claimed hers once more, muffling her cry of joy. She opened her eyes and met his gaze, the raw need reflected there sending a last shudder of completion through her. He withdrew his hand slowly and pressed a tender kiss to her temple.

"Your turn now," she said, and reached down between them to take him in her hand.

"You don't have to—" The sentence went unfinished as she slid down the length of his body and took him in her mouth.

He let out a low groan and caressed the back of her head as she teased him with her tongue and lips, delighting in her power to leave him speechless. She deepened the contact and felt him go inward, building toward his own release. A surge of fresh desire washed over her, a desire—no, a need—to give him this gift in such an intimate way. If being with him like this was so erotic and transforming, how incredible would actual intercourse be?

He gripped her shoulders and his body tensed. His climax shuddered through him, seeming to move through her body as well as his own. As soon as the last tremor left him he dragged her up beside him, cradling her head on his shoulder. Neither of them spoke for many minutes.

Eyes closed, sleep dragged at her, pulling her into welcome blankness. But before she succumbed, she wanted to say something, to let Mark know how much she cherished what they had shared together. She wouldn't be like a sappy teenager, declaring she was in love because she had had sex with a man. But being with him like this changed things, and she needed to acknowledge that. With sleep tugging at her, she fought to think clearly, to say something sincere but not too cloying.

What came out was less than articulate, more honest than she had wanted: "I never met a man who made me feel the things I feel with you," she said. "It scares me, but I don't want to run from that fear."

He caressed her back, stroking and massaging. "I've spent most of my life avoiding strong emotions," he said. "It was always easier to lose myself in facts and figures—things I could measure and control. I guess I was afraid, though I probably would have denied it if anyone had called me on it."

"Are you afraid with me?" Erin asked.

"No. With you it's as if I know there's nothing to be afraid of." His lips brushed her temple. "Try to get some rest. I think we're safe here."

Safe in his arms, she thought as she closed her eyes and settled more firmly against him. How ironic to find that kind of sanctuary now, when she had never faced greater danger.

MARK WOKE TO silvery moonlight streaming through the one uncovered window in the cabin, spilling across the sofa. The unfamiliar warmth and weight of Erin's body pressed against him made his throat tighten and his eyes sting. Days ago he had believed he had almost nothing left to live for. Now he had so much. He shifted so he could look at her, her face soft and somehow younger in her sleep, the worry lines that too often tightened her forehead banished for the moment.

His gaze shifted to the edge of the cruel collar that encircled her neck, and his jaw tightened. He would find a way to make Duane Braeswood pay for the suffering he had caused her. The collar was a particularly cruel torture, forcing her to live with the means of her own destruction.

Gently, hoping not to wake her, he lifted her chin to get a better look at the device. Maybe he could figure out how to undo that clasp, to free her of it. His hand stilled and ice water filled his veins as he stared at the band of metal, fully visible now. Where before the only item to draw the eye was the compact bomb affixed to the front, a new detail had emerged since they had fallen asleep. Now a digital readout glowed green in a black square next to the bomb. He watched as the numbers on the display changed, and he bit the side of his cheek to keep from shouting with rage.

"What's wrong? Why are you staring at me that way?"

Erin crossed her arms over her breasts and tried to pull away from him. He forced himself to assume a calmer expression. "It's okay," he said. "I didn't mean to scare you."

"What is it?" she asked again. "Something's wrong. I can see it on your face."

He gestured to her collar. "That…thing. The bomb. It has a timer."

"A timer?" She sat up straighter and put one hand to the metal.

He took the hand and cradled it in his own. "You can't feel it," he said. "It's a digital readout. It wasn't there before. It was either programmed to show up now, or Duane set it off remotely."

"What's it doing? What does it say?" Erin pulled her hand from his and tugged at the metal band, as if she might tear it away from her neck.

He stared at the glowing green numbers that slowly

ticked off the seconds. “It’s counting down time. Maybc timc until the bomb goes off.”

She clutched at him. “How much time do I have?”

“We. I’m not going to leave you alone with this.”

“How much time?”

“Twenty-three hours and thirty-nine minutes.”

Chapter Ten

“That can’t be right,” Erin said, panic like a giant hand gripping her heart. “Duane said the bomb wouldn’t go off for a week.”

“Maybe he lied. Or he had the ability to reset the timer remotely.”

She threw off the sleeping bag and reached for her clothing. “We have to leave now,” she said.

“That’s too dangerous,” Mark said, but he began to pull on his own clothing. “It’s pitch-dark out there and still snowing. If we try to leave now we’ll get hopelessly lost and maybe freeze to death.”

His words made sense, but this whole situation was beyond crazy. She couldn’t respond to it logically. “We have to reach help before it’s too late,” she said.

He put a steadying hand on her shoulder. When she raised her eyes to meet his she felt bathed in his calm determination. “We’ll leave as soon as it’s light enough to do so safely,” he said. “Meanwhile, we can spend the time gathering supplies and getting ready.”

“All right.” She took a deep breath. Everything was far from all right, but maybe she could hold on if she pretended it was. “What do we need to do?”

“I’ll start by fixing a hot meal.”

"I couldn't eat."

"This isn't about appetite. It's about survival. You'll stay warmer and keep going longer if you get some calories in you."

While he heated canned chili, she rolled up the sleeping bags and the blankets from the bunks. When he summoned her to the table she forced herself to choke down the food, which might have been sawdust in hot water for all she could taste. As she ate, all her attention was fixed on the band around her throat and the digital display she couldn't see that was ticking down the minutes until her destruction.

Mark did his best to keep her distracted. While he rigged a makeshift knapsack out of an old hunting shirt he found hanging by the front door, he had her gather the rest of the canned food, a can opener and matches to go into it.

When the sun was far enough up in the sky for them to clearly see their way, they climbed out the back window of the cabin. "We're bound to intersect a main road within an hour or two," he said. "I don't think there's any place in the state where we would be farther from civilization than that."

"I hope your brother knows some fast—and close—bomb experts," she said.

"He's FBI. They have experts on everything."

"Great." She did her best to sound optimistic, but Mark must have seen through her bluff. He patted her back.

"We're going to get through this," he said. "Come on."

If she hadn't been so miserable over the bomb and their chances for escape, she might have enjoyed the hike through the snow-covered woods. Last night's storm had left the world draped in a white coverlet that sparkled in the early morning sunlight. But the same snow that made the world look soft and beautiful all but obscured the drive leading up to the road, and left them both wet to the knees from trudging through it. Worse, when Erin looked back over her shoulder, their tracks stood out clearly in the smooth white surface.

Mark joined her in staring at the signs of their passage. "There's nothing we can do about that," he said. "We just have to keep moving and stay ahead of them."

They set out again and were both soon breathing heavily as they made the steep ascent to the road. Mark climbed up first, then turned to pull her up alongside him. A new wave of dismay washed over her as she stared at the sight before them. Twin tire tracks cut through the thick drifts, compressing the snow and making it clear that at least one large, capable vehicle had passed this way recently. "They haven't given up searching for us," she said, if only to break the stillness that threatened to smother them.

"We knew they wouldn't."

Yes, she knew Duane's men wouldn't stop until they found her and Mark, but some small part of her—the part apparently given to fantasies—had hoped they would tire of the search, or give them up for dead. This proof of how close their pursuers were shook her badly.

"Come on." Mark adjusted the makeshift pack and set off along one of the tire tracks.

She hurried after him. "Why are you walking in the middle of the road?" she asked.

"We can move faster on the packed snow. They probably already know we're up here, so all we can do is hope to outrun them."

"Why do you think they know we're here? I mean, they know we're somewhere, but they can't be sure we're right here."

She couldn't help thinking a touch of pity lurked beneath the sympathy in his expression. "I'm beginning to think there's some kind of tracking device on that collar. Setting off that timer last night, when we were stopped and thought we were at least momentarily safe, seems like the kind of mind game Duane enjoys playing."

"So what is he going to do now? Let us stumble around in the snow for a while, then swoop down and capture us once more?"

"I don't know." His expression grim, Mark clutched the rifle. "But I'm not going back with them. And I'm not going to let them take you, either, not if I can help it." He gestured in the direction they were headed. "All I know is this road goes somewhere and if we can get there before they do, we can call for help."

She fell into step behind him. He was right—they could move faster on the packed snow, and the width of the road allowed them to walk side by side. The track led steadily downhill, and she began to feel more optimistic. After half an hour or so, they spotted a signpost ahead. "Windrow, four miles," Mark read.

"Have you ever heard of Windrow?" she asked.

"No, but if it's big enough to warrant a road sign,

they probably have a phone. We can be there in an hour."

The thought of being only an hour away from rescue—even knowing it would probably be several hours after their phone call before help actually arrived—was enough to add wings to her feet. They hurried along and within another half hour reached a paved road and a second sign pointing the way to Windrow.

"I can't believe we're almost there." She squeezed Mark's arm and they grinned at each other. She forgot all about her wet, cold feet and frozen cheeks, anticipating hot coffee and a safe place to rest and share their story. This whole crazy ordeal would soon be over.

Mark opened his mouth to reply, then froze, the smile melting from his face. "Do you hear that?" he whispered.

Her stomach twisted as the distinct roar of an engine moving down the grade behind them grew louder.

MARK GRABBED ERIN'S arm and pulled her toward woods alongside the road as bullets ripped into the snow at their feet. The explosion of gunfire echoing off the surrounding rocks drowned out her screams as he pushed her behind him and slid the rifle off his shoulder.

The Hummer slid to a stop at the end of the road, the long barrels of assault rifles protruding from the front window and over the top of the vehicle, pointing toward where the two fugitives hid in the underbrush. Mark crouched in front of Erin, sighting along the barrel of his rifle. The moment he fired, the men in the vehicle would know exactly where they were hiding—but they might know that already. If he could kill one of them before they killed him, he might give Erin a chance to get away.

The world erupted with the sound of gunfire as a barrage of bullets strafed the roadside, ending only inches from their hiding place. Erin pressed her face against Mark's back. He could feel her trembling, but she remained silent. His own heart pounded so hard he thought it might burst. Tightening his hold on the rifle, he forced himself to inhale deeply and exhale slowly. The next barrage of gunfire would probably find them. He couldn't wait any longer.

He sighted in on the driver, the man's head clearly visible in the open window of the Hummer. Mark took another deep breath, held it, then depressed the trigger.

He had heard men say that in moments like this everything happened in slow motion, but for Mark, time seemed to speed up. The driver's body jolted from the impact of the shot, while the man on the other side of the car swung the barrel of his rifle in their direction. The man managed to get off one shot before Mark fired on him, too. Splinters of rock flew up, momentarily blinding him, but when his vision cleared, the man on the other side of the car was no longer visible and the vehicle was still.

"You've been hit!" Erin spoke softly, but her words conveyed her horror.

She reached for him, but he shrugged her off. "Don't move," he ordered. "There might be a third man in the car." The motion sent pain shooting down his arm, and he felt the hot stickiness of blood trickling from his shoulder. But he blocked out the pain, focused on the Hummer. Nothing moved, though the rough grumbling of the idling engine drowned out any sounds that might have come from inside the vehicle.

"Are they dead?" Erin asked.

"I don't know."

"How are we going to find out?"

He didn't know that, either. Now that the first rush of adrenaline was fading, his arm throbbed and he was having trouble thinking clearly. "One of us will have to go out there, I guess."

"I'm not letting you go." Before he could stop her, she inched forward, but she didn't, as he had feared, move toward the vehicle. Instead, she took the rifle from him and fired on the Hummer. The shots were wild, pinging into the back fenders and flattening one of the tires.

Mark's ears still rang from the blasts as he let out his breath in a rush. Nothing moved in or around the vehicle. He shoved to his feet, swaying a little as he did so. Erin moved beside him, supporting him. "You need to see to that wound," she said.

"When we're safe." He took a step forward, jaw clenched, determined not to falter or pass out. "We have to get out of here."

"How?" She looked toward the still-idling Hummer, which listed to one side on the flat tire.

"We'll have to walk."

When Mark stepped out onto the road, he braced himself for the onslaught of bullets. When no shots were fired, the second step was easier. "Wait here while I check the car," he said.

She opened her mouth to argue, but he cut her off. "Do you really want to see what's inside there?"

She pressed her lips together and shook her head. He took the rifle back from her and approached the car obliquely, gaze riveted to the interior, alert for any sign of movement. He saw the man outside the car first, and recognized the one Tank had addressed as Trey, sprawled in the road beside it, eyes staring vacantly at the sky.

The driver, another familiar face Mark hadn't bothered to name, slumped inside the car, his blood-streaked face resting on the seat, the gun lying across his chest. Mark reached inside the vehicle and switched off the ignition. In the silence that followed, he was aware of his own jagged breathing.

He moved away from the vehicle and signaled for Erin to join him. "They're dead," he said. "But we need to get out of here. There are at least three guards left who are probably still looking for us." And Duane had many more men at his disposal—foot soldiers he could send into the fray until Mark and Erin were either captured or destroyed.

"Let me take care of your wound or we won't get very far," she said.

He glanced down at his throbbing left arm, where a dark stain marked the sleeve. A wave of dizziness washed over him and he swayed.

Erin helped him to a rock beside the road, where he sat while she helped him out of his coat, then tore off the sleeve of his shirt. The wound was a perfectly round hole in his upper arm, the edges swollen and dark blood welling. Erin winced, but said nothing as she walked around to his other side and began pulling at his unbloodied shirtsleeve.

"What are you doing?" he asked.

"I need something to make a bandage to help slow the bleeding," she said. "That's all we can do until you see a doctor."

She managed to rip off the sleeve, then tore it into strips. She made a pad from some of the strips and wound another around the pad to hold it in place. With the final two strips she fashioned a makeshift sling, then helped him back into the coat, draping the left side over his shoulder. "How does that feel?" she asked.

"Better," he lied, and stood, fighting a wave of dizziness and nausea. "Let's get out of here."

ERIN RESISTED THE urge to reach out to support Mark, sensing he would push her away. He was in full-on tough guy mode right now, and maybe that was what was keeping him going. She tried to focus on safety ahead. Later, when she had put some distance between the events of the afternoon, she might be willing to contemplate how close they had come to death.

A green highway sign announced they had reached the Windrow town limits, but all Erin could see was more rock and trees—not the bustling community she had hoped for. "Do you think it's a ghost town or something?" she asked.

"I see a building up ahead." Mark put a hand to his eyes and squinted. "It looks like some kind of store." He started walking again. "They ought to at least have a phone, and right now, that's all I care about."

The store in question had a faded sign that read

McCarty's over the green wooden door. The rest of the building hadn't seen a coat of paint in this century. A rusting newspaper box and a soft drink machine with "Out of Order" scrawled across the front with black marker took up most of the small front porch. The only attempt to spruce the place up was a dented milk can by the door into which someone had stuck a trio of fake sunflowers. The flowers drooped with a dusting of snow.

Mark paused in front of the door. "Just a minute," he said. He ducked around the side of the building. When he reappeared seconds later, he no longer had the rifle.

"What did you do with the gun?" she asked.

"I hid it in the bushes. I didn't want the store clerk to think we were robbers."

"Good idea."

He started for the door again, then froze, reaching for the doorknob.

"What's wrong?" Erin asked.

He nodded toward the newspaper box. "What's the date on that paper?"

She stared at it, the headline visible through the mesh door momentarily stopping her breath: Domestic Terrorist Group Claims Nuclear Bomb.

Mark bent to study the paper more closely. "It's today's date."

Erin crouched beside him and read aloud the story beneath the bold headline: "'A group calling themselves the Patriots, believed to be based in the US, has threatened to detonate a nuclear bomb within twenty-four hours if their demands are not met.'" She looked up at Mark. "I can't read any more."

Mark jerked the handle of the machine, but it refused to budge. “Maybe we can find out more inside.”

Erin stood, nausea rising in her throat. “You told me the bomb wasn’t real,” she said.

“It’s not.” His face was pale, but his eyes blazed. “There’s no way he could have armed what I gave him. Not this soon.” He took her elbow. “Come on. We’ve got to call my brother and find out what’s going on.”

The interior of the store smelled of pipe tobacco and old dust, but the heat blasting from a wall furnace made Erin feel better as soon as she stepped inside. A man with a frizz of iron gray curls and a bushy mustache looked up from behind the front counter as Mark closed the door behind them. “I didn’t hear a car pull up,” the clerk said.

“It’s down the road a ways,” Mark said. “We had a little trouble and we need to use your phone.”

Erin had thought they would tell whoever they encountered the truth—that they had been kidnapped by a madman, held prisoner in a remote cabin and escaped, after enduring a shootout with armed thugs. But she could see how deranged that might sound to a stranger, so she followed Mark’s lead. “We just need to call my friend’s brother to come pick us up,” she said.

The old man stared at Mark’s bandaged arm beneath the coat. “You in some kind of accident?”

“Yes, and I need to call for help.”

The old man’s expression didn’t soften. “I haven’t seen you two around before. Where are you from?”

“We’re visiting the area,” Mark said.

“Don’t you have cell phones you can use?”

Erin bit back a groan of frustration. Why was this guy being such a pain about a simple request to use the phone? "We lost our cell phones," she said.

"What did you say your names were?"

"We didn't." Mark's expression was tight. Erin couldn't tell if he was in pain or merely annoyed.

"Please." She leaned across the counter toward the old man and gave him her most pleading look. "My friend is hurt and we really need help. We just need to use your phone for a few minutes."

He studied them a long moment, his expression unsympathetic. "All right," he finally said. "Come with me."

He led the way to a back room that was evidently used for storage. "The phone's back there," he said, pointing into the shadows.

"Back where?" Erin leaned forward, trying to see.

"It's on the rear wall."

Mark started into the room and Erin followed.

The door slammed, plunging them into darkness. "Hey!" she yelped.

Mark pounded on the door. "What do you think you're doing?" he shouted. "Let us out of here."

"Do you really think I'm that dumb?" Was the old man really *chuckling*? "A couple of guys stopped by this morning, said they were with the FBI and they were looking for a pair of fugitives. You two fit the description they gave me to a T. They said there was a big reward for your capture. So no, I'm not going to let you go."

Chapter Eleven

Mark squeezed Erin's arm, as much to reassure himself as to comfort her. Of all the places they might have ended up needing help, they had to wind up with a crazy man. "What did the two men you spoke with look like?" he called through the door. "Did they show you credentials?"

"They didn't need credentials. Who would make up a story like that? They were dressed in black and had big guns. They said you two were dangerous subversives who were part of this group that wants to blow up the country."

"We're not!" Erin protested. "They were lying."

"A guilty person would say that, wouldn't they?" The clerk's voice rose with indignation. "I'd rather take the word of the law than you. They left their card. It says Federal Bureau of Investigation, right there in black-and-white."

"They weren't real agents if they didn't show you their badges and identification," Mark said. "I know because my brother is with the FBI."

"Sure he is. And I'm a monkey's uncle. I'm not as dumb as I look, mister. They said there's a big reward for the person who turns you in. I'm going to call them right now, and then I'm going to start planning my vacation." His footsteps retreated.

Mark pounded a fist against the door in frustration, but all this did was send a shock wave of pain through him. "You're making a mistake!" he shouted. "Let us out!"

"We're the good guys!" Erin said. "Please, let us out!"

In answer, rock music blared, the pounding of drums and screech of guitars drowning out their calls for help.

Light suddenly flooded the space. Surprised, Mark turned to Erin.

"There's a switch here by the door." She raised her voice to be heard over the blare of music and gestured to the light switch. "No reason we have to fumble around in the dark." She leaned toward him, frowning. "You're white as a sheet. Please sit down before you fall down." She took his good arm and led him to a stack of cases of soft drinks and pushed him down. She settled beside him. "How are you feeling?"

He felt like leftovers that had sat in the sun for too long, but saying so would only worry her. He gestured for her to lean close enough that he didn't have to shout over the blare of AC/DC. "The phony agents the old man talked to must have been Duane's men," he said. "He probably sent them to talk to everyone around here as soon as he learned we had escaped."

"Why is he trying to pass that bomb off as real if it isn't?" she asked. "And why now?"

"I don't know," Mark said. "Unless he feels like federal agents are getting too close to discovering him and this is a last mad dash for power."

"What are we going to do?" Erin asked. "If Duane's men show up here there's no telling what they'll do to us."

Mark had a good idea what Duane would do to them, and it wasn't pretty. By now the leader of the Patriots had to have figured out the bomb Mark had made was a dud, even if he was trying to persuade others that it was real. He would want revenge on Mark for trying to trick him, and Mark knew he wasn't a good enough actor to convince Duane that he was still on his side, so the madman would eliminate him. And the fact that Erin was his stepdaughter apparently meant nothing, so Duane would likely kill her, too.

"We have to get out of here before Duane's men show up," he said.

"How do we do that?"

He stood and began walking around the room. Cartons of toilet paper and cases of soda sat side by side with an old tobacco display, a kid's toboggan, a broken barbecue grill and even a set of balding tires. The room was windowless, though two of the walls were fashioned of painted cinder block, which indicated to Mark that they were probably outside walls. He looked up at the ceiling and his heart jumped as he recognized the outline of what might be a hatch leading to the attic. "Help me drag these tires over here," he said, tugging at the stack.

Erin rushed to help him. She followed his gaze to the ceiling hatch. "Do you think that leads outside?" she asked.

"It probably leads to the attic," he said. "But from there we might be able to access the roof, or another part of the store. It's the only exit besides the door, so it's worth a try." He scrambled onto the stack of tires, which put him within arm's reach of the hatch. But lifting both arms over his head was impossible. His shoulder muscles cramped in agony when he tried to raise his injured limb. He settled for shoving at the hatch with one hand. At least he didn't have to worry about anyone hearing them, with that music turned up to full volume. The hatch moved easily, and he shoved it aside far enough to allow a person to climb up into the space.

But that person wouldn't be him. With only one good arm, he wasn't going to be able to lift himself up there. He looked down at Erin, her anxious face upturned to him. "You'll have to climb up there and go for help," he said.

"I can't leave you!"

"You have to!" He squatted and took her arm. "And you need to move fast, before Duane's men get here."

"Where am I supposed to go?" she asked.

"Follow the road to the next town. There's bound to be one. Stay out of sight of traffic. You don't want to run into Duane's men headed here. Find a police station or a fire station or somewhere official, and call the number I'm going to give you." He glanced around them. "Find something to write with and I'll give you my brother's number. Once you tell him what's going on, he'll take over and send help for me."

"What if Duane gets to you before I can reach your brother?" she asked.

"I'll fight him. I'm not going to give up after coming this far. Now hurry."

She found a Sharpie and tore a piece of cardboard from one of the cartons. Mark wrote "Luke Renfro" and Luke's private number on the cardboard and handed it back to her. "Put that somewhere safe and climb up here. I'll boost you into the attic. Take whatever exit you can find, and once you get outside, start moving away from here as fast as you can. When Duane's men arrive, I'll stall them as long as I can."

She climbed onto the tires with him, the uneven platform forcing her to stand with her body pressed to his. "I don't want to leave you," she said, her hands braced against his chest.

"Right now, you're the only one who can save us." He clasped her close and kissed her, a fierce embrace that he hoped told her all he didn't have words to explain—how much she had come to mean to him in their short time together and how much he hated for them to part. He had his doubts about her being able to summon help before Duane did away with him, but at least Mark would die knowing she was safe.

He tasted the salt of her tears and broke the kiss. "Don't cry," he whispered, and wiped her cheek with his thumb.

She ducked her head. "I'd better go. Give me a boost."

Awkwardly, relying on his good arm, he helped her scramble onto his back and from there into the attic. Once she was safely away, he slid the hatch back in place, then shoved the tires into the corner. When the clerk and Duane's men did arrive, Mark wanted to give Erin as much time as possible before their pursuers figured out she had escaped.

With a groan, he sank to the floor, legs stretched

out in front of him and back against a stack of boxes. All he could do now was wait, and pray that Erin, at least, reached safety.

ERIN CROUCHED IN the dark attic, the loud rock music from the front of the store vibrating the floorboards beneath her. The attic smelled of dust and mice. She suppressed a shudder, hoping no rodents were in residence at the moment. As her eyes adjusted to the dimness she could make out cardboard boxes shoved against the wall and a stack of old suitcases next to a metal floor lamp. The light seemed brighter to her right, so she moved in that direction, crouched over to keep from hitting her head on the rafters, and stepped carefully on the joists. The last thing she wanted was to crash through the ceiling onto the clerk's head.

She rounded a stack of boxes and a cry of relief escaped her as she recognized the dusty outline of a window. Hurrying to it, she wiped at the grimy glass with the sleeve of her jacket and looked down into the store's backyard. A sagging chain-link fence ran along the back and a rusted barbecue smoker sat in the shade of a barren tree. She stood on tiptoe and tried to see the ground and gulped. She guessed the drop was at least ten feet, maybe more, and though several inches of snow coated the ground, that wasn't enough to provide much of a cushion for her fall. If she was lucky, she'd escape with only a sprained ankle or a broken arm, but she didn't like the thought of risking that. Heart sinking, she turned away from the window to explore the rest of the attic.

The other end held no window, only a rusting metal vent that didn't yield when she pushed against it. The only other exit was the hatch over the storeroom, where Mark waited. The thought of him wounded and trapped spurred her on. She'd have to risk jumping out the window, but first she had to raise the sash or break the pane. She needed something to protect her from the broken glass. Maybe some old clothing or rags. She tugged at the lid of the nearest trunk and wrenched it open, coughing at the cloud of dust that rose. Trying not to think about mice, she tugged at what looked like cloth shoved inside the trunk, and yanked out a moth-eaten chenille bedspread that might have once been a bright blue, but looked like a stained gray in the dim light. The coverlet was easily large enough for a king-size bed, and its expanse gave her an idea.

She returned to the window, dragging the bedspread with her. While the music continued to shake the rafters, she hefted the metal floor lamp. Shielding her face with the cloth, she drove the lamp into the window like a spear, shattering the glass. Before she could lose her nerve, she tied one end of the bedspread to the rafter over the window and tested the knot with her weight. It held, so she cleared away as much of the loose glass as possible, and stuffed the rest of the anchored coverlet out the window, so that it trailed down the side of the house. Then she knelt on the sash, facing inward, took hold of the bedspread and began to climb down, bracing her feet against the weathered siding of the building and holding tightly to her makeshift rope.

The bedspread ended five feet from the ground, but that was close enough for her to feel comfortable jumping. She tried to yank the bedspread after her, but it held fast, so she was forced to leave it hanging from the open window. With luck, the clerk wouldn't decide to take a smoke break in the backyard and see it flapping in the breeze, giving her away.

After making sure the coast was clear, she climbed the fence, then hurried to the side of the house and retrieved the rifle from its hiding place in the bushes. She shouldered it, then crossed in back of a few buildings that appeared to be vacant. When she was sure she was out of sight of the store, she turned up toward the road. The wind had picked up, the icy breeze sending a chill through her, but the scent of snow and cedar invigorated her, and the need to reach help for Mark made her walk faster, which helped to warm her.

She had gone only a few yards when the whine of an approaching vehicle sent her scurrying for cover in the trees. Crouched low behind snowy branches, she studied the black Humvee headed into town. It wasn't the same car Mark had fired upon earlier, but it was very like it. And the wide shoulders and grim faces of the two men in the front seat of the vehicle sent fear shuddering through her. Those were two of Duane's men, she was certain. And in only a few minutes they would burst into that storeroom to take Mark away.

As soon as the vehicle passed, she began retracing her steps to the store. She didn't have time to get help from someone else. She would have to save Mark herself. She had the rifle, though she wasn't sure how much ammunition was left in the single clip, or how much good the gun would do her against both Duane's men and the store clerk, who might be armed, as well.

She'd have to find another weapon, or get to Mark in the storeroom before the other three did.

Duane's two henchmen were just getting out of the Hummer when Erin looked around the side of the building toward them. Dressed in dark suits and sunglasses, they fit the television portrayal of federal agents, though they were considerably beefier than any of the supposed Feds she remembered. One reached inside his black overcoat and she caught the glint of a handgun tucked under his arm. He looked toward his cohort and nodded, and they strode across the gravel lot and through the front door of the store.

As soon as they were inside, Erin, crouching low, scooted across the yard to the vehicle. She peered in the passenger-side window, hoping to spot another weapon or two. Duane's goons almost always carried semiautomatic weapons, and since the two phony FBI agents hadn't been carrying any long guns, she hoped to find them in the Hummer.

She spotted one rifle on the passenger floorboard in the back, but what met her gaze on the driver's side front set her heart pounding not with fear, but elation. The keys to the Hummer dangled from the steering column. The massive vehicle, with its reinforced grill, four-wheel drive and powerful engine, just might be the best weapon at her disposal.

As the blaring music inside the store abruptly died, Erin opened the passenger door of the Hummer and slid inside, climbing over the center console and sliding into the driver's seat. Holding her breath, she twisted the key and the engine turned over. Not hesitating, she shifted into Reverse, backed up, then drove around the side of the building. She floored the gas pedal as she sped toward the sagging chain-link fence. The jolt of impact with the fence thrust her back against the seat, but the Hummer rolled over the chain-link panel as if it was made of tinfoil. She kept right on driving, up to the corner of the building where the storeroom was situated. She backed up a foot or so, then stomped on the gas pedal, sending the Hummer crashing into the side of the store.

The cinder blocks and old plaster splintered against the vehicle's grille. She barely heard the shouts of the men as she drove into the building, where one of Duane's men had hold of Mark's arm. The image of the four men frozen with shock and gaping at her would remain burned into her memory forever. She aimed the Hummer toward Mark's captor and the man released him and dived out of the way, while Mark headed in the opposite direction.

Erin lowered the driver's side window. "Get in!" she shouted to Mark, then ducked beneath the dash as a bullet shattered the windshield.

Mark wrenched open the back door and dived inside. Staying low, Erin shoved the shifter into Reverse and screeched backward through the debris. By the time she reached the backyard, Mark was leaning over the backseat beside her, firing out the shattered front window toward their pursuers. The clerk and Duane's two men had staggered out of the shattered building like ants from a ruined hill, one of the thugs cradling his arm, the other firing his handgun toward the fast-retreating Hummer.

Erin made a sharp turn and the vehicle jounced over the rough ground to the road. The tires squealed as she wrenched them onto the pavement and barreled away from the store. She reached back and pulled her seat belt across her body as Mark struggled into the front passenger seat. "Are you okay?" she asked.

"My life may have flashed before my eyes when you came barreling toward me with this thing," he said, buckling his own seat belt. "I thought you were trying to run me down."

"I was trying to run over the goon who had hold of you," she said. "I trusted you to have enough sense to get out of the way."

"I don't think sense was on my side as much as good reflexes." He reached into the backseat and retrieved the rifle she had spotted earlier on the floorboard. He glanced over his shoulder in the direction they had come.

"Anyone back there?" she asked, though a check of the rearview mirror showed only empty road behind her. She had a clearer view back there than she did through the spiderwebbed glass, but she wasn't going to complain. Every mile that unrolled beneath her tires was a mile farther from the most immediate danger.

"Not yet, but that store clerk is bound to have some kind of vehicle, so they'll be after us soon."

"We'll still have a head start. All we have to do is get to some place large enough that Duane won't have influenced everyone. Then we can call your brother."

Mark shifted to face her. "How did you get hold of this Hummer? You were supposed to climb out of that attic and go for help."

"I didn't get very far down the road before I saw those two headed back for you. Even if I could have run all the way to the next town, I wouldn't have found help in time to save you."

"You could have gotten away," he said. "You didn't have to come back and save me."

"Yes, I did." She glared at him. "And I'm pretty insulted that you think I would do otherwise."

He shrugged. "No one would blame you."

"You would have come back for me," she said. "In fact you already did that—when Duane's men recaptured me in the woods."

"This isn't about keeping score," he said.

"No, this is about working together to keep each other safe. We're stronger together than either of us is on our own."

He didn't deny it and she knew she was right. Now that the worst of the danger was past, a thrill ran through her at the idea that she had saved him. She had fought past almost-paralyzing fear to do something bold and daring, and they had come out on the other side all right. They really did make an incredible team.

"You still haven't told me how you ended up with this car," he said.

"Duane's goons left the keys in it when they parked in front of the store. I guess they didn't think there was anyone around to bother it. Maybe they wanted to be sure they could make a quick getaway. I was looking for a way to get you out of the storeroom before they got to you, and decided this was it."

"Good thing they were driving a Hummer and not a sedan." He leaned over and touched the side of her face. "You're bleeding. Some of the glass from the window, I think."

Before she could protest, he pulled a handkerchief from his pocket and dabbed at the warm wetness that trickled down the side of her face. The tender gesture sent a tremor through her and broke whatever toughness spell circumstance had cast over her. She gripped the steering wheel more tightly to control her shaking, and fought the nausea that welled in her throat. "I think it's just hitting me how close we came to dying back there," she said.

He squeezed her shoulder. "But we didn't die. We're going to be okay."

"Not if we don't get to your brother—and some explosives experts—soon." She touched the collar at her throat. "How much time do we have left?"

He glanced at her throat, and the display she couldn't see but knew was there. "We've got plenty of time," he said, but the concern in his eyes told a different story.

"How much time?" She lifted off the seat, trying to see her throat in the rearview mirror.

"Fifteen hours and nineteen minutes."

Fifteen hours. The words echoed in her head. She clung to the steering wheel, fighting a wave of dizziness.

"We're going to get help," Mark said. "We still have plenty of time."

"We don't know how much time we have before Duane sets off his bomb," she said. "Or whatever it is he's threatening everyone with."

Mark punched the radio button. "I'm going to see if I can learn anything more about that."

Bursts of static interspersed with crackling strains of music blared from the speakers as he spun the dial.

Then a woman's solemn voice said, "...material recovered previously from the home where the Patriots' leader, billionaire Duane Braeswood, was believed to be living leads authorities to believe these threats are serious. Authorities are still searching for Braeswood and other people associated with his organization. Braeswood is described as a fifty-five-year-old white male, six feet tall, approximately one hundred and sixty-five pounds, with graying blond hair and blue eyes. Anyone with information as to his whereabouts and activities should contact the FBI."

The newscast shifted to a story about a professional athlete who had been arrested for assault. Mark switched off the station and sat back. "He's got to be bluffing," he said. "There's no way he armed that bomb."

"If people believe it's real, it doesn't matter." Erin tightened her grip on the steering wheel. "He's making everyone afraid and they're all listening to him. He must be in heaven."

"The description they gave is what he used to look like," Mark said. "No one will recognize him from that. Someone who didn't know would see him now and think he's a harmless old man."

"We can tell the FBI what he really looks like, and that the bomb probably isn't real," she said. She would feel a lot better if she knew how far they were from help. "Look in the glove box and see if you can find a map," she said. "Maybe we can figure out where we are and where we should go."

"Better yet, this thing probably has GPS," Mark said. "That can help us find the closest police station."

She surveyed the dash. The array of dials and

digital readouts resembled an airplane's cockpit. She didn't even recognize what half of the gauges were for. But there was one display that was familiar to her. Staring at it, she swallowed hard. "We have something else to worry about," she said.

"What is it?" Mark leaned over to get a better look at the dash. "Are we overheating? Do you think a bullet hit one of the tires?"

She shook her head and pointed to the gas gauge. "If we don't find a town soon, we're going to run out of gas and end up stranded."

Chapter Twelve

As if to confirm Erin's pronouncement, a chime sounded and an orange light on the dash flashed Low Fuel. Mark unbuckled his seat belt and leaned into the backseat.

"What are you doing?" Erin asked.

"I'm hoping Duane's men thought to carry an extra gas can, but I don't see anything back here. Do you remember seeing one strapped to the bumper or anything?"

"No. They probably planned to buy gas at the store before they left," she said.

"Which kind of defeats the purpose of a quick getaway." He settled into his seat once more. "Is Duane slipping on training his henchmen, or is good help hard to find for bad guys, too?"

"I think it's a sign he's getting too cocky," she said. "He's so sure he's going to win in the end that he thinks he can take shortcuts. Maybe that's all this threat with the bomb was—a shortcut to carrying out his 'vision.'"

"We need to find a shortcut," Mark said. He leaned toward the dash. "Let me see if I can find the GPS."

Much button pushing and second-guessing later, he

figured out how to operate the GPS, which informed him they were eighteen miles from the nearest settlement, a mountain town large enough to boast a pizza place, three churches, a gas station, a medical clinic and a liquor store, but no police.

"At least we can get gas there," Erin said. "And maybe use the phone."

"How are we going to pay for the gas?" he asked.

She set her jaw. "We can start out begging, but if that doesn't work, we could assume the roles of modern day Bonnie and Clyde and hold up the place at gunpoint. That might be the quickest way for us to get to the police, and you can use your one phone call to get in touch with your brother."

"That's fine as long as we don't run into some trigger-happy local," he said. "Let's hope begging works."

The dashboard chimed again and she glanced down. Mark followed her gaze to the warning light, which now glowed red. "We may not get a chance to beg or steal," she said, even as the engine coughed, sputtered, then died.

Erin steered the vehicle to the side of the road and rested her forehead on the steering wheel, eyes closed. "Now what?" she asked.

"We're back to walking."

"How long do you think it will take us to walk eighteen miles?" She sounded exhausted, as weary as he felt.

"It's more like fourteen or fifteen miles now," he said. "We can do it in five or six hours." Provided they didn't collapse before then. Or end up back in the clutches of Duane's men.

She lifted her head and her eyes met his. "Everything about this ordeal has felt impossible," she said. "Yet I keep on pushing forward. Maybe I'm just too exhausted to be afraid anymore."

"Or maybe you're a lot braver than you think." He leaned across the center console, ignoring the pain in his shoulder, to kiss her. Her warm sweetness revived him, the grip of her hand on his arm reminding him of all the reasons he had to keep fighting. "I'll never forget the sight of you behind the wheel of this Hummer, barreling to my rescue," he said. "If you're strong enough to do that, you're strong enough to do anything."

"I don't know how much strength I have left," she said. "But I'm stubborn enough that I won't let Duane win. There's too much at stake to give up now." She opened the driver's side door. "Come on. We might as well start walking. I'd like to get to the next town before dark."

"Take one of the guns with you." He pressed one of the two semiautomatic rifles that had been stashed in the Hummer's backseat into her hands, along with an extra clip of ammunition, and collected the other rifle and ammo magazine for himself. "We'll have to leave the one we took from the cabin behind, since it doesn't have an extra ammo clip."

"What else do they have that we can use?" She opened the door to the backseat and he moved to the rear hatch. A quick scan of the vehicle's contents revealed a gallon jug of water, two blankets, a toolbox filled with miscellaneous hand tools and a first aid kit. The glove box yielded two protein bars.

"These look like they've been in here awhile," Mark said, handing her one of the bars.

"I'm so hungry I would eat a picture of food," she said, ripping the wrapper off the bar.

He bit into his bar and chewed. It was the consistency of jerky and tasted like sawdust, but it might be enough to keep them going a few miles farther. Once they were safe again, he planned to order the biggest steak dinner he could find. And pie. Peach pie. With ice cream. He shook his head, banishing the distracting fantasy.

He opened the first aid kit and found a packet of pain relievers and swallowed them down with some of the water. "Is your wound bothering you much?" she asked.

"I'm getting used to it." The wound was a dull fire spreading out from his shoulder, but with the bullet still lodged beneath the skin, he knew it would only get worse. The pain relievers, like the energy bar, might keep him going long enough to reach safety.

He dumped the rest of the first aid kit and the water bottle into the blankets and knotted them into a bundle he could carry on his back. "Do you really think we're going to need those?" Erin asked.

"I hope not, but I'd rather not get caught out with nothing. Besides, anything we take is something Duane's men can't use."

"I don't suppose you have a knife?"

"No, why?"

"We could slash the tires."

"I used nail scissors to puncture the tire of the Hummer the two men who caught you in the woods were driving," Mark said. "That slowed them down enough for me to ambush them."

"I wish we hadn't left the ax back at the cabin."

"It doesn't matter. This Hummer is already out of gas, and unless they're carrying extra with them, it will take them a while to get it fueled up again."

"Right." She looked up and he followed her gaze toward the low bank of clouds moving in. "Looks like we're in for more snow," she said.

"We should have planned our escape for better weather." He started forward. "Come on. We'd better start walking."

BETWEEN THE FALLING snow and the need to hide each time they heard a vehicle approaching, Erin and Mark traveled at a snail's pace. With each step, Erin imagined the timer that controlled the bomb at her throat ticking off another second. Instead of moving toward safety, she felt as if she were traveling toward her own destruction.

Beside her, Mark's breath grew more labored, his face grayer. The lines around his eyes deepened in pain, and he wore the grim look of a man determined to hang on at all costs. "Let me at least take the pack," she said.

"No, I've got it," he said, but when she reached up to slip the knotted blanket from his shoulder he didn't resist. As she settled the makeshift pack across her back he lifted his head, alert. "Car coming."

They scuttled for the roadside, sliding down through the snow into the ditch and struggling up the other side to crouch in the damp grass and trees. The vehicle, a white Jeep, zipped by, the woman behind the wheel never glancing in their direction.

Erin let out a breath, her heartbeat slowing its frantic gallop. These wild dashes to safety every time a car passed were more exhausting than the walking itself.

"Let's go," Mark said. He started up the slope and reached back to offer her his hand. But before she could take it, the rock gave way beneath him, sending him hurtling back toward her in a spray of loose gravel and mud.

She tried to catch him, but he slid past her and landed hard on his injured shoulder, a sharp cry of pain piercing the air.

"Oh no! Are you okay?" She hurried to his side and tried to help him sit up.

He groaned and curled away from her. "Give me…a minute," he managed to say through clenched teeth.

She stared in horror as bright red blood blossomed at the shoulder of his coat. Had he torn open the wound again? Or worse, driven the bullet deeper? "Let me see," she said, and tried to push aside the fabric of his coat.

"Leave it." He grabbed her hand and held it. "There's nothing you can do. I'll be all right in a minute."

She wanted to argue with him, but he was right—what could she do? She wasn't a surgeon who could remove the bullet, or a nurse who could administer medication to dull the pain or fight off infection. All she could do was crouch beside him in the snowy ditch and wait for the tension to ease from his face, and for him to tell her he was ready to travel again.

The hum of tires on the wet road drew her attention and she peered through the underbrush at the burnt-orange Volkswagen bus trundling up the road toward them. She couldn't imagine Duane or one of his cohorts ever being caught in such a vehicle. When it was close enough for her to make out the Coexist and *Namaste* stickers on the front bumper, she was certain this driver, at least, had nothing to do with her malicious stepfather.

She rose and scrambled up the ditch embankment.

"Erin! What are you doing?" Mark called.

She ignored him and lifted a hand to flag down the bus. To her surprise and delight, the vehicle slowed with a screech of brakes and stopped several yards ahead of her on the shoulder of the road. The driver rolled down his window and looked back at her. White hair streamed from beneath a bright blue knit beany, the thin strands wafting in the breeze. "Are you okay, miss?" he asked.

"My friend and I were out, uh, hiking," she said, struggling to come up with a plausible story on the fly. "He fell and injured his shoulder and we need a ride to the nearest town for help."

The furrows on the man's forehead deepened. "Where were you hiking?" he asked.

"I don't remember the name," she said. "We're not from around here. We got lost and wandered pretty far off the trail. If you hadn't stopped, I don't know what we would have done. Will you give us a ride?"

"Sure I will." He climbed out of the cab and looked toward the ditch. "Is your friend down there?"

"I'll get him," she said. "Wait here a minute." She scooted back down into the ditch and into the trees.

"What are you doing?" Mark whispered when she reached him.

"I just saved us walking fourteen miles or however far it is." She slid her arm under his uninjured shoulder and helped him into a sitting position. "We'll need to leave the guns and everything else behind," she whispered.

"I don't like leaving the guns," he said.

"I told this guy we're hikers who got lost. If we show up with automatic weapons when we don't even have a real backpack, he'll know something is off."

Mark grimaced, but whether in pain or disagreement, she couldn't tell. "All right," he said, and started up the slope.

The driver was still waiting when Erin and Mark reached the road. Eyeing Mark, he let out a low whistle. "That looks like a pretty bad fall you took," he said.

"I'll be fine once we get to a town," Mark answered, moving past the man to the open side door of the van.

"Dolorosa doesn't have a hospital," the driver said. "I think they have a little medical clinic, but I don't know the hours, or if they're set up to treat anything very serious."

"We just need to get to someplace we can call my brother." Mark rested his head on the back of the seat, eyes closed, then he sat up, suddenly more alert. "Do you have a cell phone we can use to make the call?" he asked.

The man slammed the van door shut, then climbed into the driver's seat. "I don't have one," he said. "I figure if I want to talk to anyone or anyone wants to talk to me, they can wait until I'm home." His eyes met Erin's in the rearview mirror. "Don't you have a cell phone? I thought all you young people couldn't live without the dang things."

"I left mine at home and Mark lost his when he fell," she said.

Mark looked impressed. Who knew she had such a talent for creative lying?

"There's a store in Dolorosa," the driver said. "They probably have a phone you can use." He pulled onto the road once more.

"How far is it to Dolorosa?" Erin asked.

"Another forty minutes or so," he said. "Can't go too fast on these mountain roads." He laughed, a sound like wind escaping from leaky bellows. "Least ways, Sheila here won't go too fast on these uphill climbs."

"Sheila?" Erin didn't try to hide her confusion.

"My ride." Their chauffeur patted the cracked dashboard. "I bought her off an Australian guy, so the name seemed appropriate. My name's Gaither," he said.

"I'm Erin and this is Mark," she said. Now that they were off their feet and on their way to safety, she felt a little dazed.

"How big of a town is Dolorosa?" Mark asked.

"Oh, it's pretty small," Gaither said. "There's a few churches and stores and such, but nothing I'd call a tourist attraction or anything. The closest they have to that is the Pioneer Cemetery."

"What's that?" Erin asked.

"It's one of the oldest cemeteries in this part of the state," Gaither said. "People who are interested in genealogy or history, or who want to see the old markers, come to visit it, but that's about it. We get hikers and kayakers in the summer, and a few snowshoers and cross-country skiers in winter, but mostly Dolorosa is a pretty sleepy place."

Not a town likely to have a resident explosives expert, she thought, rubbing absently at the collar.

"What's with that thing around your neck?" Gaither asked.

She reached up to finger the collar, then jerked her hand away. She couldn't very well tell the old guy she was wearing a bomb, but any other explanation escaped her.

"It's the latest fashion." Mark's voice, so calm and reasonable, broke the awkward silence.

"What's with the flashing numbers?" Gaither asked.

"You've seen those fitness bracelets everyone wears these days?" Mark asked.

"Yeah. My daughter has one. I told her I don't see the point in counting your steps every day, but she said what she always says—that I'm too old-fashioned and out of touch." He snorted.

"This is sort of the same idea." Mark sat up, clearly warming to his subject. "But instead of counting steps, it counts down minutes and hours until you reset your fitness goals."

Erin fought the urge to pinch him or tell him to shut up. A fitness necklace? Did he really think anyone would fall for that story?

Gaither nodded. "My daughter would love that one. She likes everybody to think she's fit, even if she isn't." He glanced at Erin. "It don't look all that comfortable, though."

"Oh, you get used to it," she said airily.

Mark opened his mouth as if to elaborate, but shut it when she sent him a warning look.

"Thanks again for giving us a ride," she said. "Do you live around here?"

"I got me a place above Dolorosa, by the river," he said. "It's a yurt, with a woodstove and solar electric. Real cozy place. It suits me and Betty just fine."

"Betty? Is that another vehicle? Or a pet?"

He let out another wheezing laugh. "My old lady," he said. "She'd be with me today, but she's busy canning the last of the tomatoes from our greenhouse. She sent me to Dolorosa for more canning jars and a few other supplies."

Erin glanced to the back of the van, at the collection of cloth grocery bags, and tried to ignore her grumbling stomach.

"We heard on the news before we left for our hike about that madman who's threatening to set off a nuclear bomb," Mark said. "Do you know any more about that?"

"I stopped listening to the news years ago," Gaither said. "The press always distorts everything and it's all just depressing anyway."

"So you haven't heard about this terrorist, Duane Braeswood, who says he has a nuclear bomb?" Mark asked. "He says he's going to set it off if the government doesn't meet his demands."

"How would one guy get hold of the technology to make a nuclear bomb?" Gaither asked. "It's been a while since I was in college, but from what I remember, it takes more than a couple of pounds of plutonium and some fuses to do that kind of thing."

Mark's eyes met Erin's. "Maybe he persuaded a nuclear physicist to work for him," he said.

Gaither shook his head. "What a waste of an intellect. Why is this guy making these threats anyway?"

"Apparently, the leader of this terrorist group thinks the only way to fix the country is to destroy it," Erin said.

"That's like burning down the forest to get rid of a little patch of poison ivy," Gaither said.

"Do you have a radio we could turn on, see if there's any news?" Mark asked.

Gaither shook his head. "When I bought Sheila, she had an eight-track tape player," he said. "But I pulled that out a long time ago." He patted a rectangular hole on the dash. "I prefer listening to my own thoughts."

Erin sagged back against the seat. Her own thoughts were in too much turmoil to make good company.

"Don't get me wrong," Gaither said. "I hope they catch these crazies, but I don't see how me fretting over the matter will help anyone."

"I suppose you're right," she said. But she wished they could find out more, if only to see if they fit into the puzzle anywhere. Had Duane planned this ultimatum all along, or had something she or Mark had done triggered this outburst?

"Where are you two from?" Gaither asked.

"Denver," Mark said.

"Idaho," Erin said.

"Denver and Idaho. So you just met up here for a little vacation?"

"Yes," she said, and tried for a bright smile.

Gaither raked his hand over his chin, which bristled with several days' growth of beard. "Don't take this wrong," he said. "But if you're going to go hiking here in the mountains, you ought to be a little better prepared. You need good packs and emergency supplies and water. A map and a compass come in handy, too."

Mark had compressed his lips into a thin line. Maybe he was thinking about how he had set out with all those things when he had left home on his last hiking trip, a year ago. "We'll remember that next time," he said.

Erin settled back into the seat and closed her eyes. The warmth of the van and the hum of the highway lulled her to sleep. She woke with a start when the van stopped.

"We're in Dolorosa," Gaither announced. He climbed out and opened the van's side door. He peered in at them and nodded. "You're looking a lot better, Mister. I was a little worried when I first saw you, but I guess you'll make it now."

"I'll be fine." Mark climbed out after Erin and offered the older man his hand. "Thank you."

Gaither shook his hand. "Shorty will help you out." He slammed the van door. "I'd better be going. Betty needs those jars." He climbed back into the driver's seat and, with a wave, puttered away.

Chapter Thirteen

Erin took a deep breath and looked at Mark. "I guess we'd better go inside and get this over with," she said.

"Yeah." He took her arm. "Maybe I should let you do the talking. You have quite the talent for spinning tales."

"I guess I do my best work under pressure." She tried for a smile, but her lips wobbled dangerously.

Mark hugged her close. "Hang on a little longer," he said soothingly. "We're almost there."

The Dolorosa Country Store looked considerably more prosperous than McCarty's. New gas pumps gleamed on concrete islands out front, and brightly colored posters on the double glass doors leading inside advertised tobacco products, energy drinks and lottery tickets. Erin searched for a newspaper box amid the gallons of washer fluid and cases of soda stacked in pyramids on either side of the door, but saw none.

Cowbells jangled as Mark pulled open the door. The smells of fresh coffee and frying chicken made Erin stagger and her mouth water to the point she was afraid she might start drooling. She clung to Mark's arm, heart pounding as they approached the middle-aged woman behind the front counter.

"Excuse me," Mark began.

The woman didn't look up from the invoice she was studying.

"Excuse me." Mark spoke louder this time.

She raised her head to stare at him with pale brown eyes behind black-rimmed glasses, but said nothing.

"Could we please use your phone?" Mark asked. "We've been hiking and got lost. The man who gave us a ride here said you would have a phone we could use to call for help."

"Pay phone's out front." She pointed a long, orange-tipped nail toward the door.

Mark looked pained. "I fell hiking and hurt my shoulder. I lost my wallet with all our money in it."

The woman's expression didn't change.

"Please, we just need to make one phone call," Erin said.

The clerk's eyes shifted to meet hers. "If I gave away stuff to every beggar that wandered in here asking, I'd go broke inside of a month," she said.

Erin took a step forward. She wasn't sure what she intended to do, though her first impulse was to slap the smug look off the woman's face. Her second impulse was to burst into angry tears, but she doubted that would draw this woman's sympathy.

Mark put a restraining hand on her arm. "Is there someplace else in town that might have a phone we could use?" he asked. "Or is there a sheriff's office or a police department?"

The woman snorted. "You think the cops will lend you a quarter for the phone?"

It was Mark's turn to deliver the silent treatment.

"We got a deputy who swings through here every once in a while," she said. "But we don't get a lot of crime around here, so he doesn't have cause to be here often. And knowing him, he's fresh out of quarters."

Erin was exhausted, half-starved, frightened and angry and fed up. "Why can't you just be a decent human being and help us?" she raged. "All we're asking is to borrow your phone for five minutes to make one lousy phone call. We'll even call collect. Then you never have to look at us again."

The woman's eyes narrowed. "I pay for that phone, and if you want to use it, you have to pay for the privilege."

"Fine." Erin unhooked the gold hoop from one ear and laid it on the counter. "That's fourteen karat gold. You can sell it in any jewelry store for way more than your phone bill."

The woman's hand shot out and she swept the earring off the counter, then reached under and pulled out an old-fashioned black plastic corded phone. "Five minutes," she said, and turned away.

Mark seized the phone and wiped his free hand on his jeans. He punched in his brother's number, then leaned toward Erin, so that she could listen with him. The phone buzzed three time. Four times. Erin suppressed a moan. What if they had gone through all this and Mark's brother didn't answer his phone?

"Luke Renfro." The clipped voice on the other end of the line was so like Mark's that Erin might have imagined the man beside her was speaking.

"Luke." The word came out hoarse, more of a croak

than speech. Mark cleared his throat and tried again. "Luke, it's Mark," he said.

The man on the other end of the line was silent so long Erin worried he had hung up. "This better not be a joke," he said.

"It isn't a joke. It's really me," Mark said. "I need your help, Luke. I'm in a little store in a place called Dolorosa, Colorado. It's in the mountains. Duane Braeswood and his men kidnapped me and they've been holding me hostage. I managed to get away a couple of days ago, but they're looking for me."

"Give me your number so I can call you back." Erin heard scrabbling noises, as if he was searching for a piece of paper.

"It's the phone for the Dolorosa Country Store," Mark said. "I don't know the number. The woman behind the counter let us use it to make one call. Please, send someone to get us right away."

"Us?"

"I have Erin Daniels with me. Braeswood kidnapped her, too. She's his stepdaughter."

"We know who Ms. Daniels is."

Erin blinked. The FBI knew her? Did they suspect she was in league with Duane? Her stomach flipped at the idea.

"She helped me escape," Mark said.

"Is there somewhere safe you can wait for me?" Luke asked. "It may be a while before I can get to you. I don't know if you've heard about the trouble Duane Braeswood has been causing us, but we've got every available agent working overtime on this."

"I heard part of a news story," Mark said. He glanced toward the clerk, who was shuffling her stack of invoices, but clearly listening. "I have some information that can help you with that, but you need to get to us as soon as possible. We're not safe. And there's something else."

"What else?" Luke asked. "Are you hurt?"

"I have a gunshot wound that probably needs attention, but that's not the biggest problem. Before we got away from him, Duane Braeswood wired a bomb to Erin." He glanced at the display on her collar. "It's set to go off in a little over twelve hours."

"A bomb! You didn't say anything about a bomb." The clerk snatched the phone from Mark's hand. She stared at them, wild-eyed. "I don't know what kind of crazy you are, but you get out of here right this minute."

"Or what?" Mark snapped. "You'll call the sheriff? Well, go ahead. He's just the man I'd like to see."

"I won't waste my time with the sheriff." The woman slammed down the phone, reached under the counter and pulled out a sawed-off shotgun. "Get out. Now!"

Mark raised his hands and backed toward the door. Erin hurried after him. When they were outside, he wrapped his arm around her and they hurried across the road, to a treeless gravel lot where two tractor-trailer rigs and a rusting bulldozer were parked. "That woman is as nasty and crazy as Duane," Erin said when they were out of sight, and hopefully out of range, of the clerk.

"She's definitely not a people person." Mark leaned back against the bulldozer.

The snow had stopped but the clouds remained, and the air was icy and heavy with moisture. Erin rubbed her shoulders. "I wish I had one of those blankets now," she said.

Mark held out his arms. "Come here," he said.

She came to him and let him wrap his arms around her. The solid feel of him made her feel safer and warmer. "Will your brother send help?" she asked.

"He will." Mark rested his chin atop her head. "He may not be able to come himself, but he'll know people in the Bureau's Denver office, or maybe an office even closer to this part of the state. He'll send someone." He hoped the Bureau's desire to find out everything Mark and Erin knew about Duane would speed them along.

"Why do you think Luke said he knows me?" she asked. "You don't think they believe I'm part of Duane's horrible organization, do you?"

"They probably have profiles on any family members of known terrorists," Mark said. "That doesn't mean they think you're guilty of anything. But they'll want to find out everything we know about Duane. Maybe our information will help them to track him down and stop him."

"When they find Duane, what will happen to my mother?" Erin had never dared voice this question before. Maybe she hadn't believed anyone, before Mark, would understand her concern.

"I don't know the law," he said. "She might have to go to jail as an accessory, if they believe she has helped him or lied to protect him."

Erin nodded, the fabric of his shirt shifting beneath her cheek with the movement. "I tell myself she's an adult. She made this choice. But I can't believe she ever condoned the bad things Duane has done. She did what she did out of some misguided idea of love."

"Maybe the prosecutors will take that into account. You can speak on her behalf."

"At least in jail she'll be safe from Duane," Erin said.

The front door of the store opened and the clerk stepped out and looked around. Mark and Erin shrank farther into the shadows of the machinery. "Maybe she did call the sheriff," Erin said.

"I hope she did," Mark said. "At least in his custody we'll be safe."

"Unless Duane has paid off local officials."

"Do you really think he does that?"

"I've learned not to underestimate anything he will do," she said. "All his money and followers have given him an outsize ambition and an overly positive opinion of himself to go with it." She closed her eyes and snuggled against Mark. "I just want to have a bath, eat a good meal and get a good night's sleep. Not necessarily in that order." She wanted to do all those things with him. And when they woke, she wanted to make love to him slowly and thoroughly, with no worries about being interrupted, and with a whole box of condoms at their disposal.

Whether he wanted the same thing she couldn't tell, and she was afraid to ask.

A white panel van pulled up to the store and a man wearing khakis and a black leather jacket got out and went inside. Less than a minute later he came out, got in the van again and backed out of the parking lot.

Erin closed her eyes again, and was wondering if it was possible to sleep standing up when she felt Mark stiffen. She opened her eyes and pulled away from him. “What’s wrong?”

“That van is headed this way.” He nodded toward the road, where the van was already turning into the lot. The driver drove slowly until he was almost even with them and stopped, the van blocking their view of the road. The driver’s window rolled down and a middle-aged man with a softly lined faced studied them. “Rosalie tells me you folks need some help,” he said, in a voice that hinted at origins in the South.

Mark stepped in front of Erin, shielding her with his body. “Thanks, but someone is on the way to help us,” he said.

The metallic sound of the slide of a pistol being pulled back sent ice through Erin’s veins. She remained frozen in place as the muzzle of the weapon appeared in the window of the van. “Y’all want to come along quietly and there won’t be any trouble,” the driver said.

Chapter Fourteen

Mark wanted to howl in rage or lash out in fury, but such temper would be foolish in the face of the gun. He glanced toward the store across the street, but the parking lot and doorway were vacant. Behind him, Erin stood so close her trembling moved through him. She had been so strong, had been through so much. To have it all end now when they had just found each other engulfed him in a dragging sadness. "How did you find us?" he asked.

The man with the gun didn't quite smile. "We have our ways." He motioned toward the back of the van. "Get in."

"Where are you taking us?" Erin asked, as the door opened and a larger man dressed in jeans and a flannel hunting jacket climbed out and took hold of her wrist.

"Mr. Braeswood wants to see you," the driver said.

They climbed into the van, where a third man waited. Outnumbered this way, Mark and Erin would have no chance of overpowering their enemies. Duane might have underestimated them before, but not now.

Mark had thought their captors might take them back to the cabin, or even into Denver. Instead, the van cruised slowly down Dolorosa's main street, then stopped in front of a modest house, the kind that might be rented out to vacationing skiers in winter or fishermen in summer. A tattered wreath hung on the front door, the faded red ribbon fluttering in the breeze.

The front door opened and the driver waited in the van while the two guards escorted Erin and Mark into the house at gunpoint. The door slammed behind them, the sound echoing in the darkened room, which was devoid of furniture.

"Professor Renfro."

Mark turned toward the sound in time to see a wheelchair glide through a doorway to the right, flanked by two more guards. Mark took a step toward them and one of the guards pointed a rifle at him. Duane's eyes burned the intense blue of a Bunsen burner. "Don't let my injuries fool you," he said. "At my word any one of my men would kill for me, though I hope it won't come to that."

Mark waited. Better to say nothing and see if he could figure out what Braeswood wanted from them.

"I examined that trunk you tried to foist off on my men," Duane continued, the hiss and click of the oxygen tank punctuating his words. "Very clever."

"It's not real," Mark said. "You can't blow up anything with it."

Duane's head bobbed up and down, the oxygen tube jerking with each movement. "Not in the state it was in when you left it, but I have many resources at my disposal."

"You couldn't have armed that thing," Mark said. "It's impossible."

"Maybe it is. Or maybe it isn't. The Feds can't risk

the chance that I'm telling the truth, so they'll give in to my demands." His lips twisted in a distorted smile. "So you see, even though you didn't do the job I wanted, you did enough to help carry out my goals."

"What are your demands?" Erin asked.

Duane shifted cold eyes to her. "I'm demanding the immediate resignation of the president and his cabinet. I will replace them with persons handpicked for the job—men who share my vision for steering the country on the correct course once more."

"You won't get away with this," Mark said. "They'll never believe the bomb is real. It's impossible."

"They'll believe me when I tell them the esteemed nuclear physicist Mark Renfro created the device for me. I have pictures of you working in your secluded lab to show them. Your fingerprints are on the device. Your DNA is in it, in a matter of speaking. When they learn such a reputable scientist is behind the project, they'll have no choice but to believe."

"No!" Mark's vision misted with rage. "I had nothing to do with the kind of evil you're perpetrating."

"But now your name will be associated with it forever," Duane said. "When people think of you in the future, they'll remember a terrorist. Your daughter will be ashamed to tell anyone that you were her father."

Mark lunged toward the man in the wheelchair, but before he had moved six inches he was knocked to the floor by one of the bodyguards. He lay there, lip bleeding, staring up at Duane. He had thought he could never despise anyone more than he had despised this man, but Duane had found a way to increase his hatred. "I hope you burn in hell," Mark said. "If I ever find a way, I'll send you there myself."

"There is a way you could save your reputation," Duane said. "Or rather, avoid it being tarnished in the press."

"What is it?" Mark hated how quickly he took Duane's bait, but thoughts of his daughter growing up with her reputation tarnished because she shared his name—possibly even growing to hate him because of it—drove him.

"You were clever enough that I can see you are very close to creating the weapon I'm looking for," Duane said. "A few more weeks, maybe months, and you would have built a working nuclear weapon. I want you to come back to a new lab I'll build for you and finish the job."

"Never!" Mark said. "I won't be any part of that kind of evil."

Duane made a wheezing sound that might have been a chuckle. "Not interested?" He subsided into a fit of coughing. One of the guards stepped toward him, but Duane waved him away. When the coughing ceased, he wiped a tear from his eye and grinned at Mark. "Maybe I can change your mind about that."

He turned to look across the room. The door opened and a little girl edged into the room. Light brown curls formed a halo around her face and thick dark lashes framed sky-blue eyes. She clutched a stuffed elephant to her chest and looked around, cheeks flushed, lips trembling. At last her gaze came to rest on Mark. "Daddy?" she whispered.

ERIN STARED AT the girl, then the man. Mark had struggled to his feet, but now all the color drained from his face. He swayed, then sank to his knees. "Mandy," he sobbed.

The little girl ran to him and threw her arms around him. He held her tightly against him and buried his face in her hair, tears streaming down his cheeks. Erin wiped tears from her own eyes and sniffed.

"A touching scene, isn't it?"

She stiffened, and turned to find that Duane had glided his chair alongside her. "That might have been you and I under different circumstances."

"That could never have been you and me."

"Only because you weren't willing to listen to the wisdom I had to share. You always insisted on going your own way."

"Because your way is crazy," she said. "You enjoy torturing and manipulating people for your own twisted ends. Do you know how sick that is?"

His expression hardened. "It's very easy for people to dismiss things they don't understand as madness," he said. "Despite what you wish to believe, it isn't mental illness that drives me, but a clear determination to do whatever is necessary to make this country great once more. The reason we have fallen so far from our ideals is that so few people are willing to do what is necessary to restore greatness. As the good book reminds us, we must separate the wheat from the chaff, and the sheep from the goats."

"Why do you get to decide the definition of greatness?" she asked.

"Again, because I am one of the few people with the ability to see things as they should be, and the courage to take action." He gave her a coy smile. "Did you like the little gift I gave you?"

"What gift? I don't want any gifts from you."

"The necklace, of course. Very haute couture, don't you think? I even went to the trouble to gold plate it, in case you suffer from an allergy to base metals."

"What do you think it's going to do to my mother if you blow me up?" Erin asked, resisting the urge to tug at the neckband.

"When she sees what I'm willing to do to those who cross me, Helen will never think of leaving me again."

The coldness in his eyes made her shiver. But she forced herself to meet his gaze. "Let Mark and his daughter go," she said. "Find another scientist to make your bomb—one who actually believes in your cause."

"So, you've developed feelings for my scientist," he said. "And here I was beginning to think you were incapable of normal womanly affection. A female eunuch, as it were."

"You don't know anything about me," she said.

"I know everything about you." His voice grew harsher. "You may have thought you were out of my reach, but I have made it my business to know what you were up to at all times. Not many women your age have never had a successful relationship with a man—or a woman."

"You're the reason I never had a relationship," she said. "I never wanted to put anyone else in danger from you."

He laughed. "And now you've gone and fallen for the professor who is, after all, already under my control."

"Let him go," she said again, not caring if he

laughed at her affections. If she had to die, at least she could know she had saved Mark and his little girl.

"Forget about me. Let Erin go."

She and Duane turned to find that Mark had risen, Mandy in his arms. The little girl had her head on his chest, her arms around his neck, but she watched the others with wary eyes.

"Why should I let her go?" Duane asked. "If she stays you can continue your touching little romance—as long as it doesn't interfere with your work."

"Let her go," Mark said. He unwrapped his daughter's arms from around him and set her on the ground. "She can take Mandy with her. I'll do whatever you want as long as you let the two of them go free."

"No, Mark." Erin's words were full of anguish as she looked at him. It hurt to look at her, to think about what they might have had if Duane hadn't interfered.

He nudged Mandy toward her. "Go to Erin," he said. "She'll look after you."

His daughter gazed up at him, her eyes so like her mother's he felt a stab of grief—not the sharp, raw longing to be with his wife again, but the dull ache of acknowledgment that their time had passed. He had room in his heart for a new love now, but Duane was determined to take that from him, as well.

"I want to stay with you, Daddy," Mandy said.

"I know, sweetheart. I want to stay with you, too." Mark patted her shoulder. "But more than that, I want you to be safe." He nudged her again and, head down, she walked to Erin's side. She reached up and slipped her hand into Erin's, and the young woman gave her a wobbly, wet-eyed smile.

Mark forced his gaze away from them, to the broken man in the wheelchair. Rage clawed at the back of his throat as he met Duane's smug grin. How had so many people allowed Duane Braeswood's money and power to bulldoze over everything that was right and just? Why didn't more people fight back? Why hadn't *he* fought back more when Duane first kidnapped him? He had had so much to fight for, yet he had allowed this little man to take everything from him, even his dignity.

"Promise me you'll let Erin and Mandy go and I'll build you all the bombs you want," Mark said.

"But I only need one," Duane said. "And when it's done, you'll have outlived your usefulness to me and I'll have to kill you."

Mark nodded. Hearing the words out loud shook him, though Duane wasn't telling him anything he hadn't already known. But he didn't intend to give the madman a chance to end his life. Or to make use of any bomb he might build.

"Mark, don't do this," Erin protested.

"Take them into the next room," Duane said, and one of the guards took hold of Erin's arm. A second guard scooped up Mandy.

"Let go of me, you bully!" The little girl kicked and clawed at the man who held her. "Put me down." When the guard ignored her, she leaned over and bit his ear, hard. Yowling, he punched the side of her head.

Mark didn't remember lunging for Braeswood. He didn't remember upending the wheelchair and pinning the frail body to the floor. When he came to his senses again he had one knee planted on the older man's chest, his hands around his throat, the oxygen cannula ripped away. Duane stared up at him, eyes bulging as Mark squeezed.

"Let him go." The barrel of the gun was hard and cold, pressed against the back of Mark's head.

"Go ahead and shoot," Mark said. "I'll snap his neck first." He could feel Duane's pulse jumping beneath his fingers, could hear him fighting for breath.

"Don't…shoot," Duane wheezed.

The man with the gun backed away and Mark relaxed his grip on Duane's throat a little, though he kept his knee planted in his chest and his eyes locked to his enemy's. "Who has the power now?" he asked.

Hate edged out fear in Duane's eyes. "What…are you going…to do?" he gasped.

Good question. Mark hadn't exactly formulated a plan. He'd acted on instinct when the guard had gone after his little girl. "Let Megan and Erin go," he said. "Now."

"Do it," Duane said.

Mark heard movement behind him, then Erin was standing beside him, Mandy in her arms. "Mark…" she began.

"Take Mandy outside and wait," he said. "I'll be out in a minute."

He waited until the door closed behind her, then he grabbed Duane by the shoulders and hauled him upright. The once-powerful man weighed little more than a child, and his legs dangled uselessly, incapable of supporting him. "I need my chair," he said. "My oxygen."

"I prefer you helpless." Holding Duane tight to his chest, Mark turned to the closest guard. "Give me your gun," he said, and held out his good hand.

The man glowered at Mark, who responded by squeezing Duane tighter. "Give it to him!" Duane ordered.

Reluctantly, the man handed over the large pistol he had tucked in his belt.

"And your keys," Mark said.

The man passed him the keys. "Which vehicle do these go with?" Mark asked.

"Black Jeep parked on the side."

Mark took a firmer grip on Duane. "All right, Duane. Are you ready to go for a ride?"

"You'll never…get away…with this," Duane huffed.

"Maybe you haven't figured out yet that I'm a man who has nothing to lose." He held the pistol on the three guards and dragged Duane toward the door.

Once outside, he moved to where Erin and Mandy waited. He pressed the keys into Erin's hand. "Take Mandy with you in the Jeep parked on the side of the house. Get out of here. Don't stop until you get to a good-sized town. Do you still have Luke's number?"

She nodded.

"Good. When you get to a safe place, call Luke and let him know where you are."

"What are you going to do?" she asked.

"I'm leaving, too. Duane is my ticket out of here."

"Daddy, don't leave me," Mandy said.

He focused attention on his little girl. "I'm only leaving you for a little bit," he said. "I'll come get you soon and then I promise I'll never leave you again." He hoped he was telling the truth. "Right now, I want you to go with Erin. She'll take good care of you."

She nodded solemnly and looked up at Erin.

"I don't like leaving you," Erin said. "We should all go together."

He shook his head. "It's safer for you this way."

"What are you going to do with him?" She nodded to Duane.

"I don't know yet." He tightened his grip on the older man. "Though I can think of a few things I'd like to do. I'd like to make him suffer the way he's made all of us suffer."

"If you…kill me…you'll have…a legion after you," Duane said. "They won't rest…until…they avenge me."

Mark wondered if Duane was right. Would he stop Duane, only to have to contend with an even larger and more menacing threat in his wake—a tribe of followers fired up for battle by the image of a martyr?

Mark didn't have time to worry about that now. He had to make sure Erin and Mandy got away, before any more of Duane's followers showed up. "Go!" he ordered her. "I'll catch up with you as soon as I can."

Chapter Fifteen

Erin took Mandy's hand and led her around the side of the house to the Jeep. The girl climbed into the backseat and Erin buckled her in. "Are you okay?" she asked.

Mandy shrugged and looked away. Erin resisted the urge to gather her up in a hug. The poor girl had been passed around among so many people she probably resisted getting close to anyone anymore. Erin knew what that was like.

Driving away from Mark was one of the most difficult things she had ever done, but she knew keeping Mandy safe was more important than what either of them wanted. She glanced in the rearview mirror as she pulled onto the street and saw him leading Duane toward the white van.

"Where is Daddy going?" Mandy asked.

"Not too far, I don't think," Erin said. "Your uncle Luke is coming to get him soon."

"I like Uncle Luke," Mandy said. "And I like his girlfriend, Morgan, too. They're going to be married soon and I get to be in the wedding."

"Oh?" She watched in the rearview mirror as the van backed out of the driveway and started down the street. How was Luke going to find his brother if they got too far out of town? Somebody needed to keep track of him and Duane. And what about Duane's driver? Maybe a threat to Duane would be enough to keep him in line, but what if he decided to play the hero? How would Mark handle it with his attention divided between Duane and the driver?

She drove to the corner, then made a U-turn in the street. "Are we going after them?" Mandy asked.

"We're just going to make sure they're okay," Erin said.

"That's a very bad man with Daddy," Mandy said. "He took me from my aunt Claire and brought me here."

"When was this?" Erin asked.

"Yesterday. I had to spend the night locked in the back of that white van. They gave me Toaster Strudel for dinner."

A chill ran through Erin, and she gripped the steering wheel hard to control the sudden shaking in her hands. "Did those men hurt you?" she asked.

"I have a bruise on my arm where one of them grabbed me, but he has a bigger bruise on his leg where I kicked him back. After that the old guy in the wheelchair told him to leave me alone." She paused, then added, "Mostly, I was just scared and lonely."

Erin had been scared and lonely a lot in the past months and years. Duane had managed to isolate her even when he hadn't physically held her in custody. "I won't let them get to you again," she said, and vowed to keep that promise.

"Look at that funny car." Mandy leaned forward against her seat belt and pointed out the front windshield at the burnt-orange VW van puttering along in front of them.

Erin almost smiled. What was Gaither still doing in town? They made an odd parade—the white van, the VW and the Jeep, never driving over twenty-five miles an hour through the gravel streets. The van pulled into a small park, where picnic tables and a baseball backstop were visible in the distance. Gaither stopped, too, positioning his bus crookedly across the entrance to the park. Erin pulled in across the street, and left the Jeep's motor running.

"What is that man doing?" Mandy asked.

Erin wondered the same thing as Gaither climbed out of the VW. He watched the van for a few moments, then started toward it. Erin had a sudden, horrible vision of the old man being injured in a firefight, or taken hostage by Duane. She rolled down her window. "Gaither!" she called. "What are you doing here?"

He reversed course and crossed the street to them. "Hello, Erin," he said, his gaze taking in the Jeep and the girl in the backseat. "Is that your friend Mark in the van over there?"

"Yes." She tried for a smile that conveyed innocence. "What brings you back to town so soon?"

The old man rubbed his chin. "Well, I got to thinking after I dropped you off at the store. I remembered Rosalie was working today, not Shorty, and she isn't a woman overly blessed with the milk of human kindness, you might say. My conscience started bothering me, so I swung back by to check on you. Rosalie told me your friend in a white van picked you up. That struck me as kind of odd. I knew he must have been close, to reach you that quick, but you hadn't said anything about him being a local, though maybe I misunderstood." He tugged at one ear. "My hearing isn't what it used to be."

"But when you saw the white van you decided to follow it," Erin said.

"Something like that." He glanced over his shoulder at the vehicle. No one had emerged from it. "Right now I'm trying to figure out how you two went from no transportation at all to having two new-looking rides." His gaze shifted to the backseat once more. "And a little girl."

Erin sighed. "It's a really long story."

"We're waiting for my uncle to get here," Mandy said.

"Does he live around here?" Gaither asked.

"No. He lives in Durango. He works for the FBI."

Time to cut this off before Mandy started spilling their life histories. The less the old man knew about Duane and his organization, the safer he would be. "Gaither, I appreciate all the help you've given us, but we're fine," she said. "Really."

"I can't say I've had a lot of experience," he said. "But I didn't think the FBI showed up unless there was trouble. Are you in some kind of trouble?"

"We'll be fine once Mark's brother gets here." Erin tried to sound confident. "But I think you should leave, just in case there is trouble."

"Well, I don't know." He shifted his gaze toward the van. "This a lot more interesting than watching Betty can tomatoes."

"Please go," Erin pleaded.

At that moment the door to the van burst open and Duane Braeswood fell out. Mark tumbled after him, and the two rolled around on the ground, grappling for the pistol, each fighting for a firm grip on the weapon as it waved about. The driver jumped out of the van also, and pulled a gun, but the two wrestled too furiously for him to get a clear shot.

"Why am I beginning to think the two of you aren't ordinary hikers?" Gaither asked in a conversational tone.

"That's my daddy with a very bad man," Mandy said. "He kidnapped my daddy and then he kidnapped me to try to make Daddy do some very bad things."

Gaither looked at Erin, his eyebrows raised in question. She sighed. "That about sums it up," she said. She watched the two men roll around on the ground, the driver hovering over them. "I don't suppose you have a gun on you?"

"I don't believe in them any more than I do cell phones," he said.

Of course he didn't. "Right now a cell phone and a gun would come in handy," she said. She could call Luke Renfro on the phone and tell him to hurry up, and use the gun to hold off the driver.

"Looks to me like your friend is getting the better of the old guy," Gaither said.

Luke straddled Duane, one hand wrapped around the grip of the pistol. The driver moved in closer. "Great. As long as the driver doesn't shoot him," Erin said.

"I can take care of him," Gaither said.

She stared at him. "How are you going to do that?"

He stooped and picked up a fist-sized rock from the side of the road and hefted it in his palm. Then he pulled his arm back and hurled the stone, striking the driver in the head. The man slumped to the ground as if shot.

Erin gaped as Gaither brushed the dirt from his hands. "How did you do that?" she asked.

"I used to play minor league ball," he said. "It's been a few decades, but I still stay in practice." His eyes met hers. "I said I didn't believe in guns, not that I didn't believe in being able to defend myself. Now I'll see if your friend needs any help."

He strode across the street, and together he and Mark tied up Duane and the guard and stowed them in the van. Erin started the Jeep and drove to meet them.

Mark walked to the driver's side window. "You were supposed to go far away from here, where you'd be safe," he said.

"Somebody has to keep an eye on you." Her gaze met his and she felt the shimmer of heat through her. He leaned closer and she parted her lips, willing him to kiss her. Later, when they were alone, she would tell him how much she loved him, but for now the kiss would be enough.

"Daddy, can I get out of the car now?"

Mandy's question brought Erin out of her lovesick daze. Mark opened the back door of the Jeep and gingerly pulled his daughter into his arms. Balancing her on his hip, he carried her over to Gaither, and the three of them fell into conversation.

Erin unbuckled her seat belt, but she didn't get out of the Jeep. She smoothed her hand along the steering wheel and fought to subdue a storm of emotions. Of course Mark belonged with his daughter now. The child needed him, and they both needed time to heal. Erin had been a pleasant distraction while the two of them had been thrown together, but now they were back to real life. In real life a distinguished scientist and single dad didn't have a romance with the stepdaughter of the man who had killed his wife, kidnapped him and his daughter, and generally made his life hell. Erin had been a fool to ever believe otherwise.

Brakes squealed as a trio of black SUVs came around the corner, sending up rooster tails of dust in their wake. The first vehicle skidded to a halt inches from the bumper of the Jeep and a handsome, dark-haired man wearing black trousers and a black quilted jacket jumped out. Luke Renfro looked enough like his brother that Erin might have momentarily mistaken them for one another in a crowd. The two men faced each other, the one freshly groomed in black tactical gear, the other bloodstained and weary, with shaggy hair and several days' growth of beard. They were like before and after photos of the same man. They stood immobile for a long while, staring, as if trying to convince themselves this moment was real.

"Hi, Uncle Luke." Mandy broke the spell. "Daddy's back."

Luke went to his brother and the two men embraced, the girl sandwiched between them. Luke drew back and looked into his brother's eyes. "I'm sure you have a hell of a story to tell," he said. "And I want to hear it all. But right now I'm just glad you're safe."

"Duane Braeswood and one of his men are tied up in the van," Mark said. "You'll want to check out the white house two streets over, where they were staying."

Luke turned and signaled to the vehicle that had

parked behind him, and a trio of men in SWAT gear piled out and headed for the van. Then he gave a dispatcher the information about the house and told her to send a team in to check it out. "What can you tell us about this nuclear bomb Braeswood is threatening to set off?" he asked Mark.

"It's not real," Mark said. "It's a fake I made. But it's not armed."

"You made a terrorist a bomb?" The muscles of Luke's jaw tightened and Erin feared he might punch his brother.

"Braeswood killed Christy. He threatened to kill Mandy. I had to at least pretend to cooperate with him. I stalled as long as I could, then, when he upped the pressure, I made a decoy bomb."

"So he thinks it's a real bomb," Luke said.

"He knows it's not real," Mark said. "But he's arrogant enough to believe you won't call his bluff."

"Maybe he found someone to turn your decoy into a real weapon," Luke said.

"There's no way he could have gotten the material to arm it," Mark said.

"Are you sure of that?" Luke's expression was grim.

"I'd bet my life on it."

"What about the lives of innocent people?"

"If you find the bomb you can prove to yourself that it's harmless," Erin said.

Luke shifted his gaze to Erin, then walked over to her, Mark and Mandy trailing after him. "Ms. Daniels?" Luke asked.

She released her grip on the steering wheel of the Jeep and rested her hands in her lap. "It's nice to meet you, Agent Renfro," she said. She managed a smile, but his attention was already focused on the collar around her neck. "Is that the bomb?" he asked. "On the phone, Mark said something about you being wired with a bomb."

"Yes." She wet her lips. "At least, according to my stepfather it is."

Luke's eyes met hers again. "Do you know where Duane has hidden this nuclear weapon he's threatening to detonate?"

She shook her head. "No, but it's probably somewhere in Colorado. I don't think he's had time to move it anywhere else."

"We can't be sure of that," Mark said. "It's possible he shipped it to one of his followers in New York or DC or another major city. One thing in our favor, though. I don't know what he told you, but it's not a suitcase nuke. The decoy I built is in a big metal trunk. It's big enough people would notice it, and it's really heavy. It takes two strong men to move it."

Luke nodded and took out his phone. "I'll spread the word." He shifted his gaze to Mark. "Then we'll see about getting you to the hospital to have a look at that shoulder. Don't think I haven't noticed you favoring it."

"I can wait a little longer," Mark said. In the excitement of the last hour, he had almost forgotten the pain of the gunshot wound.

"Why are the numbers flashing on your necklace?" Mandy asked.

"Are they flashing?" Erin lowered the visor and craned her neck to see in the mirror. The display on the collar had changed from green to red and the numbers flashed with each changing second, a horrible pulse counting down her doom.

But it wasn't the flashing red numbers that shocked her as much as the time displayed. "This says…I've got less than an hour." She stared at Mark in horror.

"That's because no matter what you do to me, I'm still in charge!" Duane, held between two agents in black flak jackets and fatigues, screamed the words like curses. "You think you can stop me, but you never can."

The agents dragged him away to one of the SUVs, shoved him in the backseat and drove away. A second set of agents hauled away the van's driver.

"Where is your explosives expert?" Mark asked.

"He's on his way." Luke's voice was more clipped than ever, his expression strained.

"Where is he coming from?" Erin asked.

"From Denver." Luke refused to meet her gaze. Instead, he turned to his brother. "You told me we had more time."

"We did. Braeswood must have reset the timing mechanism."

Luke pulled a set of keys from his pocket and handed them to Mark. "You take Mandy and get out of here," he said. "There's a medical clinic a couple of streets over where you can get that arm checked out. I'll stay with Ms. Daniels."

"I'll stay with her," Mark said, and his words made Erin weak with relief.

"Your place is with your daughter," Luke said.

He bowed his head. Erin felt his struggle, but she knew Luke was right. "Go with Mandy," she said. "There's nothing you can do to help me anyway." It was her turn to look away, before he could see her sadness and longing for what might have been.

She listened to his footsteps walking away, then the sounds of the car door slamming and the engine starting. She bit the inside of her cheek to keep from crying out as he drove off. Even if she survived this ordeal, she doubted she would see him again. Oh, they might run into each other during a court trial, if it came to that, but he needed time to reconnect with his daughter and the rest of his family. She didn't fit into his plans.

"Sir, you'll have to leave now, too."

Erin realized Luke was speaking to Gaither, who had stood nearby and silently watched the whole drama unfold. She would have to be sure Luke knew the part the older man had played in saving them Maybe he'd get a medal.

"What's going to happen to her?" Gaither asked.

"Someone will be here soon to remove the collar and deal with it," Luke said. "For now, we need to clear the area."

An agent took Gaither's arm to escort him away. "Good luck, Erin," the older man called.

She swallowed. "Thank you." But she couldn't help thinking she had used up her share of luck a long time ago.

After Gaither left the silence closed in around her. Luke walked some distance away to make a phone call. She closed her eyes and tried to pray, but her mind was a blank. All she could think of was Mark, of the joy on his face when he had been reunited with his daughter, of his bravery in fighting off Duane, of how tenderly he had touched Erin when they had made love.

"I've been talking to headquarters about your situation." Luke Renfro was beside the Jeep again. Being with him was a little disconcerting, he looked so much like Mark—though a Mark from a different world than the one they had shared. "We discussed getting a welder or someone like that up here to cut the collar off, but our explosives experts believe it's possible the device is set up to trigger with any kind of tampering," he said.

"Yes, Duane told us it was."

"We're still trying to find an explosives team that's closer," he said. "We aren't giving up yet."

She nodded. "I appreciate that."

"For now, we have to wait. And I'm going to have to leave you alone for a bit." He looked rueful. "I have orders to stay back at least eighteen hundred feet."

"I understand."

He took a step back, but she couldn't help calling out to him. "Agent Renfro? Luke?"

"Yes?"

"I didn't have anything to do with Duane Braeswood's awful plans," she said. "He was my stepfather, but I never saw him as anything but a madman and a criminal. Maybe I was wrong not to go to the authorities with what little I knew about him and his organization, but I was trying to protect my mother. And myself, too."

"You never gave us reason to believe you were guilty of any wrongdoing." He put his hand over hers on the door frame and squeezed it. "We're going to do everything we can to save you," he said. "I'll have my brother to answer to if I don't."

He walked away, leaving her to wonder what he had meant by that last statement.

Chapter Sixteen

The FBI had commandeered a local community center two miles from the park as their temporary headquarters. Mark had elected to go there with Mandy, instead of the emergency clinic, wanting to stay close to the action in case Erin needed him. Not that there was anything he could do, but he didn't want to be traveling in an ambulance somewhere, or knocked out on an operating table, if Erin asked for him.

One of the agents showed father and daughter to a room furnished with two folding chairs and a cot. Mark sat on the cot with his daughter, marveling at the feel of her in his arms. "You've gotten so big," he said.

"You're growing a beard." She rubbed her hand across the whiskers on his cheek.

"I haven't had time to shave lately," he said.

"I kind of like it." She snuggled against him. "Do you think Erin will be all right?"

His stomach tightened. "I hope so."

"She's very pretty." Mandy looked up at him from beneath her lashes. "Do you like her?"

"Yes, I like her."

"Are you in love with her?"

How was he supposed to answer that question?

If he said yes, would Mandy think he was betraying her mother? Or worse, that he was turning his back on her? "Would you be upset if I said yes?" he asked.

"I think it would probably be okay. As long as I get to come live with you."

"Of course you'll live with me. You're my daughter and I love you very much." He kissed the top of her head. "So much."

"I love you, too, Daddy." She pressed her head against his chest. "Aunt Claire told me you might be dead, but I never believed her. I wouldn't let myself."

"I wouldn't have blamed you if you did," he said. "You had to wait a long time."

"It doesn't matter now that you're here."

They didn't say anything for a long while, and her breathing slowed and deepened. She had fallen asleep. Poor thing was probably exhausted. Later, he'd ask her what had happened with Duane and his men, though he wasn't sure he was ready to hear those details yet. Maybe he would find a counselor to help her deal with all the trauma of the past months. For that matter, maybe he would find someone to talk to himself. No telling what demons the events of the past months would leave him fighting.

He eased Mandy off his lap and laid her out on the cot. He was just standing when the door to their room opened and Luke stepped in.

"Why aren't you with Erin?" Mark demanded. Pain squeezed his chest. "Has something happened? Is she all right?"

"Nothing has changed." Luke set a brown paper bag on one of the folding chairs. "Did you go to the clinic about your arm?"

"I'll go later. Another hour or two isn't going to make any difference."

"I figured you'd say that, so I brought you some food. I thought you might be hungry."

Mark turned away. "I can't eat. Not until I know she's safe."

"We found an explosives guy who works for La Plata County," Luke said. "He's on his way."

"So you just left her alone?" Anger tightened his chest.

"There are two officers keeping an eye on her."

"But they're not with her. They don't know her. She's having to deal with this by herself."

"Mark, you know we can't risk any more lives."

His head told him Luke was right, but his heart screamed that the only life that really mattered was Erin's. "What does Braeswood say about the bomb?" he asked.

"Which one?" Luke opened one of the bags and began to set out burgers and fries. "He's already shut up and lawyered up. When he's not ranting about all the followers who will carry on his work even while he's in custody, he's reminding everyone that he is a frail old man who has suffered greatly and he's threatening to sue us."

"What about those followers?" Mark asked. "Did you arrest any of them?"

"Half a dozen or so. It was easy enough for our team to pick them out of the crowd. We've had some of them on our radar for months. But so far they're not talking, either. We're looking for more." He slid a cardboard tray of chicken nuggets toward Mandy, who had awakened and now perched on the edge of the cot. "Here you go, honey," he said. "Why don't you take these over by the window and eat while I talk to your dad."

Mark waited until Mandy had carried her lunch across the room before he spoke again, keeping his voice low. "Do you think Duane's right?" he asked. "When he says others will carry on his work?"

"I don't know. The world is full of crazies. We just try to stay one step ahead of them. We checked out the house you told us about, but it was clean. We figure he wasn't there but a couple of hours. Any other ideas where we might look for this alleged nuclear bomb?"

"There's a cabin in the mountains where he kept me and Erin prisoner. I think I could find it again, but he's probably cleaned it out by now. The last time I saw the trunk with the decoy in it, two of Duane's thugs were loading it into the back of a Hummer."

"When was this?" Luke asked.

"Two days ago."

"He could have driven or flown the trunk anywhere in the world by now."

"I'm telling you, it's not armed. It's all a bluff."

"You can't know that." Luke held up a hand to forestall any further argument from Mark. "Even if the thing isn't a nuclear device, you can fit a pretty powerful explosive charge into a trunk like the one you described. So we don't have any choice but to take his threat seriously."

"I'm not saying you shouldn't take him seriously," Mark said. "Just that the man is a liar."

"Which we already knew." Luke slid a burger and fries toward Mark. "Eat this. You must be starving."

His stomach heaved at the thought of eating anything. "I can't eat. I can't stop thinking about Erin. I'd be dead now if it wasn't for her."

"You said she helped you escape. How?"

It wasn't so much what Erin had done, but what she had motivated *him* to do. "She created a distraction and I threw acid on one of the guards. Then we ran."

"When was this?" Luke asked.

"Two days ago. We got away while two of the guards were preoccupied with loading the trunk."

"You've spent two days wandering around out there?" Luke glanced out the window.

"We spent two days running from Duane's men." He glanced toward Mandy, who was sitting in the other chair, lining up her chicken nuggets in neat rows on the cardboard tray. "I killed three of them," he said softly. "And wounded another—not counting the man with the acid."

"We'll want a statement from you later." He handed Mark a cup of coffee. "I ought to warn you there are some people who want to make it hard for you because you cooperated with Braeswood and made the bomb he's threatening everyone with."

"I didn't cooperate with him!"

Mandy stared at him, her eyes wide. Mark forced himself to lower his voice and stay calm. "I didn't have any choice," he said. "And I didn't make a bomb. I made a fake to try to placate him."

Luke put a reassuring hand on Mark's shoulder—the uninjured one. "I'm pushing hard against any attempt to prosecute you," he said. "I've pointed out to anyone who will listen that you and Erin have cooperated fully. And you're the man who finally stopped

Duane Braeswood. That's going to weigh heavily in your favor."

Mark stared into his coffee cup. "You caught the man, but you haven't really stopped anything. He's still threatening to put a big hole in the world with his supposed nuclear device. He's still trying to kill Erin." He squeezed the cup the way he wished he had squeezed Duane Braeswood's neck, not caring that hot coffee sloshed onto his hand and splashed on the floor.

Luke studied him for a long moment. "How long have you been in love with her?" he asked.

Mark set the crushed cup aside and raked a hand through his hair. "I don't know. Maybe about five minutes after I met her." Anguish tore at him. "I never told her, though."

"You'll get a chance to tell her," Luke said.

Mark glanced toward Mandy, who was singing softly to herself as she dipped the chicken nuggets in ranch dressing and popped them into her mouth. "This is a lousy time to start a relationship," he said. "I don't want to upset Mandy."

"Mandy's a resilient little girl. And that's what counselors are for—to help with transitions like that. If you love Erin, you should try to make it work with her. Don't pass up a chance for happiness."

"What would you know about it?"

"You might be surprised." He sipped his coffee. "I'm engaged. To a journalist I met in Denver when we first came to Colorado on this case."

"Really? Congratulations." Mark began to pace. Hard to imagine Luke—the brother who had always been the sworn bachelor—finally settling down. Mark looked forward to the day when his own life was settled once more. He would never take the ordinary pleasure of living for granted again. But mundane routines seemed very far away right now. “When is this bomb guy supposed to get here?” he asked.

Luke’s phone chirped. “That may be him now.” He turned to leave the room, but Mark followed him out into the hall. “Go back to Mandy,” Luke said.

“I’m coming with you,” Mark said.

“And what happens when Mandy realizes you’re not with her? Your daughter needs you, Mark. Let me take care of Erin.”

Mark fisted his hands. How many times had he heard of someone being torn over some decision? Now he knew what that really felt like—a physical pain as if he was being ripped in two. He dragged in a ragged breath. “All right. But you’ll bring her to me when this is over?”

“I will.” They didn’t say “if it works out all right” or “if she’s still alive.” But the words hung in the air between them, as real and horrifying as if they had been spoken.

ERIN FOCUSED ON a fly crawling across the dashboard, trying to shut out the sights and sounds outside the Jeep—the bright yellow police tape encircling the park with its ominous warning, Danger, Do Not Cross. Law enforcement officers from several agencies had closed off the streets leading to the park and shouted through bullhorns for people to clear the area. Luke had stopped by again a while ago to ask if she wanted anything to eat or drink, but she had refused. "I don't think I could swallow," she said.

He had nodded, his eyes full of real concern, but then he had left and she hadn't seen him again, or spoken to anyone. She was the queen bee at the center of a hive of activity, but unapproachable and dangerous.

She wondered what Mark and Mandy were doing right now. Maybe they were eating a good dinner, or taking a nap. Maybe father and daughter were merely catching up on the months they had lost, relearning each other again. She was glad Mandy had warmed to him so quickly. Her aunt must have done a good job of keeping the girl's memory of her father alive—or maybe Mark himself had been such a strong presence in her life before his disappearance that he wasn't easily forgotten.

A siren's blare jerked her from her reverie, the strident wail rising and falling and rising again as it drew near. She turned to watch a sheriff's department SUV turn in at the entrance to the park, idling a moment while officers scurried to move aside barriers, then pull up next to her.

A man dressed in something resembling a space suit stepped out, a tool bag in one hand, what looked like a small black safe with a handle attached to the top in the other. He saluted his driver, then the vehicle backed out and men moved the barriers back into place. The uniformed man made his way to the open driver's side window of the Jeep. "You must be Erin," he said.

"Yes."

"My name's Chad." He offered a hand and she shook it. "I'm here to deal with that rather unique necklace you're wearing." He tilted his head to study the device more closely. "What can you tell me about it?"

"Um, it's a bomb. With a timer. It's gold plated." She shrugged. "I don't know a lot."

Chad opened the Jeep's door. "Why don't you step out here and we'll get to work."

When she was standing in front of him, he set his tool bag on the front seat of the Jeep and opened the main compartment. "How much time does it say we have left?" she asked.

"Almost ten minutes." He placed the tip of a probe against the collar and watched the readout on a handheld monitor.

She swallowed. "Is that going to be enough?"

"I guess it had better be. Now hold still while I check this out."

She pressed her lips together, fighting the jittery nerves that made her want to scream. How could he be so calm and methodical as the seconds ticked down?

He removed a laptop computer and opened it on the seat next to the tool bag. He connected a handheld scanner to the computer and glided it slowly over the collar, studying the monitor display as he did so.

"It's okay to breathe," he said after a moment. "A good idea, actually."

She hadn't realized she had been holding her breath, and let it out in a whoosh. "Can you tell anything about the bomb?" she asked.

"I can tell a lot." He set aside the scanner and pulled out a bulky black helmet with a full-face visor. "You'll need to put this on," he said.

She gaped at him. "I don't really see the point. If

this thing goes off, it's going to take my head clean off. I doubt a helmet will do much good."

The face mask on his own helmet prevented her from seeing his expression, but his voice remained calm and reasonable. "Right now, the helmet is to protect your eyes," he said. "I'm going to fire a laser at the collar. Oh, and you'll need to hold really still. I wouldn't want to miss the collar and hit you instead."

Meekly, she donned the helmet. Chad removed something that looked remarkably like a laser pointer from his tool bag. "Okay, close your eyes and lean your head back."

Before she could ask why she needed to close her eyes, he said, "You're less likely to flinch if your eyes are closed. The light is really bright."

She closed her eyes, leaned her head back and waited.

And waited. She could hear Chad breathing, and a bird singing somewhere behind her. The rumble of a distant truck engine. A small buzzing sound.

"Okay, lean forward a little."

She did as he asked and he moved behind her. She felt something pulling at her throat and then a cool breeze washed over her as he removed the collar. She opened her eyes and stared at him. "You did it," she said.

Though she couldn't see his face, she imagined him grinning. "The laser stopped the clock mechanism," he said. "We still have to disable the armament, but we can do that somewhere else." He opened the small safe, dropped the bomb inside and slammed the door shut. "All right, let's get you out of here." He reached up to remove her helmet.

But he had scarcely laid his hands on her when the bomb exploded, shattering the world and sending them flying.

Chapter Seventeen

The explosion shook the building where Mark and Mandy were waiting, rattling the chairs and knocking a painting of a sailboat on a lake to the floor, where it rested crookedly against the baseboard.

Mandy screamed and clung to her father. "What was that noise, Daddy?"

"I don't know," he lied, picking her up and walking to the window. It took all his willpower to stay on his feet and not give in to the sick dread that swept over him at the idea that the explosives experts hadn't gotten to Erin in time.

The cacophonous wail of multiple sirens filled the air, and car after car raced past the community center, headed toward the park. "Daddy, you're squeezing me too tight," Mandy said, pushing against his chest.

"Sorry, honey." Mark set his daughter down and moved to the door. A man raced past and Mark grabbed his sleeve. "What happened?" he asked.

"Somebody said a bomb went off in the park."

"Was anyone hurt?"

"I don't know. I'm going to find out." He pulled away and raced out of the building.

Mark wanted to follow him, but he couldn't leave

Mandy here and he couldn't expose her to the carnage that might await at the park. He spotted a phone on a desk across the room and crossed to it. His fingers shook as, for the second time that day, he dialed his brother's number.

You have reached the voice mailbox of Special Agent Luke Renfro. Please leave a message at the tone.

Mark slammed down the phone and moved to the door, which the other man had left open in his haste to leave. An ambulance raced past, siren screaming. "No," Mark muttered. Then louder, "No!" He hadn't found love again only to have it torn from him.

A black SUV turned into the parking lot and parked in front of the door. Luke slid from the driver's seat, his expression grim. A dark streak that might have been blood painted the side of his face, and one sleeve of his coat was torn.

Mark gripped the door frame and watched his brother approach. Luke didn't say anything at first, merely pressed something into his hand.

Mark looked down at the cell phone. "What's this for?"

"So you can call me when you get to the emergency clinic."

Mark tried to hand back the phone. "I told you, I'm not going to the clinic. My injury can wait. What about Erin?"

Luke shoved the phone and a set of keys into Mark's hand again. "You're going to the clinic to see Erin. Go. The address is already programmed into the GPS. If you leave now, you'll get there just after the ambulance."

"Are you telling me Erin is alive?"

"Yes. And the bomb tech, too. He had already removed the necklace and placed it in a containment device when it blew. They were knocked off their feet, but they were both wearing helmets and he had on a bomb suit. He managed to shield her from most of the debris. The ambulance is taking them to the hospital as a precaution. The doctors will probably release them in an hour or two."

"How did you get this?" Mark touched the streak of blood on Luke's face.

Luke touched the spot and examined his fingers. "A sign fell on one of the sheriff's cars and trapped an officer inside. I helped pull it off and I guess I cut myself. Now go. I'll look after Mandy."

Mark clapped his brother on the back, then sprinted for the car.

"I'M FINE, REALLY. Most of these bruises are from before the explosion." Erin tried to fend off the probing hands of the emergency room physician and see past him to the next cubicle. "Is Chad okay?"

"I'm fine!" called a familiar voice. "Aren't you glad I made you wear that helmet?"

"Yes, thank you. And thank you for getting that necklace off me before it blew."

"My timing could have been a little better," he said. "I'm still trying to figure out what I did wrong."

"As far as I'm concerned, you did everything right. Ouch!" She flinched as a nurse sank a needle into her arm.

"Just a tetanus shot," the woman said. "Then you'll

be free to go." She pressed a bandage over the injection site.

"No, I am not a relative. Not yet anyway."

Erin's heart leaped at the sound of the familiar voice. She stood and was moving toward the door when it burst open and Mark stepped inside. Their eyes locked and she hesitated, not sure how to read the expression there. "What are you doing here?" she asked. "Why aren't you with Mandy?"

"Luke is with Mandy." He moved toward her, but made no move to touch her. "I had to make sure you were okay."

"I'm fine." She smoothed her hands down the front of her shirt. "Hungry and dirty and a little banged up, but I'll be fine. How are you?"

"Same as you."

"How's Mandy?"

"She's good. Amazing."

"She is amazing. You're a very lucky man."

"Yeah. If you had said that a couple of weeks ago, I would have laughed in your face, but now I know I am lucky. I have a lot to be thankful for." He took her hand, and she sensed he was about to say something important—something she was afraid would hurt too much to hear.

"Luke, I..." she began.

"Mark Renfro?"

The man who joined them in the middle of the emergency room had taken the cliché of the black-suited FBI agent and given it a twist—from his gelled, close-cropped black hair to the skinny trousers and slim-lapelled jacket of his black suit and his hipster skinny tie. "I'll need you to come with me, sir."

Mark frowned at the man. "You're interrupting a personal conversation."

"I'm sorry, sir, but your brother, Special Agent Renfro, sent me here to fetch you." He held up a badge and nodded to Erin. "You, too, miss."

Mark pulled Erin closer to his side and faced the interloper. "Who are you?"

"Special Agent Cameron Hsung." He moved the badge closer so that they could clearly see the official photo and credentials. "We need to go now. We don't have much time."

"Time for what?" Erin asked.

"I'll explain in the car."

"No." Mark turned away. "Tell Luke if he wants me he can come get me himself. I have more important things to do right now."

"Sir, if you won't come with me willingly, I have orders to bring you by force," Agent Hsung said. "This is a matter of life and death. Literally."

Erin slid her hand from Mark's. "What's going on?" she asked.

The agent glanced around the crowded emergency room. Every eye was focused on the trio in the center of the room. "Come outside," he said.

Mark and Erin followed him outside. He waited until the three of them were in his car before he said, "Duane Braeswood is threatening to set off his bomb in ten minutes if the president doesn't announce his resignation on national television. He says he can detonate it remotely, the same way he set off the bomb necklace in the park."

"How can he do that if he's in custody?" Erin asked.

"It's another bluff," Mark said. "The necklace probably had a secondary timer or other device that triggered if it was removed from your neck. There wasn't anything like that on the dummy bomb I built. And it's a dummy. It can't blow up." But he heard the doubt in his voice—doubt planted by Luke, who had pointed out that the bomb didn't have to be a nuclear device to maim and kill. And the exploding necklace Duane had fastened to Erin's neck proved the terrorist leader had at least one more explosives expert at his beck and call.

"You're among the few people who have ever seen this dummy bomb," Agent Hsung said. "We need you to help us figure out where the bomb might be, and positively identify it once it's located."

"And we need to do this in the next ten minutes," Erin said.

The agent glanced at his phone. "Eight minutes and fifty-four seconds now." He leaned forward and punched on the car radio.

"As law enforcement officials search frantically for a nuclear bomb that suspected terrorist Duane Braeswood claims will detonate in a matter of minutes, the president is preparing to meet with reporters in a live press conference. Previously, the president has stated he will not comply with Braeswood's call for his resignation and the resignations of his entire cabinet. Braeswood, leader of an extremist fringe group calling themselves the Patriots, is in FBI custody at this time, but has refused to reveal the whereabouts of the alleged nuclear device."

Mark's eyes met Erin's. "Where would Duane stash the bomb?" he asked.

She put a hand to her head, which ached from the aftermath of the explosion and from racking her brain, trying to figure out what Duane was up to. "He would want it nearby, I think," she said. "He couldn't have put it wherever it is by himself—he had to have people move it for him. At least two people."

"We're doing a house-to-house search in Doloroso right now," Hsung said. "But we're running out of time."

"Did you check the white panel van he was in?" Mark asked.

"The bomb's not there," Hsung said. "Though some evidence suggests it was at one time."

"And it's not at the house where he was staying?" Erin asked.

"We took the place apart. It's not there."

Mark pinched the bridge of his nose. "So he probably had the bomb in the van with him when he came to Dolorosa," he said. "He hid it somewhere after he got here."

Hsung turned to Erin. "You grew up in his house. You probably know him better than any of us. What would be his idea of a good place to plant a bomb? We've already ruled out the school and the county offices. We're running out of time."

"You're not running out of time," Mark said. "The bomb isn't real and Duane Braeswood knows it."

"That's right," Erin said. "He doesn't have to worry about putting the bomb where it will do the most damage. He could put it anywhere. It doesn't even matter if someone finds it after he gets what he wants from the government."

"No offense, but the rest of us aren't convinced the bomb is as dead as you say it is," Hsung said.

Erin felt a charge of inspiration. "That's it," she said. "It's a dead bomb." Her eyes met Mark's.

"The cemetery," they said in unison.

"Go to the Pioneer Cemetery," Erin told Hsung.

Hsung put the car in gear with one hand and hit a button on his phone with the other. "Get a team over to the cemetery," he said. "Erin thinks Braeswood might have put the bomb there."

The Pioneer Cemetery covered five acres at the south end of Doloroso, the site marked by an elaborate wrought iron archway, and towering lilac bushes poking their snow-covered bulk above a dry stack rock wall encircling the burial ground.

Hsung, Erin and Mark piled out of the agent's car as two armored vehicles pulled in behind them. "Where's the bomb?" the first man out of the first vehicle demanded.

"We don't know," Erin said. "We have to look." She studied the scattered monuments and markers studding the snow-speckled grass, from the moss-covered weeping angels marking the graves of infants to a black marble obelisk in honor of some long-ago dignitary. But no shining metal trunk stood out among the plastic flowers and gravestones.

She started down the broad graveled path that led into the interior of the cemetery, Mark at her side, while the officers scattered through the rest of the grounds. "If we weren't on such an urgent mission, this would almost be pleasant," she said as they passed under the arching branches of a cottonwood, the bark silvery against the winter-blue sky.

"If there are any Braeswoods buried here, Duane might think it a good joke to deposit the bomb there," Mark said.

"He wouldn't know about that ahead of time," she said. "Wherever he put the bomb, it would have to be someplace he could get to easily, but away from the front gate, where anyone passing could spot it. I'm thinking back here." She gestured toward a rear section of the grounds. "The markers over there look older. Maybe the graves are less visited." She studied the rows of weathered wooden crosses and leaning granite stones. Then her gaze rested on a plump Cupid, the quiver of arrows on his back worn blunt from years of wind and weather. "There!" She pointed toward the Cupid. "Let's try there."

They spotted the trunk when they were approximately twenty yards from the marker, sun dappling its shiny metal surface where it sat in the middle of the sunken mound of the old grave. Mark hurried toward it, one hand outstretched. He had almost reached it when a voice behind him shouted, "Stop!"

Erin turned to see Agent Hsung striding across the ground between the gravestones. "Get back," he said. "Let the explosives techs take care of that."

Mark sent the agent a stubborn look, but stopped, then retraced his steps to rejoin Erin and Hsung. The agent led them back to the entrance to the cemetery, where they waited while a trio of bomb techs encircled the trunk.

"What made you think he'd put the trunk there?" Hsung asked.

"The Cupid," she said. "Duane has always had a very twisted view of love."

A shout rose from the trio by the grave, and they turned to see them standing with arms raised. Agent Hsung's phone rang and he put it to his ear and listened. "You were right," he told Mark. "The bomb was a dud. All show but no guts."

"That sort of describes Duane," Mark said.

Hsung pocketed his phone. "You two are free to go for now," he said. "Though stay close. We'll probably have some questions for you later."

"I don't have plans to go far." Mark took Erin's hand. He led her away from Hsung and the others, to the far end of the cemetery, beneath the snow-covered lilacs. "We didn't get to finish our conversation earlier," he said.

She tensed and tried to pull her hand from his, but he held tight. "You probably want to get back to Mandy," she said. "You two have so much to catch up on."

"We'll have time." He stopped and turned toward her, forcing her to stop, too. "I was saying before that I have a lot to be thankful for, and one of the things I'm most thankful for is you."

She looked away, her heart breaking a little as she did so. "Mark, don't," she began.

"Don't what? Tell you that I love you? Too late."

"Your daughter needs you right now. You both need time to heal. I would only be intruding."

"You're right. We all need to heal. But you're wrong when you say I don't need you. I do. And Mandy needs you, too. She likes you. I think the three of us could make a family."

"How do you know she likes me?"

"She said she did."

"She might not like me as much if she thinks I'm taking you away from her."

"I thought you were done being afraid."

Erin had to look at him then. "What are you talking about?"

"That sounds like fear talking to me. You're afraid to take a chance with me and Mandy."

"I am not." Was he calling her a coward, just because she was trying to be sensitive to the feelings of a little girl who had lost her mother and almost lost her father?

"Then prove it," he said. "Show me you're not afraid to acknowledge your true feelings."

"All right, I will." She grabbed his face in her hands and stood on her toes to kiss him, a long, fierce kiss that left no doubt about her feelings for him.

He wrapped his arms around her and returned the kiss, moving from her mouth to her throat. "I was terrified when I heard that explosion," he whispered. "I thought I had lost you and never had a chance to tell you—to show you—how much I love you."

"I love you, too," she murmured, reveling in the feel of his lips gliding over her neck. "And I know I'll love Mandy, too."

Mark raised his head to look at her. "Does this mean you'll give us a chance?"

"Yes." She grinned. "If only to prove to you I'm not a coward."

"I never thought you were a coward," he said. "To me, you'll always be the bravest woman I know."

"Only because you showed me how brave I could be."

They kissed again. Pressed tightly to him, she felt

something vibrate in his pocket. "What's that?" she asked, drawing away.

He pulled out the phone and frowned at the screen. "My brother." He hit the button to answer the call.

"Did you ask her yet?" Luke's voice was clear.

"Ask me what?" Erin asked.

"Did he ask you to marry him?"

"I'm working up to that," Mark said. "Give me a chance." His eyes met Erin's. "Would you?"

"Would I what?"

"Would you marry me?"

"What about Mandy?" she asked.

"I'm thinking a long engagement will give her time to get used to the idea."

Erin pulled him to her again, to whisper in his ear, "Yes."

"What did she say?" Luke's voice sounded a long way off as Mark returned the phone to his pocket.

"You and I have a lot of catching up to do," Mark said as he kissed her again.

"Mmm. And a lifetime to do it." In a way, they were both starting over, building new lives where love replaced fear, and neither of them ever had to be alone again.

* * * * *

Look for more heart-stopping books
of romantic suspense from
award-winning author Cindi Myers
coming in 2017.
You'll find them wherever
Mills & Boon Intrigue books are sold!